Beneath a star-filled sky

"Cold?" Gray asked softly. "Your blouse is too thin, but I like it." When River's chin lifted, he added, "It makes your hair shine like gold, and shows off your curves. And if you're still cold, I can think of a way to warm you up."

Stifling a nervous giggle that would have embarrassed her no end, River managed to say primly, "I imagine you *can* think of a way, but my shawl will do the job."

"You don't really think that for a minute, and you know it," Gray said in a husky voice, and River felt a shiver trickle down her spine.

She was shivering as if she were standing knee-deep in snow and pulled her shawl more tightly around her.

Gray's soft laugh reached her on the night wind. "That's not what will help, love."

River's Dream

*

Virginia Lynn

BANTAM BOOKS
NEW YORK · TORONTO · LONDON · SYDNEY · AUCKLAND

RIVER'S DREAM
A BANTAM FANFARE BOOK / APRIL 1991

Fanfare and the portrayal of a boxed "ff"
are trademarks of Bantam Books, a division of
Bantam Doubleday Dell Publishing Group, Inc.

ISBN 0-553-28622-6

Published simultaneously in the United States and Canada

Bantam Books are published by Bantam Books, a division of Bantam
Doubleday Dell Publishing Group, Inc. Its trademark, consisting of the
words "Bantam Books" and the portrayal of a rooster, is Registered in U.S.
Patent and Trademark Office and in other countries. Marca Registrada.
Bantam Books, 666 Fifth Avenue, New York, New York 10103.

PRINTED IN THE UNITED STATES OF AMERICA

RAD   0 9 8 7 6 5 4 3 2 1

Dedicated to Sharon K. Lynn, my Texas cousin and one of my biggest fans. Your love and support mean so much to me.

And to Melba Brown of Vale, Tennessee, who listened to my ideas with enthusiasm and appreciation. Thanks, Melba, for sharing.

Author's Note

Dear Readers,

I've been asked if I really read the mail I receive. The answer is yes, I do. This book was inspired by a letter from a lady in Florida who wrote and asked me if all heroines had to be beautiful. I wrote her back and told her that the readers seemed to prefer lovely heroines and handsome heroes, but that beauty was in the eye of the beholder.

That letter started me thinking. What if a heroine was not confident and beautiful and witty? What if she was, in fact, a great deal like me, a rather ordinary person? All kinds of interesting possibilities presented themselves because of that one letter.

That was in the summer of 1988, and now *River's Dream* is completed and, I hope, being enjoyed by my readers. And, of course, the lady in Florida.

If you enjoyed River and Gray's story, please write and let me know.

Best wishes to all of you,

Virginia Lynn
C/O BANTAM BOOKS
666 FIFTH AVENUE
NEW YORK, NEW YORK 10103

I arise from dreams of thee
In the first sweet sleep of night,
When the winds are breathing low,
And the stars are shining bright.

SHELLEY, *The Indian Serenade*

The Dream

He was tall, dark, and handsome: the epitome of the Ideal Man. And this ideal man was holding a beautiful woman in his arms. His arms were strong, corded with muscle, and yet gentle when he held her.

The woman sighed a soft, languorous sigh that slipped from between her lips and stirred the strands of his dark hair. He smiled at her sigh, his sensual lips slanting to one side and his usually shadowed blue eyes glittering with warmth.

His strong hands shifted to hold her closer, cupping her slender curves to him. "You're beautiful," he whispered, his deep voice vibrating with tightly held restraint. His fingers tangled in her heavy mane of hair, then held her head still as he nuzzled her neck. Shivers raced down her spine, and she gave a soft moan when he muttered thickly, "I love the feel of your hair, your soft skin, and the feel of you next to me like this . . ."

"And I love being with you," she whispered back, arching into him with another soft sigh.

A feeling of delirious happiness swept over her as he held her, and her heart swelled with love. Nothing had ever felt this wonderful, this secure. When she was in his arms she knew that nothing could harm her, that he stood between her and the entire world. It was the best feeling in the world. She was safe. Secure. Loved.

Outside the wind blew softly, and starshine and moonlight filtered through gauzy lace curtains over the tall windows. Reclining on a satin-covered chaise, with clouds of her long, silky hair spilling over her shoulders and her lover's arms, she stretched with a luxuriously contented sigh. Her long slender legs gleamed in the moonlight as he gazed at her with loving appreciation, and there wasn't a shred of embarrassment or shyness at the glowing fires in his blue, blue eyes. She felt nothing but gratitude that he liked what he saw. And why shouldn't he? She was everything a man could want . . .

He kissed her again, his mouth moving gently, then more persuasively over her lips, stirring storm clouds of desire and emotion. She kissed him back, closing her eyes, letting love take her far above the seaside mansion where they lay lost in each other's arms. Ocean breakers crashed against the sand and filled her ears with a roaring sound, and through the tumult she heard a discordant voice. Who would dare intrude on their privacy? Who would interrupt such a warm, intimate moment?

The voice came again. Harsh, demanding, sharp.

"Drucilla!"

No, no, not yet! It's too soon . . .

"Drucilla, you're late! Wake up!" The voice was insistent and caused the seaside mansion to vanish along with the starshine, moonlight, and Ideal Man . . .

Groaning with disappointment, Drucilla opened her eyes, set to face another day. The dream was over and her Ideal Man was gone.

She sat up and glanced around the dim alcove room on the half story above Grandmother Duckworth's front parlor. When she swung her legs over the edge of the bed her feet bumped a stack of books lying on the floor. At night, when thick dark air filtered through the dingy drapes and into her tiny room, reeking with the smell of the river, Drucilla would pore over these books. They weren't her schoolbooks. Or anything else useful. These were books that transported her from her stark, dreary existence as a schoolteacher living with her grandmother into a world of love and romance. These books fueled her dreams.

Jane Austen. Thomas Malory. The Brontë sisters. She discovered authors who wove tales that took her far from the Pinch district. Knights and castles and damsels fair, brooding heroes and fragile heroines—Drucilla would fall asleep and dream about them. When she read the printed words by the feeble light of the single candle allowed her, she was one of them. She was tiny and beautiful, and a handsome man gazed into her eyes and told her how wonderful she was. It was magic.

As magical as her Ideal Man, the tall, dark, and handsome man of her dreams. Even awake she could visualize him as if he were standing at the foot of her narrow bed. He was tall, of course, but not too tall. His physique was powerful, but not so muscular that it was knotted and unattractive. And of course he was handsome, achingly so, but not the kind of handsome that was too pretty or too rugged. His complexion was dark, as befitted a man who spent a great deal of time outdoors, and his eyes were a searing blue that provided a vivid contrast to his tanned features. And his physical characteristics were not his only wonderful qualities, for Drucilla's Ideal Man was a take-charge man who believed in being forceful but fair. He wasn't a bully, but he wasn't spineless either. And he was intelligent, but not bookish. The Ideal Man was proficient at whatever he attempted, but not so perfect that he didn't make an occasional mistake. He was, after all, human. And confident enough not to mind admitting that he was human enough to make an occasional mistake.

Drucilla's mouth curved into a sleepy smile. Dreaming of her Ideal Man always put her in a better mood. It helped her face the irritations of her daily life, such as her grandmother, who was now standing on the bottom step of the dark, narrow staircase and bellowing.

"Drucilla Duckworth! You will miss your trolley if you don't get up this instant! Lazy, worthless girl," the old woman ended in a loud grumbling voice.

Drucilla shrugged, and memories of her Ideal Man evaporated in the cold light of another dreary day.

Chapter 1

*

March 5, 1888
Memphis, Tennessee

Plump, plain, and penniless. That was Drucilla Duckworth. It was a description that she glumly assigned to herself every time she looked in the dimly lit hall mirror, and it fit her well. Too well. And today was no different. Drucilla sucked in her breath and turned slightly, peering at her reflection.

The mirror's wavy lines distorted her reflection, but she didn't need an expensive gilt mirror to know that the large shape in the unattractive black dress that stared back at her needed much more than great lighting and a ballroom looking glass. Drucilla frowned and put her shoulders back, sucking in her stomach at the same time.

No use. Even if she tightened her corset until her eyes popped out, she would not be slim. There were unattractive bulges and they were all too evident. Shrugging, Drucilla let her shoulders droop. It didn't really matter. She had long since ceased to care. Why should she? No one ever looked at her with anything approaching admiration, except maybe Horace Huckaby, who had told her quite plainly that he was only interested in her mind anyway. And it wasn't as if she would be beautiful if she were slender . . .

Drucilla gave the long skirts of her plain black dress an irritated twitch. Even her clothes were dowdy, though her grandmother had pointed out on many occasions that "One could not make a silk purse out of a sow's ear," and that "a pig in a silk suit was still a pig." Not flattering comparisons, but Letitia Duckworth was not known for flattery. Or kindness either, for that matter.

At least her long thick skirts hid some of Drucilla's worst faults, and they were at least serviceable and of sturdy material. And anyway, Grandmother Duckworth was right. Drucilla was as plain as mud, and she might as well thank the good Lord above that at least she had enough sense not to dwell too long on what would never be.

"Do with what you have, Drucilla!" Grandmother Duckworth was wont to repeat, banging the tip of her cane on the floor for emphasis. "Do with what you have and leave off vain yearnings . . ."

It was good advice. At least, that's what Drucilla told herself time and again. Still, when she rode the trolley to the schoolhouse where she taught third and fourth grade, she noticed how the young men gazed at the other young women with that *certain look*. Why couldn't one of them look at her that way, as if she were made of spun glass that might shatter at the slightest touch. Would she feel wonderful or simply giddy if a young man looked into her eyes and whispered that her lips were like fresh raspberries, her complexion as smooth as pudding, her breath as sweet as marmalade, and being near her was as intoxicating as Madeira?

Neither. With all those alluring metaphors, she'd probably feel hungry, Drucilla decided gloomily and turned away from the mirror. Horace Huckaby, who also taught at the school, had given her her greatest compliment. He had told her with a stammer that she had a lovely smile and excellent teeth. Then he'd flushed to the roots of his well-oiled hair and begun sweating like a dray horse, which was quite unromantic. His well-intentioned comment had merely made her feel like a mule on the auction block.

"Notice the strong teeth, with no overbite," Drucilla imagined the auctioneer saying as he pointed out her only asset.

Assets were not Drucilla's strong point. Any vanity on her part would be ludicrous. Even if she lost weight, she still had mousy brown hair that defied every effort to curl it. It hung in her eyes if she left it loose, so she always pulled it into a tight bun on the nape of her neck, a bun so tight it made her eyes slant. Anything looser, and her hair would escape the net she used and end up hanging in her eyes or down her back in an untidy snarl. Then the school principal—ever mindful of the slightest impropriety—would frown disapprovingly and remind her that she was, after all, only there on a trial basis and had no tenure.

So Drucilla kept her hair pulled back and thick eyeglasses perched on the bridge of her nose, giving her a professional air that she was convinced was impressive. And intimidating. Some of the fourth-grade boys in her class were quite large, having been held back a year or two.

That afternoon Drucilla hung her coat as quietly as possible on a peg near the front door. No point in waking sleeping dragons, she thought, as she tiptoed to the door of the parlor. If her grandmother was asleep, she could eat her supper in peace, without listening to the familiar harangue.

Luck was with her. Grandmother Duckworth dozed with loud snorts in a stuffed chair near the cold fireplace. No cheery blaze greeted Drucilla this afternoon. No shining brass implements brightened the hearth, only a cold grate and dead ashes. Sighing, Drucilla knelt at the small hearth and began to scoop away the ashes quietly. There were only a few chunks of coal in the tin coal bucket, but they would be enough to at

least take the chill from the small parlor. A few spills of
paper, a spark from the low-burning oil lamp, and a fire
began to smolder.

Standing, Drucilla wiped her hands on her dress. It was so
black a little coal dust wouldn't hurt it, and besides, the next
day was Saturday, wash day. She glanced over at her grandmother, who slept with her pince-nez precariously balanced
on the tip of her nose and her lips slightly parted. The dingy
lace on Grandmother Duckworth's dress collar fluttered with
each exhalation of breath, and Drucilla reflected on how alike
her days were. How many times had she arrived home from
school cold and weary, only to find her grandmother asleep in
that same chair, the same lace on her collar fluttering with her
snores? Too many to count, she decided, and turned to go
into the kitchen.

Pausing, Drucilla's attention was caught by the framed
portrait of her mother. It hung on the wall, the only decora-
tion in the room. There were no other portraits, no small
decorative objects. This was the only bright object in the
dark, dim parlor, the bright gilt frame squared around a
painting of a happy young girl. Alicia had been so beautiful,
her eyes shining with so much life and laughter. Perhaps this
dreary old house had not seemed so dreary when Alicia was
alive. Perhaps it had been filled with song and sunshine
instead of the musty ashes of two lives.

A lump formed in her throat, and Drucilla's chest ached.
She missed her mother, and wondered what her life would
have been like had her parents survived the steamboat explosion. Though there was no grave for her father—she supposed
he had been one of the bodies washed all the way down to the
Gulf of Mexico—Drucilla wondered about him, too. Surely,
if Alicia had loved him, he couldn't have been the villain her
grandmother painted him to be. Perhaps he had been reckless,
but he had been young, and he couldn't have known the
Sultana would blow up that day.

And Drucilla didn't even know his name. She had vague
memories of another name, but it always remained just out of

reach, never quite recalled, and Grandmother Duckworth insisted that the name she bore was much better.

"Why keep a soiled name, when my Simon's is at least honorable?" Grandmother Duckworth had said when Drucilla asked about her father. "I changed your name so you could hold up your head, so you would not be associated with *that man*! There's no need for you to know it."

And that was that.

Black mourning drapes still hung dispiritedly at the parlor windows, reminding Drucilla of wilted vultures. The entire house had an air of gloom about it, as if the inhabitants had already died.

"Maybe we have," Drucilla murmured aloud, and was startled by the sound of her own voice. She glanced back at her grandmother, who still snored in her chair, then went into the kitchen. She had to light a lamp, then start a fire on the stove to warm her soup. The pantry was lined with jars of preserves and pickled vegetables, and there was almost half of the dried-apple pie still in the tin pie safe.

She ate three bowls of soup and two generous helpings of apple pie before she was full. Pushing back from the kitchen table, Drucilla took her plate and bowl to the tin sink and washed them out, then dried and stacked them on the sideboard. Still no sound from her grandmother, and she decided that she should prepare a tray for her. She had probably not eaten much during the day.

Scooping the last of the soup from the crock, Drucilla poured it into a bowl, buttered some bread, and cut a small slice of pie, then she lifted the tray and carried it into the parlor. The fire had warmed the room but it was still chilly, and Drucilla saw that the crocheted shawl had slipped from her grandmother's shoulders.

"Grandmother, you'll catch a cold if you do not keep warm," she scolded, crossing the room and placing the tray on a small table. "You didn't light a fire today, and even though it's March, it's still cold outside. Grandmother?"

Mrs. Duckworth did not reply but remained asleep, her head tilted at an awkward angle. A slight frown puckered Drucilla's brow, and she reached out to pull the shawl back up around Mrs. Duckworth's shoulders. That was when she noticed that the lace collar was still. And the room was quiet. Too quiet. No snores trembled in the air. Only dead silence prevailed.

A shiver rippled down Drucilla's spine, and slowly reaching out, she touched her grandmother lightly on the shoulder. "Grandmother?"

But Mrs. Duckworth could not hear her, would never hear her again.

Chapter 2

*

"What will you do, Miss Duckworth?" Horace Huckaby stared intently at Drucilla, his thin nose quivering so violently he reminded her of a ferret.

She sighed and managed to say softly, "I don't know, Mr. Huckaby."

"Of course, there's still your teaching position."

Drucilla nodded. "Yes, there is. And Mr. Winstead was kind enough to say that my tenure will be obtained within the next two years. But I'm still not certain what I should do. After all, I hesitate to stay on here alone . . ."

Her voice trailed into silence, and she looked around her at the shabby little parlor with its mourning drapes and air of desolation. Grandmother Duckworth had died on Friday and been buried on Sunday. Since the yellow fever epidemic of 1884, the dead were buried quickly in Memphis. There were no long wakes anymore, and the funeral service that morning had been short and solemn. No one had attended but Drucilla and Horace, and the priest from Saint Mary's Catholic Church a few blocks away. Mrs. Duckworth had not been Catholic, and neither was Drucilla, but no other minister was available.

Horace cleared his throat. "Have you . . . have you any funds with which to live, Miss Duckworth?" he asked delicately. "You will be all right?"

Drucilla smiled slightly. "I honestly don't know, but I am certain that I can manage on what I earn. And Grandmother must have had a small bit put back, for we never had problems paying our bills. Of course, she would never discuss such matters with me because she said I was a ninny and wouldn't know a nickel from a gold dollar." Her smile was wry. "My education did not impress her at all, I'm afraid." She sighed heavily and pressed her fingertips against her temples. "Perhaps she was right . . ."

"Oh, no, Drucilla! I mean, Miss Duckworth," Horace amended with a flush and a stammer. "You are quite the most intelligent woman I know, and . . . and I am pleased to know you."

"Thank you, Mr. Huckaby." Drucilla lifted her brows in surprise. She had not expected such a violent declaration from Horace Huckaby. He was certainly not given to extravagant compliments nor fits of admiration.

Drucilla smoothed a wrinkle from the skirt of her black crêpe dress. It was her Sunday dress, the dress she always wore on special occasions, but she had not dreamed she would be wearing it this Sunday to bury her grandmother. Though she had not, if the truth were known, loved her grandmother, Mrs. Duckworth had still represented a form of security, and now that was gone. A feeling of panic swept over her, and Drucilla willed it away.

No, I will not panic! I will manage on my own! I am an intelligent person and I can do it!

With those reassurances echoing in her head, Drucilla stood abruptly, startling Horace Huckaby, who leaped up as if stung.

"Dear me! Are you going to faint?" he cried, his eyes bulging from their sockets so far that Drucilla fought the sudden urge to laugh.

"No, of course not! The air of this parlor is stifling and I was going to open a window," she said soothingly. Stepping to the long window that had never as long as she could recall been opened, Drucilla deliberately flung wide the drapes, then blinked at the bright sunlight which streamed in. Even the weak light of March seemed overbright in the dull room that had not seen the sun in years. The light picked out the shabby details of the room with unerring accuracy: the frayed carpet and threadbare cushions, the drift of cobwebs from the ceiling, and the dust that coated the lamp tables. Drucilla ignored all that and grasped the window latch. It was stuck. After several moments of futile effort she turned to Horace.

"Would you mind, Mr. Huckaby?"

"Mind?" he repeated, blinking owlishly. "Oh. The window latch. Of course not."

But Horace Huckaby had no better luck than Drucilla at opening it, and she finally told him to stop trying.

"It doesn't really matter. I should go through Grandmother's things, anyway." Drucilla put a hand to her forehead, trying to will away her headache. How suddenly confusing her life had become. Before it had just been boring, but now that Grandmother Duckworth was dead, she would have to decide where to live and what to do, and she wasn't accustomed to making decisions. She looked up at Horace. "I must sort through things. Will you excuse me, Mr. Huckaby?"

He nodded, reached for his hat, which had been lying on the small lamp table, then turned back to Drucilla. Horace seemed poised on the brink of some momentous announcement, and his lips worked soundlessly for a moment. Drucilla stared at him.

"Are you ill, sir?"

Mr. Huckaby shook his head. "No," he squeaked, "not ill! Just—" he gulped in a deep breath of air, "—just wanted to ask you something."

When Horace abruptly dropped to one knee Drucilla's mouth sagged open in astonishment. Was the man prone to fits of some kind? Good heavens! Then, when he put his hat over his heart, she realized with a start that he meant to propose to her! How awkward!

"Miss Duckworth, though I realize it is not an opportune moment, I hope I am not too impetuous when I say that—"

"Mr. Huckaby," she interrupted quickly, "perhaps you will forgive me if I say that I am at this time in my life quite at sea as to what to do next, and could not possibly make any important decisions. While I appreciate your company and the comfort you have offered, I beg of you not to present me with any solutions or questions that might require a decision."

Scrambling to his feet, Horace Huckaby nodded his head, and Drucilla caught a faint whiff of bacon grease. That must be what he had used on his hair. But then Horace was mumbling something she didn't quite catch while backing to the front door.

Once he was gone and she was alone, Drucilla wondered if she had done the right thing. After all, it wasn't as if she'd ever had a marriage proposal before, and it wasn't likely she would ever have one again. And perhaps she shouldn't look a gift horse in the mouth, as her grandmother always said, but the thought of marriage to Horace Huckaby had suddenly been quite repulsive. He was nice enough, and she really *did* appreciate his thoughtfulness and his comfort. But he wasn't her Ideal Man.

Horace Huckaby did not fit a single requirement of Drucilla's Ideal Man, and she knew marriage with Horace would be intolerable. Spinsterhood would be preferable. And it seemed highly likely that spinsterhood was probable. But nothing was worth shattered dreams, and if she was married to someone else, she could not in good conscience dream of her Ideal Man at night.

Yes, Drucilla thought as she took up a lamp and turned toward her grandmother's bedroom, she had definitely done the right thing in stalling Horace Huckaby.

Lamplight flickered in erratic patterns along the dark hallway, preceding her in a strange collage of dark and light. How odd that sunlight could so completely fill one room yet not reach several feet beyond into a narrow hall. And how odd that she should feel so apprehensive about going through her grandmother's things. Yet it had to be done.

Sucking in a deep breath to steady her nerves, Drucilla firmly grasped the doorknob and swung open the door to her grandmother's bedroom. It was just as Mrs. Duckworth had left it. The bed was neatly turned down, the edges of the quilted coverlet forming a perfect triangle. On the nightstand by her bed stood a brown bottle of the "medicine" she took every night and several times a day. The crystal flanges that circled the nightstand lamp shimmied as Drucilla stood indecisively in the doorway, reflecting splinters of light from her lamp. On one wall a stitched sampler read Waste Not, Want Not.

She put the lamp down and stepped to the window to throw open the drapes. Sunlight flooded in. Drucilla blinked against it, then turned back to the room. She went to the small writing desk against the far wall and sat down in the ladder-back chair in front of it. Within the space of a few minutes, she was deeply absorbed in the cleaning of the desk.

Papers from thirty years before, all written in her grandmother's neat, crabbed hand, formed a growing stack. Deeds to everything from the house to cemetery plots were mixed in with receipts from the general store and the butcher shop. It appeared as if, in her declining years, Mrs. Duckworth had grown careless with her bookkeeping.

By the time Drucilla had finished going through the desk, she was almost too weary to consider attacking the trunk by her grandmother's bed. She had found the key in the top desk drawer and been tempted to stop sorting through the desk in order to open the trunk, but she'd decided against it. Somehow, whatever waited in that trunk had taken on an air of mystery through the years. Mrs. Duckworth would never tell Drucilla what was inside, hinting of things so terrible that as a child Drucilla had been frightened to touch the worn leather.

Now, staring at the locked, leather-bound trunk, Drucilla

considered waiting to open it. She was tired, and the sun had sunk down beyond the Mississippi River. It was late, but duty called. Drucilla suddenly remembered her grandmother's favorite lines from Emerson: "When Duty whispers low, *Thou must*, the youth replies, *I can*." She sighed.

Rising from the chair, Drucilla stretched her cramped muscles and slowly approached the trunk. She ran her fingers lightly across it, feeling the nicks and scratches dug into the leather. She could recall hearing her grandmother open the trunk at least once a month, hearing the lid bang against the wall.

"Now," she said aloud, her voice coming out in a strangled kind of croak, "we shall see what all the fuss was about!"

Drucilla fit the key into the lock and turned, then swung back the lid, hearing the familiar bang against the bedroom wall. It was full of papers, all neatly bound with strips of cloth and labeled. Drucilla squinted into the dim interior of the trunk. The bundles looked like old letters. A thrill shot through her. Letters from a secret lover, perhaps? Leaning, she reached for the lamp so that she could see better.

But when Drucilla opened the top letter, dated only the month before, she was more puzzled than ever. It was from a man by the name of Tyler Templeton, and the letter was short and to the point.

"Mrs. Duckworth," it read, "enclosed you will find the usual amount. Please see that River is amply cared for. As always, Tyler Templeton."

Who was Tyler Templeton? she wondered, and who—or what—was River? Drucilla refolded the letter and stuffed it back into the envelope, then selected another one. This was one from farther down in the trunk, in a packet labeled 1876. The packets seemed to be labeled according to the year, which meant that the letters had been coming for some time. The yellowed paper rustled as she unfolded the letter and began to read:

Mrs. Duckworth,

Why won't you reply to my letters? I have a right to know about River. She's my daughter as well as your granddaughter, and I love her. I know you blame me for Alicia's death, and I have suffered untold agonies for the past seven years, but hasn't enough time passed that I may be forgiven? Haven't I paid enough penance yet? Are you determined to make my own child hate me? . . .

Drucilla stopped reading. And breathing. She sat as still as a stone, stunned. Finally she sucked in a deep breath and tried to continue reading the letter, but her mind was too full to absorb any more. Tyler Templeton must be her father and he had written letters to her, about her, yet she had never known. All those years she'd thought him dead, she'd been told he was dead, yet he wasn't. Why hadn't she been told?

Staring into space, Drucilla began to tremble. Then she picked up the letter and began to read again. As she read that one and others, she began to grow angry. She was furious that the years had been wasted, furious that her grandmother had kept her father from her, and furious that she had not even been allowed to choose. How could she have been so cruel?

Delving back into the trunk, Drucilla pulled out more letters, until finally the trunk was almost empty. Only a large box remained at the bottom, and she lifted it out. It was a flimsy box of pressed paper, and sagged with the weight of whatever was inside. She took it out and placed it on the floor. Pulling off the lid, Drucilla blinked her eyes and adjusted her spectacles.

"No," she breathed softly, "this cannot be real!"

Neat stacks of money were tied with pieces of twine and nestled inside the box. Drucilla began to count it. When she reached two thousand dollars she stopped. Where had it come from?

Then she realized the truth: Tyler Templeton had sent money every month to support his daughter, only a small amount

at first, judging from his early letters, but more as he grew
more successful. Letitia Duckworth had not spent a penny of
it; instead she'd locked it away in this trunk. All those years
of thinking they were dirt poor, of wearing secondhand
clothes and having to use candles so sparingly! And in the
trunk in her bedroom, Mrs. Duckworth had kept a small
fortune . . .

Picking up another letter, Drucilla did some rapid arithme-
tic and figured that there must be close to four thousand
dollars in the pressed paper box. It was enough to do almost
anything within reason, but what, she could not imagine.

Drucilla read late into the night. She learned that her father
had left Memphis and gone to Texas after Mrs. Duckworth
had refused to allow him to take his daughter. Obviously the
old woman had told Tyler Templeton that he wasn't fit to
raise a child, that his wandering ways and lack of work
would only hurt River. *River Templeton.* Drucilla realized
with a jerk that it was her real name.

She said it aloud, rolling it off her tongue slowly. "River.
River Templeton. Hello, my name is River Templeton. How
do you do? I am River Templeton."

Rising from the floor where she had sat so long, Drucilla
stomped her feet to get the feeling back into them, then she
walked to the small dresser and picked up her grandmother's
hand mirror. She stared into it. She looked the same. Yet she
wasn't. She was no longer Drucilla Duckworth, but River
Templeton. And she loved it. She loved the name that rolled
so easily off her tongue, loved the sound of it. Would she
ever grow accustomed to it? And how would people react
when she told them that she was not Drucilla Duckworth, but
River Templeton? She could only imagine! And why hadn't
anyone in town mentioned it before, someone who'd known
her mother and father?

But then she recalled several years before, when an old
friend of her mother's had come to visit and Letitia Duckworth
had quite rudely told her to go away and never come again.
Of course. Grandmother would have effectively handled any

such matter in a way that no one would dare speak up, and after a few years no one would even care or remember.

She put the hand mirror back on the dresser. Then she sagged against it, staring into space. In the space of only forty-eight hours, her entire life had been rearranged.

Not Drucilla Duckworth . . . River Templeton echoed over and over in her mind. And she found herself smiling. Her father was alive! The last letter had been dated only a few weeks before, and his handwriting had been strong and steady. Obviously, he had given up on seeing his daughter, and must think that she chose not to see him. But it had been nineteen years! She'd only been four when her parents—no, just her mother—had been killed. Nineteen years, wasted.

"Well, that's too much time gone," she said aloud. "I intend to make up for it now."

Sitting down at the desk, she pulled out ink and pen and paper and began writing a letter. Her first few drafts were crumpled and tossed aside, then she finally penned a letter that satisfied her. And she knew what she would do with the money.

River Templeton was on her way to Texas.

Chapter 3

*

River sat stiffly, her hands folded in her lap and her mind spinning. She was on the final leg of her journey to Texas at last. With every passing mile her anxiety had quickened, and now she was absolutely terrified.

What if her father didn't like her? What if she didn't like him? What would he think of a plump, plain daughter? Alicia had been so lovely, wouldn't he expect their daughter to be the same? After all, the last time he'd seen her she'd been four years old. What if he was disappointed? What if—oh, but enough of that, she scolded herself. One shouldn't borrow trouble, she recalled her grandmother saying. There was usually enough to go around without borrowing more.

Squinting out the small, uncovered window of the stage that bore her and three other passengers toward Clanton, Texas, River adjusted her thick spectacles. They kept sliding from the bridge of her nose down to the tip because of the heat. Who would have thought it would be so hot in Texas in May? But it was. On the train from Memphis the brisk breeze that blew in the opened windows had kept the temperature comfortable. But this, this stuffy stagecoach, was like an oven! River could feel the damp sides of her black dress grow even damper and wished she had thought to purchase a cooler color.

It had been such a strange experience just purchasing new garments that she had not thought to buy anything except what she usually bought—dark, unflattering dresses. But at least they were new, and she didn't want to throw her money away just because she had it. After all, she may not stay in Texas, and then she would need money to get home on.

In his telegram, Tyler had assured her that if she did not like Texas he would send her home. But the tone of his telegram was so euphoric that River wondered if she would be able to say anything. So far, Texas seemed like one gigantic expanse of brown rock and stunted foliage. To be fair, she had to admit that east Texas had been pretty and green, but Tyler Templeton didn't live in east Texas. He lived in west Texas, and if this country was any example, she didn't think she would like it. To a girl who had been brought up among green trees and grass—even if they were several blocks away—the landscape seemed raw and primitive.

Oh, well. There she went borrowing trouble again! She would love Texas and she would love her father, she resolved. And that was that. But she didn't have to love the heat, River decided as another gust of hot wind blew in the tiny window of the stage.

She glanced up and met the amused gaze of the man across from her. River flushed. He had been laughing at her the entire way, ever since they had boarded the stage in Fort Worth. Maybe it was because of the sharp contrast between River and the beautiful girl beside her. But whatever it was that so amused the man, she was beginning to feel terribly uncomfortable.

River waited until the man looked away, then glanced at the girl next to her. Even in this wilting heat she looked fresh and lovely, as if she had just stepped out of a dress shop attired in something exquisitely new and fashioned just for her. *Disgusting*, River thought with a sigh of pure envy.

Clutching her hands tightly together over the small reticule she held in her lap, River looked back out the window. Not even stunted trees interrupted the expanse of brown horizon, and dust clouds boiled up from the wheels of the coach, filtering inside and coating everything possible, including her tongue. She coughed. Her spectacles slid to the tip of her nose again. She pushed them up and coughed again. Her hair lay limply on her neck, still bound in its tight bun, pulled back from her face in its usual severe fashion. River pushed at a stray tendril dangling in her eyes and thought how if she had been the girl next to her, no hair would be out of place.

But she wasn't the girl next to her. She was River Templeton, after spending so many years as Drucilla Duckworth, and she was embarking on a new life. It was exciting, and the other girl was probably accustomed to doing exciting things and would think River exceedingly dull. But that was all right, too, because interesting things were beginning to happen in her life. And who knew what adventure she would embark upon next? River just hoped it was something she had never done before. That left the field wide open.

She got her wish sooner than she expected.

The stagecoach gave a sudden lurch, and the two men directly across from River sat up sharply, exclaiming. An unfamiliar sound cracked in the air, once, twice, then again, and then River realized what it was. She had heard it often enough on Saturday nights in the Pinch district of Memphis. It was the sound of gunfire, and the two men had obviously recognized it, too.

"What's happening?" River cried, straining to see out the window as the coach increased its speed.

"Must be a robbery!" one of the men shouted back, and River realized that he had produced a pistol and was busily loading it.

A robbery? She shivered. She'd lived all those years in the dangerous streets of the Pinch district without once being accosted, and now here she was miles away and in the middle of a robbery! It was unthinkable. It was terrifying.

It was exciting.

River clutched at the leather strap dangling from the side of the coach. The makers of the coach must have foreseen circumstances such as this one. How providential.

The coach bounced over ruts in the road, and she could hear the gunfire racketing outside as the guard atop the stage fired back. The two men inside were also firing. The girl was still looking composed as she held to a similar strap to keep from being deposited on the floor of the coach. River was just as determined to keep her seat on the uncomfortable cushions but was finding it increasingly difficult as the coach swung wildly down the road. Her spectacles slipped completely off and were lost, and her hair began to straggle from its tight bun, partially obscuring her vision.

"Dear God!" River could not keep from moaning when the coach spun around a curve so swiftly it seemed in danger of overturning. The leather strap was beginning to cut into her palm as she clung to it, and with the perspiration of fear and heat making her hands slippery, she was in danger of losing her hold entirely.

Suddenly the coach came to an abrupt halt and River's hands slipped. Her skirts slid too, and she felt herself plunging forward in a graceless tumble of black taffeta petticoats and muslin skirts. Head-over-heels was the only way to describe her descent into abject humiliation. Through the yards of dress material now draped over her head, River could hear muffled gasps and snickers. Her cheeks flamed, and she clawed desperately at her skirts to bring them back down around her legs. Thank God for long pantalettes and dark stockings.

The Goddess, of course, was still sitting complacently while River was helped up by one of the men. She never knew which one because she was too sick with humiliation to look. She only mumbled a thick, "Thank you," and stared down at her skirts as she smoothed them with trembling hands. Nothing worse could happen now, she decided, even if the robbers took her mother's brooch and her grandmother's wedding ring. Even if they shot her.

Of course, River had been too prudent to bring much cash along with her anyway, for she realized that almost anything could happen on a long journey. Most of the money that her father had sent through the years now rested safely in a bank vault, available whenever she wrote a letter of transfer. Only a reasonable amount of cash was in her velvet reticule, hardly enough to hurt her financially or enrich a robber. And she would gladly give it all to avoid trouble.

Robbers were a funny lot, River decided several minutes later. Instead of concentrating upon the locked cash box atop the coach, the masked men herded all the passengers into a tight knot outside the coach and asked them their names. River, who had fumbled about on the coach floor for her spectacles without success, could hardly speak for the fear clogging her throat. They looked so dangerous! Heavy guns hung around their waists, and each man had a rifle. The eyes above the handkerchiefs around their faces showed no mercy, nothing but impatience.

"Hurry it up!" one of the robbers snarled when River was slow in handing him her reticule. He reached out and snatched it away, jerking River against him when the strap hung around her wrist. Another robber laughed harshly.

"Gittin' a bit too romantic, ain't ya?" he jeered, and all the other masked men heehawed with laughter. "Cain't ya jus' ast her her name without tryin' to kiss her?"

River's cheeks flushed. She knew they were laughing at her. Her chin lifted slightly, and she gazed coolly at the robber trying to disentangle her purse straps from her wrist.

"If you will wait a moment, I will undo them for you," she said with as much dignity as she could muster.

The tall robber paused, then nodded. "Okay, but hurry it up. What's yer name?" With shaking fingers, River began untangling the strap. Then the robber demanded again, "What's yer name, lady?"

"Dru-Drucilla Duckworth," she replied in a stammer, then

wondered why she had said that. She was *River* now, not Drucilla; but years of being Drucilla Duckworth were still ingrained in her. Under stress she had replied as she would have a few months ago.

With the straps successfully disentangled, the robber yanked open her reticule and examined the contents. When he scanned the few pieces of paper she carried, he tossed aside her reticule and moved on to the Goddess. River stood in trembling relief. Obviously she was not who the men wanted. And he obviously did not realize the value of her mother's brooch or her grandmother's wedding ring, or he would have kept them.

Her heart was pounding, and her mouth was dry with fear and apprehension. What did they want? Who were they looking for? Was someone important on the stage? And did they intend to kill them, or just rob them? She steadied her quivering knees and hoped that she didn't disgrace herself by succumbing to hysteria.

Now that the men's attention was focused on the Goddess, River's gaze darted from person to person. The driver was standing with his hands over his head, his pistol and rifle lying on the ground nearby. The guard had been wounded in the shooting and lay groaning on the ground. Blood seeped from between the splayed fingers he kept pressed over his upper arm. At the sight of blood River stifled a scream.

"Shouldn't someone be tending to that man's wound?" she blurted out, then wished she'd stayed silent when the robbers turned around to stare at her.

"This ain't no Sunday school picnic, lady!" the tall robber snarled. "Jus' stand there and keep yer mouth shut!"

"But he's bleeding," River protested weakly, the words coming from some unknown source deep inside her. The robber had turned away, and now he turned back and glared at her closely.

"What'd you say yer name was?"

She thought swiftly and decided it would be foolish to

change names in midstream—it would only cause them to pay more attention to her.

"D-D-Duckworth. Drucilla Duckworth."

The robber took a step toward her, his eyes dark and menacing above the mask. "Well now, Miss Duckworth, why don't you jus' tend to him, then, if you're so blamed worried about him? Go ahead."

"Hey," one of the other masked men muttered with a scalding oath, "this one ain't her, either."

Turning, the first robber considered for a moment, then said, "Mebbe it ain't a she. Mebbe it's a he. Cain't tell by the name. Check it out."

"I say it's the blonde," the first one said. "She's got the same color of hair, and she's tall and skinny."

The Goddess stiffened, losing some of her composure for the first time. She remained quiet and watchful, and when questioned replied in a steady voice. "I *am* Miss Llewellyn. May I ask why a common outlaw wants to know the *names* of his victims?"

"It ain't yer place to be askin' anything, lady!" the outlaw growled. "Which is yer baggage?"

When the Goddess pointed it out to him, it was quickly searched, the search ending only when some papers confirmed her identity.

"Hell! None of 'em are the right one!" a long-haired outlaw burst out.

River was puzzled but too frightened by her own temerity to think much about it. Obviously the robbers were looking for someone important, and she was glad she wasn't the one. How dangerous to be mixed up with men like these!

"May I tend to the guard?" she asked then, and the man gave a curt nod of his head.

"Hell yes! Tend to him! Jus' shaddup!"

River scurried over to the guard, her heart thumping wildly in her chest. She wondered where she had ever summoned the courage to speak up. Maybe the shock had made her mad.

Or maybe the heat had gotten to her. Whatever it was, she was glad she had asked because the guard was in a bad way.

She discreetly ripped away a portion of her black petticoat, although modesty mattered little now that all the passengers had already seen her choice of undergarments. River tightly bound the guard's wound with a tourniquet, silently thanking the Memphis City School system for insisting its teachers learned first aid. Of course, who would have thought that she would be applying that knowledge to bullet wounds instead of scraped knees on a school yard?

"Thank you, Miss Duckworth," the guard whispered hoarsely. River didn't bother to correct him.

"You're welcome," she replied with a smile. "I think that will hold nicely until we can get you to a doctor."

Rising, River turned to see that the robbers were going through all the baggage atop the coach. The suitcases and trunks had been flung down to the ground, where two of the masked men were prying open lids and tearing through the contents. She winced as she saw Grandmother Duckworth's trunk kicked aside, her new petticoats, chemises, and taffeta gowns spilling from it. Staying alive was what mattered now, she supposed, but that trunk held a sentimental value for her. After all, it had housed the remnants of her life for nineteen years, and it had provided the means for her freedom. A few more nicks and bangs wouldn't really hurt it, and she could always buy more clothes. The only irreplaceable item was her mother's portrait. Fortunately, none of the outlaws seemed the least bit interested in that.

Finally they were through scavenging for whatever they could find. River could hear snatches of their conversation from where she stood near the wounded guard but could make no sense of their comments. It puzzled her that they didn't seem to care that much about the cash box or the other valuables.

"It ain't gonna look good to him," a short, stocky man said. The tallest outlaw turned sharply, and his eyes narrowed over his black mask as he glared at him.

"He's gonna ask why we didn't find her."

"Mebbe it's a him . . ."

"An' mebbe he or she ain' even *on* this stage!"

The stocky outlaw shrugged. "I say we go back."

"Might as well. Take what you boys want. I intend to cut th' horses loose. That'll give us some time."

During the entire ordeal, none of the other passengers had spoken except to answer a direct question. Now the driver spoke up.

"We're miles from town! At least leave one horse so we can go for help."

"Walk," was the terse reply. "You're too damned fat, anyway. You could use the exercise."

Laughing at his own joke, the tall, lean outlaw sauntered over to the horses and cut through the holding traces, then shooed them away. Neighing shrilly, the frightened beasts bolted down the faint track that was the road, disappearing from sight over a far ridge with a flick of their tails.

Then, laughing and jeering, the masked men loaded the few things they had taken in saddlebags and rode away. The stranded passengers exchanged worried glances. How would they ever make it into town?

"Well," the driver finally said, spitting a stream of tobacco juice on the ground and hitching up his pants, "I guess I'll just have to head out walkin'."

No one argued with him. "Take a full pouch of water," River suggested practically.

The driver nodded. "Make yourselves comfortable, 'cause I won't be back for a while."

"How far is it into town?" one of the men asked.

"Oh, 'bout fifteen miles, I'd say." The driver gave a shake of his head, removed his hat and raked a hand through his sweat-drenched hair. "You'll have enough water in that barrel to last you all till I git back if you're careful and not greedy. And sit in the shade of the coach so you don't burn."

It seemed like sound advice to River, but as soon as the driver was out of sight the others began to quarrel.

"Don't use that water for washing!" one of the men said to Miss Llewellyn, who had dipped her dainty handkerchief into the water barrel and begun to bathe her face. She gazed at him so coldly he should have frozen on the spot.

"I am hot and I must cool off. If my face should burn, it will peel and be unsightly," the girl replied icily.

"If you'd sit in the shade like the driver said, you wouldn't burn!" the man retorted.

"And who gives a damn if you do?" the other passenger put in. "I'd rather be burned and alive instead of dead from thirst with a pale face!"

The guard began to cough, and River stooped beside him. "Are you all right?" she inquired anxiously.

Dust caked the guard's face, and his eyes were hazed with pain, but he nodded. "Yeah, but those buzzards'll have all the water gone if somebody doesn't watch 'em. Looks like it'll have to be you."

"Me?"

"Who else? I can't even move, and besides, you look like a girl who can take charge." He wiped a hand over his sweaty face. "You remind me of my schoolteacher."

River laughed. "I suppose that's normal enough, because that's exactly what I am. Or was." She put a hand on his forehead. "Now you need to rest and not concern yourself with the rest of us. I shall do my best to keep things under control. If you remain here under the stage, the sun should not be so hot. Shall I wet a cloth for your face?"

"And waste water? Not on your life!"

River glanced around the barren countryside. Few trees dotted the horizon, and the only shade was provided by the stagecoach and a hump of rocks several hundred yards away. She swallowed the sudden surge of fear that seemed to lodge in a palpable lump in her throat and managed a smile.

"All right, but I will bring you a sip or two for now. You'd better take it. The others are beginning to grow a bit ugly, I think."

And she was right. The three other passengers had begun

to quarrel bitterly over the barrel of water. One of the men, a Mr. Hotchkiss, was threatening to sit on the barrel to keep Miss Llewellyn from dipping her dainty hanky into it again. Miss Llewellyn retaliated by plunging her entire arm into the barrel, thereby upsetting Mr. Williams as well as Mr. Hotchkiss. River sighed. They did remind her of fourth-grade students, so she summoned up her best schoolteacher voice and strode forward.

Garbed in her dark dress and with her hair in a bun, River looked quite imposing as she descended upon them.

"Stop it! Stop it right now, I say! This small barrel of water is all that stands between us and dehydration, and I cannot tolerate your foolish squabbling another moment!"

They gaped at her: Mr. Hotchkiss with his mouth open and Mr. Williams with his brows lifted and Miss Llewellyn in a stunned kind of stare. Suddenly, instead of being intimidated by them and self-conscious of her bulk and plainness, River was in control. They were behaving like schoolchildren and deserved to be treated as such.

But despite River's judicious distribution of the water, by late afternoon it was almost gone. The small amount remaining left the situation grim. And there was no sign of the driver or help.

As the sun grew hotter, a red haze behind the far stubble of jagged mountains, Mr. Williams stood up. He turned to Mr. Hotchkiss, his jaw set.

"I'm taking the rest of that water away from Miss Duckworth, Hotchkiss. Are you for or against me?"

Mr. Hotchkiss stood also. "I have no intention of being so ungentlemanly as to attack a defenseless woman!"

"Defenseless!" Williams gave a hoot of laughter. "I would hardly call a two-hundred-pound woman *defenseless*!"

River stood as if turned to stone. She didn't mind being called a two-hundred-pound woman—even though she weighed nowhere near that. And it wasn't even that Williams intended to take away the last of the water. What stung was the obvious scorn in his voice. What had she ever done to make the man hate her? Or make him stare at her as if she was an object of ridicule, as he had during the journey?

She fumbled for her spectacles, which she had retrieved from the floor of the stagecoach, and shoved them back up on the bridge of her nose. Then she stood up. She would give Williams the water. It wasn't worth a fight. And it wasn't as if there was enough for all of them anyway.

But Mr. Hotchkiss bounded forward like a banty rooster, his hands curled into fists in front of him. He bounced several times on the balls of his feet. "All right, Mr. Williams, if you intend to fight, I'll show you how it's done!"

"Gentlemen!" River pleaded. "Don't do this! Save your energy for more important things!"

"Like what?" the guard asked from his place beneath the stagecoach. "The water's the most important thing right now."

River glanced over at Miss Llewellyn, who sat perched on the step of the stagecoach with her hands folded primly in front of her. There was not a hair out of place, and her face did not express an iota of concern for what was happening around her. River felt a surge of irritation. And to think she had envied the girl's composure! She was little more than a cold, bloodless statue.

A loud bellow of rage recaptured her attention, and River swung back around just in time to see Mr. Williams charge bull-like toward Mr. Hotchkiss. With his burly head lowered, Williams bellowed again and caught poor Mr. Hotchkiss around his middle, slamming him to the ground. The smaller man may have had some experience in the art of fisticuffs, but he was obviously a novice at barroom brawling. River gave a cry of dismay and started forward, but the guard caught the hem of her skirt.

"Leave them alone," he advised hoarsely. "The first rule of fighten' is—Don't git in th' way if it ain't yer fight."

"But Williams will hurt poor Hotchkiss!"

"Better him than you."

"Oh, won't someone stop it!" River cried out, putting her palms against her cheeks.

Conjured up as if by magic or the power of prayer, a man appeared from what seemed like thin air, flinging his large frame between the two fighting men. No one had heard his approach, and to River he seemed like an archangel from heaven.

"What the hell are you men doing?" the stranger demanded as he roughly thrust Williams to one side and Hotchkiss to the other. Williams bounded back, his face contorted with anger and his eyes glazed. The tall man caught him by the collar, whirled him around, and gave him another rough shove that sent Williams stumbling several feet before he sprawled on the ground.

River felt a wave of admiration for his ability to dispatch Williams so easily. He still had his back to her, but she noticed his unusual hat. It was worn, with a rattlesnake band around the crown. The rattles were still attached. Her stomach suddenly lurched as she noted the lethal gun belts strapped around his lean waist, and she wondered if the man was a savior or just a new outlaw.

Hotchkiss apparently wondered the same thing, because he began a rambling dissertation that the stranger halted in midsentence.

He glared at Hotchkiss, and his deep voice was cold and flat. "Control yourself, man. It looks like you're having enough trouble without fighting between yourselves."

"W-w-well," Hotchkiss stammered, "it was Williams's fault!"

Tucking his thumbs into his gunbelt, the stranger turned and looked at the other passengers, his eyes flicking from one to the other with remote interest.

River's mouth sagged open and her spectacles plunged to the very tip of her nose.

It was her Ideal Man.

Her breath caught in her throat, and she wheezed most unattractively. It was Him, the man in her dreams, the man she had thought only imaginary, the man she had never believed actually existed. At least, he certainly looked like what she had always wanted her Ideal Man to look like, which was almost the same thing.

He was tall, but not too tall. He was muscular, but with that smooth flowing of skin and muscle that had none of the bulky knots of some men she had seen. He wore snug-fitting trousers, a thin cotton shirt open at the neck, and a double holster around lean hips. His thick hair was dark, his features perfectly arranged so that he was not too pretty or too rugged. Only his eyes were different from her dream, being a clear silver instead of the bright blue she had envisioned. But one should not examine dreams too closely or they might fade away, River decided as she continued to gape at the man.

"I can guess what happened here," he was saying, "but I would still like to hear the details." His gaze flicked from the wounded guard to the passengers. "Well?" he demanded when everyone remained silent. "What happened?"

His gaze shifted to River, who stood as if struck dumb, staring at him with huge, owlish eyes. He recoiled slightly and looked away.

The Goddess stood up from the stagecoach step where she'd been sitting during the brief struggle, and stepped forward. Her voice was as cool and soft as a September morn.

"There was a robbery. The driver has walked to the nearest town for help." She paused, then added with a faint smile touching her lips, "I am Linda Llewellyn. *Miss* Linda Llewellyn."

River's heart sank. Of course. The Goddess would be interested in a man as vitally alive as this one, and it would not matter if he was River's Ideal Man. And what man would look at a gargoyle garbed in black like a crow when the impeccable Miss Llewellyn was nearby?

"Gray Morgan," the man was saying, and River sighed with bittersweet pleasure. Gray Morgan. A masculine name. A name that was as handsome as the man. It wasn't prissy, like Marion or Francis, though those were perfectly good names and commanded respect. But they would not have suited this man. Gray Morgan suited him. It was a strong name. And his voice was strong, deep and pleasant, with no harsh twang or reedy resonance.

"Those two were quarreling over the water," Miss Llewellyn was saying as casually as if it did not matter. "You arrived just in time."

She made it sound like he was a hero, and River had to admit that he was. Why couldn't she gaze up at Gray Morgan with limpid eyes and appear so fragile and dainty that he would immediately fall in love with her and sweep her away with him?

Of course such fanciful notions were out of place and quite impractical. She knew that. The guard needed immediate attention. River cleared her throat loudly, planning to point that out, when Gray Morgan turned to look at her. His silver eyes bored into hers, and his dark brows were lifted. Her words stuck in her throat.

"Yes?" he prompted. River could not speak. She stared at him dumbly.

"Did you want to say something?"

She nodded mutely, unable to speak when he was staring at her. Morgan flicked a wary glance toward Miss Llewellyn, who shrugged her shapely shoulders. Morgan turned back to River.

"What's your name?" Gray Morgan asked with a frown. His eyes narrowed slightly in concern.

River could not answer distinctly.

"D-r-ru—Riv—aarrgh!" she said, then flushed beet red.

Morgan's brows drew down in a perplexed knot. "Excuse me?"

River's tongue seemed swelled to twice its normal size, and it clung to the roof of her mouth as she tried again. "NNnnrgh . . . R-r-r—"

Morgan's polite attention wavered, and he turned toward the wounded guard.

"Drucilla Duckworth," the guard supplied helpfully.

"Ah," Morgan said, and smiled distantly at River, who was in the throes of an urgent desire to sink deep into the ground and never be seen again, like Persephone. "Perhaps, Miss Duckworth, you should stand in the shade? You seem to have gotten too much sun," Gray Morgan said. He put out a hand to steer her toward the shade provided by the coach.

River wanted desperately to let him know that she was not an idiot, but at the moment it seemed hopeless. Humiliation seared through her body in a flaming wave, overriding the knowledge that her Ideal Man was actually touching her. Her pained gaze fixed blindly on his handsome face.

That seemed to unnerve Morgan, who seated her in the shade by the guard and stepped away as quickly as possible. He then proceeded to take charge of the situation with brisk efficiency. River watched numbly.

"Hotchkiss, give some of the water in my pouch to the guard. He needs it more than the rest of you. Williams, look at the harness and see if it can be fixed. We might catch the horses."

Miss Llewellyn attached herself to Morgan with one hand on his arm, her eyes limpid pools as she looked up at him. "It was frightening! All those men, their masks and guns and rough language." She shivered and edged closer to him.

Morgan put her gently but firmly away from him. "Those men are gone now. There's no reason to be scared, and no time for it. If you will excuse me, I'm going to give Mr. Hotchkiss some instructions."

The Goddess stared at him incredulously as he walked away, then gave a sniff of disdain and stalked back to her seat in the shade. She sat with folded arms and her head turned away from Gray Morgan.

River, on the other hand, could not keep her eyes off him. She drank in the sight of him as greedily as if he was water and she was dying of thirst. She could not stop herself. It was such a shock, seeing him at last, her Ideal Man, and she could not keep her gaze from following him.

Her steady stare finally became noticeable to Morgan, and he turned to look in her direction. For the first time, he seemed a bit disconcerted, but recovered quickly and tugged his hat lower over his eyes as he ignored her.

"Hotchkiss," he said, turning his back on River, "I want you to take my horse and ride due east about two miles from here. There's a line shack. You can't miss it. I happen to know the man staying there, and he can help us round up the horses. Williams and I will repair the traces while you're gone... Are you all right?"

Hotchkiss was staring nervously at the huge gray stallion. "That horse?" he squeaked, and Gray gave an impatient nod of his head.

"That's the only one here, isn't it? Yes, *that* horse! He won't bite. Maybe."

"I'm not so worried about being bit as I am about being thrown."

"Look, have you ever ridden a horse?" Morgan cut in.

"Yes..."

"Then you can ride mine. There's a hunting rifle in the saddle scabbard. Use it if there's trouble."

Williams swaggered forward, his mouth twisted in a sneer. "I'll go for help, Morgan."

"Forget it," Gray said shortly. "I'm sending Hotchkiss."

Williams's eyes narrowed. "What? You don't trust me to come back?"

"You said it, I didn't."

For a moment it looked as if Williams might argue, but the steely glint in Morgan's eyes kept him silent. From beneath the stagecoach came a faint chuckle, and the guard said softly, "Smart man, Morgan!"

After Hotchkiss had finally managed to mount the horse and steer him in the right direction, Morgan and Williams began gathering up the baggage strewn across the road.

"How'd you know there was trouble?" Williams asked as he helped Gray pick up trunks and leather satchels.

Gray pushed back the hat he wore, then heaved Grandmother Duckworth's trunk atop the stagecoach. Garments draped from the edges, but the trunk didn't seem damaged.

Shrugging, Gray said, "I saw the horses running with their traces hanging. I figured there had been a wreck or some kind of trouble along the way."

Williams gave a terse nod. "Trouble's right! We were held up by a bunch of armed men."

"So I heard. Give a description to the sheriff in Clanton, and maybe he can find them."

"You don't seem much interested," Williams observed sourly.

Morgan paused in picking up a wooden crate. "I'm more interested than you can guess, Williams. I'm just practical about what I can do about it right now."

"Well," Williams said, "I'm leaving on the next stage. I'm not hanging around Clanton any longer than it takes to tell everything I know."

"I'm sure that won't take very long at all," Gray said, and no one but River seemed to catch the insult. She smiled with appreciation, propping her chin in her palm and gazing at him.

She was in love.

The thought startled River. And it frightened her. She'd never been in love before, never thought she would find a man to spark that elusive emotion. Yet here she was, gazing at her Ideal Man and dreaming of love, and he was shifting uncomfortably every time he happened to meet her gaze. River tried to look away from him, but the more she tried the worse it got. He would ride away after he'd helped them and she would never see him again, she thought desperately. How could she bear it?

When the hours finally passed, and the weary, travel-stained passengers were grouped on the wooden sidewalk on Clanton's main street, she edged close to those thanking Gray Morgan for his help. She stood, staring at him with huge, glass-rimmed eyes that appeared even larger behind the thick lenses. Her heart fluttered painfully, and she knew she had to speak to him.

"M-m-ister M-m-organ," she stammered, and he turned to stare at her with polite wariness. She cleared her throat and put a hand on his arm when it looked as if he would turn away. "Mr. Morgan, I just want to . . . want to say . . . I . . . I l-lo—thank you."

Horrified, she realized that she had almost blurted out "I love you." Her throat closed with embarrassment, and she hoped he hadn't noticed.

But he had. Morgan took an instinctive step away, a faint "what!" escaping before his lips pressed together. He seemed to regain control and said more kindly, "You're welcome, Miss Duckworth. I, uh, hope the rest of your trip is safe. Good-bye."

Then he was gone. He was striding quickly away as if she might blurt out another lovesick confession. River gazed after him miserably. She'd met her Ideal Man at last. This was the best day of her life. And the worst.

Chapter 4

*

River stood on the Clanton city sidewalk struggling against disappointment. It clogged her throat and filled her heart, but she managed to drown it with hope. There was always another time, another place, another life.

"River!"

Startled by the use of her new name, River half-turned and saw a big, brawny man with a shock of blond hair leap up onto the sidewalk. He was pushing impatiently past those standing there, pushing right past the blond, beautiful Miss Llewellyn and heading straight for River.

"River!" he exclaimed again, a huge grin splitting his face. She had time for only a smile before he had reached her and swung her from the sidewalk into the air as if she were a small child, as if she were still only four years old. "River!"

"Yes..."

"River! Oh Lord, River, I thought this day would never come!" he said hoarsely, and didn't seem at all ashamed of the tears streaking his tanned cheeks. His smile was wide, and he grabbed the arm of a man passing by. "Joe! This is my daughter! This is River..."

He didn't say a word about her plainness or her weight. Tyler Templeton didn't even seem to notice. To him she was beautiful. And Joe nodded and smiled and said he was pleased to meet Tyler Templeton's daughter. River's heart swelled with a surge of love that she had never thought she would be able to feel. This was her father, at long last, and he accepted her just like she was. No mention was made of the fact that her drab clothes hid a too-large frame, or that her thick spectacles hid most of her face. Nothing was said about her chignon or her shyness. She wanted to say something intelligent that would convince her father she was at least smart if not beautiful, but she could think of nothing. This didn't seem to matter to Tyler Templeton, who talked nonstop.

"I was worried sick when I heard about what happened out there," he said. "You're all right, aren't you? I was down at the sheriff's office getting up a posse when Sandy came in and said the stage was here. Are you hungry? Tired? I've got us some rooms at the hotel in town. I knew you'd be too tired to ride out to the ranch today..."

River smiled. "Well, I *am* hungry," she admitted. "The stage accommodations weren't exactly overwhelming."

"I know that well enough," Tyler said with a laugh. "Ah, let me look at you, River." He held her at arm's length, and she took the opportunity to study her father more closely.

Physically he was a powerful man, tall and imposing, with broad shoulders and a craggy face that somehow seemed to match the rest of him. His hair was short and light blond, almost the color of wheat, and though he had to be at least forty-five, he looked boyishly young. River supposed that she had gotten her large frame from her father, and that made her feel as if she really did belong. Was he thinking that she looked nothing like her mother, perhaps? That worry was banished when Tyler pulled her into his embrace again, his arms wrapping around her in a hug.

"Let's go over to Delmonico's and get something to eat," Tyler said. He waved an arm at an approaching man who was pushing toward them through the crowd. "Sandy, just put her baggage in the wagon and join us when you can," Tyler said to him, and the lanky young man with sandy-colored hair grinned.

"Aren't you going to introduce me to your daughter, Tyler?" he said with a teasing wink in River's direction. "Or am I too much of a ruffian to let on you know me?"

Tyler laughed and shook his head. "Doggone, Sandy, you know how excited I've been! I've forgotten all my manners. River, this is Sandy Dennis, one of the best ranch foremen in the entire state of Texas."

"Pleased to meet you, Mr. Dennis," River said with a smile.

He groaned. "Mr. Dennis! Please, call me Sandy or I'll begin to think I'm somebody!"

"All right—Sandy."

Sandy was already hefting River's trunk to his shoulder and starting toward the wagon, but he gave them both a quick smile and the assurance that he would meet them at Delmonico's Restaurant. Tyler wasn't really listening. He was too busy smiling down at his daughter, cupping her elbow in a big hand and escorting her down the sidewalk. He pointed out every place of interest to her, the hotel, the ladies' dress shop, the milliner, the bakery behind the general store, the livery stable, and down at the far end of town, he said, were the saloons.

"Far enough away so you don't have to worry about being forced to listen to any drunks," Tyler added with a laugh. "They get kinda rowdy at times but don't usually mean any harm. Usually. And the hotel is up here at this end, so you'll be safe."

"Good," River replied with a shudder, recalling the menacing outlaws earlier. "I'm not certain I could bear seeing one more disagreeable person, man or woman!"

Tyler's face sobered, and he gave a grim nod of his head. "I can understand that." He reached around her to open the door to a surprisingly elegant restaurant, much more elegant than River had thought a small Texas town could support.

"I sure am glad to see you here safe and sound," Tyler told River when they were seated at a table. "We're so used to the stage being late, that we didn't think much about it until Red—the driver—came strolling into town. 'Course, by the time we got up some men to go after you, here you came. I was never so glad to see that stage! You weren't harmed in any way were you?"

River shook her head. "I was only terrified." She swallowed hard at the memory. "I just knew we would all be killed, or at the least robbed of everything, but those men seemed more interested in who we were and our luggage than anything else. Odd, isn't it?"

Tyler frowned. "Downright peculiar, I'd say."

River was silent for a moment, giving silent thanks that she was here now, safe and secure and finally with her father. "The guard said the same thing."

"Pete Hankins?"

"I don't know." River smiled awkwardly. "I never thought to ask his name, though everyone else had to give their names to those outlaws."

"It was Pete Hankins, I'm pretty sure. He usually makes this run." Tyler took a sip of his coffee, the frown still on his face. "Think I'll ask him what he makes of all this, though I'm sure he's already talked to the sheriff."

"They took him to the doctor first, I imagine. He was wounded in the shooting."

Anger creased Tyler's face, and his blue eyes grew cold. "Shooting! So help me, if you had been wounded after all this, River, I would have . . . I would have done something I might regret. It's been too damned long, and to have lost you again would have killed me."

Surprised at the depth of his emotion, River reached across the table and put her hand on Tyler's arm. "But I'm here now, and I'm safe."

Tyler smiled, the anger slowly fading from his face. "Yes, you are, and I thank God for every moment we'll have together, River. I've finally got my little girl with me."

Several seconds ticked past, then River asked the question she had asked herself so many times since first reading her father's letters.

"Why didn't you take me with you? Why did you leave me with Grandmother Duckworth?"

Tyler stared down at his big hands for a moment, working his mouth. Then he looked up at her and sighed. "I wanted to take you with me, River. I fought that old harridan tooth and claw for a solid month, but she had right on her side. I had no job, no place to live—we lived with her, your mother and I—and Letitia Duckworth was not about to reside in the same house with a man who had been responsible for her daughter's death." A note of bitterness crept into his voice. "It was the hardest thing I'd ever had to do, bury my sweet Alicia, and that old woman made it even harder. I guess since she's dead now I should forgive her, but I'm finding it hard, River. You were all I had left, and I promised myself that I'd take care of you somehow. I sent money, even when I didn't have much myself, and I sent more when I could. I wanted you to come to me, but she always had a reason: You were sick or you couldn't leave school when you were doing so well or did I really mean to risk your life in the wilderness?" He smiled grimly. "I was a fool for not going back to Memphis and just taking you, but I guess maybe I felt so bad about taking Alicia away that I couldn't take you, too."

"I wish you had!" River blurted, then she paused. "I'm sorry. I didn't mean to make you feel bad, but it was so . . . so drab most of the time, and I thought you were dead all those years. Why, until Grandmother died and I found your letters, I—"

"What?" Tyler's brows drew into a scowl again. "You mean she let you think I was—that I had—why, that vicious old harpy!"

"Talking about Trucklow again, Tyler?" a voice cut in cheerfully, and Sandy Dennis pulled out a chair to sit down at the table.

Tyler's expression eased, and he shook his head. "No, you

danged eavesdropper. You're worse than an old woman when it comes to gossip, Sandy.''

''Well, whatever keeps life interestin','' Sandy said with a grin and another wink at River. ''Did you order for me?''

''Yeah, a whole hindquarter of beef!'' Tyler retorted. ''It'll take that much to fill your big mouth.''

River listened to their teasing banter with a smile, and sat back in her chair. She was happy. Her contentment was near to overflowing. She knew that she would never feel lonely or unloved again. Perhaps she had suffered some hardships during the past nineteen years, but they were gone now. And maybe she wouldn't have appreciated her father if she had had him all those years.

''How far away is the ranch?'' River asked over dessert.

''Just down the road a piece,'' Sandy replied.

River understood from the mock-solemn expression on his face that it must be farther than she imagined. ''How far is 'a piece'?''

''I'd say about twenty miles,'' Tyler answered for Sandy, and both men laughed at her expression.

''It's not that far once you're used to it,'' Sandy said. ''But the first few times, it seems like you're never gonna get there.''

''I suppose I should have realized that everything in Texas is spread out much more than in Memphis.''

''No, there's no way you could have known,'' Tyler said with a shake of his head. ''This isn't Tennessee.''

''No, it certainly isn't!'' River agreed.

Tyler leaned forward. ''Do you think you'll like Texas, River? You don't have to be afraid of hurting my feelings if you don't, and like I wrote and told you, anytime you want to go back all you have to do is say the word.''

''Well, it's different from what I'm accustomed to, but I cannot imagine being with anyone else. If you lived in . . . in *Turkey*, I'd want to be with you!'' she finished so earnestly that Tyler had to grin in relief.

Pulling a fat cigar out of his vest pocket, Tyler stuck it in

his mouth. "I'm glad to hear you say that," he said around
the cigar, "because I don't know if I could let you go back
without me, and I'm needed here."

"Yeah, especially when Trucklow comes snoopin' around,"
Sandy put in, then subsided when Tyler gave a warning shake
of his head.

"Who's Trucklow?" River asked curiously. It was the
second time she'd heard his name, and Sandy did not say it in
a kind way.

"Just a blowhard who's gotten a little greedy, honey. It's
nothing to worry about," Tyler answered, then he turned the
conversation to another subject. "There's several women on
the ranch that I think you'll like, River. Old Sandy here was
lucky enough to get one of them to marry him, though I don't
know how he did it. Must have slipped her some cactus juice
or something. Anyway," he continued with a grin at Sandy,
"some of the women are just your age. You ought to enjoy
talking to them, you know, all that female stuff you gals like
to talk about."

River didn't know "all that female stuff" women liked to
talk about, but she didn't want to say so. Grandmother
Duckworth had never approved of having friends, and so she
had long since ceased trying to be friends with anyone. She
hoped that her father wouldn't notice if the other women
didn't like her, or that she could pretend she did not care if
they didn't. But there she went borrowing trouble again,
when she just might find that she liked the women on Tyler's
ranch.

"Well," Tyler was saying, "I intend to go outside and
smoke this cigar, and then we need to turn in for the night.
We'll ride out to the ranch first thing in the morning. River. I
think you'll enjoy the ride after a good night's rest."

River suddenly realized how tired she was. It had been a
long day, and the jolting ride in the stagecoach had seemed
much longer than three days. The robbery had been a shock,
and the meeting of her Ideal Man even more so. A faint smile
curved her mouth, and her eyes took on a dreamy glaze. He

was so perfect, so much like her dreams. Though she had to admit, in her dreams he hadn't looked at her and backed away. That hurt more than she wanted to think about, and remembering she winced slightly. Somehow, in her dreams, she was always slender and beautiful, and the Ideal Man fell in love with her too. Real life didn't seem to work that way, unfortunately.

Managing a bright smile, River told her father, "A real bed and a hot bath sound like unprecedented luxuries right now!"

"Well, I think we can arrange both of them for you," Tyler said with a chuckle as they left the restaurant.

Walking beside Tyler along the wooden sidewalk that stretched down the main street of Clanton, River was struck with how much quieter it was than Memphis. The muted clink of a piano at the far end of town was the only sound that carried on the cool night wind, and she could hear an occasional burst of laughter. Other than that, it did not seem like a thriving town at all.

"Here we are," Tyler said cheerfully, pushing open one side of the double doors. "Clanton's only hotel and chief meeting place! If you can't find someone at Delmonico's, you're bound to find them at the Clanton Hotel!"

River laughed as she entered the hotel, half-turning to look back at her father. "Now I know all the best places," she said. She was still smiling when she turned back around and saw the man standing at the front desk in the lobby.

Gray Morgan.

She stiffened, and a feeling of panic swept through her. Blindly she turned back to her father. "Papa"—how easily the childhood name for him rolled from her tongue now— "Papa, I think I'd like to go straight up to my room. I am much more tired than I thought."

"Of course, honey. Just let me find that key . . . Oh, dang it, I guess I forgot to get yours. Wait here, and I'll just step over to the front desk and get it for you."

There wasn't too much she could do but stand there and wait, wait for Gray Morgan to turn around and see her and back away again. River waited in an agony of apprehension, saw her father speak to Gray and saw him laugh, then saw with dismay that Gray Morgan was turning and walking in her direction. She glanced around desperately, searching for a hiding place, anything but to stand there and be embarrassed.

Gray was frowning down at a paper in his hands and not really paying attention to where he was going as he walked across the lobby. River froze, then gave a silent groan of dismay when he veered directly toward her. She stepped aside, but not before he looked up and noticed her.

"Oh. Hello," Gray muttered, then started to push past her.

For some reason—perhaps because the sharp memory of his reaction still rankled—River smiled, pushed at the horn-rimmed spectacles on the bridge of her nose, and said, "Oh, hello, Mr. Morgan! How very pleasant to meet you again."

Gray paused, looked around as if searching for help, then shrugged. "Yes. Well, good evening, Miss Yuckwor—I mean, Duckworth."

River's eyes blazed with embarrassed anger, but her chin lifted as she decided to prolong his discomfort. "*Duck*worth, Mr. Morgan. *Duck*worth!"

Gray had the grace to look faintly embarrassed, but he still didn't back down. A tight smile slanted his mouth, and he gave a terse nod. "Whatever. Good evening."

River watched him go, his easy, loose-limbed stride eating the distance between her and the hotel doors as if afraid she would say something else to him. All right. So she had made a terrible first impression. So she had stared at him so hard that now he didn't want to be within fifty feet of her. She still had her dreams, didn't she? And now her Ideal Man had a name.

"Got it!" Tyler said at her elbow, and River gave a start. She hadn't even heard him approach, but fortunately he didn't seem to notice her distraction.

"My room is down the hall from yours, but I'm not too far away if you need anything," Tyler was saying as he escorted River up the staircase to the second floor. "Just knock on my door."

"I will, Papa. Thank you." River watched as Tyler put the key in her door and swung it open, and a forced smile curved her mouth when he turned to her. "Good night, Papa."

"Good night, River. I'm so glad you're here."

"I am, too," she said softly, and realized that she truly was glad to be in Texas with her father.

"I'll let you sleep late," Tyler said with a wink, then he leaned forward to press a kiss on her forehead. "Sleep well."

"You, too."

River leaned against her closed door and gazed at the room. It was small but nicely furnished, with a rich carpet and carved wood furniture, softly glowing gas lamps, and a dressing screen in one corner. Sandy Dennis had placed her baggage beneath the window, and she crossed the room to look out.

Leaning on the windowsill, River stared out into the street. It took a moment for her eyes to adjust to the shadows, for there were no street lamps in Clanton. She saw one of the shadows move and recognized Gray Morgan leaning against a porch post across the street. Her heart quickened its beat, and she held her breath.

Light from a window lit one half of his face, leaving the other in shadow, but she had no doubt it was Gray. She recognized his easy stance, his casual, almost lazy motions as he lit a cigarette and stuck it in his mouth. The brief flame lit his face, and River sighed.

It was just her luck to finally meet her Ideal Man and discover that he hated her. Well, maybe not hated her, but he certainly was not impressed.

River's mouth tightened with determination. Maybe she could do something about that. Maybe, with luck and tenacity, she could make Gray Morgan at least tolerate her. Possibly even like her.

She stood at the window until Gray moved away. He walked down the street toward the saloons, his boots sounding hollow on the wooden sidewalk. Sighing again, she pulled the curtains closed over her window. A light breeze puffed against them, belling them out in graceful swells.

River undressed slowly, removed her spectacles, and put them on the nightstand, then unbound the tight knot of hair at her neck and removed the net. She tugged a brush through it until her hair crackled, then slipped between the sheets of the feather bed. After turning out the gas lamp she lay there staring at the play of shadow and moonlight on the ceiling and walls, waiting for sleep to claim her.

But tonight, it seemed, sleep would not come. Time passed slowly, and she could hear every sound from the street outside her hotel room.

Sighing, she finally rose and shrugged into a high-necked cotton robe. Perhaps a cup of warm milk would help.

She tugged several times on the old-fashioned bell rope, but the maid did not arrive. Finally she realized the only way to get warm milk was to go down and ask for it. Slipping her room key into her pocket, she stepped out into the hallway. The halls were dim, the gas lamps turned down to only a faint glow. River felt her way along the hallway toward the stairs.

As she rounded the corner leading to the stairwell, a large shadow detached itself from a wall and grabbed her. She screamed, a short sound cut off by warm lips smothering her mouth. The strong odor of whisky surrounded her, and she felt hard male arms coiling tightly around her body, jerking her close. For a moment she struggled, panic rising in her throat, then she recognized her assailant.

It was Gray Morgan, and he was obviously drunk. Quite drunk. And her father had told her that all the rowdy drunks were staying at the other end of town . . .

No matter. Now was not the time to think about that, not when Gray Morgan was holding her much too tightly, his lips searing across hers. It wasn't so much a kiss as it was an invasion, and River moaned softly. Her moan only seemed to spur him on, and Gray tangled his hand in her long hair, holding her head still so that she could not twist away.

River's head swam, and her heart was pounding so hard

she could scarcely breathe. Her knees quivered, and deep in the pit of her stomach a fire began to burn, so that when he pushed aside the edges of her robe and slid his hands across her breasts, she felt a shivering tremor that had nothing to do with fear.

What was happening to her? This was insane! River dimly realized that if she did not put a halt to this now, she would very likely have her first love affair in a hotel hallway.

Summoning all her strength and courage, she gave him a rough shove that caught him by surprise. Gray stumbled back a step, and leaned against the wall, slightly swaying.

"What'sa matter, love?" he muttered thickly. "Changed your mind?"

"No, Mr. Morgan," River said as coolly as she could manage under the circumstances, "you've got the wrong love."

Reeling backward, Gray peered at her in the dim light, his brows swooping down in a fierce scowl as he struggled to focus. One hand flashed out and grabbed her by the arm, and he pushed her into the pool of light from the wall lamp.

"You're not . . . you're Miss Duckworth!" he said, and swore softly. "Yuck . . ."

River stiffened, and her voice was icy. "No, I most certainly am not who you think I am!"

She had been going to suggest that he go back to the saloon, but a strident female voice demanded from a door down the hall, "Gray! What's taking you so long?"

Shrugging, Gray reeled away from River and down the dim hallway without a backward glance. The door closed behind him, and River felt a sinking dismay. Of course. A man as attractive as Gray Morgan would have a woman, perhaps even a wife. But if he had a wife he couldn't recognize in the dark, he couldn't be very fond of her, she told herself.

River was beginning to realize that her Ideal Man had some flaws, and it was rather daunting. Ideal Man were supposed to be perfect. Of course, the Ideal Man of her dreams wasn't real and never would be, and maybe a few flaws would only make Gray Morgan that much more attractive. Maybe.

Forgetting the warm milk, and more shaken by the unexpected kiss than she had first thought, River made her way back to her room and returned to bed. When she finally drifted off to sleep, she had the most vivid dream she had ever had, and her Ideal Man did not look at her and say, "Yuck." No, he held her closely, and his lips were warm, tasting faintly of tobacco and whisky, a taste so sharp she could swear it was real, even in her sleep. Did dreams have such realism? she wondered as she tossed and turned. It was so real, so wonderful, because Gray Morgan was holding her, kissing her, telling her huskily how beautiful she was and how much he loved her. And somehow, in the dark of night, without the harsh reality of daylight, it seemed like the natural thing for him to do.

Chapter 5

*

The Double T Ranch spread for miles, and as the buckboard rocked along rutted trails over gentle slopes, River stared in amazement. "All of this is yours?" she asked her father.

"Ours. And yes, as far as you can see this way"—he waved an arm to the south—"and to that ridge in the north. East it goes for about two miles, and west, well, west is a little disputed right now."

"Disputed?"

"Yeah," Sandy Dennis put in, "but Trucklow ain't got a leg to stand on!"

"Trucklow? Who is this Trucklow I keep hearing about?" River asked.

"Pierce Trucklow," Tyler answered after a moment of silence and a warning glance toward Sandy. "He's a neighbor of ours, and there's been a bit of a dispute over water rights."

"And land rights and people rights, too!" Sandy snapped. He gave the reins a smart slap against the horses' rumps. The buckboard jerked forward, and River clapped a hand to the straw hat she wore to keep the sun from burning her face.

When she'd regained her balance and made sure the hat would remain fixed on her head, she said, "I take it that this Pierce Trucklow is a bit unethical in the manner he disputes ownership of the land."

"Bingo!" the irrepressible Sandy said, then lapsed into silence when Tyler glared at him.

"No need to frighten her, Sandy," Tyler said with a shake of his head. "She just got here. I'd like for her to stay a while."

"Sorry, Tyler, but you know how I feel about Trucklow. He cheated to get his land, rustled all his cattle, and he won't think twice about getting rid of you if he thinks he can get away with it."

"That's why we're going to do this all nice and legal-like," Tyler said evenly.

Sandy snorted. "Takes too long!"

"But in the end, it's the only way." Tyler turned to River, who had been following the conversation with a frown. "Don't worry, honey. See, Trucklow hasn't yet figured out that a man eventually loses when he plays the wrong way. I've learned that in order to win, a man has to have the law and right on his side. I've got right, and I'm working on getting the law."

"I don't really understand what—"

"See, Trucklow wants this piece of land on the western edge of my property, up on Comanche Ridge. He claims he needs the water, that his present water supply is too unstable. And he's trying to say that he was there first and I jumped his claim. I've got a good friend, though, who's agreed to check the old records. I know that piece of land is mine."

"If you ask me—and I know you didn't—" Sandy said, ignoring Tyler's frown, "there's more to it than just that water hole."

"May be, may be," Tyler agreed slowly, "but that doesn't matter. It's my land."

Sandy shook his head. "Yeah, but makes me wonder what he knows that we don't."

"I'm not at all sure I want to know some of the things Trucklow must know," Tyler observed, then deftly switched the subject. "Look, River, that corner fence post marks the beginning of the drive leading up to the house. We'll be there in a few minutes."

River turned to look, her heart beating rapidly. This was to be her home, and somehow it all seemed so unreal. In such a short time her life had changed so drastically, and she wanted to pinch herself to make sure she wasn't just dreaming. From a tiny, shabby house in the Pinch district of Memphis, to this vast expanse of land—wasn't it the stuff dreams were made of?

"There aren't any trees, are there?" she asked, not realizing how wistful she sounded. "Or much water?"

"Do you miss the river?" Tyler asked, misreading her words.

"The river?" She stared up at him blankly, seeing in his shadowed face the worry that she might prefer Memphis to Texas. "I rarely went down to the river. It was too dangerous, and besides, I could smell it from my window."

Tyler didn't say anything for a moment, just stared into the distance. Finally he shook his head. "You know that Alicia and I named you for that river. It's where we fell in love, on the bluffs overlooking the Mississippi."

"Tell me about it."

A faint smile curled Tyler's mouth as he lifted his head and began speaking, telling River how they had met at a church picnic and how he had fallen in love with Alicia in only an instant. "It didn't take me but a few seconds to know that she was the girl for me," Tyler said, his eyes seeming to see back in time as he relived the past in his mind. "And I think she felt the same way. I do know that when we eloped I was the happiest man alive. If the war hadn't come, maybe things would have turned out different. But it did come, and it changed everything."

"How did it change things?" River asked when Tyler fell silent, lost in his memories.

"Well, for one thing, my family lost everything we owned, land, houses, servants, stock—everything. Alicia and I hadn't been married but seven or eight months when Fort Sumter fell, and I was young and fool enough to join right up." He smiled wryly. "How impetuous are young men! Anyway, she was carrying you by then, and I took her home to her mama to stay while I went to war. Of course, when the war was over and I didn't have a penny to my name, we just kinda stayed on there with your grandmother." Tyler's voice hardened. "I shouldn't have listened to Alicia, but she was so soft-hearted at times, and worried that her mother would die of a broken heart if she left her, now that she was a widow. So I let her talk me into it, and it was the worst thing I could have done. That old lady almost ruined our marriage, and I reckon she did ruin your days, River. I'm sorry about that."

"You couldn't have known."

He shook his head. "No, reckon I couldn't. But I should have figured what that old harridan would do if she had a chance. She never did like me, but she wouldn't have liked any man who wanted to take her daughter away." His voice grew thick with emotion. "That's why I wanted to take Alicia upriver with me that day, to look at a house I'd found. It was small, but still in good shape, and the owner had offered me a job at the local sawmill as foreman. I just wanted my wife back so badly, that I didn't even think about how overcrowded the *Sultana* was, how it was filled with soldiers all going back home, Yankee and Rebel alike, and when the boilers blew—" He paused, cleared his throat, then continued more softly, "When the boilers blew and fire rained down, we were separated. I reached for her, but she was swept away by the crowd and I never saw her again. In those days after . . . after we found her body, I wished it was me who'd died, but there was nothing I could do about it. I still had you, see, River, and I knew that. I wanted to do my best by our daughter, and I failed in that, too.''

Appalled by the bitterness in his voice, River put her hand on his arm, turning her father to face her. "You did the best you could, Papa, and I want you to know that I've never blamed you for anything. Grandmother Duckworth was a hard woman, but I knew that even when I was very young. I've always loved you, and I love you even more now.''

Tyler pulled River into his hard embrace and hugged her tightly, completely disregarding Sandy Dennis, who had remained silent during their conversation. After a moment he let go and chucked her under the chin. "I could not ask for a more perfect daughter, River," he said thickly.

Tears wet her cheeks, too, and she gazed at him with all her pent-up years of longing and love. To be accepted so completely was one of her heart's dreams come true.

Slightly embarrassed at witnessing their conversation, Sandy Dennis waved an arm toward the front of the wagon. "We're almost there," he said. "You can tell by the trees.''

Tyler had planted trees along the curving drive that led to the house, and the buckboard rolled slowly through the shady arches that entwined overhead. There was the soft sweet smell of new-mown hay in the air, and through the trees she could see cattle grazing.

"New mamas and their calves," Tyler said, pointing to the fat cattle. "We keep 'em pretty close until the calves are old enough to get around good.''

"Where are the rest?" River asked.

"We move them around from pasture to pasture. It lets the grass grow . . .''

"And confuses rustlers," Sandy put in.

"Sandy . . .''

"All right," the foreman said with a sigh. "You're right. I talk too much.''

"Worse than an old woman," Tyler grumbled. "There's the house, River!''

She almost stood up in the buckboard as it rounded the last

curve. Slowly, a long, low building came into view. It had a Spanish-style red-tile roof and an adobe archway over the front door. Walls of weathered boards and stones made the house look as if it belonged there, and trees shaded it from the hot Texas sun. Smaller houses built of the same wood and stone and each with its own garden plot, stood behind the main house. Neat fences kept the stock away from the vegetables, and bright flowers in wooden boxes gave the houses a warm look.

"Consuela's notion," Sandy explained with a look of pride when River commented on the pretty flowers, and she decided that Consuela must be his wife.

As the buckboard rolled to a halt in front of the main house, two women came out on the stone porch. They were waving and smiling, and one of them bounded forward with a glad cry.

"Welcome to your new *casa*, Miss Templeton!" she said. "We are all so glad to meet you at last."

Tyler smiled as he helped River down from the buckboard. "This is Consuela Dennis, River. As you've probably guessed, she's Sandy's wife. Keeps him in line too. And this is Maria Sanchez. Come here, Maria, and meet my daughter."

River stared at the two young women. They were both dark-haired and dark-eyed, with rosy cheeks and smiling faces. They seemed so happy and contented, and all at once she felt dowdy in comparison. Both women wore light blouses and flowered cotton skirts that ended just above their ankles. And instead of stockings and high-top shoes, they wore some kind of leather shoe that looked like a heelless pump. And it seemed infinitely more practical in the heat.

"I'll put her trunk in her room," Sandy told Tyler when he had disentangled himself from his pretty wife's embrace. "You two go on in out of the heat."

"Oh, señorita! You must be so hot in those clothes," Maria said quickly. "I did not think. Come into the house where it is cool."

It was much cooler inside. Tyler had built the house for

comfort rather than style, and the ceilings were high and arched so that the tile floors were cool. Long windows were open at each end of the main room so that the breeze could circulate throughout the day, and double doors opened onto a patio that was shaded by thick vines curling over an open-lattice roof. The furniture was plain and simple, more functional than pretty, but appropriate. A few woven rugs were scattered across the tile floors, and a massive stone fireplace dominated one entire wall. Books lined built-in shelves, and brass lamps hung from the ceiling. For River, after growing up at Grandmother Duckworth's, the house was better than any fairy-tale castle.

"Shall I serve refreshments on the patio, Señor Templeton?" Maria asked, and he nodded.

"Good idea, Maria. I'm sure River will want to freshen up after our long ride from town."

"*Sí!* I shall show her to her room, while Consuela greets her handsome husband!" Laughing, Maria beckoned to River, who followed her down a long, wide hallway. Several rooms opened off the hall, all of them with long windows and doors that opened onto a terrace. Maria chatted amiably, offering tidbits of information along the way.

"You can use this armoire for your clothes, and your papa had this mirror put in here just for you! Oh, he was so excited when he knew that you are coming! I have never seen him so happy, Señorita Templeton. He laugh and he say, 'Will she like me? Do you think she will like me, Maria?' until I tell him that *sí!* You will like him. You do, don't you, señorita?"

River was faintly bemused with Maria's rapid flow of conversation, but she managed a dazed nod. "Of course, I like him. He—he's wonderful."

"We all think so, too. He is a good man, and . . . are you going to wear *that*?"

Pausing, River glanced down at the dress she had drawn from her trunk. "Why . . . why, yes. Why?"

Maria wrinkled her pert nose. "It looks so hot, with those

sleeves and long skirts. Why don't you wear a *camisa* instead?''

"Excuse me?"

"*Camisa*—blouse. Like this I am wearing."

River stared at her doubtfully. "I don't have anything like that, Maria. These are things I bought before I came, and they're all I have."

"Oh. Well, we shall get some things for you. If you like," she added quickly. "I do not mean to offend you . . ."

"Oh, you haven't. I just have never seen a . . . *camisa* like yours before. It does seem much cooler and more practical in this heat."

"I shall borrow one for you," Maria said promptly, and River flushed. How could she tell the slender girl that she was much too fat to fit into anything of hers?

"I—I don't think any of yours or Consuela's will fit me," River said after a moment. "We are not even close to the same size."

"*Sí*, I know that. But Rosa, she is of your thickness, and she will have many *camisas*." Maria took the dress River held and put it back in the trunk. "I will unpack for you later, and now you shall join your papa on the patio. I will bring you something cool to drink, while you rest."

River's embarrassment faded as she sat on the patio with Tyler, enjoying the cool breeze and the rich scent of jasmine. Maria brought them a fruit punch, which was a delicious concoction made with papaya and orange and lemon juices. A tray of curiously shaped sandwiches that Tyler said were meat tortillas had been placed on the table near her, and River tried one.

"This is delicious," she said in surprise. "I've never eaten one before."

"It's made from ground corn or flour, rolled thin, and garnished with shredded meat and whatever else you want to put on it," Tyler replied with a smile. "Try some of that salsa, but watch out—it's hot!"

A small dish of diced green and red peppers that River

spread liberally on her tortilla made her reach quickly for some more of the fruit punch, and Tyler laughed.

"You were right!" River croaked when she could catch her breath. "How do you eat that stuff?"

"You acquire a taste for it. You'll see. Before long you'll be putting salsa on everything, including your morning eggs."

River made a face. "Maybe if I do, I won't eat so much and be so fat."

One eyebrow lifted, and Tyler just gazed at her for a moment. "You're not fat, honey. Healthy, maybe, but not fat."

"Healthy is just a polite way of saying fat, Papa, and you know it." River's mouth twisted wryly. "I've overheard enough comments to know the truth, so don't think you have to pretend I'm beautiful."

"But you are beautiful!" Tyler protested. "Honey, you look just like your mother, and she was the most beautiful woman who ever drew a breath! How do you think I recognized you so easily yesterday?"

"Papa, please!" River couldn't look at him. He was trying to be nice, to make her feel better about herself, but she knew better. Any mirror would make a liar out of him.

"Listen to me, River." Tyler took both her hands in his and made her look up at him. "You've got beautiful blue eyes, and your mother's straight nose and perfectly shaped mouth. Your hair is thick and shiny, and your skin is clear and pale, and you've got those good cheekbones that she had—how can I make you see that you are pretty? Maybe you aren't as slender as you could be, but after a few weeks out here, you'll be in great shape. And I think skinny women look too frail and sickly anyway. Look at Consuela and Maria—do they look bad?"

River shook her head and forced a smile. "No, but they aren't as big as I am."

"So what? They aren't sticks, either." Tyler chucked her under the chin. "No more about being fat, do you understand me? I won't listen to it, and don't you dare say any more. And don't be afraid to eat!"

Laughing, River said, "All right! But don't blame me if I get so big you have to build an extra room for me."

"That's not going to happen. And so long as you're in good health, I don't care anyway."

"It would be wonderful if everyone felt that way," River said with such wistfulness that her father looked at her sharply.

"Has someone I know been rude to you?"

"No, no! But I would like for some man—I mean, some*one*— to notice me, to think I'm attractive." *Gray Morgan*, her subconscious supplied immediately, but she ignored it.

Tyler chuckled. "Oh, so that's it! You think you've got to be beautiful to be well-thought-of. Well, listen to me, honey, when I tell you that if a person cares only about how you look instead of the kind of person you are, you're better off without them."

"Why do I have the feeling that fathers all over the world say the same thing to their plain daughters?" River asked with a smile.

Tyler kissed her on top of her head. "Because fathers all over the world know what their daughters don't, that's why. Now come on. If you're rested enough, I want to show you off to my ranch, and my ranch off to you."

"Just let me change into more sensible walking shoes," River said. "I won't be but a moment."

But when River went to her room, she discovered that Maria had made good on her promise to find her some cooler clothing. Spread on the bed were two *camisas* and two brightly flowered cotton skirts. A *rebozo*, or thin shawl, lay beside them, and two pairs of leather huaraches were on the floor beside the bed.

"What are all these?" River asked helplessly, and Maria clapped her hands together and laughed.

"I told you, *señorita*! I told you I would be able to find

you cooler things! Do you like them? Rosa was glad to give them to Señor Templeton's daughter."

"But I can't take all these," River protested, "and I don't even know if they'll fit."

"They will fit. The blouses are loose, see? And the skirts are full, with a string at the top that draws them close around your waist. Here. I will show you."

"Oh, but I don't know," River began, but was swept along by Maria's determination. She bravely bore up under the girl's handling, and dutifully removed her tight corset with the whalebone stays and gave it into Maria's hands. She felt much freer, but wasn't at all sure what else the impetuous Maria planned for her.

River dared not ask. She suffered silently as Maria undid the tight bun at the nape of her neck and brushed her hair until it crackled, and she said not a word when Maria took her spectacles and put them on the dresser. They were only for reading, anyway. But when Maria tossed aside her petticoats with the comment that they were not needed, River had to protest. Finally Maria allowed her one thin petticoat of a soft white muslin, though it was obvious she thought River was being quite foolish about it.

And when the pretty Mexican girl was finished, River could hardly believe her mirrored reflection. Who would have thought that such simple garments could be so flattering? Or maybe it was the bright colors against her pale skin.

The blouse was a lightweight cotton dyed a bright yellow that made her skin take on a golden tone, and the skirt was yellow and orange and cream. Even the *rebozo* was flattering, a sheer melon color that made her hair seem lighter. Maria had loosened her hair, holding it back with a pair of pretty Spanish combs that she said were much more flattering than the tiny little net River used.

"And it still holds it back from your eyes, though you should let a little bit curl here, like this, see?" Maria said. "Your hair is nice and thick, with pretty waves, if you would only let it free."

"It gets in my eyes and looks unkempt," River objected, and Maria sighed.

"It was those ugly glass eyes you wore that looked so bad, but I will not ask too much of you today."

"Thank you," River said dryly. But Maria did not seem to notice her sarcasm.

"De nada," the girl replied. Only one pair of the huaraches fit, but Maria assured her that she would get her another pair before long.

Grinning happily, Maria said, "Enjoy your walk with your papa."

Tyler pursed his lips when he saw River. "Whooeee! You look like a Spanish princess!"

River laughed. "I *feel* like I've been through the Spanish Inquisition! Maria is quite . . . forceful."

"Oh, yes, I could have told you that. Has a heart as big as all outdoors, though. And you do look beautiful, honey."

For once in her life, River felt beautiful. The mirror told her that she was not a beauty, but the colors made her skin glow and her eyes seem brighter, and she felt so free now that she had shed her constrictive clothing that she even felt lighter. All illusions, of course, but it made Tyler so happy to think she was as beautiful as her mother that she would not contradict him.

"Oh, I brought you something, Papa," River said, and stepped back into the hallway for a moment. When she returned, she was holding the portrait of her mother, a bit worse for the rough handling it had endured, but still an excellent likeness.

Tyler's face subtly altered, his expression growing softer, and faintly melancholy. "Alicia," he whispered, and reached out to take the framed portrait. "I haven't seen this in years, River. Not since . . . not since I left your grandmother's house."

"She kept it on the parlor wall."

"Yes, I know. It was always there." Tyler held it with reverence, then glanced up at his daughter. "Besides your presence here, there is nothing that could have made me any happier than this portrait, River. Thank you."

Flushing, she said. "You're welcome."

Tyler cleared his throat and wiped away the tears that had gathered in the corners of his eyes. "Well? Shall we go outside before I make a complete fool of myself?"

Sucking in a deep breath, River put her hand on her father's arm and sallied forth to meet the inhabitants of the Double T.

Chapter 6

*

Within an hour she was totally confused. All the names and faces seemed to blend together, but she was left with an overall impression of friendliness and genuine acceptance. Most of Tyler's ranch hands were married, and River met their wives and children.

Individual wood-and-stone buildings housed the families, while the unmarried ranch hands lived in long bunkhouses. River was struck by the air of congeniality among the many diverse personalities, and mentioned it to her father.

Tyler shrugged. "Well, if a man doesn't get along, he doesn't stay. It's important that we all work well together since we're all so close every day. I found out a long time ago that I can't tolerate dissension." A faint grin slanted his mouth. "Mrs. Duckworth taught me the value of harmony in the home."

River had to laugh. "I can well understand that!" Shading her eyes with a curved hand, she turned to survey the outbuildings. Stables and a shed for newborn calves lay to one side, and low stone buildings for cool storage were dug into a hillside. Hay barns and grain bins had been built nearby, and she could see the fresh green sprouts of corn in fields on the horizon.

"You have so much land!"

"A lot of it is rock and dust. The house is on the pretty part, but there's scrub and rock not too far out. I'll show it to you tomorrow, when you've rested a bit more. I want you to ride fences with me, get to know every inch of this place as well as I do." Tyler shifted to one leg and let his gaze drift past River to the horizon. "Ah, River, this is a great country! Maybe I did wrong in showing you the best side first, but I want you to love it too. At night when the stars are out, they're so close you can almost reach out and touch them. It's like . . . like touching God."

His voice had grown soft and reverent, and River could feel his love for the land. She followed his gaze across the acres of tall, waving grasses studded with an occasional rock and a rare tree. The wind blew and the grass looked like the currents of the Mississippi River, moving in timeless freedom, undulating ceaselessly. Yes, maybe she could understand Tyler's love for this land, and it had already caught her imagination. In time, she would love it too.

River reached up just in time to prevent her *rebozo* from flying off her head as a gust of wind swept by. The material was soft and gauzy, not really of much use as a sunshade, and she could almost feel the freckles popping out on her face.

"I should have brought a hat to shade my face," she murmured, and Tyler shook his head.

"A little sun is good for you if you don't overdo it." Laughing, he added, "I don't recommend too much, though, or you'll look like a sun-dried apple!"

"That might be an improvement."

"Ready to choose your horse?" Tyler asked then, changing the subject so rapidly River was startled.

"Ch—choose my horse?"

"Yep. Everyone has to have a horse out here. It's a long way to anywhere, and unless you're an Indian, you don't want to be walking."

"Why an Indian?" she asked, her curiosity piqued. "What makes them different?"

"Indians are used to walking. Why, I know an old man who must be eighty if he's a day, and he could outwalk any young white man I know."

"Are the Indians out here . . . violent?" River asked, recalling the newspaper accounts in the *Commercial Appeal*, where she'd read of various atrocities.

"Not nearly as violent as most white men. But that's another story," Tyler said. "Ask Gray Morgan about it sometime."

"Gray Morgan?" she echoed, and her head snapped up. The mention of his name aroused immediate interest.

"Yeah, Morgan's sort of befriended the Indians around here. The Comanches got out of hand a few years back, and it was Morgan who managed to bring about a truce of sorts. The Comanches say he's got a silver tongue," Tyler said with a grin.

River was all ears. "Does he?"

"Yeah, I guess he does. Maybe that's why he decided to be a lawyer, though most people around here don't take very kindly to a man who helps out the Indians."

"A lawyer. How does he help the Indians?"

"He's the go-between for the Comanches and the BIA, the Bureau of Indian Affairs. And he's bumped heads with Pierce Trucklow over land encroachment more than once or twice. I warned him that people around here wouldn't forget how he took up for the Indians, and that they hadn't forgotten the old wars between red man and white, but he told me real bluntly that he didn't give a damn what people thought, that he was going to do what was right, come hell or high water." Tyler shook his head. "That's a direct quote, I might add."

"So, have people grown accustomed to his choice?" River asked curiously.

"Yes, and no. Everyone has to admit he's right smart, but they don't have to admit they were wrong. It's one of those situations where all Gray needs is to compromise a little, and folks will come 'round.''

River was quiet for a moment, then she said softly, ''I don't think a man should compromise his principles.''

Tyler shot her a keen glance. ''I don't either, honey. But there are a lot of folks who do.'' He pointed toward the horses milling in the corral. ''I favor that little bay gelding. Or the sorrel mare. Both are sweet-natured, with just enough meanness to make them lively.''

River dragged her attention from Gray back to the horses. ''Meanness?'' She swallowed hard, her gaze following her father's pointing finger. ''They look so big, and are you sure meanness is a desirable quality in a horse? Especially for someone who has never actually ridden a horse?''

Tyler's booming laugh rippled into the hot air. ''Honey,'' he said, shaking his head, ''before too long you're going to complain that I gave you a deadhead to ride! There's spunk in you, and once you quit worrying about whether you *can* do it and just do it, you'll be fine.''

''I hope you're right,'' River said weakly as her father unlatched the gate and pulled her inside the corral with him. The horses instantly crowded around, sniffing, whickering, nudging Tyler.

''They're looking for sugar lumps or pieces of carrot,'' Tyler explained when the sorrel stuck her muzzle into River's armpit. ''The kids around here have a bad habit of trying to make pets of them.''

River, busily dancing out of the sorrel's reach, managed a brave smile. ''Oh,'' she said. ''Oh!'' she said again as the sorrel snatched the end of her *rebozo,* pulling it from her head. The horse flipped it in the air like it was a flag, alarming the other horses, and Tyler was forced to shoo them away and retrieve River's rather soggy shawl.

''Sorry about that. Some horses are just like children. Can't resist a good prank.''

''Yes. Well, I must admit that—what's the horse's name?—''

''Brandy, I think.''

"Brandy. Well, Brandy reminds me of a young boy I taught last year, a brown-eyed lad with the devil in his eyes and loneliness in his soul. He was my favorite." River was silent for a moment, then timidly reached out and stroked the horse on the end of her velvety soft muzzle. She smiled when the upper lip curled back and the mare closed her eyes with pleasure. "I think I'll take this one."

"You made an excellent choice," Tyler approved. "She's long of leg and has a good disposition. Of course, I had Sandy put only the best horses in here for you to choose from, but she's my favorite, too."

When they stood outside the corral again, River smiled up at her father. "Do you think I'll ever fit in? After all, I can't ride a horse, I know absolutely nothing about running or even working on a ranch, and—"

"And you'll fit in beautifully," Tyler cut in. He put an arm around her shoulders and gave her a squeeze. "No one fits in at first, River. We all have to learn—and teach—as we go through life. I don't know too many people who are born knowing everything, though I've listened to a few who claim they do."

She laughed. "I guess you're right. I just want so badly to help out in some way."

"Oh, you'll find your niche, honey. Don't worry about it."

She decided to follow Tyler's advice. River didn't worry about it. Somehow, the days seemed to flow one into the other, golden days with nights so clear she saw what Tyler meant when he talked about touching the stars. The sky was so vast, like an inverted blue bowl during the day and as infinite as eternity at night. Even when it stormed, it was more powerful, more awesome than the storms in Memphis.

Perhaps that was because if she stood on a hill or in the doorway of the house and watched, she could see its approach for miles before it struck. Thick black clouds boiled over the horizon, and the tall grasses in the fields bent low. Cattle lowed nervously, and all the men put on oil slickers and rode out to keep them from stampeding.

Even the domestic animals grew nervous. One dog in particular, a medium-sized reddish-brown dog with the unlikely name of Reggie, began to howl piteously when a crack of thunder reverberated through the air.

River was standing in the doorway of the kitchen while Rosa and Consuela prepared the evening meal, and she turned at the strange sound to see the dog shivering near Consuela's feet. "What's the matter with him?" she asked Consuela, who frowned and shook her head angrily.

"Poor Reggie has never liked storms, but since he was hurt a month ago, he will hardly leave my side."

"Hurt? What happened?"

Consuela would not answer at first. When pressed, she finally said, "Your papa did not want you to worry, but you will find out one day anyway. Sandy found Reggie hanging on a fence one morning when he went out to look for some lost cattle. It had been done as a warning, but whoever did it obviously meant to kill him. They are some bad *hombres*, men who would hang a poor dog."

River shivered. She knelt down by the dog, who stared up at her with such pitiful brown eyes that she felt a wrench of sympathy. What kind of men would resort to such a cruel thing? And why?

Reggie put a white paw on her arm, and River stroked his soft fur. A patch of white on his chest gave him the appearance of a rather dapper old man with a starched shirt and tie, and she smiled.

"Poor dog," River murmured, and slid her hand under the animal's floppy ears. He sighed and laid his muzzle trustingly on her knee.

Consuela, who was pounding out flour tortillas, smiled. "I see you like dogs as well as horses, Señorita Templeton. Sandy told me that you ride well for being inexperienced."

River stood and smiled back at her. "Well, at least I haven't fallen off yet. I'm not the most graceful of women, you know, probably because I'm as large as two women—"

Consuela immediately interrupted her, asking, "Did you see Señor Morgan today?"

River's head shot up. "Morgan? Gray Morgan? Was he out here?"

"*Sí*. He rode out to talk to your papa, and mentioned that he would like to meet you sometime."

"Meet me? But he already—" River halted. No, Gray had met Drucilla Duckworth, not River Templeton. She wondered if he recalled kissing her in the hallway of the hotel, or if he even knew whom he had kissed that night. A faint smile touched her mouth. What would he say when someone informed him that Drucilla *Yuck*worth and River were one and the same? Too bad she couldn't be there to see it.

"Lucky for him I wasn't here," River said.

Turning indignantly, the pretty Mexican woman leveled a wooden spoon at River and said in her sternest voice, "Señorita Templeton, it is not good to talk bad about yourself! Your papa was right when he said you must not, and you must stop doing it."

River stared at her. "Excuse me?"

"You say bad things about yourself, about being too large or not pretty, or some silly things. Your papa, he said not to let you do it anymore, and he was right. Only, I cannot keep quiet and pretend not to notice. No, I must say what I think, and I think you hurt your papa's feelings when you are unkind to yourself."

"I don't know what you mean," River began, but Consuela shook her head.

"Yes, you do. Think about what I have said." Consuela glanced at Rosa as if for confirmation, but Rosa would not look at her. Shrugging, Consuela continued, "Señorita, I think it would hurt your papa to say those things to you. It hurts him to think you do not like yourself very much."

River curled her arms around herself, thinking. Then she said slowly, "I never have liked myself very much. I was always made to feel, well, plain and not very smart. It's been ingrained in me so deeply that I suppose I can't help but talk that way."

"But you're not plain," Consuela said indignantly. "And you are very smart! Who has told you such bad things?"

A faint smile curved River's mouth, and she said in a rueful voice, "My grandmother. I think she did it because she was afraid I would get married and move away, leaving her alone. At least that's what I've decided her reasons were. I'd hate to think she did it because she just didn't like me."

"This *abuela*, she was very bitter, no?" Consuela said.

"She was very bitter, yes," River replied after a moment.

"Sometimes people share their bitterness with even those they love," Consuela said softly. "It is a thing they cannot help, but not a thing that should be passed from one to the other."

River was silent for a moment. "And I sound bitter?" she said at last.

"*Sí*. I know you do not mean it, but when you speak ill of yourself, you sound very bitter."

"I'll try to stop," River said, "though it won't be easy. It's an old habit." A wry smile twisted her mouth, and she looked at Consuela. "My grandmother had a proverb for habits, too: 'Habit with him was all the test of truth; it must be right, I've done it from my youth.' Perhaps not all proverbs are the truth."

"Perhaps not," Consuela agreed. "And all habits are not good."

"You're right, Consuela. I shall make an effort to amend my bad habit, and make Papa a little happier."

Consuela and Rosa exchanged smiles. "Bueno!" Rosa exclaimed. "Señor Templeton will be much happy. See, now that everything else nice is happening, perhaps that bad *hombre* who torments him so much will stop, or go away."

"Who is that?" River asked curiously, and both Mexican women looked away.

"We should not say," Rosa finally mumbled, and River took a firm step closer.

"Oh, no! You're not going to do that to me again! If you can be brave enough to tell me things for my own good, be brave enough to share important information with me. What is it that everyone is afraid to tell me? I know about that Trucklow person, whom I assume you're talking about now, but I still don't know how serious it is. Is it more serious than I've been led to believe?"

Tyler's voice came from the doorway. "River, I'll tell you all about it if you insist upon knowing, though I wish you would not. Rosa, Consuela—we'll be in the living room when it's time for you to call us to the dining table."

"Papa, what is going on?" River asked when they were seated on the long couch. "I know you don't want to worry me, but all this mystery is making me think things that may not be!"

Tyler blew a long exhalation, then looked up at the portrait of Alicia he had hung on the wall as if for guidance. "Do you recall the name Pierce Trucklow?"

"Of course. He's the one Sandy mentioned, the one who is disputing your water rights."

"Yes, that's Trucklow. Well, he is behind a lot of things that have been happening lately. I've been forced to give the order for my men to wear their guns."

River recoiled. "Guns? Is it that bad? Can't the sheriff do something about it?"

"It's not that easy, River. We're a long way from Clanton, and this is a large spread. If I can't patrol it, I can't expect the sheriff to. Besides, he's got his own worries in town."

"It was Trucklow who hung Reggie on the fence, wasn't it?" River asked, and Tyler looked surprised. She nodded her head toward the kitchen. "He's scared of storms and won't leave Consuela."

"Oh. Well, I can't think of anyone else who'd do that. Poor dog. He was one of my best cow dogs, too, but I doubt I'll ever get him out again. Well, that doesn't matter. I intend to do what I can, River, but I don't want you to fear for your life."

"Please!" she begged. "Stop treating me like a child! I am not going to run back to Memphis just because there's some trouble out here, and I wish you would trust me."

It was Tyler's turn to look hurt. "I never meant that, I just—"

"I know. And I appreciate it. But I am twenty-three years old, Papa, and I am old enough to face a little more adversity in life."

Tyler stood and looked down at her. "It's just that you've had so much already, and I want to make things easy for you."

She stood up to meet his gaze. "Don't. I want to do my share. If I'm not a contributing member of this family, I'll always feel like a guest instead of your daughter."

A smile curved Tyler's mouth and he grabbed her and hugged her. "You're right? From now on, we'll discuss the bad as well as the good. Speaking of which, do you think you can make it for a ride tomorrow morning?"

River groaned. "I'm not sure! I'm still sore from the ride this morning, but I'll give it a try."

"Good. Sandy says your riding lessons are coming along great, so a few hours in the saddle will be your first test. And I hope you like what you'll see."

The next day River didn't do as badly as she'd thought she would, but she didn't do as well as her father had hoped. The mare was gentle, but spirited, and by the time they were a few miles from the house her arms were aching and her legs were numb. Maria had practically insisted that she wear men's trousers, but as River had refused to make such a spectacle of herself, they had compromised with a divided riding skirt.

"It's safer than riding with both your legs on one side," Maria had declared so forcefully, River had finally capitulated. Now she was glad she had.

Only the pleasure she derived from riding with her father over land that he was so proud of eased the pain in her muscles, and River did her best to put it from her mind.

"Why, we're miles from the house!" she exclaimed when they stopped at noon.

"Not too far," Tyler said. He removed his hat and raked a hand through his hair. "I've got to ride out to a line shack still several miles from here, honey. I don't think you're in shape to try such a long day yet, so why don't you go on back to the house for lunch. I told Rosa I'd send you back, so she'll have your lunch ready."

After a moment's hesitation, River said, "I hope you don't think I'm a quitter, but I'm going to take you up on that offer."

Tyler smiled. "You're no quitter, or you'd have already gone back to the house!" He leaned from his saddle to chuck her under the chin. "You're a trooper, River. Look, just follow this road and it will lead you directly to the Double T driveway. You'll see the trees."

She glanced at the road just ahead. Not a soul was in sight. Clearing her throat, she asked, "This road?"

"Yes, it's safe. It's way out on the open range that it's not so safe anymore. Stay on the road, now."

Wheeling his horse, Tyler waved, then kicked the bay into a trot. River tried to appear nonchalant as she waved back and reined her mare in the direction of the road. It wasn't so bad, she decided several minutes later; in face, it was nice.

The sun shimmered down, and the mare had settled into an easy walk that didn't jar River at all. A nice breeze kept the sun from scorching her, and she pushed back her wide-brimmed hat and let the sunshine beat down on her upturned face. She smiled against the press of sun and wind and let her thoughts drift. It was so quiet, with only her mare's hoofbeats and the creak of saddle leather to break the silence. It was soothing, almost hypnotizing, and River let her mind drift pleasantly.

Perhaps that was why she didn't hear the other horse approach. Startled by the sudden noise from right behind her, River let out a scream that panicked the sorrel mare. The mare bolted, and River tumbled from the saddle and into the middle of the road with a bone-jarring *thwack*.

Stunned, she lay there, listening to a symphony of birds go round and round in her head, trying to focus her eyes. Her split riding skirt was up around her knees, and her hat, though still on its string around her neck, was crushed beneath her.

"Hey!" a voice said again, and River recognized it with a faint groan of dismay. Gray Morgan. She fumbled blindly at the skirt around her knees, trying to hide her black-stockinged legs.

"Hey, are you hurt?" he said, and his handsome face swam into view at last as he knelt down beside her. She closed her eyes.

"No. Yes. I don't know."

Gray sat back on his heels. "Well, which is it?" he asked shortly. "I don't know whether to try and lift you up or not. Or if I can," he added in a mutter that she wasn't supposed to hear.

River's eyes snapped open, and she glared at him. "I don't think anything's broken, but if I am all right, it certainly isn't because of you! What are you doing sneaking up on people?"

"Hey, it wasn't my fault you were stargazing and didn't hear me," Gray shot back. He stood up in a smooth, lithe motion, glaring down at her. "What the hell are you doing way out here?"

"Right now I'm lying in the middle of the road answering stupid questions, while my horse is probably halfway to Mexico!"

He had the grace to look faintly sheepish. "Sorry. Here, take my hand."

Gray bent and put out a hand, and River took it. When he put his other hand under her elbow to help lift her from the road, she felt a tremor in her muscles. Just his touch affected her. It was obvious that he was not exactly thrilled to see her, and even less happy that he was forced to help her up from the road. Why should she let him affect her like this when he was so obviously displeased at seeing her?

It was also obvious that he did not remember kissing her in the hallway of the Clanton Hotel, River realized, and felt a sudden surge of superiority. She knew two things that he didn't: one, that she was the daughter of one of his friends, and, two, that he had kissed her one night. A smile curved her mouth as she half-stumbled on purpose.

Steadying her with one arm around her waist, Gray held her until he was certain she wouldn't fall on her face. "There. I hope you're all right, because you gave me a backache."

River took a step forward, and almost fell when her foot twisted sideways. Her gasp of pain was real. "No! Oh, I think I hurt my ankle."

"Hurt your ankle? How could you do that falling on your butt?" Gray snapped irritably.

River's head jerked up, and she pushed at the hat that had swung around on its string to dangle in front of her. "Look, you don't have to be so rude!"

To her surprise, Gray agreed with her. "You're right. Sorry. I guess I've got a lot on my mind, but that isn't your fault. You're Miss *Duck*worth, aren't you?"

River smiled at his emphasis. "Yes, but..." No, she wouldn't explain yet. Later, maybe, she'd tell him who she was, but not now. "But you may call me Drucilla," she finished, and Gray nodded.

"Fine. Let me get you over to that rock, and we'll decide what to do about getting you back to town. My horse could carry us both, I guess, but—"

"That's really not necessary," River said quickly. "I need to catch my horse, anyway."

Gray seemed relieved. "You're right. I'll catch her for you. Will you be all right here for a few minutes?"

She nodded, spreading the material of her riding skirt over her legs with nervous hands. "Yes, but do you think you can catch her? I mean, she's awfully fast."

A heart-stopping grin squared his mouth as Gray swung atop his huge gray stallion. "There's not a horse been born that I can't catch," he assured her and wheeled his horse around. Clouds of dust mushroomed into the air behind the stallion, then drifted away in layers.

"Not only handsome, but modest, too," River muttered irritably. She pushed the crown of her flattened hat back out and jammed it on her head, knowing that she must look absolutely ridiculous. Nothing was going right. Not only was her Ideal Man stubborn, rude, and arrogant, but he did not have the least bit of interest in her. That was not the way it was supposed to be, at least not in books or in her dreams. But this wasn't a dream, River reminded herself with a sigh, and Gray Morgan certainly wasn't as perfect as her Ideal Man!

Remembering that helped her be more gracious when Gray returned with her mare.

"Thank you, Mr. Morgan," she said when he heaved her up on her mare. "I will be perfectly all right now. I can have my ankle tended when I return home, so there's no need for you to accompany me."

Gray seemed only too happy to let her go on alone. "All right, but remember to listen for other riders so you don't get thrown again."

"I wasn't thrown," River reminded him coldly. "My horse bolted when I screamed."

"Okay. Fell off, then. Just be careful."

"Thank you for your concern, Mr. Morgan."

Gray was already stepping into his saddle and reining his stallion in a direction parallel to the road. "Anytime, Miss Duckworth. S'long!"

With a wave of his hand, he was gone, riding over a ridge and disappearing from sight. River wondered why he had chosen not to take the road, then decided that it must be because of her. Why did she have the misfortune to be attracted to such a callous man? She must be daft, River decided, because even Gray's rudeness had not dampened her desire.

Gloomily reflecting that she must have hit her head in the fall, River rode slowly back to the Double T. By the time she arrived at the house, she was almost too stiff to walk. Maria helped her to her room, clucking her tongue and scolding her as if she was a child.

"You overdid it, señorita! Your papa should have had more sense than to let you do it, but he did not! Ah, a hot bath will help, and Rosa will make you some tea."

But Rosa made her spiced wine instead, and as she sipped it on the cool patio, River wondered if she would ever walk again.

"You'll feel better," Tyler predicted when he came home. "A good ride will take a lot of that soreness out of you."

River gave a heartfelt groan. She had no intention of admitting that she had fallen from her horse, or he might not let her ride alone again.

"A good ride, Papa? Torture! I thought you were rather fond of me until now . . ."

Laughing, Tyler shook his head. "You'll see what I mean when you give it a try." He put his hand in his pocket and drew out a small box. "And as a small consolation for your aches and pains, I had this made for you. It was delivered today."

Surprised, River took the small velvet box and opened the lid. Her straight brows arched as she saw the delicate gold heart and fine chain.

"Oh, it's beautiful, Papa!" she said in a breathless voice.

"Open the heart," Tyler urged. "It's a locket."

With trembling fingers, River pried open the heart. A small miniature portrait of Alicia gazed up at her from the locket, and she felt a lump grow in her throat.

"It—it's the most beautiful thing I've ever owned," River said in a quivering voice. "Will you help me put it on?"

Tyler fastened it around her neck, and the locket slid

between River's breasts. She lifted it in her palm, then clicked it shut. "I'll never take it off," she said softly.

Tyler's voice was rich with satisfaction. "I thought you might like it!"

"Like it? I love it!"

"And I love you," Tyler said, and leaned over to press a kiss on River's brow.

River smiled, and realized that in spite of her unsettling obsession with a man who didn't know she existed, she was happier than she'd ever been in her life. Everything else was going so wonderfully, that she just knew one day Gray Morgan would look past the plain face and plump body and see a woman who loved him. He had to. It was fate that had brought them together.

Chapter 7

*

Three months flew by so swiftly that River could scarcely believe it. She'd grown fairly proficient at riding, and frequently rode out with her father when he checked fences or searched for lost calves. Though Tyler did not let her do any of the heavy work, he insisted that she know how it be done correctly. River was at his side constantly, and everyone on the Double T grew used to seeing the two of them together.

River had given up trying to keep up with large straw bonnets she'd first worn to keep the sun from her face, and had taken to wearing a sombrero with a chin strap instead. Though it frequently beat against her back as she rode across the pastures and rocks, the large-brimmed hat was there when she needed it most.

Now, for convenience sake, she wore her thick hair in a single braid. If strands escaped around her face, it didn't matter, and it was much easier to care for. At night, when Maria unbraided her hair and brushed it out for her—which she insisted upon doing—the girl exclaimed over how the sun had lightened her hair in streaks.

"It's pretty, señorita! It is almost as pale as your papa's hair in places, and it all mixes in with the others."

River got the hand mirror and looked for herself. She was surprised to see that it did look fairly pretty, though not at all as she'd hoped. Tyler Templeton's hair was a light blond all over, while hers had only blond streaks. The sun had also tinted her face and her arms so that by now she looked like a Beale Street serving wench, though Maria thought that, too, looked much better.

"Sí, you have color in your face now! It makes your eyes look so bright, like the sky!"

The only thing they agreed on was that River had lost some weight. Not as much as she'd wanted to, but sure enough, when she began noticing that she had to pull the string on her skirts so tight it grew too long, she realized that she had shed some of the excess fat around her waist and hips. And oddly enough, she wasn't even hungry.

She still ate heartily, and when they'd been out all day on an exhausting ride, she came home ravenous, but her appetite was easily assuaged. The weeks of constant riding had hardened her muscles, and River felt better than she had ever felt in her life. It was pure pleasure just being alive.

The only fly in the ointment was Pierce Trucklow. He had grown bolder. Several ranch hands had reported being shot at when they were out alone, and dead cattle had been found in remote areas of the ranch. Fences had been mysteriously cut, cattle suddenly disappearing, some line shacks burned. And then word filtered back that there was a bounty on Tyler Templeton's head.

"That dirty bas—" Sandy Dennis began angrily, stopping only when he remembered that River and Consuela were listening. "Look Tyler, Trucklow's getting too brave! I say we hire our own men like he has, or at least—"

"Hire gunmen, Sandy?" Tyler shook his head sadly. "I'm not going to do that. You know I'm not going to do that."

Sandy groaned and banged his fist against his forehead. "I know. I just hoped you'd listen to reason."

"Why should Papa hire gunmen?" River asked.

"Because Pierce Trucklow has hired two of the most vicious cutthroats in the territory, the way I hear it," Sandy shot back. His mouth twisted, and his florid face grew even redder. "Had them imported all the way from New Mexico!"

"Now, Sandy, don't get yourself so excited," Tyler said soothingly. "For all we know, they could be new hands."

"Yeah? Well, since he hired them, things have been happening around here!" Sandy leaned forward, pressing the knuckles of his hands against the tabletop. "And you ain't gonna like this, but I heard rumors that he was behind that stage 'robbery.' Only he wasn't looking for cash."

Tyler just stared at him. "I had a suspicion he was behind it, Sandy," he said evenly, "but I can't prove it any more than you can."

River glanced from one to the other. "What was he after if not money?"

"You," Sandy said shortly.

"Me?"

"You'd make a good bargaining point," Tyler explained with a grim smile.

"But if they were after me, then why didn't they—oh! I know why—I said my name was Drucilla Duckworth." She gave a soft laugh. "I was so upset, and I guess I forgot my real name."

"It is a good thing for you that you did," Consuela put in with a gasp.

"No," Tyler corrected grimly, "it's a good thing for Trucklow that she did. It would have been a grave error for him to take River."

Rising, Tyler pushed back his chair and lay a gentle hand on River's shoulder. "I'm going into town in the morning, River. Still want to come with me?"

River's heart quickened. Of course she did. There might be an opportunity to see Gray Morgan, and she wasn't about to pass that up!

Nodding, she said calmly, "Yes, I thought I'd pick up

some slates, chalk, and books for the youngsters here. They need tutoring, and I've got plenty of experience at it."

"Tutoring?" Sandy echoed in surprise, and River nodded.

"It was Papa's idea."

Shrugging, Tyler said, "I realized one day that some of the children on this ranch couldn't do simple mathematics without a struggle, and it occurred to me that River could help them."

Sandy laughed. "Has anyone informed the victims? I mean the pupils?"

"Oh, no," Tyler said with a wide grin. "We're going to wait until the last minute so they don't have a chance to run away."

Consuela shook her head doubtfully. "The Delgado *niños* are not going to be easy to convince they must learn to read and write," she warned.

"No, but they'll be persuaded," River said. "At least, I hope they will."

"If anyone can persuade them, you can," Sandy said. "And if you can't—try bribery."

"Use Rosa's cookies," Consuela suggested.

"Or big sticks," Sandy muttered.

"We'll be gone several days, maybe a week, Sandy," Tyler said. "I've got some more business to take care of, as you know. The price of beef is rising, and I'm going to hold out for the highest this time. Besides, I thought River could kinda dress up a little, maybe buy her a few gowns and let me take her to dinner at Delmonico's. After all, we'll be there a few days until I finish up my business." He winked at his daughter. "How does that sound, honey?"

"Wonderful!" she exclaimed, and it did sound wonderful.

River let her mind wander to Gray Morgan again, as she often did. Would he be in Clanton? If he was, would he even speak to her? And, she asked herself with a kind of desperation, why did she want him to notice her? He'd been hateful, arrogant, and, well, rude. His "Yuck" that night in the hotel still lingered in her memory, though she'd tried to forget it.

She'd tried to forget his kiss, too, but that had not been easy, either. Even though it had been intended for someone else, she dreamed of that kiss at night, dreamed that he would kiss her again one day. And if he ever did—River stopped herself. No point in borrowing trouble, as Grandmother Duckworth had always said.

Sometimes trouble did not have to be borrowed, River decided the next day. Sometimes it came calling on its own.

It was Saturday, and the day started off pleasantly enough with the long ride into town, the casual chatter between herself and Tyler. Dust rose thickly from the road as the wagon rattled and rumbled over ruts and ridges, and by the time they reached Clanton, both of them were caked with dust.

After renting rooms at the hotel and removing some of the dirt, Tyler and River met in the lobby.

"Uh, River, why don't you go on to the dress shop, and I'll just mosey on down to the saloon and have a beer. My throat's awful dry," Tyler said with a shamefaced grin that made her laugh.

"Coward! You just don't want to be seen going into a feminine domain!"

"True enough," he admitted, "true enough! But you tell Lucy Tower to put it on my bill."

"You have a bill at the dress shop?"

"Not now, but I reckon I will after today." Tyler gave her a swift peck on the cheek. "It's been a good year, and I can afford it—get all you want. Besides, your old duds are beginning to look kind of funny now that you've, ah, changed."

"You mean lost weight," River retorted and stood on her tiptoes to give him a kiss. "It's all right. I'm not that sensitive anymore. And besides, I've changed!"

She'd changed, all right, but she hadn't realized how much until she stood in front of the tall mirror in the dress shop and stared at her reflection. Lucy Tower buzzed around her like a bee, chatting aimlessly about nothing as River tried on new gowns.

"It's all the rage back East," Mrs. Tower was saying as she fussed over River, smoothing wrinkles and straightening the hems. "And it certainly does flatter you, dear!"

"It certainly does," River agreed in astonishment. A wraparound overskirt and snug-fitting basque made her curves take on the shape of an hourglass. The solid-color jade-green overskirt was pulled up before and behind, leaving the pretty striped underskirt to peep through. A pair of bows tethered each point where the skirt was fastened, and matching ribbon trimmed the hem.

"And this one, too!" Mrs. Tower insisted, pushing forward a gown. "It will accentuate your coloring so nicely!"

River ended up choosing several gowns. Her favorite was the deep mustard dress with the puffed sleeves and fitted waist with the dropped-yoke skirt. A coffee-colored piping edged the sleeves and was stitched lengthwise along the split edges of the skirt, and a small brown rosette was fastened at the point on the yoke where the pleated split began. It was fashionable, elegant, sophisticated, and River could not resist staring at herself in the mirror.

"Oh, and you must have the matching hat!" Mrs. Tower said, "though it's rather a shame to cover up your pretty hair."

Startled, River allowed Mrs. Tower to place a small, flat-brimmed hat atop her hair. The mustard color seemed to bring out the golden streaks the sun had bleached into the mousy brown of her hair, and the hat dipped low over one eye, providing a saucy, perky look that River could not have ever imagined achieving.

"You know," Mrs. Tower was saying as she fussed about straightening the skirt and tilting the hat, "the new styles are much more comfortable. Bustles are out, thank heavens, and corsets are much, *much* looser! Not that you really need one, dear, but of course, tiny waists are *the* thing! And a nice bosom, too, but you don't even have to pad as some of my customers do." Mrs. Tower laughed her loud laugh again, a startling trait from a woman who appeared so dainty and demure. "It's amazing what we women suffer in the name of fashion, isn't it!"

Rather dazed, River could only nod wordlessly. It was hard for her to recognize the girl in the mirror as herself. Clothes certainly did change one's appearance! Why hadn't she realized that long ago? Years of humiliation could have been avoided if she'd only bought the correct style of clothing, she decided.

But that wasn't quite true. River did not realize that she had changed a great deal in the past three months. Gone was the faintly hangdog look that had usually set so darkly on her face, and gone, too, were the thick spectacles that she'd always worn. Maria claimed she had no idea where they were, but River suspected a conspiracy aimed at keeping her from wearing the hated "glass eyes," as Maria called them. Usually too busy to bind her hair in the familiar chignon, River left it in a looser, more flattering style now, with soft waves on each side of her face. Except when she was out riding. Then she wore her thick hair in a long braid, and when she took it down at night it shimmered in rippling waves down her back. The sun had gilded River's face a light, peachy color that brought out the intense blue of her thick-lashed eyes, and a constant smile changed her entire expression.

It was a completely different River Templeton who ran into Gray Morgan on the sidewalk in front of Delmonico's.

"Oh! Excuse me," River said when she bumped into someone. She'd been sneaking a glance at her reflection in the window and hadn't even noticed that a man had paused in front of the restaurant to open the door for a companion. Then River recognized the man, and the breath caught in her throat. "Oh!" she said again.

Gray Morgan smiled slowly. "I think I'll survive," he said in that deep, husky voice that still haunted her dreams at night. "I wasn't really paying attention to where I was going, anyway."

She stared at him speechlessly. Not only was he being polite, but he was smiling at her. And there was none of the usual condescension or irritation in his expression! The shock cleared her mind of any intelligent comment she might have made.

River could think of nothing clever to say, though she was certain a thousand witty comments would come to mind later. She gulped. She smiled. She balanced on one foot in the open doorway.

"Did I step on your foot?" Gray Morgan asked when he noticed her stance. He put out a hand to grasp her arm, and River wanted to sigh with pure pleasure. As always, his touch made her weak and queasy inside, and her heart fluttered wildly. "Did I hurt you?" Morgan repeated.

"You must have, Gray," a feminine voice purred, "because she can't even speak for the pain!"

Then River noticed Morgan's companion. She was slender, with dark eyes and dark hair, and the girl's smile was cold and brittle. A pang of dismay struck River. She'd managed to ignore the possibility that Gray Morgan might be married or engaged. Why hadn't she bothered to ask someone?

"N-n-no," River managed to stammer as the girl's eyes narrowed with malicious glee, "I—I stubbed my foot. You were not responsible." She wished desperately that she could sink into the sidewalk as Morgan released her arm and stepped back to frown down at her.

"Are you certain you're not just being polite, Miss—?"

River's heart lurched. *No, not Yuckworth again!* she prayed silently. Maybe she should say something before he did, anything. "What's in a name?" she quoted. "That which we call a rose by any other word would smell as sweet..."

Gray stared at her with an uplifted brow, and River flushed. How silly of her to quote Shakespeare to a man draped in gun belts and wearing a hat with a rattlesnake headband!

"*Romeo and Juliet*. Act two," Gray said after a moment, and River was startled.

"Why . . . yes! You are an admirer of Shakespeare?"

Shrugging, he said, "Oh, not really. I've just read a bit of the Bard now and then."

He was frowning, and his piercing silver eyes seemed to look right through her as he said, "You look vaguely familiar. Don't I know you from somewhere?"

Stunned, she stared up at him with her mouth slightly open. She shut it with a snap. He didn't remember her at all! It was worse than she thought!

"Gray Morgan!" a masculine voice called out.

All three in the open doorway of Delmonico's turned as Tyler Templeton approached with a broad grin.

"I see you've met my daughter, Morgan," Tyler said as he took Gray's outstretched hand and gave it a hearty shake.

"Well, not quite. We were in the process of exchanging names after I stomped on her toes," Gray explained. He turned to look back at River. "We hadn't gotten to the introductions yet."

River realized with a sudden shock that he truly did not recognize her, did not recall the plump, plain girl from the stage or the girl he had startled from her horse one day. He'd probably done the most merciful thing and put her completely out of his mind.

With renewed confidence, River smiled at Gray Morgan and decided not to remind him. After all, he had met Drucilla Duckworth, and now she was River Templeton. It was like being given a second chance to make a good first impression, and although he stood there with a woman companion glaring at her over his broad shoulder, she was going to take full advantage of it. Even if he was married, at least he wouldn't consider Tyler Templeton's daughter a complete idiot.

"How do you do, Mr. Morgan?" River said. "My father has spoken quite well of you."

"Has he?" Gray grinned. "I'm surprised! He asked me for

a favor three months ago, and I still haven't gotten that information he wanted.''

"That's not your fault, Gray," the girl interrupted. "You know how bureaucratic tangles take so much time."

"Miss Lassiter's right," Tyler said. "I haven't blamed you for it, Gray. And now that we have run into each other, why don't we have lunch together? I promised River I would treat her to Delmonico's finest, and we'd love to have you two join us."

Oh, yes, River begged silently, *do join us!*

"Well, Treena," Gray said, turning to the girl, "why don't we?"

But Treena Lassiter did not seem at all pleased at the idea, though she forced a stiff smile since Gray was already pulling her forward into the restaurant behind Tyler and River. River could feel the girl's dark eyes examining her and wondered what she was thinking.

It wasn't long before River knew exactly what Treena Lassiter must be thinking. And she couldn't really blame her, though she wasn't about to refuse the opportunity. What was the old saying about all's fair in love and war? This looked like it could turn out to be both.

"You ought to come out and see my prize cow," Tyler said when they were seated at a table, and Gray nodded.

"Are you keeping this one in the house too?"

"What?" River asked, looking from Gray to Tyler. "In the house?"

"Your father used to keep cows in the first house he had, an old sod house with a dirt floor. Needless to say, he didn't have many visitors. In fact, I think my father and I were just about the only people around who'd go visit him."

Tyler shook his head ruefully. "Well, I'd bred her to that expensive bull of Charley Snyder's and I didn't want to risk anything happening to her."

Gray grinned. "I had to stop Matt from doing the same thing this past winter when it snowed. You know how Ma is about her clean house, and when Matt brought in a new calf, she just about went through the roof!"

Treena Lassiter said distastefully, "Your brother Matt shows a remarkable disregard for others' feelings."

Gray gave her a frowning glance, and his voice grew cold. "You and Matt never have gotten along for longer than two seconds anyway, Treena."

The girl's delicate brow lifted, and her top lip curled slightly. "I should think not," she said with such a wealth of contempt that even River shriveled with dismay.

Clearing his throat, Gray turned back to Tyler, his back stiff and a muscle twitching in his lean jaw. River looked from Gray to Treena and saw the icy glitter of satisfaction in the girl's eyes.

"Gray," Tyler said into the sudden silence, "I'm going to be in Clanton for several days, tying up loose ends with some business deals I'm conducting. I hate to leave River on her own so much, but perhaps Miss Lassiter could drop by to visit." Not noticing Treena's recoil and River's start of dismay, Tyler continued, "I've yet to show her any of Clanton's star attractions!"

"Sorry, Mr. Templeton," Treena said quickly, "but I am much too busy this week. Perhaps another time."

Tyler's face fell, but River was relieved. "Certainly, Miss Lassiter," Tyler said. "Perhaps another time."

Gray cleared his throat. "Look, Tyler, I've still got my office at the end of the street, and I'm winding up some paperwork for the BIA. I'll be in town all this week, so I'll drop by to talk to you about that information you wanted." Gray flicked a glance at River. "Since you'll be busy, I'll show your daughter around for you. It's the least I can do for an old family friend," Gray added, ignoring Treena Lassiter's sudden gasp of anger.

Tyler laughed. "Did you have to say old?"

"Long-time, then," Gray amended. "You and my father were the first two white men in this area. Only the Comanches lived here before you two arrived."

Tyler nodded. "Yeah, and we had a time of it, too! I miss Mike Morgan."

Nothing was said for a moment, then Gray said, "Things are quieter now."

"Especially since you're mediator between the BIA and the Comanches," Tyler said. He shook his head. "I still think it's a good idea for you to use your law degree here in Clanton, Gray. There are plenty of folks who could use a good attorney."

Gray shrugged carelessly. "I'm not that interested right now. I'm helping out on the ranch, and anyway, with Trucklow's fancy city lawyer hanging out a shingle, why should I bother?"

"Because folks trust a hometown boy, not some slick city man with a fast tongue and faster hands!" Tyler retorted.

Grinning, Gray agreed. "Mr. Doss does have fast hands when it comes to taking money, I've heard! Just as long as it's not mine, I don't care."

"You should, Gray. These people are your neighbors."

"I think I remember that a lot better than they do," was Gray's quiet answer, and Tyler did not pursue the subject.

"Well," River said into the awkward silence, "I appreciate your offer to show me around, Mr. Morgan, but I am sure that it would be a great inconvenience, and—"

"Oh, let him do it, River!" Tyler interrupted. "I won't have to worry about you sitting in that hotel room all day by yourself, or wonder if you're getting too bored. And besides, who knows when I'll have the time to show you around?"

Avoiding Treena Lassiter's cold glare, River muttered a helpless, "Thank you. I am delighted."

The truth of it was, she *was* delighted. And she didn't care if Treena Lassiter liked it. After all, it wasn't as if she were any competition for the cool, beautiful brunette, and a girl like River had to take her small pleasures where she could. Her straight brows arched over her eyes, and her full mouth suddenly curved into a smile. Why not give in gracefully? After all, she would love being in Gray Morgan's company for several hours! It was one of her dreams come true, and she didn't mean to ignore the opportunity.

Chapter 8

*

River inhaled deeply, scarcely able to believe that she was chatting so casually with her Ideal Man. What a turn her life had suddenly taken! Just a few weeks before, Gray Morgan had been coldly distant, barely civil, and extremely arrogant. Now, because he didn't equate her with the plump, plain girl he'd first met, he had offered to be her escort for the next week.

Something in River rebelled.

Perhaps it was because she wanted to be liked for herself, as Tyler had once said, or perhaps it was because she knew that one day Gray would inevitably put two and two together and realize that River Templeton and Drucilla Duckworth—or *Yuck*worth—were one and the same. Gray's ''Yuck'' still lingered in her memory as if burned there with one of Tyler's branding irons. River had an idea.

She smiled politely at Gray and said, ''I always go to church on Sunday mornings, Mr. Morgan. Since being in Texas, I've not had the opportunity. I'm certain you won't mind escorting me to church tomorrow morning?''

Gray looked nonplussed, and River knew that if Grandmother Duckworth heard her claim she went to church every Sunday she would roll over in her grave! Treena Lassiter made a choking sound, and even Tyler looked a bit surprised.

"Church?" Gray repeated, and looked from River to Tyler as if suspecting a joke. Then he shrugged. "Sure. I'll take you to church."

"I certainly do appreciate it, Mr. Morgan. It will be so *uplifting* for both of us."

Gray gave her a wary stare, and River returned it coolly. A small smile pressed at the corners of his mouth, and he inclined his head slightly in her direction. "I'll pick you up at eight in the morning." He stood and pulled out Treena's chair. "It should be interesting to discover who's more uplifted," was his parting comment, then he shook Tyler's hand and left.

Tyler beckoned for the waiter, then leaned forward to say, "River, I didn't realize that you went to church. Why didn't you tell me?"

She cleared her throat. "Well, uh, I just didn't think it was possible. I mean, it's such a long drive into town and all. But it doesn't matter that much to me, really it doesn't."

"Are you certain?"

She nodded vigorously. "Oh, yes, I'm quite certain," she said.

Tyler glanced up as the waiter approached the table. "I'd like to pay now," he said, but the waiter shook his head.

"It's already been taken care of by Mr. Morgan," he said, and Tyler sighed.

"Morgan's always doing that to me," he muttered, and River's brows lifted in surprise.

Well. Gray Morgan may be rude and arrogant, but at least he wasn't a parasite! River made a mental note in the growing checklist of flaws and attributes for her Ideal Man.

Gray arrived promptly at eight the next morning. He met River in the hotel lobby, and she almost tripped when she saw him. Gone were the six-guns strapped to each hip. Gone was the felt hat with the rattlesnake-skin headband. She decided what was left was devastatingly handsome, and she almost wavered in her resolution to make him pay for his past insults. It took all her strength to school her features into an expression of nonchalance and to walk across the lobby.

"Good morning, Mr. Morgan."

"And good morning to you, Miss Templeton," the paragon of male beauty said with a mocking bow.

River swallowed hard. Her gaze drifted from the top of his dark, gleaming head, over his broad chest with the wine-red vest, flicked over the semi-cutaway coat, skimmed the trim trousers, and lingered on the shining demiboots. All he needed was a gold-headed cane, and the image of a dandy would be complete.

"Do I pass inspection?" Gray asked, inclining his head in a sardonic manner.

"Almost," River managed to say without wheezing.

"Almost?"

"No watch fob," she replied promptly.

"Ah, the watch fob. How could I have forgotten?"

"Yes. How could you?" River smiled as she tugged on her gloves. "But, I suppose you'll do."

"So kind of you to say so," Gray commented as he held open the lobby door for her.

River sailed past him with a much more confident air than she felt. Inside she was a quivering mush. The only way she could keep from fawning over him was to repeat silently, *Yuck, yuck, yuck.* It sharpened her resolve to make him pay for that one short syllable of humiliation.

But standing next to Gray in church, using the same hymnal, River found it extremely difficult not to forgive him. She could sense the surreptitious glances in their direction, knew the other parishioners were wondering who that was with Gray Morgan, and guessed that they were all wondering why he was in church. From the few comments and bug-eyed stares they had received—plus the minister's shocked, "Why— why—hello, Mr. Morgan''—River had deduced that he had never attended the Clanton Methodist Church before.

And later, when Gray cupped her elbow in his palm and escorted her out the church doors and down the wide steps, he confirmed her deduction.

"I hope you're happy," he muttered in her ear, and his breath whispered across her neck and made her shiver. "I will never live this down."

River feigned an astonished expression. "Never live down going to church, Mr. Morgan? Why, I'm shocked!"

"So is everyone else in Clanton," Gray shot back. He raked a hand through his hair as they paused on the walkway in front of the church, and his silver gaze narrowed on River's innocent face. "If I didn't know better, I'd think you've been talking to my mother," he said in a flat tone.

River smiled. "Your mother must be a very fine woman if she's been after you to go to church," she said.

"She is a fine woman, but she doesn't give a tinker's damn if I go to church. I was talking about your tactics, Miss Templeton."

When River would have asked what he meant, Gray took her arm and turned her in the opposite direction from the church. His long legs outdistanced her quickly, and River almost had to trot like a horse to keep up. It was not very dignified, and she finally told him so.

"Please! I'm racing to keep up, for heaven's sake!"

Gray slowed and gave her a measuring glance. "I don't know what it is about you, River Templeton, but there is something that I can't quite put my finger on."

River blinked her eyes innocently. "What do you mean?"

"If I knew what I meant, I probably wouldn't be having this conversation," he snapped.

Because he was right, and because she felt slightly guilty but more justified, River suffered with righteous indignation.

"Mr. Morgan, if you would prefer not to show me about town, I will be more than glad to release you from any obligation you might feel! All you have to do is say that you retract your offer, and it is done."

Wheeling around, Gray stared down into River's face. His jaw was set and his eyes were shadowed. "I never back down on a deal," he said shortly.

"Ah, and I am a deal?"

"You are Tyler Templeton's daughter, and I was trying to keep you from being bored and a drag on your father while you're in Clanton. If you're not enjoying my company, I can take you back to the hotel and forget the entire thing. It's up to you."

River hesitated. While she was enjoying the brief power she'd wielded over him, she could sense that Gray was not a man who would stand for it for very long. And once he was gone, it would be hard for her to think of a good reason to lure him back. She capitulated without a qualm.

"I apologize if my manner has suggested that I am not enjoying your company, Mr. Morgan. On the contrary, I am enjoying it very much." River smiled and hoped that he would know how sincere she was. "I merely wanted you to know that I was not forcing you to keep your offer if you chose not to do so. I realize that you think a great deal of my father."

"Yes, I do." Gray stared down at her for a moment, and his eyes began to soften slightly. "Hungry?" he asked abruptly, and River almost sighed aloud with relief.

"Starved!" she answered truthfully.

"Well, Delmonico's is the only restaurant."

"That sounds wonderful."

Gray gave her a wry smile. "And you sound too perky to be real, Miss Templeton."

"Kind of reaffirms your faith in the human race, doesn't it?" River countered, and Gray grinned.

"Kind of."

Lunch was pleasant. River found that she could actually

talk to Gray Morgan without either stammering or snarling, which was preferable to their usual conversations. He had a quick wit that he didn't mind exercising, and a surprising knowledge of some of the things that interested River.

"*You* have read *Wuthering Heights?*" River asked with a slight gasp.

One dark brow rose, and his mouth curled in a mocking smile. "Why do you find that surprising?"

"Well, I . . . uh . . . it just doesn't seem like a literary work that would interest you."

"Oh, I suppose you think I'm more interested in a detailed analysis of Attila the Hun's march across Gaul."

"Well, yes, something like that. I mean, most men just don't read romantic novels."

"I found it more morbid than romantic. Heathcliff was a man driven by demons and vengeance, not love."

"But he was so dark and brooding, so . . . exciting," River finished lamely when Gray's mouth curled in a mocking smile again.

Leaning across the linen-draped table, Gray lowered his voice. "So you find demon-driven men exciting, do you? I'll have to remember that, River Templeton."

The husky timbre of his voice sent a shiver down her spine, and River caught her breath at the shadowed intensity in his eyes. Steeling her quivering nerves, she managed to smile calmly.

"Only fictional madmen are exciting, Mr. Morgan. Reality is a bit more . . . exhausting."

Gray sat back in his chair and laughed. "How disappointing. Do I detect a hint of cowardice in you?"

"Oh, no—a *large* streak. I discovered a while back that I prefer all my adventures to be in print."

"I'm sure you'll find a dearth of adventures in Clanton, Miss Templeton. Life here goes along at a snail's pace."

"You can call me River, you know. It's much easier to say than Miss Templeton."

"I thought you'd never say that." Gray smiled at her over

the rim of his coffee cup, and River's heart skipped a beat when he drawled, "And I prefer Gray. It's friendlier."

"Somehow I thought you were a man who didn't care about being that friendly," River teased.

His brow arched again as he said, "I don't. Only to a few certain people."

River sat back in her chair and took a hasty sip of coffee before she committed the social sin of gurgling happily. When she could speak without gurgling, she said, "I'm delighted to be among those few, Gray."

"As your host," Gray said when they had finished their coffee and he'd paid the bill, 'I should walk you down to the courting tree. It's one of Clanton's big attractions."

"Courting tree?"

"Maybe I should say *only* tree." Gray pulled out her chair and put one hand on the small of her back, a small gesture but one that made River's knees weak and her throat tight. "It's a tall oak at the end of the sidewalk, which, I might add, is also one of Clanton's attractions."

"The sidewalk?"

He nodded and reached around her to open the door. "It was just built last year. Before that, everyone walked in the street, even when mud and water could swallow a team of mules without a trace. Our city fathers decided to pool the tax money and build the sidewalk before any more innocent citizens were lost."

Laughing, River half-turned to look up into his face. He smiled down at her, and because they were both looking at each other, neither of them saw Treena Lassiter. But she saw them.

"Well, isn't this a cozy Sunday afternoon walk!"

The spite-filled words bit into River's pleasant haze, and she turned in surprise to see Treena.

"Why, hello, Miss Lassiter," she began, but Treena was not even looking at River.

"Gray, dear,"—the "dear" had a sardonic inflection—"have you forgotten our engagement?"

River's heart dropped to her toes. Engagement? As in a marriage commitment, perhaps? Gray's answer gave her momentary relief.

His tone was slightly impatient when he demanded, "What engagement, Treena? We had no plans."

"Yes, we did. Victor Overton and his wife invited us to their house this evening."

"I didn't know anything about it, and if I had, I still wouldn't go. I don't like Victor Overton and you know it."

River looked from one to the other as the conversation bounced back and forth like a rubber ball, Treena insistent and wheedling, Gray adamant and sarcastic.

Finally Gray put up a hand, and his voice was harsh. "Treena, I am not going. That's final. And before you think of another argument, I should inform you that I have previous plans with River."

Both River and Treena stared at Gray with surprise.

"*River?* What plans?" Treena demanded, and her voice grew shrill. "I don't believe that you—"

"I promised my mother we would ride out to the ranch so she could meet Tyler's daughter," Gray interrupted with a snap. "Now, would you like to drop this before I upset you even more?"

Treena's body went rigid. Her fingers curled into the soft material of her stylish gown like cat's claws, and her dark eyes shifted from Gray to River.

"I see." Ice coated the two words. A brittle smile curved Treena's painted mouth, and she was obviously struggling for control as she looked at River. "I had no idea you were still squiring Tyler's plain daughter around town. You are *so* duty-minded, Gray!" Her laugh was hollow, and River cringed from the wealth of sarcasm and dislike in Treena's expression. The brunette sidled close and put a clinging hand on Gray's arm as if River was not even in Texas, much less standing right beside them. Her tone was low and intimate, caressing, as she looked up at Gray with a softer smile.

"I'll forgive you this time and I'll make the apologies to

the Overtons, but we can talk about it later. You know where I'll be. After taking three months to do so, the workmen are through painting and papering my house. And I have so many new things to show you, so—I'll be waiting there."

"Don't spend your inheritance before you get it," Gray drawled, and the brunette shrugged.

"There's plenty of it left, Gray. You should know that well enough."

River wondered what they were talking about but would have cheerfully bitten her tongue in two before asking. It was probably better that she didn't know. Treena Lassiter left a bad taste in her mouth, and the enmity in the brunette's eyes was unmistakeable. No, there would never be a friendship there!

Gray offered no explanation when Treena had sauntered back up the sidewalk, her hips swaying provocatively for his benefit. River winced and turned away.

It was on the tip of her tongue to ask if he'd meant the invitation to his ranch, but Gray's face was closed and she swallowed the question. He'd let her know if he'd meant it, she was sure.

But then he said, "Forget it," and River decided he must mean the entire episode.

"Now, about this courting tree?" she prompted, and he relaxed slightly.

"Ah yes, the tree. Well, it has been suggested that it double as a hanging tree, but that sort of puts a damper on any courting folks might want to do in Clanton. And as there is only one big tree, it's been the subject of a rather lively debate at times."

"I can imagine," River said with a smile. She was too conscious of Gray's hand on her back, of his easy hold on her, to pay much attention to the conversation or even where they were going. The distasteful confrontation with Treena Lassiter began to fade from her mind, and River found herself concentrating on a thousand details about Gray Morgan.

She watched the play of expression across his face as he

talked, his casual acknowledgment of greetings from passersby, his easy, almost lazy stride as they strolled down the wooden sidewalk. Everything about him fascinated her.

"So, this is the tree," Gray said when they reached a towering oak with a small iron bench built beneath it. "What do you think?"

Reluctantly dragging her attention from his handsome face to the tree, River admired it briefly. "It's lovely," she said.

Gray laughed. "Lovely? Not awe-inspiring? Majestic? Mighty?"

"All of the above," River returned promptly. "Lovely, awe-inspiring, majestic, mighty."

"Much better!"

Gray seated her on the bench and sat down beside her, his long legs sprawling straight out in front of him. "I really did mean that invitation, you know," he said.

She turned to look at him. "What invitation?"

"To meet my mother and brothers this evening. Don't look at me like that! It's not so bad, and they don't bite. Too hard, anyway," he amended with a grin.

River's heart soared, and she had trouble keeping her excitement hidden as she affected a casual attitude.

"I imagine that if I can survive falling off my horse, I can survive your family."

"You," Gray said with a laugh, "haven't met my family!"

"Are they anything like you?"

"I have five brothers who make me look like a saint," Gray said. "And if that's not enough to scare you, I should warn you that my mother abuses every one of us whether company is there or not."

It was hard for River to visualize anyone—man or woman—abusing Gray Morgan, but she could tell from his indulgent smile when he spoke of his mother that he would allow her any liberties.

"That alone will be well worth the visit, I'm sure," River retorted.

Gray's brow lifted, and one corner of his mouth curled up.

"Is that so? Well, we'll see if you sing the same tune after tonight. I warn you—the Morgans can be extremely overwhelming at times."

Don't I already know that? River asked herself with an inward sigh. Gray Morgan had already overwhelmed her, and he hadn't even tried.

Chapter 9

*

Tyler was delighted to hear that River was going to ride out to the Morgan ranch to meet Mrs. Morgan. "Oh, Nancy Morgan is quite a woman," he said. "Since she was widowed twelve years ago, she's raised all those boys alone."

"I understand she thinks a great deal of you, too," River said with a nervous smile. She could not rid herself of the butterflies that had taken up residence in the region of her stomach. Her smile wavered slightly as her gaze shifted from her father to the new gowns she'd spread out on the bed in her hotel room. She was debating on which one to wear. The bright green shirtwaist with the striped skirt and matching underskirt, or the brown and yellow plaid with the dropped-yoke skirt? Both looked extremely flattering on her, and she wanted to look her best. After all, who knew when Gray Morgan might decide to fall in love...

River almost laughed aloud at her whimsy, and Tyler smiled as she stifled a nervous giggle.

"I take it that you are pleased at your invitation," he said. "It's a nice ride out to the Rocking M, and Nancy Morgan is an excellent cook. How she feeds all those boys is a mystery to me, but she obviously manages."

"Yes. Obviously—" She paused. "Papa, which gown do you think looks the best?"

"The gold plaid," Tyler said promptly. "It brings out the nice color in your hair."

River laughed. "I didn't think you'd noticed!"

"Not notice my little girl? I notice everything! And I also notice that it's almost four, and Gray Morgan will be here any minute." Rising, Tyler gave River a swift peck on the cheek. "I'll stall him in the lobby while you dress."

Suddenly the thought of being alone with Gray Morgan was frightening. Not that she thought he would harm her, but that she might do or say something foolish. After all, there was still a lot of Drucilla Duckworth in her—clumsy, inarticulate Drucilla, who had gazed mutely and adoringly at Gray and made a complete, utter fool of herself! River grasped her father's arm.

An edge of desperation tinged her voice as she asked, "What are you doing tonight? Don't you want to go with us?"

"Some other time, honey. I've got unfinished business to take care of tonight. I think I can get top dollar for my beef, and I'm haggling over the final price."

"Oh. Well, good luck."

"See you in the morning," Tyler said with a cheery wave of his arm, and he left, shutting the door behind him.

Steeling herself, River slipped out of her robe and picked up the gold plaid dress. Why was she so nervous? It was only Gray Morgan, her Ideal Man, the man she had fallen in love with at first sight. Why be nervous, indeed!

When she was finally dressed and standing in front of the cheval mirror in one corner of the room, River was glad she'd chosen the gold plaid. It fit her new curves in a flattering style, and made her skin glow with color and her eyes seem brighter. River gave a brief nod of satisfaction.

"I may be just a pig in a silk suit, as Grandmother

Duckworth used to say, but this certainly is a *pretty* suit! I bet she'd roll over in her grave if she saw me now," she said aloud. She turned, admiring the alluring sway of the skirts. Gray Morgan could not ignore that! Even Treena Lassiter's stylish gowns were not as pretty as the one she was wearing, and it gave River renewed confidence.

Her confidence didn't fade when she accepted Gray's assistance into the rented carriage. His strong hands circled her waist and lifted her onto the high seat, and River hoped he couldn't feel the rapid thud of her heart at his touch. No trace of her inner turmoil showed on her face as she smiled calmly and thanked him.

"My pleasure," Gray said, letting his hands linger a moment too long. The brim of his felt hat shadowed his eyes and face, and the gunbelts buckled around his lean waist glittered in the bright sunlight, reminding River of the last time he had lifted her.

The memory of her humiliation at his caustic comments intruded suddenly, and River's voice was sharper than she intended.

"I'm not too heavy, am I?" she snapped. But as Gray did not associate the much heavier Drucilla Duckworth sprawled in the middle of a road with the lighter River, he merely shook his head.

"No, of course not."

"Good. I wouldn't want to hurt your back."

Gray gave her a strange look before shrugging and saying, "No danger of that."

Smoothing her skirts over her knees, River struggled for composure. She would not allow Drucilla to intrude and ruin her evening with Gray!

When Gray stepped up into the buggy and took up the reins, she managed a warm smile and a casual question. "How far is it to your ranch?"

"Not but about ten miles. It shouldn't take but an hour to get there—unless we take our time."

River pretended to consider this. "Perhaps we shouldn't tire the poor horse too greatly. What do you think?"

Grinning, Gray flapped the reins over the horse's rump and it broke into a trot. "I think you're a scheming little baggage, River Templeton, and I've never been able to resist scheming women!"

It seemed to River that he was doing a remarkably good job of resisting her, but of course it would never do to say something like that. She settled back into the cushions of the buggy and contented herself with small talk and silent admiration as they rode slowly out to his ranch.

"Well, here we are," Gray said all too soon. "The Rocking M."

"M for Morgan, of course," River observed.

"Of course."

The ranch spread out before them in a familiar pattern. Holding pens, corrals, and outbuildings stretched beyond the main house built of weathered logs, and several smaller buildings haphazardly dotted the area. It was a neat ranch, but smaller than the Double T, and River could tell that there must have been lean times in the past.

The buggy swayed down the rutted track leading to the house, and River saw the tall, lean figure of a young man waiting on the porch. Gray groaned.

"Your brother?" River guessed.

"I'm not so sure. My mother tells me he is, so to keep the peace I don't argue. When you meet him, you'll understand why I don't always claim him."

A boisterous whoop sounded as the buggy rolled to a halt, and the tall youth leaped to the side of the vehicle before it completely stopped.

"It's about time!" he said cheerfully, and his face was bristling with good humor and curiosity. "So this is Tyler Templeton's little girl? Heck, Gray, I thought you said she was—"

"Matt, why don't you go and tell Ma we're here?" Gray

broke in, and his fierce glare had the effect of silencing his brother in midsentence.

Shrugging, Matt leaped down from the buggy. "She knows. Here, Miss Templeton, I'll help you down."

"I'll do it!" Gray snapped, and Matt grinned.

Ignoring his brother, Matt reached up to help River down from the buggy, whispering loudly, "Don't mind him! He's not really my brother, but a foundling. We just humor him to be nice."

River couldn't suppress a smile. "Really? That's exactly what he said about you."

Matt thumped a finger against his temple and winked. "He has an old injury, but we try not to talk about it."

"Try not talking at all," Gray drawled as he set the brake on the buggy, and Matt lifted one brow in an exact imitation of his brother.

River laughed delightedly. "You're very good at that," she said approvingly.

"I ought to be. I've had years to study him." Matt backed off as Gray approached, holding his hands out in front of him. "Okay, okay! Supper's almost ready, and Ma's expecting you."

It was Matt who swung open the front door and ushered River in, Matt who pulled out a chair for her and introduced her to Nancy Morgan, a tiny, energetic woman who was a study in perpetual motion. River supposed she'd have to be, with her house full of grown and half-grown sons.

They ranged in age from Gray at twenty-six, to young Andy at twelve, and looked like stairsteps. All wore the same family resemblance, with only slightly varying shades of hair. Nancy Morgan's soft brown hair was flecked with strands of gray, and her eyes were the same clear silver as her oldest son's. She kept up a steady stream of conversation as she cooked the meal and placed it on the long table dominating one room.

"How is Tyler, Miss Templeton?"

"Please, call me River. He's fine."

"It's been ages since I've seen him. Why, the last time was—*put this platter on the table, Robert*—when he rode out here to see if we were all right after a storm came through. Oh, it was a bad storm, with high winds and"—*thwack* went the wooden spoon across an offender's knuckles, and young Andy quickly withdrew his hand from the plate of biscuits. Hardly breaking stride she continued—"heavy rains. We could always count on Tyler to show up to help. He's done that since my husband was killed when Andy was just a baby."

River flinched as the wooden spoon cracked across bare knuckles again. This time it was Chance, a lanky teenager who just grinned and shrugged.

Her gaze searched for and found Gray, who was leaning against the mantel over the stone fireplace and watching her. His slow smile made River flush, and she looked back at Nancy Morgan.

Seeing Gray in a family atmosphere softened some of his harshness, and she could see him relax. Here he was at ease with himself, not as guarded as he normally was. The constant wariness he usually wore was gone, and River found this new Gray even more attractive than ever. She hadn't thought it possible, but it was true.

She was seated beside Gray at the meal and was fully conscious of his warm presence next to her, the occasional nudge of his elbow or the press of his thigh against hers under the table. River found it increasingly difficult to eat or to concentrate on the conversation, which flowed like spring rain around the long table.

"Anyway," Nancy said as she stepped around the table refilling bowls and platters, "Tyler never will accept my thanks. I know Tyler Templeton, and he—*put that napkin in your lap!*" River winced as Matt received the spoon across his head "—would not dream of letting anyone help him, though Lord only knows how many others he's helped. Tyler has a way with making things work, somehow, and he'll work though all this mess with that bully Pierce Trucklow."

River had the dazed thought that Nancy Morgan was rather a small bully herself, but saw from the wide grins on her sons' faces that they loved it. None of them gave more than a casual protest when she bullied them, and River could see they adored their feisty mother. It was obvious in the way they'd say, "Aw, Ma!" when she spatted them with the wooden spoon, and it was obvious in the way they leaped to help her when she'd allow it.

"So," River cleared her throat and said, "you don't like Mr. Trucklow either?"

"No one with any sense does, but that's neither here nor there."

"Let's not talk about Trucklow," Gray said, and his mother sliced him a quick glance.

"That suits me. Did you bring me any newspapers to read? I'm getting behind on what's happening in the world."

After the meal, when subjects from the Bureau of Indian Affairs to whether Grover Cleveland would run for president again in 1893 were debated on the front porch, River had more time to observe Gray's familiarity with his family. A faint feeling of envy tinged her thoughts, envy from never having known the closeness these people shared. What would it feel like to be part of such a close-knit group? To know that though they vehemently disputed one another's opinions and even called each other numbskull, they would stand up for one another at the first sign of trouble? River couldn't imagine.

She found herself included in their lively debates, her opinions demanded and discussed, disputed, dissected, and eventually dismissed, but thoroughly respected. There was a good-natured tone to their disputes, and none of them became angry at the various insults tossed back and forth.

"That's just our way of expressing our opinions," Matt whispered to her when her shock became obvious. "And besides, Jamie knows he's got the brain of a peahen."

"Better than having no brains at all!" Jamie retorted,

which started another discussion as to how much brains peahens had.

Gray was leaning against the porch post and smoking, and a faint smile crooked his mouth as he watched River enter into his brothers' debates. She held her own, and even made a point or two before being drowned out by their racket. She was about the most learned blonde he'd ever met. Well spoken and quick witted, too, not to mention warm hearted. It had been a long time since he'd felt so at ease in his childhood home, but it'd been a long time since he'd been a child. Adulthood had been thrust on him earlier than some. As the oldest, he had been his father's right hand, had constantly been at his heels. He'd been with Mike Morgan when he'd been killed, and the memory still stuck in his heart like a burning thorn.

Straightening, Gray flipped the stub of his cigarette to the porch and ground it out with his boot. He looked up and met his mother's gaze, and knew what she was thinking without her saying a word.

"She's just a friend, Ma," he said softly, and Nancy Morgan smiled.

"Really?" she murmured, and turned back to her knitting with the mysterious little smile lingering on her lips.

"*Really*," Gray emphasized, then flicked her an annoyed glance. When his mother refused to look at him again he abruptly announced, "I'm going to talk to Robert."

"Whatever you say, dear."

Gray glowered as he stalked from the porch and into the yard. His brother was perched on a split log bench, and looked up with a smile at Gray's approach.

"Jamie and Matt are trying to steal your sweetheart," Robert said, and was startled by the vehemence of Gray's reply.

"Look, she's not my sweetheart, she's just the daughter of an old friend!"

"Easy, Gray, easy," Robert said. "You don't have to get upset about it."

"I'm not upset!"

Robert studied Gray's thunderous expression for a moment, then shrugged. "Sure. Whatever you say." He cleared his throat. "Do you feel like evening up our old score? I'm still behind by a match."

"Wrestling?"

"Unless you're afraid . . ."

Gray was already unbuttoning his shirt and tossing aside his hat, and Robert grinned.

"Hey!" Matt said. "They're going to wrestle again!" He abruptly abandoned his place beside River and flew down the steps.

All the brothers immediately filed into the yard to watch, and some lively conversation followed. River watched in complete bewilderment. She'd not heard the gist of the conversation between Gray and his mother, nor Gray and Robert, but she had noticed Gray's dark mood. Now she turned to Nancy Morgan.

"What are they going to do?"

Mrs. Morgan smiled and shook her head. "Roll around in the yard and get dirty. It's a game they give themselves points for, though I don't see why. I should win for being able to get the stains out of their clothes."

"Oh." River still didn't understand.

"It's all in fun, and they rarely get mad. It gives them a thinly disguised way of letting out their aggressions, I suppose," Nancy said as she squinted at the sock she was knitting. "It's better than snapping at one another and starting a real argument."

"Yes, I guess it is."

River sat on the top step of the porch and watched as Gray and Robert stripped to their pants and bare feet. They circled one another like wary cats, tensed and ready, waiting for the first move. Her gaze fastened on Gray, on the smooth flow of the muscles in his brawny arms. Sunlight glittered in his dark hair and over his bare skin, and she felt a thrill as she watched him move with all the grace of a wild animal. He reminded her of a wild animal at this moment, as predatory and dangerous as any wolf or wildcat.

It was Gray who made the first move, lunging toward Robert and catching him around the waist, one foot hooking behind his brother's leg to bring him crashing to the ground with a heavy thud.

"Point for Gray!" Matt shouted.

Robert bounded back up instantly and launched himself at Gray with a growl. They grappled, straining against each other, muscles flexing.

To River, the wrestling match degenerated from a game to a serious contest when Robert and Gray seemed to be getting too brutal.

Worried, she glanced at Nancy.

"Is it still play?" she asked in a small voice, and Nancy Morgan shrugged.

"Until they draw blood, it's still play."

"Do they ever draw blood?"

"On occasion. They they stop."

"Oh." River glanced toward the two men glistening with sweat and determination. "Is that the rule?"

"One of them." Nancy's hand fell comfortingly on her shoulder, and River looked up at her. "They won't hurt each other."

That was hard to believe when she could hear the rough pants and grunts, could hear Jamie, Chance, Matt, and even young Andy shouting things like, "Grab him! Knee him! Get him in a headlock!"

She didn't even know whom they were shouting for, and suspected they didn't either. Whoever was losing, she supposed. River shuddered.

Nancy Morgan laughed. "It's good exercise, River, I promise you. They'll all be good as new when it's over. A bit bruised and scratched, maybe, but just fine."

And River discovered that Nancy was right. When the match was over and Gray and Robert were good-naturedly shoving each other as they washed off with a bucket of cold water, Matt came back to sit beside River.

"Wasn't that great?" he asked cheerfully, and River gave him a wide stare.

"Great?"

"Yeah! Gray won. He always does."

"Oh."

Seeming not to notice River's silence, Matt went on to retell every point of the match, explaining how if Robert had not feigned a fall, and if Gray had not taken advantage of his being off-balance, no point would have been made. Before Matt could add more, River interrupted.

"You really admire your brother, don't you?"

Taken slightly aback, Matt shrugged and said, "Sure. I guess I do. He always wins, no matter what he does."

"Always?"

"Well, almost always. There's been a time or two he's been whipped, but not often. And he got even." Matt grinned, and River thought how much the two brothers resembled each other.

"So, you think winning is always the most important thing?" River asked, and Matt shook his head.

"Naw, but it sure beats being whipped. Of course, Gray says the important thing is justice. He even quotes some ancient verse about it."

River's interest quickened. "Do you remember it?"

Matt thought a moment, then quoted softly, "'Only the actions of the just/Smell sweet and blossom in their dust.' Or something like that," he ended with a faintly embarrassed smile.

"No, that's right," Gray said from the bottom step, and River turned quickly to watch him walk up the stairs. He was still bare-chested, and his hair was wet from the water bucket and slicked back on his head. His gaze flicked from Matt to River. "So you have my brother quoting sixteenth-century verse, I see."

Standing, Matt brushed at the dirt on the seat of his pants

and couldn't quite meet Gray's speculative eye. "Aw, I was just telling her that line you always say about winning."

"As usual, you've missed the entire point, Matt. It's about justice, not winning." Gray slanted his younger brother an amused smile. "But you're still young. You'll learn."

Matt scowled, and River put in quickly, "No, Matt said it was about justice."

Flicking River a glance, Matt blurted, "I don't need you to defend me!" and bolted down the steps of the porch.

Surprised, River stared after him as Gray jackknifed his long legs and sat beside her. "Don't worry about Matt. He's not really mad."

"That's easy for you to say . . ."

Gray shrugged. "Yeah."

River tried not to look at his bare chest, at the dark pelt of hair that curled at his throat and narrowed to a V at the waist of his pants. Hard ridges of muscle banded his chest and stomach, and blue veins snaked the sinewy muscles in his brown arms. She made a concerted effort to look away, to stare across the ranch toward the distant peaks.

As if sensing her discomfort and deciding to be perverse, Gray reached out and began to knead the back of her neck with his fingers. River jumped slightly, and he grinned.

"You seem tense," he murmured, and she swallowed the sudden lump in her throat.

"No, no," she lied, "I'm fine. Just . . . concerned about your brother, that's all."

"Matt? He'll be fine, I told you."

River tried to ignore the warm fingers against her skin, the gentle pressure as he massaged the muscles of her neck. His hand reached up under the loose bun on the nape of her neck, loosening the ribbon that held it, letting her hair fall freely over her shoulders and down her back.

"You ought to always wear your hair down," Gray murmured and River shivered.

"It—it gets tangled."

"So? Brush it."

Acutely conscious of Nancy Morgan still sitting in her rocking chair only a few feet away, and of his brothers milling about in the yard, River tried to keep her reaction under control. She inhaled deeply and steadied her voice.

"That's easy for you to say."

"Back to that again?" Gray took his hand away and sat up straight. "Why do you think everything is easy for me to say?"

River turned to look at him. "Because it is. Somehow, I have the feeling that you're not the most sensitive of men."

Gray grinned. "That's easy for you to say."

River had to laugh, and when Gray rose to his feet and held out his hand for her to take, she put her fingers in his palm. He tugged her to her feet with an easy pull, and she leaned into him for the space of a heartbeat before pulling away in confusion. It was too unsettling, pressing against his bare chest, knowing that he was fully aware of how he affected her, and she lifted her chin slightly and tried to look remote.

"Ready to start back to Clanton?" Gray asked, and she nodded.

"Yes, it'll be dark soon."

The sun had already begun to drift toward the horizon when they set out from the Rocking M with Nancy Morgan's voice ringing in their ears.

"Come back soon, River! And you can bring Gray with you if you like . . ."

"That's mother-love for you," Gray muttered, but he was smiling. "So—what do you think of my family?"

River stared toward the pink-and-crimson sky, at the tattered shreds of cloud that hung in lacy froths above the distant mountain peaks. A thumbnail moon glowed softly in the eastern sky, almost speared by a far peak, and stars were beginning to glitter in pinpricks of light. Twilight settled gently around the buggy.

"I think your family is very warm and loving. They're different from what I expected."

"What did you expect? Wild wolves?"

She laughed. "Something like that."

"You've been listening to too much gossip." Gray flapped the reins against the horse's rump and the buggy rolled faster. River caught at her still-unbound hair when it whipped her face, holding it with one hand.

Nothing was said for several miles as the land rolled past, and River was content just to sit and watch Gray. It didn't seem possible that she was alone with him, with the man who had haunted her dreams since the first time she'd seen him. Was it possible that dreams come true? That if one wanted something badly enough, it could come to pass? If it was, then there would be a happy ending to her life. So much had already happened, and to be with her Ideal Man seemed fated, even if he was not quite as she had pictured him.

"Have you ever seen stars on the ground?" Gray asked, abruptly breaking her reverie and startling River.

She pushed heavy waves of hair from her eyes where the wind had tossed it, staring at him in the dusk. "N-no."

"I'll show you some."

He reined the buggy to a stop and set the brake, then leaped down. River glanced around at the empty landscape. It had grown almost dark, and the land glowed with a faint sheen. Grasses waved, undulating in the slight breeze like currents in a river, and in the distance a coyote howled.

"Where?" River asked, but Gray didn't answer. He put his hands on her waist and lifted her from the buggy to the ground. For some reason, River's heart was thudding in an erratic tempo, and when Gray silently took her hand to lead her to a ridge above the road, she hesitated.

He turned to look at her in the dim light. "What's the matter?"

Feeling faintly foolish, River shrugged. "Nothing. I can't see where I'm going, that's all."

"You don't have to see. I can. Just keep holding my hand."

That's easy for you to say, River thought, but she followed him blindly.

When they crested the ridge, Gray waved a hand toward the meadow below. "See the stars?"

River gasped softly. Stretching below them was a field of tiny fireflies, all twinkling like stars in the tall grasses. "It looks like a carpet of stars!" she exclaimed softly, as if afraid of startling them with her voice. "I've never seen anything quite so beautiful!"

"Yeah, I thought you'd like it."

The dusk shimmered like magic, and River knew that Gray was going to kiss her. It seemed only natural for him to turn and pull her into his arms, to tilt her head back with his thumb under her chin and press his lips against hers. His mouth was warm, moving across her parted lips in a sweet, gentle kiss that was vaguely disappointing.

Where was the fire and passion of that night in the hotel? That night he had seared her very soul with desire? Did he feel that for other women, but not her?

Some of River's disappointment must have been evident, because when Gray released her, he was frowning.

"What's the matter?" he asked. "Did I scare you?"

"Scare me? Oh, no, you were quite . . . gentlemanly."

"Gentlemanly?" Gray seemed a bit taken aback. Then he said coldly, "Ah, I forgot. You prefer brooding, demon-driven men."

"No, no, that's not it," she began, but Gray had jerked her close again, and this time his kiss was anything but gentlemanly.

His mouth seared across her parted lips with a ferocity that was frightening, and she could feel the hard press of his body into her curves. A moan escaped her as Gray forced her head back under the brutal urgency of his mouth. Digging her fingers into his shoulders to keep from falling to her knees, River's breath came in small, rough gasps. His hand caught in the tangled waves of her hair to hold her head still when she would have pulled away, and his other tugged at the buttons of her dress. Dazed with the force of his embrace, River didn't offer a protest when his hand slipped into the open edges of her dress, did not try to pull away when his fingers caressed her bare breast.

The night air slid across her skin and made her shiver, and still she did not pull away. The sudden onslaught had stunned her, and she was too confused by his actions and her own reactions to protest. It was only when Gray's head followed the path his hand had taken, his lips moving intimately across her bare breast, that she was jerked to awareness of what he was doing, what she was doing.

"Oh! Stop!"

Gray's dark head lifted, and his silver eyes glittered dangerously. "Stop?" he repeated softly.

Half-sobbing with reaction and fright, she nodded. "Yes, please."

"Am I being too gentlemanly for you?" he asked harshly.

"Oh, you—you misunderstood," River said when he released her and stepped back.

"I don't think so."

Her head snapped up, and she held the edges of her dress together as she glared at him. Just because there was truth in what he said did not lessen her anger.

"I don't think you know the definition of *gentleman*, Gray Morgan!"

"Maybe I don't. At least, not your definition."

Seething with anger and humiliation, River reacted instinctively. Her arm swung up and her palm crashed against Gray's cheek with a loud crack. Gray did not move. He stared down at her with narrowed eyes, and a muscle in his jaw leaped as he clenched his teeth.

Gulping, River realized that she had just provoked him into rage, and realized, too, that they were miles from anywhere. She stood as if turned to stone, holding her breath and waiting for his reaction. Seconds dragged by as if weighted with rocks, then Gray turned away and stalked back down the ridge toward the buggy.

River had the brief fear that he was leaving her stranded

before he growled over his shoulder, "Come on if you want to ride back to Clanton. It's a long walk."

If there had been another way to get back into town, River would have gladly taken it. But there wasn't. And she wasn't at all certain she wanted to sit beside a furious Gray Morgan for another five miles. But at least he did not seem interested in prolonging their argument.

Which was just as well, River reflected when she climbed unaided back into the buggy, flouncing down on the seat and avoiding Gray's cold gaze. He seemed to be a man balancing on the brink of violence, and she certainly did not want to be the one to give him a shove.

As the few miles left to town passed in a blur, River had the sinking feeling that she might never see Gray again, and it saddened her. She found it hard to dispel the huge lump in her throat, even when he politely walked her to the door of the hotel and told her good night in a barely civil growl.

That night her dreams were painful, with images of Gray superimposed over the hateful face of a stranger. It was confusing, and she woke up sobbing, wondering if she would ever see Gray again.

Chapter 10

*

Maybe she wouldn't have seen Gray again, if not for a stranger. It wasn't the stranger of her dream, but she did not think about that until the incident was over.

Disconsolate because of their argument and not wanting Tyler to know, River pretended that Gray was going to come for her again that day. After breakfast Tyler went on to conduct his business, leaving River at loose ends. For the first few hours she stayed in her hotel room and tried to read, but that soon grew stale.

Restless and miserable, River decided to walk down the street and stare in the shop windows. Even that was better than moping around the tiny, stuffy hotel room and thinking of Gray.

River strolled slowly down the wooden sidewalk. She felt utterly alone, with no one to talk to, nothing to do. Everyone in town was busy with their own lives, and she was at loose ends. Maybe she should walk down to the general store and buy the slates, books, and chalk for her pupils at the Double T, but then again, she had all week to do that. And right now, she wasn't in the best of moods.

Sighing, River decided to wait. It would give her something to look forward to. She paused to stare in the windows of the local pharmacy, noting the rows upon rows of glass bottles and the modern display of perfumes in a case.

"May I help you, miss?" a man wearing an apron asked from the open doorway, and River turned with a start.

"Oh, no. I'm just looking," she said, then walked on. She hadn't gone far when the rumbling sound of hoofbeats thundered down Clanton's main street. Curious, River turned to watch as a large group of horsemen rode by at a fast pace. A beefy man with a rough, craggy face headed the group. He was the only one who looked as if he *might* be decent, River thought as they passed. The others all looked like itinerant drifters, with unshaven faces and hard features. Two of them wore patches over one eye, and all of them wore enough guns to outfit a small army troop. Some of them wore ammunition belts crisscrossing their chests, and rifles sprouted from saddles like porcupine quills.

"Who are those men?" River couldn't help asking a man who had paused to stare at them with a tight face.

He flicked her a glance. "Trucklow and his men," was all he said, then he moved on as if he was afraid he had said too much.

So that was Pierce Trucklow, River mused. He looked like a man who would not worry about the company he kept. No wonder he and her father were at odds. Tyler would not long suffer a man like Trucklow, a greedy man who hired obvious criminals and villains. She repressed a shudder.

River hesitated about continuing her walk, then had the rebellious thought that Pierce Trucklow and his men would not stop her from going about her daily life. After all, they did not even know her, and she certainly didn't know them! No, she would continue her walk, not inviting trouble but not allowing a man's reputation to make her run like a frightened rabbit.

Her skirts swished along the wooden boards, and she lifted

them slightly to keep them from soiling. As she passed the saloon, River had to sidestep a man who stood in front.

"Excuse me," she murmured politely when he stepped in her path, and waited for him to move. He didn't. She looked up with a frown and saw the man gazing down at her with narrowed eyes. He was dirty and unkempt and looked as if he had been riding the trail for weeks. One of Trucklow's men? she wondered.

"Excuse me," she repeated firmly, and took another step to go around.

"Excuse *me*," the man mocked her, grinning and revealing two missing teeth as he swept his hat from his head and gave her a sardonic bow. "What's your hurry, little lady?"

River thought swiftly. No one else was nearby, and a call to anyone in the saloon might bring worse than this man. "I'm meeting someone," she said quickly.

The man leaned against one of the porch posts. "Yeah? And who would that be? I might know him."

"I doubt it," she said. "Now please move out of my way."

"Don't get fresh with me," the man said with a touch of anger in his voice. "Do you think you're too good to talk to me?"

"No, just too busy." River stood her ground, not certain what she should do but hating to turn tail and run. Her chin lifted, and she eyed the man boldly. "If you do not remove yourself from my path, sir, I will be forced to call upon someone to remove you."

A gust of unclean air wafted to her nose when he shifted position, and he leered down at her. "I don't think so, little lady. There ain' nobody in this town who's gonna try it."

"Gray Morgan will," River threw at him, and the man laughed aloud.

"Gray Morgan? Hell, it'd take three of him and a dog to scare me!"

"How about one Morgan and two Colts?" a voice asked softly, and the man gave a jerk of his head, his hand dropping to the edge of the long coat he wore. "I wouldn't try it," the voice warned, and River's knees went weak with relief when she saw Gray.

She would have flung herself at him, but Gray gave her a quick shove that sent her stumbling into the street. "Stay there," he ordered tersely, and she didn't dare argue.

Clinging to a hitching post, her stylish hat tilted awkwardly over one eye, River watched with wide eyes as Gray turned back to the man from the saloon.

"We had a run-in last year, Brogan," he was drawling, and the man gave a tight nod.

"Yeah. I remember."

"Do you? Since you're back in town I thought maybe you'd forgotten."

Swaggering forward a step or two, Brogan said, "You don't own this town, Morgan."

"No, I don't. But I feel a moral obligation to keep it clean of trash. That's you, Brogan."

Brogan's face darkened with anger, and he blustered, "I have a right to walk down these streets or drink in this saloon! And what's more, Mr. Trucklow brought me into town."

"Now, that's not really a good recommendation," Gray said softly. His gaze flicked to the double saloon doors, where a burly man was stepping out.

River gasped. It was Pierce Trucklow. The huge man paused, and a grin slid over his face.

"Ah, it's Gray Morgan! How pleasant."

Gray's eyes narrowed. "Too bad I can't say the same for you, Trucklow."

A flicker of annoyance passed briefly over Trucklow's face before he hid it with a smile. "Still angry about your Comanche friend, Gray? He asked for what he got."

"I don't think so."

"When a man trespasses—red or white—and doesn't heed warnings to leave, then he gets shot. It's plain and simple and the law backs me up."

"Sometimes the law protects the wrong man, Trucklow.

And as for trespassing, it hasn't yet been decided who's trespassing—you or the Comanche."

Trucklow laughed harshly. "You never have been a man who can listen to the truth, Morgan!"

A tight smile curled one side of Gray's mouth. "The Comanche have a saying about that, Trucklow: 'When you tell a man the truth, it's best to have one foot in the stirrup.' Maybe you should remember that."

Bewildered, River looked from one to the other, and finally Pierce Trucklow seemed to notice her. His smile widened, and he leaned against the porch post and gazed at River for a long moment.

"Who's your pretty little friend, Morgan?"

Gray's reply was short. "You know who she is."

Aware that her hair had come loose and was dangling in front of her eyes with her stylish hat, River self-consciously pushed at it as Trucklow and the two men who had come up behind him stared at her. She began to feel like a plump goose in a poultry shop as they looked her up and down, and a slow flush pinkened her cheeks. Lifting her chin in an unconsciously defiant gesture, River stared back at Trucklow without letting her gaze falter. He chuckled.

"Ah, you must be Tyler Templeton's daughter," he said, and she stiffened.

"And if I am?" she shot at him in a steady voice.

"I'm pleased to finally meet you, Miss Templeton. My earlier efforts to gain an . . . introduction . . . have failed."

"So I heard," Gray answered for her. He pushed the brim of his felt hat back from his face so that Trucklow could see his eyes, and warned softly, "Let it drop."

Trucklow seemed amused. "My dear fellow, I have no ill intentions toward anyone. I'm just trying to make my fortune in my own little way, as everyone else is doing. Except you, of course, and you seem to be interested only in fighting for lost causes."

"It's not over, Trucklow."

The big man nodded slowly. "You're right, Morgan. And it should be interesting to see who wins."

"Tell your dog to stay out of my way," Gray said, and pointed to Brogan. "Next time he bothers a friend of mine, I won't think twice about putting him out of his misery."

Brogan took an angry step forward, but Trucklow's arm shot out to bar his way. "Leave it be, Brogan," he said, and the man halted. Only his eyes followed Gray as he turned to River and took her by the arm.

"Come on," Gray said as he half dragged her back up the street with him.

River remained quiet, only slicing him wary glances now and then as he escorted her up on the sidewalk and past the shops she had just passed. She tried to keep up, but Gray's long legs outdistanced her, so that finally she had to ask him to slow down.

"Gray. Please . . ."

Slowing at last, Gray looked down at her. His hand, which had been painfully grasping her arm, loosened its grip.

"What were you trying to do?" he snapped. "Start another war?"

"I don't know what you mean."

"Can't you stay out of trouble for a few hours? Did you have to get in Brogan's way?"

Growing angry, River shot back, "I was taking a walk, Gray Morgan, and that's all! The wretched man barred my way and would not let me pass. What kind of town is this, where a woman can't even walk unescorted down the street?"

"All right, all right." Gray dropped her arm and tucked his thumbs into his gunbelt, gazing down at her flushed face for a long moment. An occasional pedestrian passed by, and River had the distracted thought that none of the more sedate citizens seemed to frequent the far end of town.

"Look, unless you want to invite trouble, just stay at *this* end of the street. Do you think you can do that?"

"I'm positive I can manage it now that my memory's been jogged," she said, glaring back at him. "It seems that my trusted guide forgot to remind me of that yesterday when he walked me down to the famous courting tree—''

"Yeah," Gray broke in, "I guess I did."

There didn't seem to be anything else to say, and they stood there awkwardly. Then Gray shrugged.

"Are you hungry? Delmonico's front door is right here."

River pretended to consider, ignoring the hopeful leap of her heart. "Yes, I could eat a bite," she finally said when it looked as if Gray might retract his obscure invitation.

Without speaking, Gray reached around her and shoved open the door to the restaurant, sweeping one arm forward in a mocking gesture. River sailed past him as if he had graciously bowed, and steeled her determination to make amends. After all, though Gray Morgan had a few flaws that she hadn't counted on, he was still her Ideal Man.

"Where's Tyler?" Gray asked when they had ordered their meal. "Still wrangling over the price of beeves?"

River lifted her shoulders briefly. "I suppose so. I haven't seen much of him since we've been in town."

She gazed at Gray over the rim of her coffee cup, remembering the man who had accosted her, and Gray's swift reaction. "How did you know I was in trouble?" she asked. Gray's silver eyes flicked up to meet hers, and her heart skipped a beat.

"I was across the street. I saw you walking, then I saw Brogan stop you."

He'd seen her walking, yet had not joined her. Was he still angry?

He must be, because he wasn't offering much conversation. "What was Trucklow talking about? What Comanche?" she asked then, and Gray frowned.

"A friend of mine," he said shortly.

When he didn't elaborate, River hesitated. Dare she ask more questions? He certainly didn't seem to be in the mood to answer them. But then Gray was shaking his head, and he looked back up at her.

"It's not a big secret. I'm a mediator between the BIA and

the Comanches on occasion. When I was a kid, I used to ride with them. I had a good friend, a blood brother. We met when his horse threw him and broke his leg, and I killed a panther that was about to have him for breakfast." A faint smile slanted his lips, and some of the coldness left his eyes. "His name was Redhawk, and he stayed at the ranch with us for a while. After he healed, we still stayed friends. Sometimes I would stay with the People, and sometimes he would stay with me. It wasn't a big deal back then when I was only seven or eight, but a few years later it all changed when my father was killed."

His voice trailed into silence, and his eyes clouded with memories that River could not see or understand.

"The Indian wars?" she prompted softly, and Gray gave a short nod.

"Yeah. Of course, there had always been war between white man and red, but when the buffalo slaughter started, it grew worse. The buffalo represents an entire way of life to the Indian. It provides food, clothing, shelter, and security. Nothing is wasted by the Indian. But now the buffalo are almost gone, hunted and slaughtered from trains for their hides, then left to rot on the plains. There's not much left for the Comanche anymore."

"But I thought Congress was providing for them?" River said with a question in her voice.

Gray's laugh was bitter. "Oh yes, they've provided, all right! Last year Congress passed the General Allotment Act, or the Dawes Act. What a stroke of genius. That act is intended to break down tribal bonds and make farmers of the Comanches—*farmers,* for Chrissake! They were warriors, and now the government wants them to plow dust and grow crops. What a joke. Naturally, it's not working."

River noticed that Gray's hands were clenched into fists on the table, and she saw the white lines bracketing his mouth as he thought of the injustices to his friends.

"Can't they be shown how to farm, though? I mean, they can't be warriors forever."

Silver sparks flashed from his eyes as he growled, "If you can find someone who can grow corn in solid rock, I'd like to meet them! The president subdivided tribal lands and awarded family sized plots to each individual. But the catch is, the best tribal land was designated as 'surplus' and sold to white men. The Comanches—and Apaches and Navajos, et cetera—were given barren rock to cultivate. And that is what the quarrel with Trucklow is about."

"He was sold fertile land," River said softly, and Gray nodded.

"Yeah. It was Redhawk's old hunting ground, and when he tried to provide food for his starving family, he was shot. Naturally, not much is going to be done about an Indian getting himself shot on white man's land."

"Did Trucklow acquire his land illegally?" River asked.

Gray shrugged. "That's what I'm trying to find out. It just takes so damned much time, so much cutting through bureaucratic tangles—kind of like what Tyler's going through. I sure wish I could prove Trucklow got his land unfairly. And so do the Comanches." He smiled, a smile that didn't quite reach his eyes. "That's one reason Trucklow has so many hired guards. He's afraid he's going to wake up one morning with that red scalp of his hanging from some Comanche brave's lodgepole."

"Scalp?" River echoed with a shudder.

Gray grinned. "Yeah." He reached across the table and lifted a stray strand of her hair in his palm. "Hair like yours would be a real prize to a Comanche—especially if it was still attached. A few years back, you'd have brought many ponies in a trade."

River tried not to react to the touch of his hand, to the slow, hypnotic smile on his lips. "A few years back?" she repeated in a croaking voice.

Gray still held her hair, and his hand grazed the soft curve of her cheek. "Too bad bartering white wives isn't so much of a good deal anymore."

Clearing her throat, River sat back in her chair and managed a weak smile. "I see."

"Do you? I wonder."

River was silent for a moment, then she asked, "Don't you resent the Indians for killing your father? I mean even though the men responsible may not have been your friends, doesn't that matter to yo—"

"Indians?" Gray stared at her, then laughed shortly. "It wasn't Indians who killed my father, River. It was white men who didn't like Mike Morgan's refusal to massacre a sleeping village. That was right after the Battle of Little Big Horn up in Montana, see, and sentiment ran high for a while."

River sat back in her chair. "I see," she murmured, thinking that the situation was much more complicated than she had dreamed.

Now she understood why Gray Morgan was contemptuous of his neighbors, why he preferred using his education and law degree to help the Comanches rather than the white men. It made her heart ache to know that he had lost his father to people whom he'd trusted. She looked up at Gray. She had to ask, even though she knew the answer.

"Was Papa involved in all that?"

"Tyler? No, he refused to be involved too. He'd always let the Comanche hunt on his land as long as they didn't steal his beef. He's also been known to give them cattle in the winter or spring when they're hungry, but the men who killed my father didn't have a quarrel with Tyler." Gray's mouth twisted bitterly. "My father's murderers justified their actions on the basis of my friendship with Redhawk. We were 'Indian-lovers,' see."

Horrified, River realized that Gray must blame himself in some way for his father's death.

"But those men were caught and punished, weren't they? I mean, they aren't still . . . still here?"

Wearily, Gray rubbed the stubble of new beard on his jaw. "No, they weren't caught and they weren't punished. Most of them wore masks, but I know who they are and they know who they are. Nothing has ever been said, but none of us have forgotten.''

He stood abruptly, shoving back his chair. ''Are you finished?'' he asked, clearly too upset to remain sitting. It would have been awkward to say no, and she'd lost her appetite anyway, so she just nodded.

''Yes, of course,'' she murmured.

They didn't talk on the way back to the hotel, each lost in their own thoughts. Twilight colored the town in soft roses and violets, reminding River of the previous dusk, and she sighed. The quarrel between them had begun because of her, and even though Gray had reacted harshly, she couldn't say it was all his fault.

''Gray?'' she said when they reached the hotel, ''I'm sorry about last night.'' She didn't want their misunderstanding to go unresolved.

She held her breath as he looked down at her, his brows drawn down over his eyes in a frown and his mouth thinned to a straight, tight line. Would he forgive her? Would he ever want to see her again?

Then his expression softened slightly, and a half-smile pressed at the corners of his mouth. ''Maybe I better walk you up to your room,'' he said, and River knew he was willing to forget the incident.

''Do you think Brogan might come here?'' she asked as he opened the hotel door for her.

''Not really, but there's no telling who might be in the lobby.''

River knew he meant Trucklow, and her eyes grew wide with apprehension as she looked quickly around the wide room. Horsehair settees and ornate chairs dotted the carpeted area, and small serving tables held the evidence of recent occupation, but the lobby was deserted except for one old man dozing in a corner.

''Looks safe enough,'' she said with a relieved smile.

''I'm sure it is, but this is the only hotel, and Pierce

Trucklow is in town tonight,'' Gray reminded. "Where's your father's room?"

"Down the hall from mine."

"It might be a good idea if we stop by and tell him you're back."

But Tyler—assuming that River was with Gray—hadn't returned yet. No one answered their knock on his door, and they walked to River's room. She was reminded of the last time she had stayed in this hotel, and how Gray Morgan had found her in this very hallway and kissed her so ruthlessly. It was a most disturbing memory, and River tried to push it to the back of her mind as they stopped in front of her room.

"I'll just check it out," Gray said, taking her room key and opening the door. He stepped in first, his gaze sweeping the room, then he beckoned her in. "It's okay."

Uneasy at his caution, River sidled into the room with a nervous laugh.

"Maybe I should hire a bodyguard," she suggested with another weak laugh.

"I'll be watching out for you," Gray said shortly, and River turned to look at him.

"But your office . . . room is at the other end of town."

A flicker of annoyance crossed his face. "I *know* where my office is."

She stiffened. "Sorry!"

Gray swept off his felt hat and raked a hand through his hair with a sigh. "Look, I didn't mean to be rude. It's just that I'm trying to figure out how to keep you safe until Tyler gets back."

Alarmed, she said, "Do you think I'm in danger, then?"

"No, but I don't trust Trucklow any more than I'd trust a snake."

Her gaze flicked to his hatband. The rattles shook with a slight clacking each time he moved his head, and Gray followed her gaze. He grinned.

"That's what happened to the last snake I didn't trust. I'll need a bigger hat for Trucklow."

Laughing, some of River's tension eased. "So, do you intend to stay here with me until Papa returns, then?" she asked as she began to remove her hat. She moved to the mirror in the corner, watching Gray's reflection over her shoulder. He shrugged.

"I'm not crazy about the idea of sleeping on a couch, and I'm even less crazy about what Tyler might say if he found me sleeping in your bed."

Just the thought made River's eyes widen, her blood congeal into sluggish gel, and her breath wheeze in her throat. She struggled against her physical reaction and managed to ask lightly, "Does Papa's opinion matter that much to you?"

Gray's clear gaze found hers in the mirror, and his eyes narrowed in speculation as he said flatly, "Yes, it does."

She turned and tossed her hat to the bed. "It does to me, too." A faint smile curved her mouth, and she found that she was suddenly nervous with Gray towering by the door and looking at her with a strange expression. "Would you like some wine?" she babbled, aware that she was babbling but unable to stop. "The hotel left a carafe and glasses in here for some reason, though I rarely drink. It does funny things to me, you know, makes me all light-headed and chatty, and—"

"And it sounds like you've already been drinking," Gray cut in. He moved to the small table where a tray and carafe had been placed. "Maybe some wine will slow you down."

River nodded, lacing her hands tightly together and silently admonishing herself not to revert to Drucilla Duckworth. She had to be serene, calm, cool, sophisticated, if she wanted to impress Gray with her wit and charm. And she realized that she wanted that very much. With each passing hour she was falling more under his spell, becoming more infatuated—in love?—with him.

"Thank you," she said calmly when Gray pressed a glass of wine into her now only slightly quivering fingers. River took a huge gulp, then smiled tremulously at Gray. "It tastes good."

He swallowed his wine in a single gulp and set the empty glass on a table. "It's not bad, but I prefer beer."

She hastily gulped another sip as Gray began to pace the room restlessly. What kind of small talk would interest him? And after the evening's deep conversation, what could she say that wouldn't sound inane?

"Look," Gray finally said after he'd stared out the open window for the fifth time, "I think everything's all right. Why don't you just write a message for Tyler and tell him to keep an eye on you, and I'll give it to the clerk at the front desk."

River set her half-empty wineglass on the table beside the bed. "Oh. That sounds like a good idea." She crossed to the small writing desk opposite the bed and took out a sheaf of paper with THE CLANTON HOTEL imprinted at the top. After scribbling a brief message, she folded it and gave it to Gray.

He shoved it into his shirt pocket. "Lock your door when I leave. And don't open it for anyone, unless they identify themselves first and you know them."

"That narrows the field down considerably," River said, then answered the question in his eyes, "I don't know anyone in all of Comanche County but people from the Double T and you. And your family," she added.

Gray grunted. "Then you shouldn't be opening your door." He slapped his hat against his lean thigh for a moment, then shrugged. "Well, I guess I'll leave."

For a moment River had the crazy thought that he might kiss her again, but he didn't. Instead, he pivoted on his heel and stalked to the door, opening it and looking out into the hall before turning back to look at her.

She stood there indecisively, then said softly, "Good night, Gray."

"G'night. Lock the door," he reminded her. Then he stepped out and shut it behind him.

River crossed to the door and turned the key in the lock, listening as she heard Gray's boot steps fade away in the hallway. She leaned against the closed door and shut her eyes. A long sigh slipped out and hung in the air for a moment.

"I must be mad," she whispered to the empty room. Then she laughed softly and said, "Only a madwoman would be talking to herself like this!"

River tried not to think about Gray as she undressed and pulled out a nightdress, tried not to think about the night before when he had kissed her and she hadn't really wanted him to stop. Only her sense of propriety—only what she knew she should do instead of what she wanted to do—had kept her from yielding to him gladly on that star-studded ridge under the night sky.

Tossing her cream-colored lawn nightdress atop the bed, River sank down on the mattress and unbraided the rope of hair at her neck. Too many strands had escaped from her neat braid, and she would have to rebraid it in the morning. She shook her head, and sun-gilded hair rippled in shimmering waves down her back. She finger-combed it, not bothering with the hairbrush atop the dresser, then stood up to shrug into her gown.

A faint glimmer of reflection from the mirror caught her eye, and River paused with the nightdress still draped over one arm. Was that really her reflection in the mirror? Was that really her? She hadn't taken the time even to glance at her reflection unless she was dressing to meet Gray, but now she stepped closer to the cheval glass and stared.

Slowly reaching out one hand, River lightly touched her image in the mirror. Her hair was loose and waving around her face, framing it in a cloud of soft color, making her sun-honeyed skin glow. The gold locket Tyler had given her reflected the gaslight in tiny splinters, and she curled her fingers around it. Her blue eyes fringed with thick, dark lashes looked faintly sleepy, probably the effect of the wine she'd drunk too fast. But it was her body that drew her most critical attention.

All the bulges and folds of surplus flesh were gone.

River stared. Her breasts were high, round, and firm, not

too large but not too small, and her waist had narrowed to a span that Gray could easily have circled with his hands. The swell of her hips was gentle, and her thighs were lean and hard from all the riding she'd done with her father. Was it really her? Was it really River she was seeing in the mirror? Drucilla Duckworth had disappeared, vanished as if by magic, sleight of hand, the magician's box.

A faint smile curved River's mouth. Perhaps she wasn't strikingly beautiful, or even pretty, as Trucklow had said, but she was attractive. And maybe Gray would notice.

Slipping the thin lawn gown over her head, River lifted the wineglass Gray had given her and drained the rest of her wine. She should sleep well tonight, she thought drowsily as she turned out the gas lamp and slipped beneath the covers of the bed. And all her dreams should be dreams of Gray . . .

Chapter 11

*

Maybe it was the small amount of wine she'd drunk that made her sleep so soundly. Or maybe she was just dreaming such wonderful dreams that she did not want to wake up, but whatever it was, River never heard them come into her room. She knew nothing and had only an instant's warning before something struck the side of her head and she spiraled into a black void.

Waking was painful. And suffocating. River could not tell if it was night or day, and found to her consternation that she could not move her arms or legs. Something scratchy and musty was pressed close to her face, wrapped around her body, and cushioning her against a steady jounce that made her ribs ache. There was also a vaguely distasteful rag stuffed into her mouth so that breathing was difficult and screaming impossible.

Another jounce and she could hear voices from outside her dusty prison.

"Dammit, Riggs! I done told you not to be so loud!" came a faintly whining voice.

"It ain't me, Webster! It's you, you lop-eared mule!" said a fretful voice.

River held her breath as her kidnappers clumsily lowered her. Would she hit the floor—ground?—at any moment with a hard thump? Unfamiliar hands roughly shifted her around. She wished she could see, could know what was happening around her.

"Act like we're just movin' this carpet," came one of the voices again—Webster? Riggs?—and River realized that she must be rolled up inside a carpet. From the pervasive odor, she thought it must be an *old* carpet. She was bound so tightly it was useless to try and escape, and she was becoming dizzy from the continual jolting.

Inhaling as much as possible through her squashed nostrils, River hoped that whoever had her would unroll her soon before she suffocated to death. It was so stifling that she could almost ignore the bruising, rib-cracking jolts. And she was so terrified that she hoped she did not become overwhelmed with tears. If her nose filled up with tears, that would kill her for certain.

"Ow!" came one of the voices again, and River could feel herself being shifted, harsh hands handling her so roughly she began to struggle. "Ow! It's like holdin' a live snake, Riggs!" the whining voice protested, and River's body was gripped even tighter.

Perhaps if she wiggled hard enough, there was a chance for freedom. River wriggled again, harder, hoping whoever had her would at the very least unroll her, at the most, release her.

As she struggled, River first heard more curses, and then felt weightless as she was swung through the air, felt the sickening sensation of falling, then the bone-jarring thud of a hard landing. Then she heard the shots, the brittle burst of gunfire that made her blood freeze. What if a bullet hit her? She was, after all, rolled up inside an old carpet. Would anyone know that the carpet was alive, that it was River? She struggled to keep moving so that someone would notice.

Then she realized that perhaps she wasn't really being rescued. Maybe it was another gang. Maybe her captors would be the victors. She was not quite certain why she was being kidnapped anyway. Who could possibly want her—

except for Pierce Trucklow, she reminded herself, and felt a cold shiver of terror.

Her brief worries vanished quickly as she heard more shots, more curses, then the pounding of booted feet. River waited in an agony of fear for the next development in this horrible nightmare. She almost wished she could pinch herself to be sure she was awake but knew from the aching of her body that she must be. No nightmare was so painful.

She lay there and heard the distant hum of activity, footsteps, a few muffled voices, then nothing. It was almost an anticlimax when she felt the carpet being tugged, and she braced herself as she was rolled along the ground like a ball.

Suddenly light exploded in her eyes and there was a heavy gush of sweet, cool air—air that didn't smell of dust and old tobacco. River's eyes had trouble adjusting to the rapid change, and she had to blink several times to clear them of a teary haze.

"River!" came an achingly familiar voice, and at last her eyes began to fill with relieved tears. It was Gray, and he had rescued her, her knight in shining armor, her Sir Galahad, her Ideal Man. If her throat hadn't been so tight, she would have called his name as he removed the gag from her mouth.

When she was finally able to focus on him, River saw that Gray had rocked back on his heels and was staring at her with lifted brows. There was an odd light in his eyes as his gaze raked her, and she suddenly remembered that she was wearing only a thin nightdress. A faint flush stained her cheeks pink, and her arms automatically crossed over her breasts, which had the effect of making Gray's mouth slant in a crooked smile.

Feeling foolish, River cringed deeper into the carpet that she'd been so eager to leave, noticing the crowd of people behind Gray. A rumble of voices filled the lobby, and she closed her eyes so she didn't have to see them staring at her.

"Are you all right?" Gray asked. She nodded blindly, too miserable to open her eyes.

She heard him laugh softly and felt a spurt of indignation.

"I hope," she ground out, "that you are enjoying yourself at my expense!"

"Come on, sweetheart," Gray said with another laugh, "let's get you out of here."

Scooping her from the musty carpet into his arms, Gray stood and began to force his way through the crowd. River put her arms around his neck and buried her face against his chest, breathing in the now-familiar scent of tobacco and whisky.

"Move back," he said as he pushed past the curious. "Move back."

"Gray," someone called, "Curtis went after the sheriff for you!"

River felt Gray pause and turn, heard the contempt in his cold voice as he said, "Then Curtis can tell the sheriff what happened."

"But . . . but aren't you going to have him find out who did this?" the same voice asked, and River opened her eyes and looked up at Gray's hard face.

There was a wealth of scorn in his eyes, and his lip curled as he shook his head. "I wouldn't send Wentwhistle to look for a lost dog."

It grew so quiet in the lobby, a dropped pin would have sounded like a load of bricks, and River put her face back into Gray's shoulder as he walked across the lobby and up the flight of stairs. The gaslight flickered on the walls in eerie shadows as he retraced River's earlier path down the hallway, and Gray kicked open her door.

"I need to talk to Papa."

He shook his head.

"He's not back. There was a note delivered by Doug Fenster's boy that Tyler will be staying the night out there."

"Doug Fenster?" River repeated slowly. "I don't know him."

"I do. Don't worry about it. Tyler's all right."

River put her head back against his shoulder, then felt him

pause, felt the gentle descent of her body back onto the hotel bed from which she had been so rudely removed earlier.

For a moment she felt bereft, abandoned, then Gray returned and pressed a glass of wine into her hands. River took it blindly, her fingers automatically closing around the glass stem as he guided it to her lips. The wine didn't taste as good now as it had earlier, but it did have the effect of steadying her hands and the erratic pop of her lungs. She took another sip, then sagged back into the fat feather pillows again as Gray took back the glass. She closed her eyes, avoiding his narrowed stare, but she could feel him looking at her. Her skin seemed to burn wherever his gaze traveled.

"What happened?" Gray asked as his hands swiftly and methodically made an impersonal check of her arms and legs. "No broken bones" was his matter-of-fact diagnosis. River's head rolled back and forth on the fat feather pillow, and her voice seemed faraway.

"No," she agreed in a foggy whisper, "no broken bones." Opening her eyes at last, she looked up at him, at the angles and planes of his face, not quite able to meet his eyes yet. The light was behind him, throwing his face into shadow, hiding his expression. For some reason, River felt a twinge of fear.

"What happened?" Gray repeated, lowering his body to the bed. River felt the mattress sag with his weight, and finally looked into his eyes.

They were cold and flat, betraying nothing, giving her no hint of what he was thinking, and she inhaled deeply to give herself courage. The events of the night had completely unnerved her.

"I don't know," she said softly.

He gave an impatient shake of his head. "I'm not asking for rhyme or reason, River—I am asking you what happened. Can't you just tell me what you recall, for Chrissake?"

"You don't have to swear!" she said angrily, and saw him smile.

"Ah, that's better. What do you remember?"

Glaring at him, River told him all she could recall, remembering to mention the two names she'd heard.

"Riggs and Webster?" Gray repeated with a frown. "I've never heard of them."

"Well, I'm glad to hear they aren't friends of yours," River snapped.

Ignoring her, Gray asked, "How did they get in?"

"How do I know?"

"I'm the one asking questions, you're the one answering them."

"Well, ask questions I know the answers to!" To her horror her eyes began to fill with tears, and Gray's tone softened.

"Oh, God, spare me tears, at least!"

Choking on a sob, River said, "I can't help it! It was horrible, and now you're being mean to me!"

There was a moment of silence, then Gray handed her one of her handkerchiefs. River sniffed and blew her nose, knowing that she had ruined her credibility with him. It was just too much. She'd had a horrible day, a perfectly horrible day, and Gray Morgan wasn't showing a shred of compassion.

"Are you through now?" Gray asked when her sobs grew fainter, and she looked up to glare at him with teary eyes.

"Maybe yes—maybe no!"

A half-smile hooked one corner of his mouth, and his eyes were warmer now, not as distant. "At least you're coherent."

"Oh, just leave me alone," she muttered, tossing the wadded hankie to the bedside table.

Gray's gaze slid over her again, this time not dissecting and dismissing her as impersonally as an inanimate object.

"I'm not sure I can do that," he said, and her head jerked up.

"What do you mean?"

He didn't answer. Instead, he reached out and lifted the gold locket she wore, holding it in the palm of his hand for a moment. "Who gave you this?" he asked softly, turning it in his hand.

"Papa. My mother's portrait is inside."

His fingers grazed her breast as he held the locket, and River drew in a sharp breath at the touch. Her heart began to pound, and her throat grew tight with some reaction that could only be—anticipation. Yes. That was it, she decided—anticipation.

She began to tremble. Despite the cool breeze that was blowing in the open window, she wore a thin, sleeveless nightdress. Earlier she'd been cold, but now, River felt a burning flush go from her neck to her toes. Even her eyes felt hot. She marveled at the contradiction of her physical response, the heat of her flesh and the cold lump in her throat.

Gray placed the locket back in the shadowed valley between her breasts, his fingers lingering against her warm skin. It was quiet in the room, and River was certain he could feel the rapid thudding of her heart beneath the backs of his fingers. Her eyelids felt heavy, heated, her skin sizzling to the touch. The sensitive nerve endings along the surface of her skin almost vibrated as Gray's hand dragged slowly across her shoulder to her arm, then down to lift her wrist to his lips.

Shivering, River closed her eyes as he kissed the tiny pulse throbbing in her wrist, then the heel of her palm, then each finger. Deep in the pit of her stomach a fire coiled, writhing upward to spread throughout her body, until she felt as if the entire room were ablaze.

"Gray, . . . what are you . . ."

"Don't talk," he murmured against the inside of her elbow. His mouth moved up her arm, paused while he untied the tiny green ribbons that held up her gown, then pressed against the madly fluttering pulse in her throat when River gasped with shock.

"Oh, but . . . !" She reached for the bodice of her nightdress, but the fine lawn material had already slipped down, baring her breasts. When her arms moved to cross over her body, Gray grasped her wrists gently but firmly and pulled her arms out to the side.

"No. Don't cover yourself against me."

Why is he doing this, River wondered with another gasp. *Why am I allowing it?*

It was insane. Yet, deep inside she knew she had invited his touch, knew she had longed for him from the first moment she'd seen him. She'd dreamed of him every night, thought of him every day, made herself sick with longing for him, and now he was holding her, touching her, kissing her as she'd always dreamed he would.

Yet something was wrong.

It took her several moments to realize that the most important part had been left out—no words of love had passed between them.

And by the time she realized it, it was too late. She was caught in a trap of her own weaving, caught as neatly as a fly in a web, struggling more against her own desire than Gray's.

Her nightdress was gone, tossed aside, and Gray had stripped away his clothes and was lying half over her, his lean, hard body pressed intimately against her curves. One hand cupped the weight of a breast in his palm, while the other moved slowly over the curve of her ribs, down to the flat plane of her belly. Moaning, River tried to regain some detachment, but Gray's mouth closed over the peak of her breast and she could think of nothing but the moment.

Instinctively her hands came up to hold his head, to let her fingers trace small, circular patterns on his strong jaw, to wander to the dark crisp curls of hair down his neck. Her hands danced through his hair, explored the breadth of his shoulders, traced the ridge of his spine down to his hips. She arched against him, returning kiss for kiss, caress for caress.

She was lost, and Gray knew it.

Gray had known it from the moment she'd rolled out of the carpet and onto the lobby floor. Out of respect for Tyler, he'd tried to ignore the invitation that had been in her eyes since he'd met her at Delmonico's two days ago, especially when he'd realized that River wasn't aware of the message she was sending with every glance, every touch. Normally, he found it easy to avoid a woman he did not want, but the trouble with River was—he did want her.

When he'd looked down into her blue, blue eyes two days ago and caught the glassy sheen of admiration in her gaze, he'd known how she felt about him. Her mobile face was too transparent, and she'd obviously not had much practice in hiding her emotions. But until the buggy ride back from the Rocking M, he hadn't known that he wanted her, too.

He'd thought he could give her a sweet, tender kiss and remain distant. But he hadn't. The real reason he had avoided her wasn't because he was angry, but because he was too attracted to her.

And when River had rolled out of that carpet with her thin nightdress draped over ripe curves and looked up at him as if he was a knight in shining armor, Gray had wanted to take her then and there. Only hard-won restraint had checked him until he'd brought her upstairs.

He'd almost decided to get out of her room as fast as he could, but River's pleading eyes and soft curves had made him linger too long. Now he could not leave even if she ordered him to go.

"Relax," Gray murmured against River's soft, trembling lips. His hands gently ran through the wealth of her hair and pulled her head closer. His fingers began to stroke the tiny sensitive spot behind her left ear, and River shivered with the force of his touch.

She had no idea what to expect next, and she wondered if he could tell. It wasn't her fault, really, for no one had ever told her exactly what went on between a man and a woman. Grandmother Duckworth had certainly never divulged such information, and on the two occasions that River had brought it up, the old lady had expressed such shock at her granddaughter's lewdness that River had never mentioned it again. So River had only the vaguest imaginings about what occurred between men and women at this particular time—that, and the not so vague urgings of her body.

And that was a shock. Oh, she knew what to expect if she

believed the novels she had read, about starlight and moon-light and all that, but what happened to her reflexes had been a complete mystery until now. Now she discovered that her heart didn't work right, and that low in the pit of her stomach was that strange, fluttering sensation like the slow burning of a fire. There was also the thick, sluggish movement of the blood through her veins, rather like molten lava might move down the slopes of a volcano, hot and fiery and spreading flames. River's lungs had ceased to function normally and starved her body of needed oxygen by refusing to work properly. She couldn't breathe when Gray touched her . . . there . . . or when his lips left her mouth and moved in tiny little kisses along the line of her jaw and up to her earlobe. And she felt as if she was moving in a thick haze, her limbs weighted and languorous. For a brief instant River was frightened, but then Gray's harsh, demanding mouth slanted across hers in a kiss so hot and passionate that she could think of nothing but an end to the urgent fires that drove her.

Beneath the rounded curve of her hands River could feel Gray's tight-muscled chest, could feel the irregular beat of his heart. She arched against him, her hips insistent, her cries soft and wordless.

"Ready, love?" Gray muttered against her ear, his hands moving across her moist curves in caresses so intimate that she gasped.

"Oh, Gray—I don't know—it's all so strange . . ."

"Put your arms around me," he ordered, and she was glad to have him tell her what to do next.

Obediently, she curled her arms around his neck as Gray slid between her thighs, one knee nudging them apart. Still keeping her arms around his neck, River felt him lift her slim hips, felt the velvet heat of him against her, and gasped again.

"River, hush, River, it's okay," Gray said against her mouth, capturing her lips with his and kissing her until she relaxed. Then, as she lay in a haze of false security, he moved forward with a swift thrust that caught her by surprise.

There was no time for her to protest, no time for her to do more than cry out. She lay there, her eyes a wide, drowning blue, looking up at him with an accusing stare.

"Sorry, love." He kissed her swollen lips, his tongue sliding between them to fence lightly, teasing her from reproach.

Kissing him back, River held her breath when he began to move again, but discovered that there was no need to be afraid. Instead of another sharp pain, there was only an expectation, a rising need that swelled higher and higher until only Gray could ease it, only Gray could give her release.

And when it came, in wave after wave that made River think of an ocean, she cried out and clung to him, sobbing like a small child.

Slightly disgruntled, Gray pulled away and stared down at her. "Are you hurt?"

She shook her head, and he smothered back damp tendrils of blond-streaked hair from her eyes.

"What, then?" he asked as she hid her face against him.

"I'm so happy," she said into his shoulder, and he could feel the wet tears against his bare skin.

"Well, don't drown me with happiness," Gray muttered in a cross voice, but his mouth was curved in a smile.

River gave a slight sniff. "You're not nearly as mean as you'd like to be," she observed, and he laughed.

"If this is your notion of love talk, I'm not impressed."

"What's your notion of love talk?" River tilted back her head to ask. Her breath caught in her throat when he leaned down to kiss her again, his lips lingering on the arch of her throat, moving down to the small, fluttering pulse in the hollow. "Oh," she said, then, "Oh! Maybe I should take lessons."

"Oh, no, love," Gray whispered against her breast, "you don't need any lessons at all."

Chapter 12

*

Stirring, half-awake and half in the shadowy world of dreams, River tried to turn over but couldn't. Something was keeping her from it, and she fumbled with the tangled quilt for a moment before realizing that it was caught. A slight frown knit her brow, and she gave the snag a push. The snag protested.

"Hey . . . what are you trying to do?" drawled a sleepy male voice, and River's eyes flew open.

Could she be dreaming with her eyes open? Then she knew that she was not. Last night had been no dream, and the man in her bed was no dream. He was as real as the bruises on her body and the vague soreness between her thighs.

River lay stiff and still, hardly daring to glance at Gray, afraid he would be looking at her with that mocking light in his eyes.

"It's too late to change your mind," came the soft reminder, and River put her hands over her face.

"I'm not changing my mind." Her voice was muffled by ten fingers, and Gray laughed.

Prying down her fingers, he recognized the smoky blue worry in her eyes, and his smile faded. "Sorry?" he asked.

"Are you?"

So that was it. Gray relaxed back into the pillows and folded his arms behind his head. His gaze shifted from River's sleep-flushed face to her curves that still bore the marks of his passion. Reaching out, he let one finger slide over her shoulder to her breast, then down over her ribcage to her stomach. Her body quivered at his light touch, and Gray smiled again.

"No," he finally answered. "If you want confessions, you need to walk down to the Clanton Methodist Church. There are plenty of people there who will bare their souls for you."

"I don't want soul-baring." River sat up, pulling the quilt up to her chin and wrapping her arms around her bent knees.

Gray's voice was curious. "What do you want?"

Without looking at him, she shrugged. How could she tell him that she wanted to hear a simple "I love you?" It would be meaningless if she had to ask, and her stubborn streak would not let her say it first. Never since that first horrible time she had almost blurted it out, River had not even been tempted to say it aloud.

Sitting up, he swung his legs over the side of the bed and began to dress. She watched silently. There were to be no tender moments this morning, she supposed, and that was just as well. She wasn't certain any of her newfound resolves could bear up to more of Gray's lovemaking. Her gaze followed him as he dressed, stepping into his pants and shrugging into his shirt as casually as if he had an audience every morning. River's heart sank. Maybe he did. Maybe she was only one of many. Or was it Treena that he loved?

Steeling herself, River lifted her chin. It would not be very poised of her to degenerate into a frenzy of accusations that would either anger or amuse him, and anyway, she had not asked for, nor had he made, any promises.

Still, she could not help the lurch of her heart when he turned back to smile at her. Her gaze flicked from his bare chest beneath the open shirt back up to his eyes, and she managed to smile back at him.

Gray picked up his boots and sat on the chair beside the bed. "I'd suggest that you dress too, because if I know that half-witted sheriff, he's going to be here first thing this morning," he said. "And he's going to have a lot of questions in his pocket, so be ready for them."

River's eyes widened, and she leaped from the bed, clumsily wrapping the quilt around her as she stumbled for the dressing screen in the corner.

"I need a bath!" she said wildly. "I need to get my clothes on. Do you really think he'll be here soon? Oh, and you've got to . . . got to . . ."

Gray's mouth twisted. "I get the idea, sweetheart. And that's why I got dressed. Not only do I prefer the sheriff not knowing where I spent the night, I'd much rather Tyler not know, either."

River's face paled. Tyler. She'd not thought about her father finding out, not thought about how hurt he'd be if he knew that she and Gray had . . . had slept together without a single word of love or marriage being mentioned. He'd be so disappointed, and she couldn't stand that!

Whirling, she stared at Gray with blue eyes as big as pools. "What if he does? Oh, what would I say?"

Gray was tugging on his boots, and he looked up at her with a faint expression of annoyance. "If he does, I imagine *I'll* be the one explaining, not you."

"Oh, but you don't understand, Gray! I mean, he would be so upset with me, so disappointed that I would behave like—like this."

Standing, Gray stomped his feet down into his boots and grinned. "You didn't sound so upset last night," he reminded softly, and River flushed.

She had trouble meeting his clear silver gaze, the mocking lights that she knew would be in his eyes. "It's not that I'm upset, it's just that I don't think Papa would understand."

Buckling on his gunbelts, Gray cocked a dark brow at her.

"I think Tyler would understand a lot better than you think he would, but I'm not in a big hurry to tell him about it, either." He slid one of his Colt Peacemakers from its holster and spun the cylinder with a clicking sound, squinted down the barrel, then slid it back into the leather holster with a smack. "Unless you want the entire town to know that you've *been behaving like this*," he said, "I suggest that you hurry, or you'll be meeting Sheriff Wentwhistle au naturel. Then everyone from the Methodist minister to the one-eyed dog at the saloon will know that you've *been behaving like this*."

"You seem to think this is funny!" River snapped.

Gray stood with one long leg bent, his thumbs tucked into the front of his gun belt, his mouth twisted into an amused smile. "Funny? A little strange, maybe, but not funny."

River's chin lifted defensively. "I just don't want Papa to be disappointed in me, that's all."

It was on the tip of Gray's tongue to say, "You should have thought about that earlier," but he didn't. One look at the uncertain misery on River's lovely face stilled the quick words. Instead, he reached out and dragged her to him, tossing aside the quilt and ignoring her gasp.

River felt the cold press of his gun belt in her bare stomach, and abrasive scrape of his Levi's against her legs, and the warm feel of his arms around her back as he held her tightly.

"Don't worry, love," he said against her parted lips, "it'll all work out."

She would have liked to ask exactly what he meant by that, but his rough, searing kiss removed any vestige of coherence, and she found herself melting into him. When he had kissed her thoroughly, leaving her breathless and unable to stand, he set her on the edge of the bed.

"Are you all right?" Gray asked, and River gave a mute nod of her head. He grinned. "You'd better hurry, then. I'll go down and stall the sheriff until you get there."

When the door had shut behind him and River sat there numbly staring at it, she wondered how matters had progressed so swiftly. It had only been two days, and now she was intimately involved with a man who had existed only in her dreams until a few short months before. And he didn't even know who she really was, that she was the same plump, plain girl who had elicited a ''Yuck'' from him when they first met.

She put her face in her palms. She could never tell him now, never confess that she was Drucilla Duckworth as well as River Templeton. He'd never understand.

River's head snapped up. What if someone accidentally told him? Papa, perhaps, or even Sandy Dennis. River's throat closed. Gray would never believe her reasons for not telling him. He would just think she'd planned the whole thing to make a fool of him, and she knew how he would react to that.

''Great!'' River muttered, rising from the bed to paw through the small dresser drawer for her underthings. She'd have to bathe with cold water from the washstand pitcher, but there wasn't time to worry about such trivia when she had other, more important, matters on her mind, such as Gray and Drucilla, the planned abduction, the sheriff. And her father.

By the time River stepped into the lobby of the hotel and crossed to the sofa and chairs where Gray and the sheriff were sitting, she was more composed. Her hair was neatly combed into a loose knot at the nape of her neck, and she wore a high-necked, long-sleeved dress that covered some of the marks Gray had left. Unfortunately she could not so easily hide the soft glow in her eyes or the slight flush on her cheeks when she happened to meet Gray's gaze, and Sheriff Warren Wentwhistle was quick to notice.

His small, dark eyes darted from River to Gray, who was now staring at him coolly, and the sheriff smirked. He didn't like Gray Morgan anyway, hadn't liked him since he was an arrogant kid. Now he was an arrogant man, but a man not many wanted to cross. It galled Wentwhistle that he had to deal with Morgan. And he wondered why a decent man like Tyler Templeton would let Gray Morgan anywhere near his daughter. But Templeton had always been like that, an easygoing man, well liked in the community. Even he liked him, and that was saying something.

Wentwhistle rocked back on his heels. "So you're Tyler Templeton's daughter," he said. River nodded.

The sheriff was short, stocky, and balding, and she did not like the sharp glitter in his eyes when he looked from her to Gray, but River tried to keep her voice pleasant.

"How do you do, Sheriff? I understand that you're going to investigate the ordeal last night."

"That's right. Morgan tells me you heard their names. What are they? Did you get a look at their faces? Did you hear anything else?"

River tried to answer as best she could, keeping her voice steady even though she shuddered at the memory.

"Any idea why they'd want to take you from your room like that, Miss Templeton?" the sheriff asked when she'd finished.

When River began to shake her head, Gray said shortly, "I already told you—Trucklow."

The sheriff looked at Gray furiously. "And you can't go around accusing a big man like Pierce Trucklow of something you can't prove!"

Gray's eyes were hard. "Is there anyone else in Clanton who dislikes Tyler? Enough to try to get at him through his daughter?" His voice deliberately cold, Gray said, "Think for a change, Wentwhistle. Think about what it is Trucklow wants from Templeton, and what he's prepared to do to get it. It should be obvious even to you . . ."

"Now see here, Morgan," the sheriff said angrily. "I've had about enough of you! The law in Clanton don't go around arresting folks who ain't done nothing wrong—"

"*Or* folks who have," Gray said with a dangerous glint in his eyes. "Don't think I've forgotten, because I haven't."

River swallowed the sudden lump in her throat. They were no longer talking about her abduction but about things that had happened long before she'd arrived in Clanton. And they both were growing angrier by the minute.

Gray was smiling, a smile that did not reach his eyes. "There's no statute of limitations on murder, Sheriff."

Wentwhistle didn't say anything for a moment, just looked at Gray. Then he shrugged. "You're not as smart as you think you are, Morgan."

"Maybe not, but I'm smart enough not to get mixed up with a man like Pierce Trucklow, and you can't say that. How does it feel to be owned?"

"One of these days, Morgan, you're going to step on the wrong side of the law, and when you do, I'll be waiting!" The sheriff bristled with hatred, and his dark eyes were narrowed almost to slits as he glared at Gray.

"I doubt it. I know a lot more about the law than you do. I studied it—you were elected to it. And maybe there's something that can be done about that, too."

Spinning on his heel, the sheriff growled, "I'll talk to you later about your *abduction*, Miss Templeton," and stalked out the door of the hotel.

River just stared at Gray. "I must say," she said after a moment, "that I don't think he intends to find the men who tried to kidnap me."

Gray shrugged. "He wouldn't have even if you'd given him their address, love. They're Trucklow's men, and Wentwhistle isn't going to buck Pierce Trucklow." He raked a hand through his thick hair and smiled at her. "Hungry?"

She wasn't really, but she wanted to be with Gray so she said, "Yes."

"Let's walk down to Delmonico's," Gray said as he took her arm, and River nodded.

"Is Papa back yet?" she asked him. "Or do you know?"

"No, and yes."

"No—and yes?"

"No, he's not back, and yes, I know."

"Gray," she said with a sigh, and he turned to look at her as they stepped out onto the sidewalk, "do you think Papa will be too upset when he finds out about last night?"

"Well, he's not going to *like* the idea of two men trying to kidnap his daughter, if that's what you mean."

"That's not what I mean at all!" River said with a snap of irritation. "I meant . . . I meant about later."

"Oh. That."

"You don't have to sound so disinterested," River muttered.

"Look, love, I don't know why you're so worried about it. Do you intend to tell him?" Gray countered with an edge of impatience in his tone.

"No-o."

"Neither do I. And neither will anyone else. So just forget it."

But it was hard to forget how she'd lain in his arms, his whispered words, and the feel of his mouth on her lips, her neck, her breasts . . . River's heart lurched. Was it so easy for him to forget the intimacy they'd shared?

River remained silent through most of breakfast.

"You're awful quiet," Gray commented, as he poured his third cup of coffee.

She managed a smile. "Am I?"

His cup clattered to the saucer, and his lips thinned. "Look. Don't expect more than I can give, River."

Her head snapped up. "Is that a warning?"

"Call it a suggestion."

River stared at him with drowning blue eyes, and he met her gaze without flinching. There was something so engaging and so vulnerable about her that Gray had the irritating thought that she appealed to his finer instincts. That was unsettling enough, but when he thought about the night before, he had the disquieting feeling that she had gotten to him more than any woman ever had. It had been extremely disconcerting to discover that he'd wanted her badly enough to risk his friendship with a man who'd been father and friend to him since he was a kid.

Gray was a man accustomed to casual relationships, not the kind that meant emotional entanglements. Yet now he found himself already emotionally involved with a wide-eyed girl with a baby face and the innocent stare of an infant. And he knew better. He knew not to become involved with an inexperienced girl who gazed at him with stars in her eyes, but he had. And he had only himself to blame for it. There was only one option left him, but it was all he could do.

When the dismal meal finally limped to an end and River's breakfast lay almost untouched on her plate, Gray stood abruptly.

"I'll walk you back to the hotel," he said. "Then I've got some things to take care of."

River knew what he meant, and she nodded, trying not to look too forlorn and bereft. She knew she shouldn't let him see how miserable she was. He had obviously decided to abandon her.

Before he could say more, she rose and spoke quickly, "I have some errands of my own, Gray. There's no point in you walking me to the hotel. And . . . and I'm busy later this evening, so I don't think I'll be seeing you again before we leave for the ranch."

She managed a bright smile and stuck out her hand for him to shake. Gray flicked her an incredulous glance, then shook his head.

"I doubt if I'll ever understand women," he muttered as he shook her hand.

"Yes, well, you have that in common with other men, I've heard," she said, her words tumbling out as she tried to back away from him. Just the touch of his hand was enough to weaken her resolve, but she was not about to let her Ideal Man tell her he didn't want to see her anymore! Gray still held her hand, and one eyebrow lifted in his familiar mocking gesture.

"If I didn't know better, I'd think you were trying to get rid of me," he said.

"No, no, it's just that I'm busy. Well. Have a pleasant day."

River brushed past him, leaving him standing at the dining table and staring after her with an appraising gaze.

What was it Grandmother Duckworth used to say about borrowing trouble? Or was that *trouble always comes in twos and threes*? No, that was deaths. River shook her head. Whatever it was, she hoped she could persuade Tyler to take her back to the Double T at once.

But later, Tyler was too intent on the sheriff's investigation to leave town. No explanation suited him. He was furious, and appalled that he had not been around when she needed him.

Pacing the floor of her hotel room, Tyler shook his head angrily. "And I suppose Sheriff Wentwhistle has done nothing?"

"I don't know. Gray Morgan talked to him. He asked me a few questions, and that was all."

"I don't like it, River, I just don't like it!" Tyler said again and again, shaking his head. "I want to talk to Gray about it. You said he stopped them?"

Nodding tightly, River wondered how she could suggest that her father speak to Gray elsewhere. After all, she had no intentions of forcing her company on anyone, and Gray had made it perfectly clear that she shouldn't expect too much of him.

Tyler strode purposefully toward the door. "Meet us in the lobby in an hour, honey," he said over his shoulder. "I want to get to the bottom of this!"

"But Papa—" The door closed on the rest of her protest, and she sighed. Being with Gray and yet not being with Gray was going to be the hardest thing she had ever done.

At lunch however, River discovered it was not as bad as she'd thought it was going to be. While he did not speak to her, she felt Gray's clear gaze come to rest on her again and again. River remained silent while he and Tyler discussed Pierce Trucklow and the possibility of conducting their own investigation into the foiled abduction. But she could have sworn there had been more than casual interest in his eyes. And afterward, when Tyler announced his intention to go and talk to the sheriff alone, Gray put out a hand, halting River's retreat.

"I'll escort River to dinner," he said. River stared at him, wide-eyed. "Join us for dinner, Tyler."

As soon as Tyler had left the lobby, River snatched her arm from his grasp. "You don't have to be nice to me when my father isn't here," she snapped.

"I know. What makes you think I'm being nice to you?"

"By taking me to dinner."

"All right," Gray drawled, "you pay for it."

When River gasped with outrage, she saw the glint of amusement in his gaze, and paused. "Are we patching up our quarrel?" she asked after a moment.

"It was your quarrel with yourself. But if you want to say that we're patching up our quarrel," he added quickly, "that's fine with me."

River didn't pursue the conversation. She was just happy that he had invited her to dinner. It must have meant he wanted to be with her. Even though their conversation was stiffer and more awkward than it had been since she'd arrived in Clanton, River was content being with him. He seemed to be putting himself out in an effort to be charming, and brought up no awkward topics.

After Tyler joined them and the meal was finished, they all stepped out onto the dusty sidewalk.

"Well?" Gray asked Tyler with a faint smile. "Did you talk to the sheriff?"

Tyler nodded glumly. He did not seem at all pleased by his interview with the sheriff.

"I knew you wouldn't be," Gray observed, and Tyler gave a short shake of his head.

"The foolish old . . . man," he ended with a glance at his daughter. "He refused to even consider that Pierce Trucklow might be behind it!"

"Did you tell him about our confrontation with Trucklow and his men yesterday?" River asked.

"Yes. And he said it was between Morgan and Brogan, not Trucklow."

"But Pierce Trucklow was standing right there!" River burst out. "And he was the one to give Brogan orders. Why doesn't the sheriff want to at least talk to him?"

"Talking wouldn't do any good," Gray pointed out harshly. "The only thing Trucklow recognizes is action."

"Now, Gray," Tyler said, "we've talked about this before."

"Yeah, and I'm still of the same mind. But I see that you are, too." Gray shook his head. "Let's walk down to my office and talk. I'll put on some coffee while we discuss the bond issue Trucklow's trying to put through."

"The one the city commissioners voted on?"

"*Tried* to vote on. I got there before the meeting ended and took care of that."

Angrily Tyler said as they strode down the sidewalk, "What is the matter with our town council? They know it has to be put to a citizen's vote . . ."

"And they know that most of the citizens are getting fed up with Trucklow and are likely to vote it down," Gray pointed out. "That's why they called a special referendum."

"The investment bond issue?" River asked. "The one that will bring in more enterprise? But isn't that good for the town?"

Gray didn't say anything for a moment. They crossed the street in silence before he spoke. "It seems that Trucklow has managed to convince our Clanton commissioners to put up bonds for a railroad. The only trouble is, there's not much in Clanton to lure a legitimate railroad. It's not the county seat, it doesn't have a university or even more than one hotel . . ."

"But Trucklow promises all that will change if he gets the railroad through," Tyler said. "Naturally, the town fathers are interested. They just haven't thought far enough ahead, to what will happen if the railroad doesn't come through and Trucklow is director of the project."

"But where will the railroad go?" River asked. "Through what land will it run?"

"That's part of Trucklow's scheme. He wants the land belonging to the Comanche, and he's almost gotten it." Gray unlocked the door to his office. "Our citizens don't mind that so much, and they can't seem to see the handwriting on the wall for their own land."

"This is ridiculous!" Tyler stormed. "After what he did to the Comanche, I should think every decent citizen would be able to see his intentions!"

River sat down in the chair Gray pulled out. "What did he do to the Comanche?" she asked.

Gray answered, his voice tight, "Took four barrels of whiskey with him to a talk with three of the old chiefs. By the time the entire tribe finished off the last of the whiskey, the chiefs had sold Trucklow more than five million acres of their alloted land at twenty cents an acre." He rattled a battered coffeepot as he spoke, and set it on a small pot-bellied stove.

River's mouth opened slightly, and her blue eyes grew wide with indignation. "But that . . . that's robbery!"

"It didn't get through Congress, but it didn't get the Comanche their land back, either. Somewhere between public outcry and justice, greed entered its ugly head."

"They haven't gotten their land back?" River asked.

"I hear it's going to be opened to white settlement later this year, if it's not granted for a railroad." Gray didn't say anything for a moment, then gave a philosophical shrug. "'The evil that men do lives after them; The good is oft interred with their bones.'"

"Platitudes, Mr. Morgan?" River couldn't resist saying. "You're beginning to sound like Grandmother Duc—my grandmother," she ended lamely. Her gaze fell, so that she could not quite meet Gray's eyes. She could feel his interested stare, then heard his soft laugh.

"I'm being compared to your *grandmother*? How novel of you," Gray said in a voice rich with amusement.

"You'd have to . . . have to have known her," River mumbled without looking up.

Gray shook his head. "I know you, and that's enough." When her head jerked up in indignation, he dug into a file on his desk, saying, "Tyler, I got this for you. It took me some more fancy talking before Doug Fenster finally got up enough guts to write it down."

Tyler's face brightened, and River rose to try and peer over the edge of the paper Gray had given him.

"This is just what we need, Gray!" Tyler said with a huge grin.

"Not quite, but it will help."

"What is it?" River finally asked when her curiosity could no longer be held. "A will or something?"

"A deposition," Gray said. "In your father's favor, I might add."

"Deposition?"

"About my land survey, honey!" Tyler exclaimed. "Don't you see? Now I've got some legal paper that backs up my claim."

"No, no, not yet," Gray warned. "I took his deposition, but until the case is heard by a judge, nothing is final."

"This Fenster," River said, "he's the clerk who wrote down the deeds in the survey office?"

"Well, you've got it a little confused, but basically that's right," Gray said. He poured coffee into three chipped cups. After taking a cautious sip, he set his cup on the cluttered desk. "Fenster filed the deeds and survey reports, but in a 'mysterious' fire a year ago—right before Trucklow made his claim—everything was destroyed from the year that Tyler filed. And then, mysteriously, Fenster up and quit. And so when Trucklow claimed Tyler had never filed and the land was up for grabs, there was no one to corroborate Tyler's story."

"And Papa got him to agree to the deposition?"

"Sort of."

Tyler snorted as he picked up his coffee cup. "Hmmph! It wasn't until you showed up out there that Fenster agreed to it, and you know it, Gray. He was just plain scared, and that's all."

River looked from one to the other. "How did you get him to agree?"

"I promised Trucklow wouldn't know about it until the day it came to court," Gray said. "Apparently, Trucklow has made the same kind of threats he's made to others—including you, Tyler. That's why I didn't mention trouble."

"You still should have told me about River immediately," Tyler said.

"In front of Fenster, and scare him out of agreeing?" Gray shook his head. "That would have been all he needed to hear, and he would have grabbed up his wife and kids and gone to California on the next train."

"I doubt it," River observed, and both men looked at her. "The closest train depot is over a hundred hot, dusty miles from here."

Laughing, Tyler teased, "Yet, you got here!"

"After a horrible stagecoach ride," River began, then froze. She thought she could feel Gray's narrowed gaze on her, a question in his eyes.

Tyler shook his head. "Not to mention the ro—"

"Papa"—River interrupted him desperately—"are we still planning to return to the ranch tomorrow?"

"No, honey. I had planned to stay another day or two." His face creased into a worried frown. "Are you ill? Do you want to return? Are you still upset about last night?"

"No, no, I'm fine. Oh, I was terribly upset, of course, but nothing drastic." River managed a smile, though she could still feel Gray's thoughtful gaze. "I just wondered, that's all."

Please, please, she begged silently, *don't say anything else about the robbery. Papa! Then Gray will surely be able to figure out that Drucilla Duckworth and River Templeton are the same person, and he'll never trust me again!*

But to River's relief, Tyler didn't mention the robbery or stagecoach journey again. Instead, he expounded on several theories concerning Pierce Trucklow, and River's mind drifted from the conversation. At the moment she didn't give a whit about Pierce Trucklow, Brogan, or even Riggs and Webster. At the moment all her energies were focused upon Gray Morgan.

It was becoming increasingly apparent that if she planned to keep company with Gray, she would have to tell him about Drucilla. Sooner or later it would come out, and then he would regard her as a fraud, impersonator . . . or worse. Although she did wonder on occasion if she shouldn't withhold the truth long enough to punish him a bit more for his "yuck," River didn't want to take too big a risk. After all, there was the rest of her life to consider!

She invented several happy endings in which she would confess, they would laugh together, he would tell her it didn't matter and they would fall into each other's arms. It could be a tender moment, perhaps even a turning point in their relationship. A slight smile curved her lips as she envisioned them in their own home, surrounded by chubby-cheeked children that all looked just like their father. How wonderful their life together could be, how—

"River!"

Starting, she glanced up with a guilty flush to see her father and Gray staring at her. The vision of married bliss vanished in a flash.

"River," her father repeated, "are you quite sure you're all right?"

"Yes, of course," she muttered in embarrassment. "I was only thinking of . . . of a novel I read last night." *Why does Gray have to look at me like that?*

"Last night?" Tyler echoed, and River suddenly recalled her busy evening of near abduction, fierce kidnappers, stray bullets, and passionate lovemaking—the last of which Tyler knew nothing about, of course. No wonder he was looking at her strangely. He must be wondering when she'd had time to read a novel.

"Yes, it was, uh, to distract me from my near escape."

She glanced briefly at Gray's amused face. At that moment she wished that he was anywhere but across the table from her listening to her babble. To make it worse, the expression on his face made her wonder if he knew what she'd been imagining.

"Oh," Tyler said, and River felt a guilty twinge about lying to him. Maybe it had been a white lie, but it was still a lie.

"Sin has many tools, but a lie is the handle that fits them all" rang in her ears, and she groaned. If only Grandmother Duckworth's platitudes did not come back to haunt her!

"Are you certain you aren't ill?" Tyler asked again. River decided to capitulate. She needed to escape.

"I believe I *am* feeling unwell, Papa. It's just the tension and excitement, of course."

Gray said, "I'll walk her to the hotel, Tyler. I have a few more questions I want to ask her anyway. And if I'm not mistaken, Anna is saving you a cold beer down at the Emporium."

"Anna?" River echoed. She stared at her father, who had flushed to the roots of his blond hair.

"Anna, the new waitress at the saloon." Tyler cleared his throat. "She, ah, knows I like my beer cold, so she keeps it in the icehouse. Whatever the customer wants, you know!"

"I see," River said, and realized that she had not considered the fact that her father might have another life too. Why hadn't it occurred to her that he might see another woman? Had she supposed he would grieve for Alicia forever?

Forcing a smile, River gave the back of his hand a fond pat. "Enjoy your beer, Papa. I'm going to go back to the hotel and read myself to sleep."

Tyler still looked faintly embarrassed as he stood and gave River a swift peck on the cheek. "Yes. Well. I'll see you in the morning, honey."

"I'll join you shortly," Gray told him, and escorted River from his office. Night had begun to fall, and he walked her down the empty sidewalk. "From the look on your face I take it that you didn't know your father enjoyed female companionship.''

River peered at him through the gathering shadows, her voice cross. ''Of course, I didn't know! But it's not as if I mind, I mean, after all—''

''Yes, after all, you have your life too.'' Gray had parrotted her earlier thought so closely she recoiled.

''I believe that you said that about Anna on purpose, so I would think Papa wouldn't be *too* shocked if he found out about . . . things. Didn't you!''

''Maybe.''

Nothing else was said for a moment as they walked slowly in the shadows formed by dusk and buildings.

A cool breeze swept down the street, lifting strands of her hair from her face. River lifted her chin, much too aware of Gray beside her, of his lean-muscled frame and the hint of tension in him. She felt it herself, felt the same drag of conscience, and maybe even—regret?

Their footsteps echoed on the almost-deserted sidewalk, and she wondered if Gray had regrets, if he was wishing he had not allowed their intimacy. Dust rose from the street, but she wasn't sure that was what caused the tightness in her throat. She turned toward him when they reached the doors of the hotel.

''You don't have to be nice to me because of my father. And you don't have to pretend something you don't feel. And I won't make a scene if you never visit me again.''

It had taken all of her courage to say those words, and she waited with dread for his response. The light through the half door left one side of Gray's face in shadow, and she could see only one corner of his mouth turned up in a smile.

''You think you've got everything figured out, don't you, River?''

She nodded. ''Yes.''

''Well, maybe you have,'' he replied softly, and swung open the door.

It was another enigmatic remark, one that left her just as

much in the dark as she was before. River preceded him into the lobby. She didn't know if she expected or wanted him to walk her to her room, to wait for an invitation inside, but it didn't matter anyway, because he very formally held out his hand for her to take.

Fuming, River placed her hand in his and he gave it a perfunctory shake. "Good night, Miss Templeton," he said politely and precisely, then turned and walked back out the hotel doors. She was left standing in the lobby staring after him and wondering.

Chapter 13

*

Still slightly nervous at being in the same hotel room as before—it was hard to believe no others were available—River found it difficult to sleep. Finally, after tossing and turning and reading and rereading the slim volume of Dickens she'd found in her room, River fell asleep. It was hot, and a desultory breeze came and went through the opened window, barely stirring the lace curtains. She kicked off the sheet and the quilt and lay in her thin nightdress, dozing fitfully.

Her dream came and went, seeming real one moment, drifting into a hazy collection of vague images the next. One moment Gray was there, smiling at her, the next he was pushing her away. River ran after him, crying out, but her Ideal Man was gone, disappearing in a thick mist.

She sobbed, and the noise sounded loud even in her dream. And when she felt a hand stroke her cheek in a gentle caress, she turned blindly to it, trying to see through the mist.

"Shhh, love," the disembodied voice said, and because dreams were never very clear on who said what, River just accepted the voice.

She smiled, and the hand moved down her cheek to the

curving arch of her throat, then the bodice of her gown. A fresh, cool breeze whispered across her skin, sliding over bare arms and legs, where her gown had been.

Stirring, she arched toward the voice again, and the hand still caressed her, still traced arousing paths over her curves and hollows. When warm lips covered her mouth River moaned softly. It was so real, so real . . .

River . . . River.

At first she thought it was part of her dream, but when the voice called her name again, River's eyes opened and she saw a dark shape bent over her bed. A scream formed in her throat but was quickly smothered by a hand over her mouth.

She struggled against it until she clearly recognized Gray's voice muttering, "Keep still, or you'll have the entire hotel up here!"

Relief flooded her at the same time as the realization that Gray had removed her nightgown. She scrabbled for the sheet. "What are you doing in here? How'd you get in? And where is my nightdress?" River hissed.

"One question at a time," Gray said as he sat on the edge of the bed. "I'm here because I want to talk to you. I came in the opened window—the same way Riggs and Webster did last night, I'm willing to bet—and your nightdress is on the floor."

"Give it here," she said crossly as she slid one arm from beneath the sheet to snatch it away from him.

"Modesty at this late date?" Gray teased, and she felt rather than saw his gaze on her in the dim light that filtered in the open window.

"What did you want to talk about?" she snapped as she slid the nightdress over her head and fumbled about beneath the sheet until it was twisted down over her hips and legs. "Couldn't it wait until morning?"

"No."

"Why not?"

"It's hard to believe you can think of so many questions when just awakened."

Still holding the sheet up to her chin, River's eyes became adjusted to the dim light, and she saw that Gray's expression was slightly blurred. There was a strong scent that she hadn't noticed at first but could now identify as alcohol.

"You've been drinking."

He grinned. "And such acute senses, too."

"I repeat—what do you want?"

"I want you to be quiet and listen for a minute." He stood up and strode to the window. River saw his shadow against the light, saw him lean out, heard the scrape of something across wood. "Did you hear that?" he turned back to ask.

"Well, yes, but it wasn't very loud."

"That's what I thought too."

"Tell me what you're doing," River begged. "You're making me crazy!"

"It's an experiment, love. See, Riggs and Webster did what I just did. They climbed up the porch posts onto the porch roof, heaved a carpet up here—all without being heard by anyone—and then proceeded to wrap you up in it as snug as a bug in a rug."

She groaned. "Your metaphors are not amusing!"

"I couldn't resist."

"Try harder next time. Well, now you know how it was done. Prove it."

"Ah," Gray said, "that's going to be a little more difficult."

He returned to sit on the edge of her bed again, and River gazed at him warily. "Do you think you can?"

"Prove it?"

"Yes."

"Sure. All I have to do is catch them."

River eyed him closely, noting the lift of his brows and the speculation in his gaze. He was up to something. She was certain of it. "And how do you intend to do that?"

"Ever been fishing?" Gray asked casually, and she shook her head. "Too bad. Then you might know how easy it is to catch something with bait—"

"Oh, no! I may not fish, but I'm familiar with rat bait, and if you think I'm going to volunteer to put myself in danger just to—''

''Catch a couple of rats?'' Gray finished for her. ''Why not?''

''Gray!''

''Listen, love. Why don't we give it a try? If Trucklow is too smart for us—fine. We'll try something else. If not, we can put him out of your, and Tyler's, way. Don't you want to help out your father? Do you want him to lose part of the Double T? He's worked hard all these years, and he always tried to take care of you. I can remember him talking about you, how he sent you money every month and extra money at Christmas and your birthday . . .''

Burying her face in her palms, River moaned softly. ''Don't appeal to my nicer side,'' she said from between her fingers. ''I don't have one.''

''I suspected as much.'' He pulled her hand down from her face and held it between his palms. ''Listen, love. I'd watch over you.''

''Is that supposed to be comforting?''

''Well, I haven't done such a bad job of watching out for you up to now.''

''Except that you made love to me when you really didn't mean it,'' River blurted. When the words were out, she shivered with a pang of regret. Gray dropped her hand and looked at her through narrowed eyes, his silver gaze as cold and flinty as steel.

''Are you suggesting I forced you?''

River's chin lifted slightly, and even though she would have cheerfully retracted her words, she couldn't do it without appearing foolish.

''Maybe not *forced*, but I think that there were certain misrepresentations, perhaps,'' she finally said.

''Misrepresenta—I don't think so. You read into the situation what you wanted to see. I never made any promises to you.''

Her chin quivered slightly at his flat tone. ''Well, I just

don't understand what I'm supposed to think, what I'm supposed to feel!''

Gray was silent for a long moment, then he said, ''The Comanches have a legend that fits this situation. Maybe I should tell it to you.''

''Will it help me understand what you're trying to say? Or not say?''

He shrugged. ''If you let it.''

She stiffened. ''I'll keep an open mind.''

Gray's teeth flashed in the dim light, and he laughed softly. ''Good.'' Rising from the edge of the bed, he went to stand against the wall, his face in the shadows and his arms folded over his chest. ''Once there was a young Comanche brave who had gone up into the mountains to hunt,'' he began. ''It started to snow, and so he started back down the mountain. He came upon a rattlesnake, coiled up against a rock and shivering with cold.

'' 'Take me with you,' the snake said to the brave. 'Put me under your shirt to warm me. I am cold and will freeze to death up here.'

'' 'I can't do that!' the brave said. 'You will bite me and I will die.'

'' 'No,' the snake said, 'I would not bite one so kind as to help me.'

''So, the brave picked up the snake and put it beneath his shirt and continued down the mountain. When he reached the foot of the mountain where it was warmer, the snake bit him.

'' 'But you promised you would not bite me!' the brave said as he lay dying.

''The snake hissed, 'You knew what I was before you picked me up,' then slithered away and left the brave to die.''

River was silent when Gray had finished, just staring at him in the moonlit, silvered room. ''Well, it's an apt comparison,'' she muttered after a moment. ''I suppose the point is that I knew how you were before we made love, and you want me not to expect any promises you never made, right?''

"Something like that. Not now, River. I never made any promises, because I can't."

"I see."

"I wonder if you really do, but there are more important things to worry about right now."

Her throat tightened. What could be more important than her love for him? In her books, the men were always desperate to be with their women . . . so desperate they often went to extreme measures—like Mr. Rochester—to marry them. Could Gray be so different from the men in books?

"Such as?" she managed to ask.

"Such as luring Trucklow into a trap. Are you brave enough to give it a try?"

"Appealing to my better side didn't work, so now you're going to appeal to my pride, right?"

Gray grinned. "Whatever works."

"All right, but I will haunt you forever if they kill me, Gray Morgan!"

Pushing away from the wall, Gray leaned over and took her face between his palms. "You haunt me now, River Templeton." He kissed her, a soft, fleeting kiss that left her hungry for more, aching with emptiness, then his hands fell away from her face and he straightened. "Now, all we have to do is get Tyler to agree," he said as casually as if he had not just turned her world upside down again.

"Tell him one of your stories," River muttered. "That ought to get him."

Gray's laugh was soft. "He's heard them all, or I would."

Shifting beneath the light sheet, River thought that Gray was a far more complex man than she'd ever imagined. In fact sometimes she felt that she didn't know him at all . . .

"Why are you so concerned with my father's problems?" she asked.

Gray took his time in answering. He pulled a small pouch from his pocket, built a cigarette, then lit it. A thin curl of smoke rose, then drifted lazily away on the hint of a breeze through the window.

"Tyler's problem with Trucklow represents more than just one man against one man. Ever since Trucklow showed up here a year and a half ago, there's been all kinds of trouble. If he's allowed to get away with it, he'll progress to the next ranch, then the next, until he has all of Comanche County in his back pocket. I can't and won't allow that, even if my friendship with Tyler didn't enter into the situation. And besides, I haven't forgotten Redhawk."

River nodded. Of course. His Comanche friend whom he said Trucklow had murdered.

Gray stretched lazily, reminding River of a great, lithe cat. He said softly, "I better go. It's late, and we need to catch Tyler early in the morning before he has a chance to make other plans."

Flushing at the sudden, unbidden wish that he wouldn't go, that he would stay and hold her as he had the night before, River hoped he couldn't see her face in the dim light. He already knew too much about her feelings for him, had guessed too closely what she longed to hear.

"I'll see you in the morning," she whispered. "Only, I don't know if my father will be as easy as I am."

As it turned out, Tyler was more adamant than River. He shook his head and roared like a lion, declaring he would never endanger River's life so foolishly.

"So, you'll just wait and let them pick the time and the place, right?" Gray asked him.

Tyler whirled and looked at him. "What do you mean?"

"Do you think they're going to give up? Do you think Trucklow won't try to get all the aces? Hell, Tyler, he's not a man with the patience to wait years. He'll try to force your hand, and there's always the chance he'll succeed."

Blowing out his cheeks in frustration, Tyler glanced from Gray to River, and his face softened. "I can't risk her," he said after a long moment. "I just can't risk her."

"But you'll agree?"

Tyler's mouth twisted wryly. "I'll agree, but we better make darn sure River's not in any danger!"

"Count on me for that," Gray said, and Tyler nodded.

Only River wasn't as certain. Her heart began to pound erratically whenever she thought about the man Brogan and his cruel eyes. The memory of Riggs and Webster, though not as terrifying, was just as unsettling.

Spreading out a sheet of paper on the desk in Tyler's room, Gray said, "Here's what we'll do . . ."

River flapped the reins across the rented horse's rump with a sigh of disgust. Another day of riding alone and her hands were chapped and her arms ached from guiding the hardheaded horse over lonely roads. There had not been a sign of any kidnapper, or even a sign of a passerby while she had—for all outward purposes—driven up and down the same road looking for wildflowers.

Wildflowers, for heaven's sake! According to their plan, which didn't sound quite so brilliant now, River was supposed to take a box of paints and an empty canvas and pretend to be painting the wildflowers that grew in patches along the road outside Clanton. She had quite dutifully set up canvas and easel on a deserted stretch of road and painted some perfectly dreadful flowers that Gray said looked more like a nest of snakes. But aside from a few strange looks she'd received from townspeople when she'd openly loaded the hired buggy, no one had come within five feet of her.

"And now," she muttered aloud as the wind whipped her hair from her face, "everyone in Clanton thinks Tyler Templeton's daughter is a lunatic!"

It was the second day of her futile activity, and she was sick of it.

"I refuse to go out again," River said firmly when she rounded the shelf of rock where Tyler and Gray waited in the searing sun. Sawing at the reins, she glared at them both. "It's bad enough that I have to sit in the sun and paint squiggles, but we haven't caught a single rat with our 'bait.' "

She noticed Gray looked just as disgusted as she felt, and River's irritation eased.

"Well," he said, pushing back his hat to look at Tyler, "shall we call Sandy and Juan Carlos in?"

"Might as well." Except Tyler didn't sound disgusted or upset. He was relieved that nothing had happened, that Trucklow had not attempted to abduct River again. "Maybe Trucklow has decided to forget about it."

"I wouldn't bet my last gold dollar on it." Gray uncoiled his long frame from atop the rock. "Maybe we weren't as slick as we thought. Maybe he got wind of our plan and decided not to play."

"You're probably right," Tyler acknowledged with a sigh. "Well, we can't sit around waiting for him to jump forever. We've got to get back to business."

"Yeah, but be sure and keep a guard on our bait. I'd hate to hear that you dropped the fight because Trucklow managed to snag your last ace."

"Why is it that I'm beginning to feel like a hand of poker?" River asked crossly.

Grinning, Gray mocked, "Because you're the queen of hearts?"

If only that were true, she reflected. Hurt, she shot back, "I might as well be, since I'm being manipulated by a knave!"

"Very good," Gray approved. "Your metaphors are improving."

Tyler ignored their banter and said thoughtfully, "We're going back to the Double T tomorrow. Since Trucklow is still in town, he's bound to know it. Why don't you find out why he hasn't gone back to the Bar None, Gray? After all, the committee meeting has been cancelled for now."

"I already did." Gray tugged his felt hat with the rattlesnake hatband lower, shading his eyes. "He's here for the same reason you are—to negotiate with the agent from the Chicago Beef Concern."

"Chicago?" River echoed. "But that's so far away to ship cattle!"

Tyler smiled. "I know, honey, but don't you remember what I told you about shipping cattle back East?"

"Yes, but I thought they, uh—I guess I wasn't listening."

Even Tyler was amused, and Gray laughed outright.

"I'm glad you pay such good attention," Gray mocked.

She was irritated by their comments, but it was true that she hadn't paid attention to their discussions. In fact her attention had been solely focused on Gray, but she never would admit that.

"Tell me one more time," River said shortly.

"We drive the cattle to Fort Worth, where they're loaded on trains for Chicago," Tyler explained patiently. "Sometimes agents come here so they can get the best beef without having to barter in Fort Worth. It beats the competition, and I get more money since my cattle look a lot better before they've been walked halfway across Texas."

"Why do you have to go so far?"

"Because—as you might recall—there are no closer shipping points. Railroads are notoriously unable to put railheads anywhere near where they'd be useful."

The day had been warm, and River's hair was moist with perspiration. She pushed at the strands in her eyes. "It's too bad there isn't a rail line closer."

"You're beginning to sound like Trucklow," Gray said in a dry voice. "Are you considering joining the opposition?"

"Don't be ridiculous! A railroad would be nice, but I don't want to cheat and lie to get one here."

Tyler shook his head. "Progress will eventually reach Clanton, and it will reach it without men like Trucklow. I just wish some of our commissioners could see that."

"In case you haven't noticed," Gray said, "there's more and more cattle competing for the market. If Clanton-area ranchers can't get their cattle to market more feasibly, it won't be long before agents don't bother to come down here anymore."

"That's what I hear," Tyler said with a worried frown. "Are you now in favor of the railroad, Gray?"

"I've always been in favor of it, just like any intelligent citizen or rancher. It's just that Trucklow's methods get my back up."

"Well, maybe someday the railroad will come through," Tyler said, then shrugged. "I'm not worried about being out-priced by Trucklow. He doesn't take care of his cattle, and mine are healthy and fat."

"Yeah, but he rustles fat, healthy cattle, remember."

Losing her patience, River snapped, "Why doesn't someone *do* something about the man if he's so bad?"

"You've talked to the sheriff," Gray shot back, "so you tell me!"

"It's hopeless."

"No, no, honey, nothing's hopeless," Tyler soothed. His gaze was thoughtful, noting River's flushed cheeks and the odd glitter in her eyes. She'd changed since she'd arrived. But lately she seemed different, some indefinable something that he couldn't quite identify, and Tyler was worried. His voice was soft when he said, "I think we need to get back to the ranch in the morning, honey. This visit hasn't exactly been as relaxing as I'd hoped it would be."

But I don't want to be so far away from Gray, River said silently. She needed time for him to see her and remembered Grandmother Duckworth's adage "Out of sight, out of mind." Aloud she said, "It will be good to get home again."

On her last night in Clanton, Gray took River to a town festival.

"Why haven't I heard anything about it?" she asked in surprise when he'd asked her.

"You have been a little busy the past few days," he pointed out. "There are handbills stuck up all over town. But today's Friday. A lot of people will be driving in for the festival and staying because tomorrow is Saturday, when they buy whatever supplies they need."

"Oh. Well, of course I'd like to go. What shall I wear?"

Gray seemed amused by her question. "Wear whatever it is that females wear, I guess. Most of the country folk wear their best Sunday clothes to something like this."

Glad for an excuse to shine, River dressed in her best. She wore the jade green dress with the ribboned underskirt, and perched a saucy new bonnet atop her hair. She felt pretty as she looked in the oval mirror in her room, and was glad that Gray's last few hours spent with her would leave him with a flattering memory. It was much better than the hot, dusty face she'd presented him the past two days! Or the first time he'd seen her, wearing a dowdy dress and with her hair pulled back in a tight bun.

The image of that black crow, Drucilla Duckworth, faded completely from her mind when she spotted Gray waiting on her in the lobby. He was dressed casually, in a pair of narrow-legged pants and blue chambray shirt, open at the neck. River thought he looked more handsome than ever. For an instant she felt a pang of regret that this would be their last night together—perhaps forever. But she refused to allow any sadness to ruin their evening.

Tyler, Gray, and River strolled down the wooden sidewalk toward the end of town where the festival was being held on the church grounds. Handbills proclaimed that for a nominal fee of fifty cents a ticket, ice cream and cake would be served, with further refreshments being sold at long tables set up on the grounds. Proceeds would help pay for a new church organ.

Paper lanterns swung from poles, giving the festival a glittering gaiety, and River was surprised at how many people milled about.

Laughter filled the air, and she could hear what sounded like band instruments tuning up. "Music?"

"A concert at eight o'clock," Gray said. "The Clanton musicians are not the best, but they sound decent. You might enjoy them."

River read one of the handbills: "A quartet composed of Curtis Weaver, Doctor Parrott, Mrs. Mullen, and Miss Lassiter will favor the citizens with their fine singing voices at half past eight tonight." *Treena Lassiter?* But she did not ask Gray.

Wooden planks had been joined together to form a platform for the musicians, and a large square area had been cleared for dancing. When the music began, Gray bent River a mocking bow and asked for the privilege of her company in a waltz.

Flushing, she glanced from Gray to her father, and Tyler smiled. "Go ahead," he urged. "I see an acquaintance I haven't seen in some time. You young people enjoy yourselves. After all, that was the reason I brought you to town, River."

River slipped her hand into Gray's outstretched palm, sucking in a deep breath when his other hand moved to the small of her back. His palm pressed against her in a light caress, and she felt her heart give an unsteady pop when his hand shifted slightly. Did he feel the same charge of electricity that made her senses quicken? She stared up at him with a suddenly shy smile, and he smiled back. He swung her onto the planked dance floor and pulled her into his arms. His breath was warm against her ear, and River shivered as he pressed his body close to hers. It brought back such vivid memories, and she wondered if he ever thought of that night too. Was it just another night, another woman to him? Or did he ever think of her in a more tender way? And would he miss her when she was gone?

"Relax," Gray murmured against her ear.

A hot flush stole up to stain her cheeks, and she could not help stiffening even more. She remembered another time he'd told her to relax. Noticing her nervousness, he drew back to look down at her.

"What's the matter?"

"Nothing," she lied with a forced smile. "I just have not . . . not danced much."

"Nothing to it." He pulled her close again. She could feel the cold bite of the buckles on his gunbelt, and wondered why he always seemed to be wearing them. Few other townsmen did.

Gray's hand moved from the small of her back up to her neck, pulling gently at the knot of hair on her neck. "You know I like your hair free. Why do you always wear it in that damn bun? You look like a schoolmarm when you do."

"Oh, Gray!" she protested softly when he freed her hair to let it hang down her back. But inwardly she froze a little. Did the hair remind him of Miss Yuckworth? She knew it wasn't proper to let it go free, but it *was* her last night with Gray. Finally her common sense won and she reached back to fix the damage. He caught her hand in his.

"Don't. I like to watch the light in it, and watch it around your face."

"But it's ... it's ..."

"It's what I want," he said softly, and the warm gleam in his eyes made her voice catch in her throat. She was aware that people were staring in their direction, aware that his hands were moving much too possessively and familiarly over her back.

"Gray," she whispered around the lump in her throat, "people will talk."

"They've always talked, and they'll talk whether you give them an excuse or not. Do you really care?"

"Of course I do." But she wondered if she meant it. Grandmother Duckworth had taught her to care if people talked about her, but she only minded if they were repeating ugly rumors. And how could anything between her and Gray be ugly?

Because he was still holding her more closely than he should, and because she was worried that Tyler might see and disapprove, River tried to make their conversation perfectly conventional.

"Where did you go to law school?" she asked, hoping to distract him.

He laughed softly, obviously aware of her ploy. "Chicago." Then he swung her around, and her skirts belled out in a graceful swirl as she leaned back to look up at his handsome face. At least he wasn't wearing that horrid hat, she thought with a dreamy smile. She hated the hatband, especially after his story about the snake and the Indian brave. It was too much of a reminder that she was not supposed to fall in love with him or expect him to fall in love with her.

"Did you like Chicago?" she asked softly, growing hazy with the wonderful evening, the soft lights, and the man holding her in his arms. Dancing was such a lovely way to be held . . .

"No. It was dirty and crowded and smoky. I missed the open sky and the clean wind and the emptiness."

River felt his hand shift to press against the small of her back again, holding her hard against him. She could feel his lean thighs even through her thick skirts, and swallowed hard at the direction of her thoughts. What was it that her grandmother used to say? Something about the wages of sin is death? Was it a sin to long for a man as she longed for Gray Morgan?

She looked up at him, and he was smiling down at her with a faint glitter in his silver eyes that made her heart lurch. Gray's smile lingered, curving up the lips that—River suddenly recalled—had touched various parts of her body, and she felt a slow fire curling in the pit of her stomach. How did he do this to her? How did he make her respond so quickly with just a touch or a word? And could everyone see, did everyone around them notice that she was weak with longing for him?

Maybe not everyone, but one certain woman did. And that woman was coldly, deadly, furious.

"Well," Treena Lassiter said as she halted by their side, "I see that you are enjoying making a spectacle of yourselves!" She preened, smoothing her elegant green taffeta skirts and patting the brim of her new straw hat.

Flushing, River wrenched away from Gray, but he kept a tight grip on her arm.

"Spectacle, Treena?" Gray mocked. "How odd that sounds coming from you."

Stiffening with indignation, Treena glared at him, and River began to feel invisible as the brunette snapped, "It is even more odd watching you make a fool of yourself!"

Something flashed in Gray's eyes, something that made even Treena take an involuntary step backward.

"Oh, Gray," she said in a rush, "I didn't mean that. I don't know what comes over me at times." She paused to wet her lips, and her voice was too forced to cover the edge of desperation. "I've been under such a strain lately, with all the business details . . ." She batted her eyes.

"Such as your *uncle's* will?" Gray asked with a biting sarcasm that River didn't understand.

Treena's dark eyes narrowed to glittering slits, and her mouth tightened, making her sulky, pretty face seem only sullen. "It's too bad you had to mention that."

Gray's eyes flicked from her to the crowd, then back. "I thought you were supposed to sing, Treena. You'd better hurry, or they may start without you."

"I don't care about that."

Shrugging, Gray started to turn away, reaching out for River's arm, but Treena wasn't defeated.

"Gray! Gray, you've been so busy lately, and there are so many things I have to tell you—when is a good time to discuss them?"

"I'm busy now, Treena," he said in a flat, bored tone that made the brunette flush. "And if it's about the same thing, I'm disinterested as well."

Her high color remained as Treena flung back her head, and her fingers tightened on the velvet riticule she carried. "It's not *all* business," she said after a moment, then added with a soft, seductive laugh, "There are other, more *relaxing* subjects we can discuss, as I'm certain you may recall."

At the word "relaxing" River's heart fell, and there was a thick lump in her throat at the implied intimacy. Of course. She was foolish to think Gray would not take what Treena offered—lovely, slender Treena in her taffeta dress and French perfume—and why should he have refused what River offered too? What was it Grandmother Duckworth had once said about not buying the cow if the milk was free? Or something like that, anyway, and she *had* thrown herself at Gray's head. Perhaps it would be best if she left gracefully now—the situation could only end in embarrassment if she stayed much longer.

But when she tried to pull away gently, Gray's hand coiled around her waist with a biting grip. "Stay here," he commanded, without even glancing at her, and River's chin tilted up in indignation.

"Look, Treena," Gray said, "we've had this discussion before. This is not the time or the place to talk about it."

Treena's dark, hot gaze shifted to River, then back to Gray, and she said coolly, "I understand. Of course. I just wanted you to know that I didn't lie to you."

Gray's face was cold, his tone impatient. "Knowing how I detest liars, I would think you'd have enough sense not to lie to me, Treena."

She didn't know what they were talking about, but River's heart sank even further. *She* was the biggest liar of all. What would he think when he found out about Drucilla Duckworth? If he could be this cold and harsh to a beautiful woman like Treena, then he would certainly feel no qualms about being even more savage to River when he discovered her lies.

Calculated tears pricked Treena's eyes, softening them to a dewy sheen as she lowered her gaze briefly, then glanced back up at Gray with diamond-spangled lashes. "Oh, then that is why you are with this—that is why you are so angry. Please don't punish me for my impetuous words, Gray. Not this way."

Gray made an impatient motion with his hand. "As usual, you have missed the entire point, Treena. And your theatrics— while admirable—don't work with me. You should know that by now. So, if you will excuse us . . . ?"

The implied dismissal was not lost on Miss Lassiter. Not at

all. Treena's trim figure stiffened, and there was a bright flare of anger in her eyes as her gaze shifted from Gray's handsome face to River's embarrassed expression. There was no mistaking the flush of love in the silly cow's eyes, Treena decided, and she had seen the possessive hand on her back. So. That was the way things had gone. And while she had foolishly sat back and waited for Gray to cease squiring Tyler's plain daughter around town, the sly baggage had snatched him right from under her nose!

Flinging back her dark head crowned with the stylish hat bristling with curved feathers, Treena managed to smile. "All right, Gray. I see that you are still angry with me. You'll get over it. You always do. And I'll be waiting for you like I *always do*." Her smile encompassed River, who stood there like a stone as Treena added in a confidential whisper, "I'm sure you understand how men must keep their pride over things like silly arguments, Miss Templeton. We women must simply wait until their ruffled feelings are soothed. And Gray always returns—"

"Treena," Gray said harshly, but the brunette laughed gaily.

"All right! You know where to find me, love," she said, and rose swiftly to her toes to press a kiss on Gray's cheek. "Until later." Then she was gone, sweeping away in a rustle of silk and perfume.

"Forget her," Gray said when he looked down at River's wide blue eyes and dismayed expression. "Treena lives to be theatrical. She can't seem to tell the difference between the truth and what she wants to be true." He shrugged. "That's her problem."

But River had the daunting thought that it was her problem too. Gray just did not know that she had lied to him, was living a lie in fact. She chewed at her bottom lip. It was strange that she'd forgiven him for calling her Miss Yuckworth. All she worried about now was a way to confess that she was not just River Templeton, but Drucilla Duckworth too.

Drucilla Yuckworth.

Unfortunately, no answer presented itself.

For the rest of the evening River tried to concentrate on being with Gray, on enjoying the present. But as he walked her back to the hotel and they stood in the faint glow of lamplight shining through the windows, she was distracted.

"Where's Papa?" River asked as they paused on the sidewalk in front of the hotel.

"I think he said something about a . . . cold beer," Gray said, and River understood.

"Oh. Well, good night."

"What? Aren't you going to invite me to your room for a glass of wine?" Gray smiled down at her, and River's heart did a flip-flop.

"W-w-wine?"

"You know, a beverage made out of crushed grapes and fermented for—"

"I know what it is! I just didn't know that you liked it that well," River said without a stammer. "It's made out of dandelions or berries, too, you know." Her heartbeat quickened at his casual shrug, and afraid that he would decide not to linger, she added, "Would you like to come up to my room and have whatever is there?"

"*Whatever* is there?" Gray repeated with a mocking smile that made her flush again. "That sounds very interesting, Miss Templeton. I'm right behind you . . ."

The walk to her room was all too short, and they were alone. Her fingers shook as she poured and handed him a glass of wine, and she jerked when he said, "Grapes."

"What?"

"Grapes. The wine is made from grapes, not berries or weeds."

Swallowing the sudden lump in her throat, River managed a nod and smile. "Yes, I think you're right."

"I'm not going to attack you, you know," Gray said as he seated himself in a tufted chair that looked much too small for his large frame. "Disappointed?"

River slammed her glass to a table. "No! Why on earth would I be disappointed?"

"Because you've been expecting it ever since that first night," Gray said.

Because he was so close to the truth, River stood there staring at him silently, not knowing what to say. He took a sip of his wine, gazing steadily at her over the rim of his glass, and she turned away to look out the window. Why did he make her so uneasy?

"Isn't there a difference between being attacked and—and being in love?" she asked a moment later, keeping her eyes fixed on the rim of her wineglass.

She heard him rise from the chair and set the glass on a table, felt him come to stand right behind her, and the hair on the back of her neck fluttered beneath his even breaths. Gray's hands closed around her arms, and he turned her slowly to face him. When she couldn't lift her eyes to meet his gaze, afraid of the mockery she would see in those clear silver eyes, he tilted back her head with a finger.

Gray's eyes were shadowed, but there was no mockery in them, no contempt or amusement. His voice was soft and deep.

"River, I'm not going to pretend I don't want you. I do. But it's got to be on my terms. Right now I can't promise you what you want . . . or deserve. And it may be a long time before I can. Do you understand?"

She didn't, but she nodded anyway. It had occurred to her as she stood there quivering in his light grasp, that she would take Gray Morgan on any terms. She only hoped that she could live with it later, and damned herself for being a weak coward. If she just hadn't dreamed of him for so long, just hadn't fallen in love with him so quickly, then maybe she could have refused, insisting upon her rights as a woman, as a person.

But it was far too late for that.

Not waiting for an answer, Gray was kissing her, his mouth crushing against hers hungrily, his hands moving to the

buttons of her gown and unfastening them with a swift
efficiency that startled River. She was lost, lost in an emotion
much too strong to combat, and even when he lifted her into
his arms and carried her to the bed across the room, she did
not offer a protest.

Filled with urgency, River helped Gray undress, helped him
unfasten his shirt and toss it aside, rubbing her hands over his
hard-muscled body. Her fingertips teased the dark pelt of hair
on his chest, roamed over his broad shoulders and down his
arms, then back up to cradle his face. She tried to memorize
his features, the glittering silver eyes with the faint sun lines
at the corners, the dark arch of brows winging over them, his
high cheekbones slashing down, and the strong, determined
shape of his mouth. If she could only commit his face—every
facet of it—to memory, then she would always have him with
her.

But Gray was in no mood for lingering caresses and long
kisses. He wanted to feel her body close around him, feel her
golden curves and hollows as near to him as a woman could
be to a man. Each satiny swell, each velvet fold of her,
belonged to him at this moment. The surge of possessiveness
surprised and angered him, and he took her more roughly
than he intended.

"Gray!" came a soft, startled voice, and he looked down
into River's warm blue eyes and relaxed his hold.

"Did I hurt you?" he murmured against her throat, and she
shifted slightly.

"A little," she whispered into his ear, her hands caressing
the muscles in his back, moving lightly down the ridges of his
spine.

"Let's try it again, then," he muttered. "Easier this
time."

The bedsprings squeaked a protest as Gray shifted to lie
next to her, his hand exploring her body until she writhed
with the same urgent yearnings he'd felt. He took his time,
loving her with soft touches as well as the hard drive of his

body. River cried out, arching against him, digging hills and valleys into the bed linens with her heels.

At first she'd been vaguely frightened by his urgency, but now she was driven by the same compelling force. She reached for release, moaned a protest when Gray seemed to withhold it purposefully, then sighed with delirious pleasure when he pressed forward at last. She quivered as he took her from an unfulfilled longing to the peak, and when she felt the shuddering release, cried out against him.

"Gray, oh, Gray," she half sobbed, and he soothed her with soft words and gentle kisses.

"No, don't say anything," River murmured when Gray lay on his back and gazed at her with half-lidded eyes. "I don't want you to ruin this perfect moment."

Gray laughed softly. "You're right—it's pretty damned perfect."

Chapter 14

*

Even perfection had its flaws, River discovered to her extreme dismay. The night was over too soon, and then she and her father bid Gray farewell and drove back to the Double T.

She intended to pass the time without Gray by throwing herself into the busy preparations for the cattle drive, but River found it more difficult than she'd imagined. Somehow her complacent life on the Double T was not the same.

Instead of counting the cattle being passed through a chute into a corral, she found her attention wandering and had to let one of the ranch hands take over. He gave her a curious glance, lifting a length of rope that was used to count the cattle. With swift, expert hands, he tied a knot for each longhorn passing through the chute, a much more effective method than River's "One, two, three."

And at the branding, when she was supposed to press the hot iron quickly onto a bound, bawling calf, she could not bring herself to do it.

"It doesn't really hurt them anymore than it hurts for you to burn your finger a little," Tyler told her, but River backed away.

"I'm sorry."

"That's all right, honey," he said, but she could tell he was a bit disappointed in her. "Why don't you help Rosa and Maria in the kitchen?" he suggested then. "They might need someone to help them put together the food supplies."

Somewhat shamefaced, she walked slowly to the kitchen behind the main house. River paused in the open doorway with the red dog at her heels, saying, "I came to help!" The large room was a bustle of activity, and no one made her feel she was a failure for not remaining outside with her father and the hands.

"Ugh!" Maria said as she poured flour into tin canisters. "I cannot stand the cows' *moo moo moo* and the smell of burning hair. I do not blame you for coming in to be with us, señorita."

Flashing Maria a grateful smile, River proceeded to check off the list of supplies needed for the men going on the long drive.

"Flour, sugar, coffee, beans, salt meat, salt, pepper, dried vegetables, fruit, liniment, bandages, whisky—" She looked up in surprise. "Whisky?"

Rosa laughed, her plump face flushed from the heat of the ovens. "They use it as medicine as well as drinking," she explained.

"Two cases of it?" River asked incredulously. "Are they expecting some kind of epidemic?"

"They will be gone for several months," Maria replied. "And anyway, sometimes they have to use it as a trade for fresh food from farmers or Indians."

"Oh. Sounds dangerous to me. Is Sandy going too?" River asked, wondering how Consuela would be able to bear her husband being gone for months at a time.

"*Sí*. He was going to stay here, but one of the men quit today, so now he must go." Maria shrugged. "Consuela, she is used to it. And he will bring her something pretty when he comes back from Fort Worth."

"Who quit?" River asked idly as she counted the boxes of

salt and cones of sugar, almost tripping over the red dog at her feet.

"Juan Carlos. He has been here for three years, and all of a sudden—phhht! He quits." Maria shook her head. "He is not very smart, that one. He will not like working for anyone else."

"Perhaps he went back to Mexico," Rosa said, but Maria shook her head again.

"No, I heard him tell Pepé and Bob that he is going to work for a *norteamericana*, a very beautiful *norteamericana* who will pay him much money. They laughed, and Juan Carlos got angry and said it was true."

"I wonder whom he was talking about?" River asked, and both women shrugged.

"Perhaps in New Mexico. Or Arizona," Maria said. "It does not matter."

No, River reflected, it didn't matter. Right now, she couldn't think of anything that truly mattered but Gray Morgan. He dominated her thoughts so much she wanted to scream, to push him out of her mind and heart and never think of him again. But she couldn't. At night, when she lay in her lonely bed and shadows played across the floor, she thought of the night Gray had slipped into her hotel window. None of even her favorite books could compare to the sensuality and romance of that night. She couldn't even read them anymore. The words were pale shadows of reality. Part of her wished he would slip into her room, but she realized that Tyler would never understand that.

And besides, Gray had told her he had his own cattle drive to organize, the shipping to market of the Morgan beef. Although his brothers handled the cattle drive, Gray, as the oldest, was always there. It was tradition, he'd said with a mocking laugh. Late spring and early summer saw many herds headed to shipping points. And with all his brothers except Andy and Matt going along on the drive, Gray would be needed at home.

As she helped pack supplies for the drive, she wondered if

Gray was doing the same thing. Somehow, it made her feel a bit closer to him.

"Rumor has it," Tyler told River later that afternoon, "that the Comanches are up in arms about their land rights, and that will heavily involve Gray as the mediator."

"Do you think Trucklow is behind the new violations to their land rights?" River asked. They were on the terrace enjoying an unusually cool breeze from the north. River's thin *camisa* and flowered skirt fluttered with each gust.

"According to the Comanche they are, and I suspect that they're right. They usually are about that kind of thing."

Tyler tamped tobacco into his pipe and tried to light it, sucking noisily on the stem. His attention was riveted on the pipe, so that River was startled when he asked, "How well do you like Gray Morgan, River?"

She froze at the question. "What . . . what do you mean?"

"I mean, how well do you like him? Does he seem like a fine young man to you, or do you have any complaints?"

River wondered if her father suspected something or if someone had told him. Or if he'd just guessed. Or perhaps he just wanted to know how well she liked Gray Morgan. She licked her suddenly dry lips and managed to answer casually, "Oh, I think he's nice enough." *Nice enough?* she groaned silently. "I mean, he and his family are decent people, and Gray doesn't seem lazy or slothful."

Tyler's mouth slanted in a wry smile. "I know all of that, honey. I just wondered what you thought of him as a man."

"He's very handsome," she said abruptly, and knew that wasn't what Tyler wanted to hear either.

"Yes," he said with a sigh, "I've heard women say that before."

For some reason, that irked River, and she said more sharply than she intended, "I'm not a person to be fooled by appearances!"

"I never meant to insinuate that you were," Tyler said. "But you've spent time with him, and I thought perhaps you'd formed an opinion."

"I'm sorry, Papa. I didn't mean to snap at you," River said softly. "To be honest, I don't know what to think of Gray Morgan sometimes. One minute he's charming and polished, and the next, he looks and acts like a brutal outlaw! If you had seen him that day with Trucklow and Brogan . . ."

You would have been as impressed as I was—and as frightened, she thought.

"Oh, I've seen Morgan in action. I know exactly what you mean," Tyler said. "I suppose it is a bit unnerving to the uninitiated. Well, I just didn't want you to think you had to be nice to him for my sake, that's all."

River stifled a laugh. Hadn't she paraphrased that very same sentiment?

Evening shadows were beginning to fall, drifting about the house and muffling the sounds of lowing cattle and laughter from the other houses down the hill. The red dog was curled at River's feet, as he frequently was. Idly, she let her hand fall to play with his silky ears, and the dog nestled closer.

When he suddenly bristled and began to bark, River sat up with a jerk. Tyler turned toward the door leading from the house, then laughed and said, "You've got the dogs barking at you, Morgan. Come on out and join us."

River's heart did a flip, and she wondered if she looked as disheveled as she suddenly felt. "Hush, Reggie," she admonished the still-barking dog, and Gray's glance slid toward her.

"Strange name for a dog," he said, sauntering out onto the terrace with the easy, almost lazy gait that made River think of the time he'd confronted Brogan with the same insouciant air.

Smiling, she said, "It was the name of a hero in a dime novel that Consuela read. She liked the sound of it."

"What brings you out to the Double T?" Tyler asked as Gray sat down in a chair with a rattle of spurs and hatband.

"Trucklow," he said, and even River sat forward to listen.

"More trouble?" Tyler knocked his pipe against the heel of his hand.

"For Trucklow. I just came from town by way of Doug Fenster's place. I've already warned him, so now I'm here to warn you."

"About what?" River cut in, unable to wait another moment.

"I got that plat I sent to Austin for," Gray said, referring to the map of the property. He swung her an amused glance. "And the deed, and the survey report. Trucklow doesn't have a prayer of proving any claim at all to that land up by Comanche ridge."

"Dammit, that's great!" Tyler burst out. "So he's done for?"

"Not until the circuit judge comes into town, and that won't be for another week."

"Just think," River murmured with a sigh of satisfaction, "all that trouble he's gone to over a little bit of water hasn't done him a bit of good!"

Gray spun his hat on one finger. "I still don't think that's what this is all about anyway. I think he's got another reason that concerns his city development plans."

"Well, whatever it is, I'm just dang glad it's almost over and done with." Tyler's voice was thick with relief. "Then Trucklow will go on and leave us alone."

"I wouldn't count on that, either," Gray said. "I've asked some questions, and some of the answers aren't that satisfactory. Trucklow was involved in a land scandal a few years back with a man by the name of Isaac Kalloch. Kalloch and he managed to fast-talk the Ottawa Indians out of about twenty thousand acres of Kansas land to sell to developers for a city. What Kalloch couldn't swindle, Trucklow stole. They made a pretty pair until Kalloch—with the help of a few senators and congressmen—started buying up land for railroads, hotels, dairy industries, sawmills, and any other enterprise that promised a profit. Trucklow struck out on his own, maybe seeing the eventual end Kalloch would find in San Francisco. Kalloch was shot by a man he'd defeated in the election for mayor. Trucklow had disappeared by that time, and wasn't heard of again until 1886—right before he came to Clanton.''

"Whew! Trucklow is a pretty devious operator," Tyler said.

"He had an excellent tutor." Gray frowned down at his hat. "That's why he's able to make so much trouble for the Comanches as well as deceive our town commissioners. He knows the ropes. And he knows people in high places."

"So do I," Tyler said, and Gray looked up at him.

"I know the governor of the state of Texas."

"Ross?"

"One and the same. Lawrence S. Ross and I met in Austin a few years back. We had some mutual interests, struck up a conversation—that was before he was elected to governor last year, you understand—and he told me if I ever needed anything, get in touch with him."

"Keep that in mind." Gray stood and hooked his thumbs into his gunbelt. "We may need him before this is over with."

"Care to stay for dinner?" Tyler asked after a moment.

Gray shook his head. "I need to get back to the ranch. Robert and Jamie are still organizing our drive, and I've got to help." He shot River a grin. "By the way, my little brother Matt is madly in love with you."

"Me?" River echoed with a gulp. "Why?"

Gray's brow lifted, and he shrugged. "He sets his sights high, I guess. Anyway, he gave me this to give to you next time I saw you."

As he dug into his pocket, River wished it was Gray who had been thoughtful enough to bring her a token of his regard. And why hadn't he? Didn't he care as much about her as his brother obviously did?

"What is it?" River asked doubtfully when Gray had put a foreign object in the palm of her hand.

He laughed. "It's a good-luck charm. Buffalo bone and bird feathers, tied together with . . . well, it's an Indian charm.''

"Do I wear it?"

"Only if you don't want any close friends," Gray said with a grin. "It stinks."

Clearing her throat and avoiding the dog who was leaping at the charm in her hand, River said, "Please tell Matt I appreciate the thought. And that I am very pleased."

Gray tugged his hat on. "I'll tell him."

"Don't go yet, Morgan," Tyler said. "I've got something I want to show you. It's in my office, so if you'll just chat with River for a few minutes, I'll go get it."

It was quiet on the terrace after he'd gone. River stood uncertainly, not knowing what to say. After all the nights of thinking and dreaming of Gray, he'd given her a token from someone else. Did he think of her at all? She shivered and pulled her *rebozo* more closely around her shoulders as a stiff breeze curled across the terrace.

"Cold?" Gray asked softly. "Your blouse is too thin, but I like it." When River's chin lifted, he added, "It makes your hair shine like gold, and shows off your curves. And if you're still cold, I can think of a way to warm you up."

Stifling a nervous giggle that would have embarrassed her no end, River managed to say primly, "I imagine you *can* think of a way, but my shawl will do the job."

"You don't really think that for a minute, and you know it," Gray said in a husky voice, and River felt a shiver trickle down her spine.

"So—maybe I'm wrong."

She *knew* she was wrong. Just being this near Gray and remembering . . . well, remembering, was igniting that slow fire in the pit of her stomach again, but unfortunately, it did not warm her. No, her hands were icy, and she was shivering as if she were standing knee-deep in snow. River pulled her shawl more tightly around her.

Gray's soft laugh reached her on the night wind. "That's not what will help, love."

She sliced him an irritated glance. "I know!" she shot back, "but it's what I have for now."

His hand lifted to graze her cheek gently, and in the purple haze of dusk that shrouded the terrace he could see the glitter in her eyes and the soft trembling of her mouth at his touch.

"It's all you *want* for now. You may think you're ready, but you're not, River."

"I don't know what you're talking about!"

"Yes, you do. You're still too full of guilt and platitudes to accept some things."

"I don't understand."

"I won't argue the point." He pulled her close, and River stiffened. "Don't be silly," he muttered in her ear. "I'm not going to ravish you here with your father in the next room."

"I didn't say you were," she snapped back, too embarrassed to admit that she was more afraid of her own reactions than his.

Trembling and angry at herself, she stood silently beside him, much too aware of how close he was, his amused stare, and her desire for him to take her right there on the terrace. Her blood was coursing rapidly through her veins, and every nerve ending was throbbing with need and longing. She had to do something or say something that would ease the tension before she melted into his embrace and begged him to take her off with him.

"It's a beautiful night," she said awkwardly.

"Yes it is. Who's playing the guitar?"

Then River heard the music that had been softly playing and realized that she'd been so caught up in her thoughts, she hadn't paid any attention to it.

"Some of the men play guitar and trumpet. They often play at night, and everyone dances."

"Do you?"

Gray's voice was as caressing and intimate as if they were in bed, and she had to clear her throat before replying.

"No, I never have."

Catching her by the hand, Gray said, "Let's dance tonight, then, River. There's a pretty moon and stars, and the wind is soft." He pulled her close, his body fitting to hers, and began to move her across the tiles. "Do you know what they call a moon like this?" he murmured in her ear, and River shivered uncontrollably.

"No . . ."

"A hunter's moon. It's full and bright for hunting."

"Are you hunting?" she asked around the lump in her throat.

His soft laugh stirred the loose hair in front of her ear. "Yes. I'm hunting you, love."

It was the perfect answer.

The moonlight was waxing bright, filtering through leaves and trees, casting erratic patterns on the terrace. A sweet, heavy fragrance of night-blooming flowers drifted on the wind, seeming to surround them with magic. It *was* magic and she didn't want the spell to end.

When Tyler returned to the terrace with a law book in his hand, River sighed as the spell was broken.

"Here's what I wanted to show you, Gray," he was saying, then paused when he saw them. "Oh, did I interrupt something?"

"No," Gray said. "We were just enjoying the music."

He pulled away from her. River hoped she'd heard a note of regret in his voice that Tyler had returned.

While the two men discussed the upcoming case, she murmured a good-night and went to bed with her dreams and memories, the red dog right behind her.

Events progressed much more quickly than Gray or Tyler had thought. The circuit judge arrived in Clanton a week early and demanded that the case be either tried or postponed indefinitely.

"Another point for Trucklow," Tyler said grimly, "but this time I'm ready for him!"

"What do you mean?" River asked.

"Everything seems to fall into place for him, but I have the goods this time!" Tyler tapped one finger on a thick envelope. "This time, Trucklow cannot fight point and detail of the law. And besides, Gray Morgan has agreed to argue the case for me.''

River sat up sharply. "He has?"

"He has." Tyler smiled. "It didn't take me too long to talk him into it. I think he was just waiting for me to ask him."

"So, when do we go?"

"Day after tomorrow, honey."

"So soon?"

"I'm ready, River. I've been ready for over a year."

The court hearing went like a dream. River could hardly believe it, sitting stiff and straight on a bench in the dusty store that was serving as the Comanche County court room. She listened to Gray—a steely eyed, scathing, predatory Gray, clad in his tailored suit and red vest—list point and detail why Pierce Trucklow did not have a case. Gray highlighted his discourse with readings from a thick volume entitled *Blackstone's Treatises*.

"Not only does my client, Mr. Templeton, have riparian rights to his land, but he does, indeed, have all rights to the land as surveyed in 1877. And this survey," Gray said loudly to drown out the immediate objection by Trucklow's attorney—a nervous twitch of a man with a ferret face and a bulging briefcase—"was filed in Austin, our state capital."

There was a buzz of voices in the crowded store as Gray produced the plat for the judge's perusal. After a careful study of the map, the judge peered over his spectacles at the two attorneys in front of the table.

"I was under the impression that all the records were destroyed in a fire, Mr. Morgan," he said. "Isn't that the reason we are having this case in court? Because no proof of boundary lines could be produced?" He rattled the paper. "Where did you get this?"

"The records clerk—Mr. Fenster—recalled that back in seventy-seven he had been in the habit of sending all deeds and survey reports to Austin to be recorded because his storage space was limited. With the building of the new county court house, he ceased the practice. But not before sending Mr. Templeton's survey report."

"Objection, Your Honor," Trucklow's attorney said. "How does the court know that this is a true record? Mr. Morgan could very easily have fabricated this report with the help of his witness, Mr. Fenster. In fact, I would even go so far as to suggest that he did in fact do such a thing—"

"I can produce signed affidavits stating that these are true and certified copies, Mr. Doss," Gray drawled. "Would you care to see them?"

"It appears that you have been very thorough, Mr. Morgan!" the judge said as he skimmed the documents Gray put on the table. "I would be interested in knowing how you obtained these."

"Since I've always dealt honorably with the clerks, Your Honor, one who happens to work in the Austin courthouse was quite happy to do the necessary work. He searched through old books and files until he found these." Gray's smile was slightly mocking as he eyed the city-slick attorney.

Leaping to his feet, Pierce Trucklow boomed out, "They are forgeries! They have to be!"

The judge frowned and rapped his gavel on the table. "Sit down in my court, sir! You are out of order!"

Trucklow pointed a finger at Gray, and River shivered at the malice in his face as he ground out, "Don't make enemies in high places, Morgan!"

"If you're referring to yourself, Trucklow," Gray said, "I'll take my chances."

The gavel rapped again, and Mr. Doss went to Pierce Trucklow and begged him to be seated. The huge man gave his attorney a look that would have shriveled rock, and wheeled around and out of the courtroom. Several men followed him, among them Brogan, who turned to smirk at River.

Matt Morgan—standing in the back of the courtroom with his mother and brother—made a move as if to go after him, but Nancy Morgan put one hand on his arm and shook her head.

A large portion of the crowd had hastily parted after Trucklow's exit, and as the gap closed behind him, the judge ruled in favor of Tyler Templeton. A ragged cheer rose, gaining momentum as Matt and Nancy and River pushed forward to congratulate Gray and Tyler.

"Attaway, brother!" Matt Morgan said, grinning so wide with pride that it looked as if his face might split at any moment. "I knew you could do it!"

"Was there ever any doubt?" Nancy Morgan asked, beaming with such maternal pride that some of the pleasure faded from Matt's face.

"No, I guess not," Matt said shortly. "Not for Gray. He never fails at anything."

No one heard the faint edge to his voice except River. As she gazed at him in surprise, Matt forced a huge smile. The tall, gangly youth grabbed River and swung her around, and when she protested, set her back down and took her hands in his. "Kiss me, River!" he shouted, and she laughed as she made a rapid retreat.

Townspeople crowded close, some of them to talk to Gray and some to talk to Tyler, but all to offer words of support.

None of the celebrants, however, noticed a rigid figure at the back of the feed store. Treena Lassiter stood with cold, glittering eyes, watching as Gray put a casual arm around River, his touch light and possessive. She noted the faint glow in River's eyes when she looked up at Gray, the way she leaned into him ever so slightly, as if familiar with him.

"How cozy!" She spat the words between clenched teeth, then spun on her fashionable heel and stalked from the store. He would pay. Yes, Gray Morgan and that ridiculous, cow-eyed girl would both pay for this outrage! And much sooner than she had originally planned.

Chapter 15

*

"So," River asked her father cheerfully as they stepped out of the makeshift courthouse and onto the sidewalk, "what do we do now?"

"Celebrate," was the prompt reply.

Even Gray laughed at Tyler's wide grin and exuberant face. "Don't celebrate too soon," he warned. "I don't think Trucklow likes the decision."

"An appeal?" Tyler guessed, and Gray shrugged.

"That's not likely. An appeal would only confirm the decision, and even Mr. Doss can see that. Trucklow would only be wasting time and money. No, I meant I think he may try to—"

"Gray!" an imperative feminine voice cut in, and they all turned to see Treena Lassiter standing at the edge of the sidewalk. "I need to see you," she said, ignoring both his family and friends.

"Uh-oh," Matt Morgan muttered under his breath. "The she-cat's on the prowl!"

"Matt," Nancy Morgan reproved with a hard jab of her

finger in his back, "mind your manners. Your brother can handle his own affairs."

Matt nodded but managed to wedge himself protectively between River and Treena, who had flashed her rival a fierce glare.

"Treena," Gray said, "I'm busy right now. Maybe later."

"No," the girl shot back, "now!"

Gray would have refused, but Tyler, anxious to avoid any public confrontation, urged him to speak to her in a more private place.

"We'll meet you at Delmonico's," he added when Gray shook his head. Tyler put one hand in the small of River's back to guide her down the sidewalk, and the remaining Morgans followed.

River did not want to leave Gray with Treena, but she couldn't say anything without appearing foolish. She remained silent, her heart in her throat, wondering what the girl had to say to Gray.

Nancy Morgan tried to lighten the suddenly tense atmosphere. "That certainly was a fine trial, Tyler!" she said in a bright voice. "And didn't Gray present a good argument?"

"Yes, a mighty fine argument," Tyler agreed with a forced laugh. "I was very impressed with him."

"How about a party?" young Andy suggested. "We always have parties when we're glad about something."

A genuine laugh burst from Tyler, and he ruffled Andy's brown hair. "Now, that's not a bad idea, Andy! I think a party would be just what we need right now."

Sidling close to River, Matt said softly, "Don't worry about Gray. He's not one to be where he doesn't want to be. He'll join us quicker than that!" He snapped his fingers and smiled at her.

"Oh, I'm not worried at all," River lied. "Not at all."

But as an hour passed, then two, River found that the constant smile on her face made her jaws ache, and she could tell from the strain on everyone else's face that Gray's continued absence was quite noticeable. Where was he? What were he and Treena talking about? Or doing? Matt was right when he'd said Gray didn't stay anywhere he didn't want to be, so her only assumption could be that he wanted to be with Treena. River was miserable.

Finally the interminable meal at Delmonico's was over, and Gray still had not arrived.

"Well," Tyler said into the awkward silence that followed their departure from the restaurant, "I guess River and I will stay in town tonight. Nancy, are you and the boys going back to the ranch?"

Hesitating, Nancy Morgan's clear gray gaze, so much like her oldest son's, rested briefly on River's miserable face before shifting to Tyler. "Gray drove us into town with him, and I suppose we'll wait."

"I can drive the buggy, Ma," Matt said harshly. His youthful features were creased into angry lines, and his brows were lowered into a scowl. "Gray can get back home if he wants. He knows the way."

Nancy's hand rested briefly but warningly on her son's arm as she said gently, "I'm sure there's an excellent explanation for his tardiness. Until we hear it, we can't judge."

Some of the ice in the region of River's throat began to thaw. Mrs. Morgan was right. And it wasn't fair to condemn Gray before he'd explained.

But when Gray joined them in the lobby of the Clanton Hotel, he didn't offer an explanation. He was no longer in his tailored suit and red vest, but was once more wearing his Levi's, shirt, and gun belts. His felt hat was slanted atop his head, shading his face.

"You're late!" Matt snapped angrily, and Gray just looked at his younger brother with an uplifted brow.

"Yeah."

Nothing else was said for a moment. Everyone waited in silence for his explanation, and when it was apparent none was forthcoming, Tyler said into the growing tension, "Well, Gray! We've decided to have a celebration on the Double T."

Gray's gaze flicked to Tyler. "That right?"

"It was my idea, Gray!" Andy boasted with a pleased grin. He seemed unaware of the tension.

Gray smiled faintly. He reached out to ruffle Andy's brown hair. "You'll think of any excuse for a party," Gray said. "You just like to eat."

River said nothing and tried not to look at Gray. She certainly didn't want to sit there with her heart in her eyes, or be as obvious as Matt. But she was dying to know where Gray had been, and if he'd been with Treena, and if they had patched up a quarrel, or if. . . . A dozen doubts flew at her, and she tried not to think about them.

"We'll have the party Saturday," Tyler said, "before the boys leave on the cattle drive Monday. That way everyone can join in. It'll be a good send-off for them."

"They'll be too hung-over to ride," Gray observed dryly. "I remember your last party."

"Well, some of them did dip into the whiskey barrel a little too freely, I'll admit," Tyler said with a laugh. "But that was a long time ago. Maybe they've grown wiser."

"I doubt it. They've had time to forget their headaches by now," Gray said, and at last his gaze slid to River's closed face. She didn't look at him but remained silent, then stared down at her hands twisted in her lap.

She could feel his gaze, could feel Matt's vibrating anger, could sense Gray's mocking amusement. River had rarely felt so awkward or uncertain.

Without preamble or explanation, Gray reached out and took River's hand, lifting her up from the settee where she sat. "Come with me," he said, then said over his shoulder to his startled mother and the others, "We'll be right back."

"Where are we going?" River asked as Gray propelled her out of the lobby and down the sidewalk to a short alley.

"Right here." Gray turned her, pushing her up against the outside wall and propping one hand on each side of her head. "Listen to me and don't ask questions," he said. "I want you to be careful—very careful. Don't ride alone, and don't go off with anyone you don't know that well."

"But what—?"

Impatiently, he shook his head, and his eyes were hard, glittering slits in the dim light streaming from overhead. "Don't ask a lot of questions, River. Just be careful. Tyler can't be with you every moment of the day. If he could, I wouldn't bother telling you any of this."

"But you haven't told me anything!" River protested. "You just brought me out here to frighten me out of my wits and that's all!"

"No," Gray said, "that's not all." Before she could speak his head lowered and his mouth seared across her lips without warning, burning, igniting a slow, curling fire in her. A soft moan escaped her, and her head tilted back under the onslaught of his mouth, her eyes closing.

River inhaled deeply—then stiffened. There was the unmistakable scent of expensive French perfume clinging to Gray. She broke away abruptly, glaring up at him with blue sparks in her eyes. "You're wearing her perfume!" she said in a snarling gasp.

Gray seemed amused, and his mouth twisted. "Do you like it?" he mocked, then grabbed her hands when she would have whirled away. "Look, you know that I was with Treena for a short time. You saw her come up to me. Don't act like the wronged woman, for Chrissake, because it was nothing like that."

"But you reek of her!" River said before she could stop herself. Why couldn't she just be cold and silent? Why did she have to let him know that she cared so much?

"Why do you think I changed clothes?" Gray asked with a shake of his head. "That damned perfume she wears gets on everything, and . . . don't be questioning me, River. I can't answer all your questions."

"Oh, you can't? Well, I assure you that I won't question you again, Mr. Morgan," she said between her teeth. "In fact, I will be delighted to stay as far away from you as possible!"

Gray just looked at her. "I can see this conversation has

ended for the moment. I'll talk to you when you're more rational."

"Rational? I'll tell you what's rational, Gray Morgan! Rational is not listening to one word you have to say!" She slid quickly under his arm and fled to the hotel doors, flinging them open and barreling straight into Matt Morgan's arms.

Matt took a surprised step back, his arms instinctively closing around River. "What have you done to her?" he demanded of his brother. "Why is she crying?"

"I'm not crying," River half sobbed.

At the same time Gray said, "How the heck do I know why she's crying?"

Clumsily patting River's hair, Matt looked from Gray to his mother, who stood in the doorway just behind him.

"River," Nancy Morgan said quietly, "I think you need to join your father. He's worried about you."

Nodding and unable to look at any of them, River wiped her eyes with the handkerchief Nancy quietly produced, then fled into the hotel without a backward glance. Matt, bristling with anger, was quickly shushed by his mother when he would have spoken to Gray.

"Let's go home," Mrs. Morgan said, and no one said anything as they walked down the sidewalk.

It promised to be the grandest party in the history of the Double T. Tyler had huge pits dug into the ground and lined with stones, then had fires built to roast whole hogs and sides of beef. Rosa, Consuela, Maria, and River spent hours in the kitchen planning dishes, baking bread, pies, cakes, and confections. Sandy and several of the men built long tables on sawhorses, strung lanterns, and laid a dance floor, complete with raised platform for the musicians and their instruments.

The morning of the planned celebration dawned crisp and clear, and River woke early. She lay in bed, one hand over the side to fondle the silky ears of the dog on the floor. Reggie was always there, faithful and loyal, with tail wagging and love shining in his eyes. Somehow, the red dog had become River's without her knowing it. Perhaps it was because everyone on the ranch was too busy to pet him or do more than offer a kind word now and then.

"Oh, Reggie," River whispered, and the dog looked up at her with a quizzical expression, "I don't know what I'm going to do." The red nose quivered with sympathy. "Should I be cool to him? Or should I forgive him? Is there anything to forgive?" One floppy ear twitched forward, and she stroked it, sighing. "I almost wish I'd never met him, never known he exists." Another sigh escaped her, and she turned back over to stare at the shadowed ceiling.

"Love is blind," Grandmother Duckworth had said about Alicia, and River completed the verse aloud, her voice soft and sad, "and lovers cannot see the pretty follies that themselves commit."

Whining, the red dog sat up and gazed at her piteously. His golden eyes fastened on River's face as if he could help, or wished he could, and she smiled through the silent tears streaking her cheeks.

"The main difference between dogs and men," River said to the animal, "is that when you love a dog he doesn't bite you."

Swinging her legs over the side of her bed, she rose to dress, the red dog at her heels. She had to dispel her despondent mood before guests began arriving, before the Morgans arrived. It just would not do to let everyone know how distressed she was over Gray's actions—least of all, to let Gray know! Let him think she didn't care that much, that he could have a dozen Treena Lassiters. She would laugh and enjoy the festivities as if she hadn't a care in the world, as if she had never loved Gray Morgan at all.

"Where are you going so early?" Maria asked as River strode through the kitchen with determined energy.

"For a morning ride," came the determinedly cheerful reply. "It's a brisk, cool morning, and I haven't ridden in several days."

"Be careful," the Mexican girl called after her. "You know how Señor Templeton worries."

"Oh, I will," River promised. "And I'm taking the dog with me."

After saddling her mare and fielding questions from the men busy with final preparations for the celebration, River rode out of the stable yard and up a gentle slope behind the ranch. The red dog loped behind her, tongue lolling from his mouth, eyes bright with anticipation.

River wore a pair of trousers and boots, and her light shirt did not keep out the early morning chill. It was invigorating instead of uncomfortable, and she spurred the mare to a canter. Wind whipped her cheeks to a bright pink and burned her ears. The mare's rhythmic hoofbeats over the rocky ground and hard-packed dirt of the prairie resounded in her ears, and River urged her on. Riding was an excellent way to clear the mind, she decided as her worries and troubles diminished.

It helped put things in perspective. Gray had been with Treena. Well, so what? He'd come back to her, hadn't he? He had not stayed with Treena, and maybe there really was a good explanation for his prolonged absence and the strong scent of French perfume on him. He'd been right when he'd said she didn't want to listen to him, because she hadn't. She'd reacted—overreacted—and now she was sorry.

Instead of being cool and distant to Gray, she would be sweet, charming, attentive. And she would certainly listen if he felt like explaining again, although—knowing Gray—that was not likely.

Somehow, her Ideal Man had grown much more stubborn than in her daydreams. Of course, he was more handsome too, and that made up for the stubbornness by a wide margin, she decided.

Tilting up her face, River smiled into the growing day. Everything would be all right, she just knew it. The sky was a brilliant blue haze, with the early sun slowly climbing over saw-toothed ridges and rolling hills. Sucking in a deep breath,

River thought that it was the most glorious day she had seen in a long time. And somehow just the bright promise of the day calmed her jumbled thoughts as she reined the mare to a halt and surveyed the world. The red dog finally caught up, panting, his eyes glittering with pleasure. He flopped to the ground, tongue lolling and sides heaving.

When the mare shifted beneath her, pawing at the ground impatiently, River laughed. "All right!" she said as she reached forward to pat the mare's gleaming neck. "We'll ride on."

Nudging the mare's sides, River let her break into a gallop, then an easy canter. It was far easier to ride a horse that was running smoothly than one that was jolting along in a gallop, she'd learned. And the red dog had no trouble keeping up with the slower gait. When the fresh horse flattened out in a dead run along a ridge top, River let her go. The whistling sound of wind and thundering hoofbeats filled her ears, and when she finally slowed the animal, her ears rang.

Lather flecked the mare's sides and neck, and River decided to turn back at a walk to cool her down. It had been an exhilarating ride, but now she was much too far from the house. Somehow, without realizing it, she had left Tyler's land and ridden across the road. It must have been habit, because before the trouble with Trucklow accelerated, she had been accustomed to taking this same route.

Whistling for the dog, who had gotten behind, River nudged the mare a bit faster. "Reggie!" she called when there was no sign of him. "Reggie!"

When she had ridden only a few yards, River heard a strange sound. At first she thought her ears were still ringing, but then she realized it sounded more like a whine or a wail. It sounded again, louder this time and closer, and she immediately decided Reggie must have been caught in one of the traps Tyler's men put out to catch the coyotes that stalked the herd on occasion.

Spurring the mare forward, River crested the ridge where the sounds were originating. Her stomach lurched at the thought of Reggie in a trap. He was only recently fully recovered from his injuries, and she couldn't bear the thought of the dog suffering again.

But when River rode over the ridge and down the brush-studded slope, she didn't find Reggie caught in a steel-jawed trap. He was being held by a man, half strangling him with a thick rope looped around his neck. Three other men stood by, watching.

"This your dog?" Brogan asked with a cruel laugh as she reined her mare to a halt.

River's horrified gaze flicked from the dog to Brogan. "Let him go!"

"Sure." Brogan released the rope, but as the dog half stumbled, then broke into a run toward River, he pulled his pistol.

"No!" River screamed, and kicked her mare. As the horse leaped forward Brogan's pistol went off, and she heard the dog yelp as he somersaulted through the air, then lay still. River's heart fell, and she sawed on the reins at the same time as Brogan leaped for her, one hand snagging the bridle. River lashed at him furiously with the end of her leather reins, kicking at him with one foot she managed to free from the stirrup. "Damn you!" she sobbed as he dragged her from the saddle. "Damn you!"

Laughing, Brogan wound his hand in her hair and shoved her facedown on the ground. "If you don't want what your stupid mutt got, you better be quiet. And still," he added when she struggled.

With angry, pained tears streaming down her face, she was yanked back to her feet and shoved roughly into the arms of another man. River glanced around for Reggie's body, but the dog was not in sight.

The man holding her whispered, "He crawled into the bushes to die, I think."

Startled, River glanced over her shoulder. The short, skinny man holding her was looking at her with something close to sympathy in his eyes, and she was immediately wary.

"Why are you telling me that?" she asked slowly.

"Because I used to have a dog too." He glanced over at Brogan, who was grabbing the skittish sorrel mare. "Be quiet like he said. I don't want to hurt you."

"Then why have you got me?" River muttered but lapsed into a sort of stunned silence as she kept her eye on the tall, lanky outlaw catching her mare.

"You're just supposed to hold her, not romance her," Brogan shot at the man gripping River's arms. His dark eyes narrowed. "Do I have to worry about you going soft on me, Riggs?"

Riggs? River gave a start. Riggs and Webster, the men who had tried to abduct her! Why, she knew these men. She'd seen them with Pierce Trucklow at the Emporium Saloon in Clanton the day Gray had confronted Brogan. Gray had been right all along about Trucklow engineering that foiled abduction. And he was obviously right about Trucklow not giving up too.

Tilting back her head to glare at Brogan, she said more bravely than she felt, "You'd better release me at once. When my father and Gray Morgan discover that I'm gone, they will know who's behind it."

Brogan's menacing laugh curled into the air. "Let them do all the lookin' they want, little lady. They ain't gonna find you at Trucklow's."

River swallowed the sudden lump of cold fear in her throat.

"Here," Brogan was saying to a stocky man with a balding head and wide eyes, "send her horse running in the wrong direction. By the time they find it, they'll think she's been thrown or something. That ought to buy us enough time."

Enough time for what, River wondered. Her legs were shaking and her throat was dry. She felt nauseated and prayed that she would not disgrace herself by throwing up all over her shirt. Why hadn't she listened to Gray's warning? Her foolishness had cost her not only her dog's life but perhaps her own.

"Mount up!" Brogan ordered curtly when the sorrel mare

had been slapped into a thundering run away from the Double T.

At the moment River was too confused to know where she was. She had to watch the route, she reminded herself as her hands were bound behind her and she was heaved atop another horse. Riggs mounted behind her, his arms on each side of her body, and kicked his horse into a jarring trot.

As they rode away from the bottom of the ridge, River looked over her shoulder for Reggie. There was no sign of the dog, nothing but bare, dry ground and stunted mesquite and brush. As frightened as she was, she couldn't help the wave of grief that clogged her throat and filled her eyes.

''Aw, don't cry,'' Riggs muttered in her ear when he felt the warm splash of a tear on the hand holding his reins. ''I won't hurt you.''

River cried silently, and the landscape passed in a haze of watery browns and greens as they rode across the ridge and toward the horizon.

Chapter 16

*

"Where could she be?" Tyler muttered anxiously, scanning the horizon beyond the Double T for what must have been the hundredth time in thirty minutes.

Sandy Dennis shook his head, his brow drawn into a tight knot. "Damned if I know! She knows to hurry back, and not to be gone long. Do you think that skittish mare throwed her?"

"Threw her," Tyler corrected absently. "I don't know. I think she's learned to ride pretty well by now."

"Guests are beginning to arrive, señor," Rosa said as she entered his study. Her plump hands laced and unlaced fretfully. "What shall I tell them?"

"Tell them to enjoy themselves," Tyler replied after a moment. "And ask some of the men if they'd mind joining me at the corral." He paused. "Is Morgan here?"

"No, Señor Templeton."

"Let me know when he arrives, please, Rosa."

A long sigh puckered Tyler's mouth, and he shook his head. "She wouldn't stay gone this long unless something was the matter, Sandy."

"I know."

"Let's get some men to ride with us, and we'll fan out over the ranch and look for her. Do you know her usual route?"

"It changed after this business with Trucklow started. But she can't have gone far."

"She's been gone since first light, Sandy, and now it's almost noon. That's a long time." After another short pause Tyler said, "I'm going to change into my riding boots. And I'm going to get my pistols."

Sandy's eyes widened and he nodded, but he said nothing.

By the time Gray arrived, Sandy was giving out orders. "We'll fan out in groups of five, traveling a mile apart, going in four directions. That ought to pretty well cover most of the area close to the ranch. If we don't find her that way, we'll meet and reconsider."

"Reconsider what?" Gray caught only Sandy's last words.

"River's gone," Tyler replied, sliding from the top of the corral to approach Gray's stallion. "She left early this morning to ride and hasn't come back."

Gray didn't say anything for a moment. His gaze flicked from Tyler's worried face to Sandy's, then back. "She still got that little sorrel mare?" he asked, and Tyler nodded. "We'll find her," Gray said as his brother Matt joined the group.

"Find who?" Matt asked, and one of the other men gave him a brief explanation. "I'm going, too," Matt said at once, and no one argued. It would take all the manpower available to cover the large expanse of the Double T.

When the men were all mounted and ready to ride, Rosa, standing nearby with her hands still twisting, lifted a shaking hand. "Look! Señor Templeton, what is that?"

All heads swiveled, but it was only a small, limping silhouette against a far ridge. "It's only a dog," someone said in disappointment, but Sandy Dennis had broken into a run.

"That's not just any dog," Tyler burst out, "that's her dog!"

Sandy reached the red dog first. Weary and weak from loss of blood, the dog lay down to wait. Then he saw a familiar face, his tail thumped once, then twice as Sandy knelt beside him.

"Here now, old boy, what's happened to you?" Sandy murmured. He touched the matted hair on the dog's shoulder, then stared down at the smears of blood on his fingers.

Rising as Tyler reached him, Sandy said grimly, "He's been shot." The implications were obvious.

"Shot!" someone echoed.

"Get him to the house," Tyler said heavily. "Rosa can care for the dog while we look for . . . River."

"If we can follow his blood trail," Gray Morgan said, "we stand a better chance of finding River."

Half an hour later, the men reached the trampled scene. It had been Gray who had followed the faint traces of blood over ground and rock, and he dismounted to kneel beside bent grass and overturned rocks.

"There were four of them besides River," he said. He pointed to one of the tracks. "There's a Y-shaped nick on one of the horseshoes."

"Anything else?" Tyler asked, bending to peer at the tracks.

Gray stood. "Yeah. One of the men has holes in the soles of his boots."

Faintly disappointed, Tyler said, "I was hoping for something a little more definite."

"Is River's mare shod?"

Tyler nodded.

"Too bad. It's easier to track a barefoot pony."

Gray wandered around the area for a few minutes, pausing occasionally to study some tracks. Finally he rose and looked at Tyler.

"One horse went that way," he said, pointing east with a jerk of his thumb. "The others went north."

"They split up?" Matt guessed, and Gray shook his head slowly.

"I don't think so. Maybe they turned her mare loose. If they did, we need to find it to know for sure."

"I'll find the mare," Matt said, eager to do something besides stand around. "In case they removed saddle and bridle, what's it look like?"

"Sorrel, with a white blaze and four stockings," Gray said, and Matt vaulted to his horse and rode eastward.

"I didn't realize you'd ever been riding with River," Tyler observed distractedly, and a faint smile flickered on Gray's mouth.

"Actually, I haven't. I just saw her mare once. Look, we need to have a plan. When we find her, we can't all go riding in at once. They'll see us coming ten miles away, and that could only endanger River. Why don't you and the others go back to the house and get some rest? I'll find her."

Tyler shook his head. "Do you think I could rest knowing that my daughter is in danger?"

Bending one leg at the knee, and staring down at the ground with his thumbs hooked in his gunbelt, Gray said so softly only Tyler could hear, "I think you know I'll do what's right. I know she's your daughter, but I'm not going to risk her because you want to be there. Trust me, Tyler, and if I don't find her tonight, we'll all go tomorrow."

An agonized expression creased Tyler's face as he pondered, but he finally gave a brief nod. "All right, Gray. I know you can track like a Comanche, and you must have something up your sleeve. But if you come back at daylight and tell me you couldn't find her or rescue her, I'm riding."

"Fair enough."

Turning, Gray grabbed his saddle horn and vaulted atop his stallion with a smooth motion that reminded Tyler of a Comanche brave. He didn't take off in a cloud of dust as Matt had but rode slowly away, his gaze fixed intently on the ground.

"Come on," Tyler told Sandy and the others, "let's go wait."

An hour after her abduction, River had almost decided that she was destined to die atop a jouncing horse. Then, after what seemed like more hours of riding, splashing through creeks that rose to her knees, and pounding over hard ground that paralyzed her strained muscles, she slowly became aware that they had stopped. She was so tired she could barely see, and was only vaguely aware of her surroundings. Dazed, she heard the buzz of soft voices and a scrabbling reminiscent of rats on wood as she was lifted from the horse and was set on the ground. Immediately, her legs buckled and she collapsed in a heap.

"Omigod," came a concerned voice that sounded like Riggs or Webster. "Help me!"

A firm pair of hands gripped her under her arms and around her waist, and she was gently aided up an incline and through a door. She knew it was a door because she could feel the wooden frame as she bumped into it, but her vision was blurred with weariness and the tears she had shed. A sharp, acrid odor assailed her as she stumbled into the small shack, and she coughed.

"I forgot to open the damper on the stove," an apologetic voice said, and Brogan cursed.

Startled at the sound of his voice right behind her, River jerked, and fell back. Arms caught her before she hit the ground, and she was lowered to a thin, bare mattress.

Hands gripped her tightly, digging into her arms and making her cry out. Immediately she bit her lip, not wanting Brogan to know he had hurt her.

A harsh laugh penetrated her daze, and River shivered. "Don't hurt, does it?" came the jeering voice. His grip grew even tighter. "If it hurts, you just let me know about it," Brogan taunted.

River did not utter a sound or try to move away. If she reacted, she knew he would only hurt her more. Then he was dragging her back up from the mattress, his hands moving over her body as she tried to shrink away. Pain could be tolerated, but his degradation was more than she could bear.

"Stop it!" she said sharply.

"Don't you like it? I'm a lot better than Morgan, I can promise you," Brogan said with another harsh laugh. One hand moved to rip at her blouse, and River tried to jerk away.

"Ah, let her alone!" the nameless outlaw protested. "We ain't got time for that. You know our orders, and I'm ready to get out of here. Let's leave her with these two and go."

Brogan gave River a final, hurting pinch that wrung a soft moan from her. "I still say we should at least get some fun for all our troubles," he muttered as River cowered on the sagging mattress. She wished she could see more clearly, wished her hands weren't tied, wished she were anywhere but here. And when she heard the door open, she prayed that Brogan was leaving.

"Have you two got your instructions straight?" Brogan asked in a sharp tone, and Riggs answered him.

"Sure. Don't we always?"

"*No, you don't always,*" Brogan mimicked. "Keep the girl here, and keep her alive for now. This is your last chance, do you understand? Foul this up and you're both dead men!"

Even River shivered at the menace in his tone, and right now she didn't care if he did kill the others.

"But them other times weren't our fault," Webster whined. "That Morgan fella come along a'fore we had a chancet to get outa there."

"Like I said—no mistakes!" Brogan warned, and River suddenly realized that he must be leaving Riggs and Webster behind. That fact opened up a new array of possibilities. Riggs was at least faintly sympathetic.

Through the loud, overpowering fear pounding in her skull, she heard Brogan say, "We're gonna ride. We'll be back. You know what you have to do."

A shiver traced icily down River's spine. Was part of their

orders to kill her, perhaps? Was that why she'd been brought here?

The thought brought fresh tears to her eyes, and even when she heard the door slam behind Brogan she couldn't feel a bit better.

River, however, was in no immediate danger. Riggs and Webster, she soon discovered, weren't the fiercest of outlaws. Neither were they the tidiest of men. Once Brogan left, she sat up on the mattress and looked around her at the filthiest shack she'd ever seen in her life. She sat silently appraising the two men, who grew flustered at her steady stare.

Both wore long, open coats. One man was short and so skinny he looked cadaverous. The other was short and round, with the kind of face that would still look cherubic when he was eighty. Both men appeared to be in their thirties, and both of them wore gun belts tied snugly around their waists. Somehow, in spite of the blatant display of weaponry, the duo looked more ridiculous than dangerous.

Perhaps it was because the gun belts were tied tight and high instead of left loose and low on their hips. To River, it looked as if they would have to reach under an armpit to find their pistols. Thinking that, she almost giggled.

When she sat up straight, silently appraising them, Riggs mumbled something about going outside, and left. Then River was alone with Webster, who didn't seem at all pleased with her steady gaze. He looked away and busied himself at a table cluttered with old papers, opened tin cans, empty bottles, and an assortment of half-eaten food.

Realizing that he might be easily intimidated, River took a step closer to him.

"Aren't you *scared*?" she said suddenly, startling Webster. The short, round-faced outlaw jerked to look at her.

"What do you mean?"

She looked at him scornfully. "You know that my father will come after me. And if he doesn't, Gray Morgan will," she added more confidently than she felt. Gray might, after all, still be angry with her.

Webster recoiled. "I ain't got no quarrel with Gray Morgan."

"You do now," River said. She pushed at the blond wisps of hair straggling in her eyes, and looked at her tightly bound wrists. Some of her initial shock was wearing off, and as she recovered her aplomb, she recovered her wits. "Untie me," she said in her most authoritative tone.

"Un—untie you?"

"Or at least loosen the ropes," she said crossly. "If you don't, the blood cannot circulate."

Hesitating, Webster gazed at her with wide, doubtful eyes. Just as he was wavering the door opened and Riggs returned.

"She wants me to untie her," Webster said.

Riggs frowned. "No. We can't take any risks."

River's hopes sank. "What are you going to do with me?" she demanded in spite of her gnawing worry.

Webster and Riggs stared. "Do with you?" Riggs echoed at last. "We ain't going to do nothing with you. We're just supposed to keep you here."

"How long?"

"Now, see here," Riggs began indignantly, "you ain't supposed to be asking so many questions!"

"If you were in my place, wouldn't you be asking questions?" River retorted.

"Mebbe," Webster acknowledged with a glance at Riggs. Both men shuffled their feet, then exchanged another glance. They were an odd contrast, as gawky as young geese and just as awkward.

"Well," Riggs capitulated, "I guess we could loosen the ropes up a little. Will that make you feel better?"

"Some," River conceded with a sigh. She held out her hands like an obedient child as Riggs told Webster to tend to the ropes.

"Me?" Webster echoed with a trace of indignation. "Why is it always me? I have to start the fire, cook the meal, clean the shack—"

"Well," River said tartly as she held out her hands, "it

certainly doesn't look to me like you've been overworked!
This place is filthy."

Webster's mouth drooped and his eyes widened. "That
wasn't nice," he reproved so sadly that River was startled.

"I'm sorry," she surprised herself by saying. "I didn't
mean to hurt your feelings."

What was she saying? She was apologizing to an outlaw
who had kidnapped her and was partially responsible for the
shooting of her dog!

River buried her face in the cup of her tied hands. It had
been a long, stressful day, and she wondered if she was losing
her mind. Brogan's ferocity, and now the mild menace of
Riggs and Webster, had affected her brain, she decided.

"There, there," Riggs said, coming to pat her back in an
awkward attempt to comfort her. "It's not so bad. And we
won't hurt you, really we won't."

"Then why are you keeping me here?" River inquired in a
voice muffled by her hands. She didn't look up. She didn't
dare. If she did, and saw ludicrous expressions of concern,
she would begin laughing hysterically and they might think
her mad enough to shoot. "Why?" she repeated in a choked
whisper.

"We have to," Webster said, adding quickly, "but it won't
be for long! As soon as your Pa does what Tr—our boss
wants him to do, we can set you free."

River's head snapped up, and her brief descent into hysteria shifted to anger. "So that's it! I knew it! I knew that
pompous, vicious, evil, wicked man was behind all of this!
And to hire a man like Brogan, another savage killer, to carry
out his nefarious plans is just beyond reason!" Her blue eyes
snapped with fire, and Riggs and Webster took a quick step
back. "And you!" she added, sensing an advantage, "you
two have the unmitigated gall to mouth blithe platitudes of
comfort! How dare you pretend you're decent human beings,
when you're holding an innocent person against her will in
order to force another innocent person into giving up that
which he's worked hard for!"

Webster slid Riggs a puzzled glance. "Did you get all that?" he whispered loudly. "I didn' unnerstand a lot of them big words."

"Never mind," Riggs said with a sigh. "She don't think we're very nice, that's all."

"Maybe she's right," Webster said after a moment.

Both men looked at River, who stared back at them.

An impasse of some sort had been reached, and she knew she had to take advantage of it now.

"Look," she said in her most cajoling voice, "why don't we come to an agreement?"

"What kind of agreement?" Webster asked.

"You—as my jailers—must keep me here. But there's no reason why we can't get along as well as possible under the circumstances. Right?"

She looked from Riggs to Webster until they both nodded their heads, looking faintly bemused.

"Right," Riggs said.

"Then I'd like to suggest, gentlemen, since we must be here in this small, filthy shack for an undetermined length of time, we work together to make it habitable."

"There she goes with them big words again, Riley," Webster muttered.

"I mean we must clean it," River explained, and Webster looked around.

"It ain't so very dirty," he began, but even Riggs made a disgusted sound.

"She's right about that, Walter," Riggs said. "We can't expect her to think it's clean when it ain't. Females think different about what's clean and what ain't, remember."

River hid a smile. Thin, lanky Riggs looked as awkward as if pinned together in a mismatch of arms and legs. His movements were disjointed, his head bobbed on his skinny neck like a puppet's. And his voice was just as awkward, a high-pitched shriek instead of a normal baritone. He wore baggy trousers pulled up well above his waist, and his gun belt cinched the material into puckers. A checkered shirt covered his thin chest, and like Webster, he wore a long cattle-man's coat, a kind of duster that hit him midcalf. High leather boots that had seen much better days covered his legs to the knee, and his striped pants were tucked into the top. All in all, he looked shabby and disreputable, but not dangerous.

River began to feel much better. Her situation didn't seem nearly as grave as it had earlier.

"If you'll just untie me now?" she said, once more sticking out her hands.

With the ropes untied, she began to rub at her wrists to restore the circulation. Brogan had tied them so tightly deep purple grooves were cut into her soft flesh, and even Riggs made a shocked sound.

"I'll be fine," River assured him. "Let's get to work on this cabin."

Within the space of two hours, she and the outlaws had cleaned the cabin and put a pot of beans to boil on the small potbellied stove in one corner. Exhausted with her day's ordeal, River sagged to the mattress—now covered with a clean blanket dredged up from a cupboard—and lay down.

She was so tired she fell asleep almost instantly, and didn't even know when Webster gently draped another blanket over her bruised body.

"She's a pretty little thing," Webster whispered to Riggs, and the outlaw nodded.

"Yeah. I just wish Trucklow hadn't of made us take her. If I'd known, we wouldn't have gotten involved in all this, Walter."

"Yer right, Riley." Webster sighed. "Workin' for him ain't quite what I thought it'd be."

Both men gazed down at River's pinched face and the tawny mane of hair tangled across the rough blanket.

Chapter 17

*

It was dark when River awoke with a jerk. She stared up at the ceiling, knowing she wasn't at home but not quite able to remember where she was. Then the memory hit her, and she turned her head to look for Riggs and Webster.

They lay on the floor, snoring, their boots for pillows and a thin blanket for their bed. River almost smiled. They weren't so bad. Misguided maybe, foolish maybe, but not really evil like Brogan or Trucklow.

Easing one leg then the other over the side of the bed, she slipped slowly off and stood there. Someone had removed her boots, and she couldn't find them in the dark. No matter. What mattered most was escape. Riggs and Webster might not be so bad, but Brogan would come back.

Sliding one foot slowly across the floor, then the other, River made her way to the door. Then she cursed the fates. Obviously, they had not quite trusted her to remain asleep. A heavy metal bolt barred her exit. She glanced around at the two outlaws. They were still asleep. A faint glow from the embers in the stove revealed their darker silhouettes.

Stumped, River stood there in an agony of indecision. A

loud noise such as the metal bolt would surely wake them, and then she might not have another opportunity to escape. They would certainly watch her more closely then.

Sucking in a deep breath to steady her nerves, River decided to take the chance. It might turn out to be her only one. Slowly, ever so slowly, she let her fingers slide over the cold iron bolt, exploring the contours to find the latch. The thick finger of iron slid into a U-shaped clasp, was turned, then jerked back by a small hook forged on one side. It would be terribly noisy unless done with delicate precision.

River grit her teeth together, then slid the iron bolt as slowly as possible from the clasp. It scraped, metal on metal, a grinding mutter that could escalate into a shriek if she pulled too fast.

In what seemed like minutes but was only seconds, River had undone the latch, and the heavy wooden door creaked forward. She froze. Had they heard it? Would they waken? No one moved, and she could hear the uninterrupted cadence of snores.

As silently as possible, she slipped out the open door and into freedom. She stood for a moment as her eyes adjusted to the light from a waning moon. To one side was a leaning structure that she assumed stabled the horses, and she wondered if she dared approach the animals.

One loud neigh or whinny of greeting, and Riggs and Webster would waken. It was too risky, River decided, and began running.

Rocks and hard ground tore at her stockinged feet, and she winced but kept running. She ran until her sides ached and her throat hurt from the harsh, ragged gulps of air. When she stopped, the night was eerie. Nothing moved for miles, not even the wind. No one was near, neither man nor beast, and while that was comforting in one way, in another it was disquieting.

When she paused for breath, she wondered if she was running in the right direction. If only the sun was up, then she could tell from its position where she was, but it was just the moon hanging in the sky, the moon and a thousand bright stars.

For some reason River recalled the first night Gray had kissed her, and how the fireflies on the ground had looked like a seas of stars. She had behaved so foolishly that night. But she had behaved foolishly on several nights since then, she reflected as she pushed up from the rock where she sat and stumbled on.

River tried to recall where the moon had been on the night she and Gray danced on the terrace of the Double T. Of course, it had been much earlier in the night, but if the sun rose in the east, didn't the moon? Then, it should be hanging over the ranch's western edge, right? She struggled to remember, and a snatch of verse came to mind.

" 'Hark, what light in yonder window breaks? It is the east, and Juliet is the sun . . . ' That was it!"

River's brief smile of satisfaction faded as she realized that east encompassed a lot of territory.

Wearily, River passed a hand over her eyes. She was so confused. And her feet hurt. Her sides ached and her throat was dry and raspy. She stopped and stood for a moment, staring around her in an effort to recognize the landscape. It all looked the same, sloping ridges dotted with brush and stunted trees, an occasional outcropping of rock, and always the mountain peaks in the distance, rimming the velvet blue of the night sky.

A coyote howled, its wail hanging in the air for a moment before being joined by another, then another, and River shuddered. What if she was attacked? Though timid in nature, a pack of coyotes might consider her fair game, like a lone calf or a crippled cow.

River ran again, faster this time, sliding down a rocky arroyo that tore at the skin of her face and arms, stumbling yet continuing. In spite of the chill desert night, she could feel the sweat dampen her shirt. Her stockings were gone now, torn to shreds. The trousers she wore had one knee out.

Several times she thought she heard pursuers, and she stopped to hide in a clump of bushes, her heart pounding so hard she knew it could be heard. Then she realized that the hoofbeats had been the beating of the blood in her ears, felt foolish, and rose to push on.

It was her worst nightmare. Running, feeling as if the shadows of evil were right behind her, hovering like the giant dark wings of a hawk.

And she had no idea where she was going, no idea how to get home. She was lost, running for miles.

Finally, falling down another steep arroyo, River just lay there when she reached the bottom. She closed her eyes. *It's over. I'll lie here until I die. They'll find my bleached bones.*

She folded her hands across her chest as if holding a flower and arranged her legs in a perfectly straight line. If she was going to be found dead, she refused to be unladylike. Then she happened to think about her tangled hair, and she sat up and finger-combed it into some semblance of neatness before she lay back down on the rocky floor of the arroyo. Time passed. She heard the rustle of night creatures in the brush. She heard the wings of a hawk as it soared overhead, and shuddered, but she remained still. Her toes grew cold and numb, and her feet began to itch. Then her nose itched, and she scratched it.

Finally, when a pale glow lit the eastern sky, River sat up and decided she was going to live. She'd watched that sun rise from her room before, and she rose wearily to her feet and began to walk toward the eastern horizon.

Matt Morgan nudged his mount forward, staring at the ground as he'd seen Gray do so many times before.

"I don't know what he finds when he does this," Matt muttered aloud. "All I can see is rocks and dirt."

He lifted his head to squint into the distance. The sun rose behind him, glistening over the flat land that stretched for miles. Far ahead of him rose the ridges of the Cap Rock

Escarpment, saw-toothed ridges that rose from two hundred to a thousand feet into the air.

Splashing through Indian Creek, Matt rode his horse up the muddy slope and reined it to a halt. He peered down at the ground again, straining to make sense of the cuts and prints in the mud.

"What are you doing here?" a harsh voice demanded, and Matt's head jerked up, his hand flashing down to the pistol strapped to his thigh. "Whoa, little brother!" the voice said, and the pistol lowered as he recognized Gray. Gray eyed him thoughtfully. "You're pretty damn fast with that thing," he said, and Matt nodded.

"Yeah. Sorry about that. Reflex action." There was a pause, then he asked, "Did you find her?"

"Yes and no."

"I hate it when you say that!" Matt flared.

Gray's brow rose mockingly, and he leaned forward in his saddle. "I found where she was."

"Was?"

"Yeah, *was*. By the time I got there, our daring little victim had escaped. She left behind two very penitent outlaws."

"I'll bet they were by the time you got through with them," Matt said.

"Actually, I think they were grateful it was me and not Brogan or Trucklow."

"Where are they?"

Gray gestured with one arm, and Matt looked beyond him to see two horsemen tied to their saddles, looking abashed and more than a little bruised.

"You brought them with you?" Matt said with wide eyes.

"Had to. They started to blubber like babies when I said I was leaving them behind. Something about preferring me to Brogan, though I'm not quite sure I like that."

"And River?"

"I lost her tracks."

Matt's jaw sagged. "You lost her tracks?"

"Hell, it was like following turkey tracks! They wander aimlessly, criss-crossing, backtracking, and when she went through some kind of thicket, I lost them."

"So you're quitting? Just leaving her out there?"

"Have I ever quit before a job's done?" Gray asked softly, and Matt mistook his softness for indifference.

"I don't know what's the matter with you!" Matt snarled so fiercely Gray's eyes narrowed. "You treat her like she's nothing, like she's some kind of . . . of Treena Lassiter! If you ask me, you're better off with a cold, calculating female like Treena. At least you can't hurt her."

"Matt—"

"If you're not going to look for her, I will!"

Nudging his horse into a trot, Matt rode away, leaving Gray staring after him.

It wasn't fair, Matt reflected, just not fair. Gray was always the one who got everything, while everyone else got the leftovers. And that seemed to include women. He'd liked River from the first, thought her sweet nature and shyness much more appealing than bolder females. And with her big blue eyes and long, curling lashes, slow smile and soft, drawling accent, Matt thought River the most wonderful of women. That's why he didn't understand his older brother's attitude toward her—especially when River's feelings for Gray were so apparent. Maybe Gray had no feelings, Matt amended sourly.

Kicking his horse up the next ridge, Matt rode down the crest, zigzagged back over another ridge, and out onto a rutted road. He turned to look behind him but saw no sign of Gray. Shrugging, Matt trotted westward down the road.

That was when he saw it: a ragged, stumbling figure on the road. Pale hair shone in the sunlight, tumbling down around shoulder and back, and Matt spurred his mount into a gallop.

"River!" he shouted, and she hesitated, seemed poised as if for flight, then abruptly sat down in the middle of the road at Matt grew close enough for her to recognize him.

"Matt," she croaked as he slid from his horse and ran to

her. "Oh, Matt! I thought you might be—I thought I would never get . . . home . . ."

The last word trailed into silence as River pitched forward into Matt's arms. Hot, scalding tears streaked her cheeks and burned onto his arm and young heart, and he held her for several minutes, just rocking back and forth, stroking her hair, murmuring nonsensical sounds that his mother had used to comfort him as a small boy.

Then, slowly, he rose to his feet and pulled River with him, still holding her, letting her cling to him.

"I was so frightened," she whispered into his shirt, and Matt nodded.

"I know, I know. Here. I know you want some water."

River gulped thirstily, and water ran down her chin and onto her shirt, making mud out of the caked dust.

"Ready to go home?" Matt asked, and she looked up at him.

"More than you can imagine!"

Matt grinned at the thread of strength in her voice and heaved her up to his saddle before mounting behind her. "It's not nearly as far riding as it is walking," he said, reining his horse back around.

They rode over the ridges and down through Indian Creek. River leaned back into Matt with a relieved sigh and closed her eyes. She didn't open them until she heard Gray's voice only a few feet away.

"I see you found her."

Why did he sound so mocking, she wondered as her eyes opened. And Matt sounded so defensive, so belligerent!

"Yeah, I found her," Matt was saying.

"Was she alone?" Gray asked, his eyes as flinty and hard as granite as he raked River's disheveled frame with an appraising gaze.

Acutely aware of Gray's searching gaze and bewildered by the tension, River looked from one to the other. "What's the matter?"

"Nothing," they said in unison.

"At least we agree on something," Gray commented. River's throat tightened.

Something was the matter, something they didn't want to tell her. Her glance drifted to Riggs and Webster, who sat miserably atop their mounts. What had happened after she'd escaped the cabin? How had Gray found them? Had he faced them alone?

"Papa?" she said shakily. "Is my father all right?"

"He was when I left him yesterday," Gray said. "And he's expecting to see you this morning, so the quicker we get back to the ranch, the better he'll feel."

"She's riding with me," Matt said.

Gray merely shrugged. "Suit yourself."

As Gray wheeled his big stallion around and kicked it into a swift canter, dragging Riggs and Webster behind him, River turned to look up at Matt. "Has something happened?"

"Not unless you want to count the fact that you were kidnapped, your dog shot, and your horse found in the next county," Matt replied in a voice that sounded so much like Gray's that she was startled.

"You sound just like Gray."

"Is that anything to say to someone who just rescued you from the very jaws of death?"

"What are you and Gray quarreling about this time?"

"And *you* sound just like Ma!" Matt said, making River laugh shakily.

"Thank you. I happen to think your mother is a wonderful person."

"She is."

River's gaze darted ahead to Gray. He didn't even glance back at her, didn't act like he cared if she had been found, was alive, or unharmed. Did he? Did he care at all? Had she been deceiving herself all along? After all she'd been through, she didn't feel like making excuses for him anymore. He was unfeeling. Cold. And she'd imagined him as her Ideal Man . . .

"Tell me about my dog," River said, her voice flat. "Is he . . . is he dead?"

"I don't know, River."

"What about the men who kidnapped me? Are we taking them to the sheriff and telling him about Brogan?"

Again Matt shook his head. "I don't know."

"Do you think something will be done about Trucklow this time? Will Sheriff Wentwhistle pay any attention?"

Shrugging helplessly, Matt said, "I don't know the answers to any of those questions. No one does until the time comes. Trucklow may get off."

"I'll bet Papa has something to say about that," River said grimly.

Tyler Templeton did, indeed, have something to say about Pierce Trucklow. A lot to say about Pierce Trucklow. And he said it all to the sheriff.

Wentwhistle leaned back in his chair and listened with a thoughtful frown as Tyler and River told what happened. Occasionally he would flick a glance toward Gray, who leaned casually against a far wall and gazed at the sheriff from beneath the brim of his hat. Gray's stare seemed to unnerve Wentwhistle, who shook his head when Tyler finished his story.

"Well, if what you say is true—"

"It is true!" River said angrily.

"Hold on a minute, little lady!" The sheriff rubbed at his jaw. He gazed at River, dressed in shirt and pants like a boy, then heaved his bulk up from the chair. He reached for his hat and tugged it on. "I reckon I'll ride out to that line shack and see for myself."

"Why bother, when we brought Riggs and Webster in for you to question?" Tyler asked impatiently.

Wentwhistle's jaw thrust out in a stubborn slant. "I said I want to see the shack for myself. You say it was on Trucklow's land?"

"Up near Comanche Ridge," Tyler corrected him.

"But that's your land."

"I know, Sheriff. The curs used my line shack!"

"In other words," Wentwhistle began, "you want me to arrest Trucklow's men for trespassin'."

Tyler's patience snapped. His voice held a hard edge River had never heard before. "Sheriff, I want you to do what you were elected to do. If you cannot or will not, I will take steps to see that you are replaced—"

"Are you threatening me?" Wentwhistle blustered.

"No," Tyler said. "I am telling you that I will personally contact Governor Ross and inform him of the situation so that he can make his own investigation. What he finds would of course be up to him—and you."

"Governor Lawrence S. Ross?" The sheriff wheezed a bit unsteadily. Then he said sharply, "He ain't gonna listen to some angry rancher from Comanche County, not when he's got an elected official down here that—"

"Ross and I are well acquainted with one another, Sheriff. He will know that I don't cry wolf."

Stymied, Sheriff Wentwhistle looked from Tyler to Gray and back. He wasn't quite willing to risk his own neck, but he wasn't quite willing to be bluffed, and he wasn't sure just how well Tyler knew the governor.

"I'll look into it," Wentwhistle said finally.

Gray pushed away from the wall. "I told you this was a waste of time, Tyler. This yellow-livered fool isn't going to do a damn thing."

"Hey!" Wentwhistle's face grew red. "You can't speak of an elected public official like that."

"You weren't elected this last time; you were bought and paid for by Pierce Trucklow," Gray said, "and a man is still entitled to his opinion. You've heard mine."

"Stay out of my way, Morgan," the sheriff said.

Gray laughed. "I can assure you that we won't cross paths again, Sheriff, since you never leave your safe, comfortable chair."

River cleared her throat, and both men turned to look at her. "Please," she said softly, "I just want to find the person responsible for what happened to me. I don't want to be afraid to ride alone again, or to walk down a street. Do you understand, Sheriff?''

Wentwhistle stared at her for a moment, then relaxed. "Yes, ma'am, I do understand. And I'll do what I can to help you, but keep your friend here out of my way."

Nodding, River stepped between the sheriff and Gray on her way to the door. Tyler followed, and Gray backed the few steps to the door without saying another word.

When the door had closed behind them, River turned to look at Gray. "What's the quarrel between you and the sheriff? You never have told me."

"And I won't," Gray said without an instant's hesitation.

"You were right, Gray," Tyler said into the bristling silence between them. "The sheriff isn't going to do anything."

"Oh, he may slap a charge of trespassing against Brogan and the others, but that's about all." Gray was quiet as they walked down the sidewalk in the afternoon sun that spilled into Clanton.

"Every man in Comanche County will know about this," Tyler said. "It should influence the next election. And so will Governor Ross, if I don't miss my guess."

"That doesn't help us now," Gray pointed out. He looked at River from beneath the brim of his hat. Her face was pale and still marked with faint violet bruises from her ordeal. His mouth tightened. "I'm riding out to the Bar None and have my own talk with Trucklow. Care to come along, Tyler?"

"Please don't do it, Papa!" River said. "It's not worth it. He's dangerous, and that man Brogan is just a cold-blooded killer. Wait, and let the sheriff—"

"It's our turn now," Gray broke in. "Matt or Sandy can see you back to the Double T."

But Matt and Sandy insisted upon going with Gray and Tyler, and it was Nancy Morgan who rode beside River with a rifle in her lap and a frown on her face. Two of the hired hands followed the wagon at a close pace, and the small caravan rocked over rutted roads to the ranch.

"They're idiots," River muttered. "If they come back at all, they'll probably be shot to pieces."

"Oh, I have a little more faith in them than that," Nancy soothed. She reached out to pat River's hand. "You've got to accept that your father as well as my son are men. And men don't sit back and wait for others to do what should be done."

"But why can't he wait on the law to take care of it?" River asked, still confused.

Nancy was silent for a moment, then said, "I'm afraid that after witnessing his father's murder, Gray doesn't have much faith in the Clanton sheriff."

River turned to look at her. "Wentwhistle was involved?"

"No, but he didn't stop it, and he never looked for the men who were." Nancy's gaze was fixed on the far peaks. "Mike wasn't a man who'd back down, just like Gray. I can understand your fear, for I felt it often enough myself, but in the end, if you don't accept the way they are, you will only make what time you have together unhappy. I would not have changed Mike, except perhaps to make him a little more cautious." Her smile was wan. "You may not believe this, but Gray is more cautious than his father was. It was Gray who tried to get Mike to come home, to choose his words with care. But nothing would do but that Mike refuse to temper his words with good judgment. The silly, stubborn mule." Her last words were said fondly, and River shook her head.

"And they shot him?"

"Yes," Nancy said, "they shot him. That was twelve years ago. It really affects a fourteen-year-old boy to see his father shot."

There didn't seem to be anything to say to that, so River remained silent, thinking about the boy who had seen his father killed, the man he now was.

She turned abruptly to Nancy. "I want to be in town when they get back there with Trucklow."

The older woman just stared at her for a moment.

"Don't you hate waiting and wondering?" River persisted. "Worrying?"

"You know," Nancy said after another moment of silence, "I think I do!"

The wagon turned around in a wide arc, then rattled back up the road toward Clanton.

Chapter 18

*

Nancy Morgan stopped the wagon in front of Gray's small office across the street from the Emporium Saloon. She gave River a quick smile, then turned to the two men who had accompanied them to the Double T.

"Why don't you gentlemen wash some of the dust from your throats, while Miss Templeton and I wait at the hotel?" Nancy smiled at the men. "Oh, and you can inform anyone who asks that we'll be waiting for them."

"Do you think they will . . . will come back soon?" River asked, unable to voice the fear that her father and Gray might not come back at all.

"Not soon, maybe, but they'll be back. I have faith in them." Nancy smiled. "Let yours grow a little, honey."

" 'We walk by faith, not by sight,' " River quoted softly. Nancy looked at her curiously. "Part of my grandmother's legacy?" River said. "She had a proverb for every occasion, appropriate or not. Although I am determined not to misuse them."

"Only time and experience will help you there." Nancy smiled again.

"Ah, and to quote my dear grandmother, 'Experience keeps a dear school, yet fools will learn in no other.' I have a very strong sympathy with that particular sentiment, I'm afraid."

"You shouldn't. You're certainly no fool," Nancy said firmly. "And now, why don't we just go back to the hotel and wait on our loved ones?" She tucked a hand through River's arm. "It's so nice to have another woman to talk with, to worry with. Though I know they try, there are times when my sons just do not understand me. I have discovered that there is a vast difference between male and female that has nothing at all to do with anatomy."

Flushing from Nancy's casual use of the term "loved ones" in regard to Gray, River agreed, "I have noticed that very thing since meeting your son."

"Rather trying at times, isn't he? He always has been."

To River, who had never really known her mother, the rapport between her and Nancy Morgan was something she had only dreamed of. She realized with a pang that Nancy could be a wonderful substitute.

"The lobby is certainly crowded today, isn't it?" Nancy commented when they sat on a settee in an alcove and sipped from glasses of iced lemonade.

River felt vaguely uncomfortable, fully aware that she had gathered more than a few shocked stares at her attire. She may have been able to ride her mare more comfortably in her trousers and shirt, but it certainly wasn't proper for sitting in the lobby of the Clanton Hotel!

"Perhaps I should have waited elsewhere," River murmured when a man stared at her over the rim of his spectacles. "I seem to be drawing unwelcome attention."

"Nonsense. And I think you look quite fetching in those trousers, something not many females do, you know. But you are so slender and trim, that they fit you wonderfully."

Still unaccustomed to being called slender, River flushed, and the high color in her cheeks made Nancy Morgan think once more how becoming River Templeton was. And instead of being vain, the girl was overly modest, another excellent trait as far as Nancy was concerned.

Shrinking back in her chair in the small alcove, River tried to disappear. She was self-conscious and couldn't help lifting a hand to smooth her hair.

Nancy smiled. "I think I'll just walk down to Lucy Tower's shop for a moment. Wouldn't you like to come with me? It would take your mind off . . . things," she said when River gave a quick shake of her head.

"No. I think I'll wait here. Papa and Gray might return at any moment."

"I doubt they've done more than reach the Bar None by now," Nancy said, but River would not be moved.

River scooted back in her chair after Nancy left, as if trying to make herself invisible. The ice had almost melted in her glass, and she gave the pale lemonade another swish. Where was Gray? What was he doing? Was he hurt, or perhaps, wounded and suffering? And her father . . . Tyler was such a proud, upright man he would not compromise with Trucklow in any way.

They were dangerous men, and River knew it all too well. It was only by the grace of God that she had escaped the less-dangerous Riggs and Webster with little more than bruises and scratches from the thorn bushes she'd plunged through in her headlong flight. And her poor dog. Reggie was still alive, but his wound was critical. Rosa was still tending to him when Gray and Tyler had pulled River from the house to ride into Clanton. If it hadn't been for Reggie, they would have wandered over acres of land before they'd found where the struggle had taken place, and she might not have been found before Brogan caught up with her.

River shivered at the thought, and a voice floated softly to her ears.

"Cold in June? My, my, Miss Templeton, you aren't very hardy, are you?"

River's head snapped up to see Treena Lassiter gazing at her with spiteful dark eyes.

"Do you mind if I join you for a moment?" Treena continued, sitting without waiting for a response. She smoothed silky skirts over her legs, lay her reticule in her lap, and smiled at River.

"How can I help you, Miss Lassiter?" River asked in a wary voice.

Treena folded her hands primly over her reticule, somehow reminding River of Linda Llewellyn, the Goddess on the long journey from Fort Worth, the cold, icy statue with no feelings for anyone else.

"Why, it will be yourself you'll be helping," Treena said with a light little laugh. "And Gray."

River's interest quickened. "Gray?"

"Ah, I thought that might intrigue you. Yes, Gray. I have come to bring you a message from him."

"A message from Gray?" River repeated, feeling like an echo. "What do you mean? When?"

"Now," Treena said with a shade of annoyance. She chose to ignore River's other question as she smoothed the gloves over her small, dainty hands. Clasping her velvet reticule and looking down her nose at River's trousers, Treena said, "If you will come with me, I'll take you to him."

"Come where?"

Treena stood abruptly. "Really! If you don't want to see him, just tell me, and I will be more than happy to tell him so, Miss Templeton!"

Hesitating, River wished Nancy Morgan had not left the hotel. Treena looked so insistent that she suspected Gray might be wounded, or worse. It did not then occur to her that Tyler would have come for her, or that they had not yet had time to get back from the Bar None.

"Well, let me leave a message for Mrs. Morgan at the front desk. She was here with me, waiting on Gray. Should we not wait for her?"

"No. There's no time for that."

Treena's voice was adamant, and River rose, setting her watery lemonade on the table. "Very well."

"I'll leave a message at the desk," Treena said firmly, "while you go do something with your hair."

River's hand automatically went to her hair, and she found the braid half-undone and dangling over one shoulder. "But if Gray needs me now, does how I look really matter?"

"Do you want him to see you disheveled?" Treena shot back as she stood and stared down her long, thin nose at River. "It's up to you."

"No. No, I will be with you in a moment."

When River emerged from the ladies' room she found Treena waiting impatiently, tapping one foot against the floor and staring out the front window. As River walked with the girl down the wooden sidewalk, she thought to ask, "Where are we going?"

"To my house," Treena said calmly, and River's heart sank.

Why would Gray go to Treena's house, unless . . . unless something had happened, and as it was on the edge of town, they had stopped there? A thousand thoughts flew round in her fevered brain, and by the time they reached Treena's neat frame house on the very fringe of Clanton, she was almost beside herself with worry.

"Where is he?" she asked when she stepped into the empty living room.

Treena removed her gloves and tossed them to a table before replying off-handedly, "Oh, he'll be joining us very soon. He wants you to wait here."

River perched nervously on the edge of a settee and looked around her. The room was furnished ornately, with heavy chintz draperies and overstuffed chairs, lots of gold braid and fringe, and a profusion of green plants.

A tiny smile flirted with Treena's mouth as she pulled the braided strings of the velvet reticule to open it. She snaked one hand inside, and when she withdrew it she held a very small, very lethal pistol.

River half rose in alarm, but Treena gestured with the tiny weapon, and River slowly sat back down.

"Isn't this an interesting little toy?" Treena asked so casually she might have been speaking of a puppet or jack-in-the-box. "It's a Remington Elliot .22, often used by gamblers or hidden in bodices. This tiny little ring is the trigger, and this pistol has five very deadly shots before I have to reload."

Licking suddenly dry lips, River managed to ask, "And to what do I owe this fascinating lesson in weaponry?"

Perching on the arm of a chair, Treena leveled the pistol at River. One leg swung back and forth in an idle motion, and the feline smile never left her lips.

"Gray Morgan has a great deal to do with this lesson, Miss Templeton. May I call you River?"

River shrugged, her eyes fastened on the pistol. "As you seem to hold all the aces, I'd say you could play your little game any way you like."

"How astute of you!" Treena's eyes sharpened. "You see, River, until you came to our small town Gray Morgan was exclusively mine. Since your arrival, he seems to have been distracted. Now, while I'm certain that your . . . attractions . . . won't last that long, unfortunately it's extremely irritating to me. I'm sure you understand."

"I understand irritation. Threats are less understandable," River shot back. She was growing more nervous with each passing moment.

"Threats? Dear me, how melodramatic we are!" Treena mocked. The short barrel of the pistol waggled. "Please be good enough to remain still and quiet. This trigger, for some reason, has a tendency to go off if just slightly jostled. I would hate to shoot you accidentally."

Slowly River said, "Then to remove any danger of that, why don't I just leave?"

"Oh, no, that won't do at all!" Treena laughed. "I mean to shoot you, and when I do it will be no accident."

"Mrs. Morgan will be here shortly," River began, then paused. Of course Treena would not have left a message, and she—fool that she was—had walked directly into this trap!

"I can see by your expression that you realize that won't

happen," Treena said quietly. Her dark eyes glittered with a faint light. "I have thought of everything."

River stared at her. "Have you thought of how you'll explain my death or disappearance to Gray?"

"I won't have to. Pierce Trucklow will be blamed."

"But at this moment," River said, "Gray's riding out to the Bar None to bring Trucklow into the sheriff's office."

Treena seemed unperturbed. "I doubt he will. By the way, how did you enjoy your little stay with those outlaws? Did they abuse you at all? I hope so."

Locking her fingers around one knee, River tried to keep calm. Nothing would be gained by panicking now, and as Treena held a loaded pistol, she had to keep Treena calm too.

"It wasn't too bad," River replied after a moment. "Did you plan that too?"

Treena smiled. "How clever you are! I warned Gray that if he . . . if he did not cooperate, I would ruin things for him. He thought I meant Trucklow. I was talking about you, however." Rising from the arm of the chair, Treena began to pace the room with short, quick strides. "I was very careful, you know. Obviously, since you are here instead of dead, I was not careful enough. I should have used my own men and not depended on the idiots Trucklow hired. My hireling was quite dependable, if a little greedy."

"What do you mean?"

"I bribed someone from the Double T to give me the information I wanted, but he became greedy. He wanted more to keep quiet. Silly fool!"

River's throat tightened. "You mean, you killed him?"

Treena made a distasteful face. "Don't be absurd! I'm not a killer!"

"Yet," River muttered, eyeing the pistol.

The brunette's hand wavered slightly, but she giggled; it was an odd, irritating sound that sent a chill down River's back.

"Perhaps it is. Well. I have plans that cannot go wrong this time. And Pierce Trucklow will have to cooperate. After all, even though I obtained the information for him, he was the one who actually engineered the entire escapade. And my accomplice is safely tucked away for the moment, so don't hope for a sudden repentance.''

River couldn't imagine who Treena meant, and her mind cast about wildly for clues. ''I don't think you are clever enough to do anything like that,'' she said at last, hoping to goad Treena into revealing more. For a moment, River imagined herself as a female Sherlock Holmes from *A Study in Scarlet*. She hoped that she could really be as tricky—and that Treena wasn't a reader.

''Oh, no? It was I—*I* who coaxed Juan Carlos into telling me how you ride out early every morning. It was I who convinced that silly Trucklow to let his lazy men wait until you were foolish enough to do so again! And it would have worked, except those stupid idiots allowed you to escape! Trucklow would have his land, and I would have Gray again.''

''Do you really think Gray can be forced?'' River countered. ''As soon as I was released, he would be with whom he chose.''

Treena smiled nastily. ''Not if you were dead. That was part of my bargain with the incompetent Mr. Trucklow! I was not to be involved, but as soon as he had what he wanted, he was to . . . dispose of you.''

An icy chill shivered down her back as River gazed at Treena's face. Suddenly the brunette did not seem so lovely anymore, and she wondered why she had ever considered her a rival. She was a threat, a deadly threat, but had never been a rival.

''I see,'' she said slowly, ''and now that I'm still here and not *disposed of*, what do you intend to do?''

''I have it all planned,'' Treena said as lightly as if they were discussing a party. ''Remove all your clothes except for your underthings.''

''Remove my clothes?'' River repeated, and Treena gave an impatient wiggle with the pistol.

"Yes! Now! While I wouldn't enjoy murder, I might not mind wounding you."

Slowly, River stood in the neat, cozy little living room and removed her boots, trousers, and shirt. She stood shivering with fear in her thin chemise and pantalets.

"And take off that locket too," Treena said. She pointed to the gold chain and locket River wore around her neck.

"No! My father gave me that, and it has a portrait of my mother inside—"

"It doesn't matter. Just take it off." Treena laughed shortly. "You're fortunate to know who your mother and father are, my dear. I never had the chance. I was left as a baby with an *uncle*, who was delighted to have a little girl to fondle. But that is another story. I left him and came west with someone else." She waggled the pistol. "When he died in a barroom brawl, I was left truly on my own. So you see, I've always had to live by my wits."

"And Gray?" River asked tightly. "How does he enter into all of this?"

"I met Gray Morgan when he was in law school, and he agreed to untangle the legal snarls of my uncle's will. I did not dream he was such a puritan about some things."

"Such as murder?"

Treena laughed. "Among others. Anyway, I followed him out here, invented a tale of investment with my inheritance, and waited for him to fall in love with me." She frowned then, her eyes glittering. "He's so picky about meaningless details. What does it matter if a paper is truly legal, as long as a bank will accept it?"

Confused, River just stared at Treena, her mind racing. The brunette was obviously unbalanced. But then Treena was pointing the pistol at her, demanding that she pick up her clothes and accompany her.

A strong wave of Treena's perfume assailed River's nostrils, and she was reminded of a foreboding prophecy: "And all the perfumes of Arabia will not sweeten this little hand," Shakespeare had said in *Macbeth*, a tale of madness and murder. Treena was not above murder, and she *had* to think of a way to get free!

Her teeth chattering with fright, River had to make her way down a steep flight of stairs into a dark, unlit basement. It smelled dank and musty, and there was a fetid odor that reminded her of a barnyard.

But it wasn't until Treena lit a lantern and hung it from a hook that River could see the man chained to a wall and staring at them with wide, hollow eyes. River screamed, and the sound echoed over and over in the basement.

"Shut up!" Treena snapped, and slapped River across one cheek.

Reeling, River fought to remain on her feet. When she turned back to the man, she saw the fear in his eyes.

"Juan Carlos," River murmured, "I thought you went to work for—"

"A beautiful *norteamericana*," the Mexican finished hoarsely. "*Sí*, I thought the same. Only she is a she-devil, *diabla*! *Por Dios, Madre de Dios!*"

"Oh, be quiet," Treena said impatiently.

River looked at her for a long moment. "All this time," she said softly, "I've thought Pierce Trucklow was the true enemy."

"Pierce Trucklow is just an inept swindler, a second-rate man with second-rate dreams. All he's worried about is trying to get a silly little piece of unimportant land. When the railroad is built, a town site can be built almost anywhere. Lots can be sold, commercial property leased—"

"Railroad?" River repeated dazedly. "Through Clanton?"

"Across Comanche Ridge, and down the plain . . . ah, I see that you've finally made the connection." Treena shrugged. "I told Trucklow that once my plan went through, Comanche Ridge would be his by default, but he didn't believe me. Or trust me. Whichever, he's a fool."

"But how . . . ?"

"It's simple. My *uncle* was a member of the Texas legislature. Using his connections, I've been working on a land grant approval for that Comanche land Trucklow let slip through his fingers, including Comanche Ridge. Once the grant is approved, one hundred and twenty-five thousand acres will be donated to our corporation for the railroad. Of course in order not to pay taxes, I intend to sell off most of it.''

"But the state cannot take away my father's land," River began.

Treena smiled. "It can in order to build a railroad, my dear. If the owner refuses to sell it to the state for a nominal fee, it is simply appropriated.''

River's gaze flicked to the man in chains sitting against the cellar wall. "So how do I fit in? And Juan Carlos?''

Treena turned to the terrified Mexican. "He has a very simple choice to make. He can put on your clothes—a gown would have been preferable, but these will do—and disguise himself as you. Or he can stay chained down here with the rats until he dies of starvation.''

Shuddering, River looked from Treena to Juan Carlos. "I don't know what you think his wearing my clothes will accomplish. He may be close to my size, but one close look at him will be enough to convince anyone that he is not me. Why, his hair is short and dark, and his coloring is darker, and—''

"That doesn't matter. He just needs to wear them out of my house right now. Witnesses must see you leave, you understand. The clothes will be found later. And the locket.'' Treena gestured with the pistol. "Switch clothes with her, Juan Carlos. I will unlock one shackle at a time, so don't get any ideas.''

There was a rattle of chains as the Mexican slowly shuffled, his hands trembling with weakness. He'd obviously been chained for some time without food. River's eyes dilated, then focused on the clothes Treena was holding out to him.

"*Switch* clothes?'' River couldn't help repeating. Her breath came short and fast, and the dark cellar walls began to recede. *No, no, don't faint now!* she told herself, and inhaled deeply of the musty air. What would Holmes do?

Treena smiled viciously. "You, my dear, are going to take Juan Carlos's place in the cellar."

Frantic with fear, River surged toward the steep stairs, but Treena lunged after her and caught her by her long hair, swinging her around.

"Don't be stupid!" Treena snarled. "I could easily shoot you!"

River summoned courage and strength at the same time and brought up her right arm. Her fingers curled into a fist, and she punched Treena squarely in the mouth. She had the brief satisfaction of seeing Treena fall, then she pivoted and ran again. Her legs seemed too numb to work properly, and she half fell, half scrambled up the narrow steps as she heard Juan Carlos shouting encouragement at her.

Then she heard his high-pitched warning, "Look out! She is going to shoot!"

A deafening explosion ripped through the air, and River felt a burning pain on the right side of her head. Shadows swayed alarmingly, and she heard Treena behind her as if from a great distance. The kerosene lamp overhead seemed to sway, and then grew dim, and River fainted.

"Dammit!" Treena swore. "What if someone heard the shot? And I'm bleeding. If she has scarred me, I shall kill her with my bare hands, so help me!"

Juan Carlos prudently remained silent, even when Treena unlocked his chains and ordered him at gunpoint to put on River's clothes and locket. "And put yours on her," Treena said with another nudge of the pistol.

The Mexican obeyed, though his hands were trembling and he was faint with deprivation.

"This is not right, Señorita Lassiter," he said once, and she shoved the short barrel of the pistol against his neck.

"Shut up! Don't talk to me about what's right. I know what's right for me and that's all I care about." There was a short pause, then she told him to drag River to the far wall and lock her in his empty chains. "Unless you both wish to languish down here?"

Silently the Mexican did as instructed. The long chains rattled heavily, and he felt a pang of regret that his foolishness had caused his old employer's daughter so much trouble. It was his fault, his greed had seduced him, and he resolved to do what he could to stop Treena Lassiter.

"Excellent," Treena said when he was through. "Now come upstairs with me. And bring the kerosene lamp."

He hesitated, glancing at River's blood-streaked face. "Shouldn't we leave her some light down here? The rats, they don't like the light, and it gets so dark—"

"Bring the lamp!" Treena repeated sharply, wagging the gun, and he obeyed. The door to the cellar closed behind them, shutting out the light and plunging the dank room into black shadows.

River, barely conscious, moaned softly. She had heard Juan Carlos's objections, had wanted to speak but had not dared. Pain throbbed in River's skull and she could feel the steady drip of blood down the side of her face. She tried to move, but found the heavy chains dragged at her arms and legs. River scooted along the floor, shivering with cold, until she could sit up with her back against the wall. As her eyes grew accustomed to the dark she found that she could make out a tiny sliver of light that threaded beneath the cellar door. And she could hear Treena and Juan Carlos talking.

The Mexican's voice lifted in agitation, and River heard Treena speak sharply again.

"Shut up! My mouth is bleeding and my looks may be ruined, and you want to talk to me about right and wrong? I think *you are insane* . . . hey! Stop it! Be careful with that lamp until I'm ready. What are you doing, you crazy idiot?"

Through the dull throbbing in her head, River could hear sounds of a scuffle, the grunts of pain and heavy thuds, then the crack of a pistol shot. She jumped, held her breath, wondering who had been shot, then jumped again when another shot sounded. There was a shattering crash, then silence.

Then, more terrible than the shots or the screaming, came the unmistakable scent of smoke. River held her breath for a moment, let it out slowly, then inhaled again. No. She had not been mistaken. She smelled smoke.

"No!" she moaned desperately. "No!" She tugged frantically at the chains bolted to wooden supports. "Help me!" she screamed finally, hoping someone upstairs would relent and come to her rescue. "Please, help me!"

Almost hysterical with fear, she pulled at the shackles around her wrists and discovered that one of them was loose enough to slide over her hand. Gritting her teeth, she tugged at it until her skin was scraped raw. Finally one hand was free, and she repeated the same painful process with the other. *Bless Juan Carlos,* she thought as she freed her ankles. He had not fastened the chains around her legs, but left them loose, so she could escape.

Weeping with relief, River felt her way to the stairs, guided by the sliver of hazy light from above. But relief died as she tried the door and found it locked. She beat on it with both fists, screaming for help, but no one replied. Sagging against the locked door, she panted for breath, coughing as smoke curled around her.

But there were no sounds from above, no footsteps or voices, and River knew that both Treena and Juan Carlos must be unconscious or dead. And if the kerosene lamp had been knocked over and set the house on fire, she would die too.

Thick black smoke began to seep beneath the cellar door, and River coughed as it burned her lungs. It stung her eyes and nose, creeping down the stairs with greedy fingers, and she knew the flames would soon follow. The house would burn down over her head and fall in, and no one would ever find her body, she thought with a sob.

River felt her way back down the steep, narrow stairs and around the dank cellar walls. There were no other doors or windows, no exit that she could find. As the smoke grew thicker, drifting down in layers, she crawled across the floor into the crawlspace. Water dripped down the stone sides in small rivulets, and she pulled old mattresses and furniture across the entrance. It would slow the smoke and fire, she hoped, at least long enough for someone to see the flames and arrive to rescue her.

Curling her aching, bruised body into a ball, she put her head on her knees. Fingers of smoke slowly penetrated the makeshift barrier, stinging her nose and eyes, and she pressed her face close to the damp wall. It was over. She could hear the crackle of the flames now, hear the wood burning overhead and the hiss and pop of pine as it caught fire.

Closing her eyes tightly, River thought of her father. Then she thought of Gray, visualizing his mocking face and eyes the color of smoke. Would he miss her? Had he loved her as she'd loved him? She'd never know now. This was the end of all her dreams. . . .

Chapter 19

*

Gray Morgan was not in a good mood. Neither were Tyler and Matt. Hardly anyone spoke as they rode toward Clanton from the Double T.

"Why d'you suppose Ma and River stayed in town?" Matt asked the empty air, and no one answered at first. Tyler seemed lost in thought, weary, his blond head bent.

It was Gray who finally replied. "Because if something can be done easily, they won't. That is why we're riding another twenty miles instead of doing something worthwhile."

"Now, Gray," Tyler reproved in a soft voice. "They must have thought we would be returning to town with Trucklow, and decided to wait there. If we didn't know he wouldn't be there, they didn't either."

Gray didn't respond. His thoughts focused on Pierce Trucklow. Something bothered him about the entire situation, more than just Trucklow's greed and methods. He seemed to know too much. How had he known they were coming after him? There had been no sign of him or his men at the ranch. Why? Gray had to ask himself.

The question bothered him more the closer he got to

Clanton. A shadowed moon flirted with clouds, and silver light flickered erratically over the rutted road. Hoofbeats pounded in a matching cadence, and Tyler, Gray, and Matt rode abreast. The early night was quiet, with a brisk wind coming up from the south.

"It's not close to dawn, is it?" Matt asked in surprise a few miles closer to Clanton.

Gray, his mind puzzling about other matters, flashed his brother an annoyed glance. "No. It's not even close to midnight. Why?"

Somewhat sheepishly Matt muttered barely loud enough for Gray to hear, "Because I saw that glow on the horizon and thought it was the sun coming up, I guess."

"What glow—" Gray asked.

Tyler pointed. His voice was strained as he said, "Look, Gray!"

Gray looked. Up ahead, in the vicinity of Clanton, a reddish glow appeared on the horizon. Because of the flat land between town and riders, it was easily seen. There was only one explanation for it, and it was an explanation that seared into each man's brain as they stared at the red-and-orange light spearing the night.

"Fire," Tyler breathed softly, and Gray nodded grimly. Fire was the most feared disaster on the plains. It could ravage an entire town if unchecked, and it was hard to check a fire without ample water. Fortunately, Clanton had deep natural wells, but the process of getting water to fire was painstakingly slow.

Spurring on their horses, they urged the weary animals on, eating up the remaining miles to Clanton.

But when they arrived at the outskirts, they could see that the situation was serious. Flames had leapt from one house at the town's edge to another, and soot-streaked men were passing water buckets in a line, trying to save the houses not yet afire.

Bucket, shovel, and wet gunny sacks were being used until the town's small man-powered fire pump could be dragged to a cistern and put in efficient working order. It was rapidly apparent that Clanton's volunteer fire brigade had not been effectively organized.

"Whose house is that?" Matt asked, reining his mount in beside Gray.

"Treena Lassiter's," Gray said. He pushed back his felt hat, gazing through narrowed eyes at the structure fully engulfed in flames. It was an inferno, a blazing ruin. He slid from his stallion, which was snorting and half rearing with fright, and started toward the line of men at a run.

"Where you going?" Matt called, then noticed that Tyler had dismounted, too, and was advancing toward the bucket brigade. Shrugging, Matt slid from his horse and let the reins dangle. No point in hitching his horse to a post that might go up in flames, he thought as he followed his brother.

Before he reached him, someone grabbed Matt's arm, spinning him around. He staggered back a step before recovering, muttering, "What the hell—? Oh, sorry, Ma. Are you all right?" he asked, grabbing her by the shoulders.

Nancy was as white as a sheet, and her silver-gray eyes were glassy. She shook her head. "No! Oh, Matt, how can I tell Gray?"

"Tell Gray what?"

"Yeah," Gray said from behind them, "tell Gray what?"

Nancy turned, looking much older than Gray had ever noticed. Her soft brown hair with the faint gray streaks straggled over her face and shoulders, and a spiderweb of lines fanned out from her eyes and pinched her mouth. Gray suddenly felt the bite of dread at his vitals.

"Tell Gray what?" he demanded again, more harshly, ignoring Matt's protest. Nancy sobbed, then pointed toward the house.

"She . . . she's in there!"

"Treena?"

A shake of her head, then a nod, and Nancy said with a supreme, visible effort at control, "Yes, and . . ."

"Who?" Gray glanced toward the crumbling house, the

flames licking at timbers already collapsed. The heat seared them even from a distance. "Who?" he demanded even more harshly.

"River, Gray. Oh it's River!"

Her words ran together in a sort of shaking sob, as if it was one word instead of several. Gray looked up and over her shoulder to see Matt's shocked, desperate face. Giving his mother a quick squeeze of comfort, Gray reached around her to grab Matt, who had already spun on one heel toward the house.

"Don't!" Gray said sharply, and braced himself for Matt's inevitable reaction.

Matt pivoted back to face him, his right fist coming up to crash into Gray's face, but Gray's arm blocked it.

"You don't even care!" Matt screamed, his voice rising above the clamor of the fire brigade and the shrieking wood burning. "You don't care!"

Quickly, savagely, Gray's open hand jerked across Matt's face, spinning him around.

"You don't know how I feel," he said quietly when Matt looked back at him. "You have no idea."

And because it was true, and because Matt's young heart was almost breaking, he looked down at the ground and broke into a sob.

"No, Gray. No, Gray, don't let it be!" he pleaded.

Steeling himself against the pain piercing him like a bowie knife, Gray sucked in a deep breath filled with smoke and agony.

"I can't stop what's already happened, Matt. And I think we need to be with Tyler right now."

Tyler. Matt turned, and a glance at his mother's face was enough to tell him that Tyler Templeton did not know who was in that hell.

"Who's gonna tell him?" Matt whispered, looking at Gray. Then he understood something that had been eluding him for a long time. He understood that even though Gray could be harsh, aloof, taunting, distant, he shouldered responsibilities that Matt could not. And in that instant all past resentments were forgotten.

"I'll tell him," Gray said quietly as he turned toward the line of men passing buckets.

Gray walked toward Tyler, his face grim, his stride steady. When he reached him, Tyler just looked at him. He wiped a soot-streaked hand across his brow as he met Gray's steady gaze, and his mouth worked soundlessly.

"What is it, Gray?" he asked at last.

"Ma just told me . . . That's Treena's house, Tyler."

"Treena? Poor kid." Tyler sounded sad. "Someone said there were two bodies in there . . ." His voice trailed into silence as he realized the meaning of what he said.

"Tyler, I hate to—"

"Don't say it, Gray."

Gray cleared his throat, wondering how anything could hurt so bad and not leave a visible wound.

"I have to say it, Tyler."

"No!"

"Tyler . . ."

Matt appeared in the swirling smoke and bits of ash floating down like fiery snowflakes. His youthful face was ravaged by grief and pain. Broken sobs burst from his throat, and Tyler's stoical denials faltered. As Tyler's hard-held composure crumbled, he jerked Matt into his arms and they both sobbed as if infants.

Gray, feeling his throat tighten, pivoted on his heel and stalked away.

"Gray," Matt called, breaking away from Tyler and half stumbling after his brother, "Gray, where are you going?"

When Gray spun around, his eyes were flat and cold. There was no emotion in them, nothing but the reflection of the leaping flames. His voice was toneless.

"Why?"

Matt's young face had aged in the past few minutes, and his voice was deeper, older, haunted.

"Because I want to go with you."

Gray just looked at him, then flicked a glance toward Tyler and his mother, who had soundlessly come up behind Tyler and offered her comfort. His gaze shifted back to Matt.

"Come on."

"Gray!" Nancy burst out, guessing where he was going. "Wait and take someone with you. Your brothers can go..."

"There's no time to wait for them," Gray said shortly. "They're too far away and time is running out."

"What's the plan?" Matt whispered as they lay flat on their bellies watching Pierce Trucklow's house.

"I don't have one."

Startled, Matt jerked his head to look at Gray. "What do you mean you don't have one?" He could feel Gray's careless shrug.

"Just like it sounds, Matthew. I don't have one."

Matt lapsed into silence at Gray's terse usage of his given name. High overhead a fickle moon cast shadows across the Bar None. Lights gleamed inside the sprawling log house in a deceptively welcoming glow.

Gray's voice was tight. "This is for River," he said, and Matt knew then that Gray had loved her.

After a quick glance at Matt, Gray rose in a half-crouch and ran across the perimeter of Trucklow's house. He skirted the edge, still running in a half-crouch, one pistol drawn and held at his side. He halted in a clump of sage, looking up at the second story. A light was on in an upstairs room, and he watched it closely.

Every muscle in his body was tense; he was ready for whatever happened, ready for Trucklow. There was no emotion in him, no reaction. He'd deliberately drained body and mind of anything but purpose.

A rustle to one side distracted him for a moment, then Gray glanced up at the window again. He saw the faint shadow of movement and heard the low rumble of Trucklow's voice. A quick look around him showed no evidence of guards, and Gray rose from the brush. He ran forward and paused in the deep shadows of the house, then stuck his gun in his belt before grasping the smooth contours of a porch post.

It didn't take but a moment to climb the post to the second-floor roof, where he took pistol in hand again and crouched in the shadows. He recognized Trucklow's voice. A harsh glitter frosted his eyes, and his mouth tightened.

"Hell no!" Trucklow was saying to someone. "I'm not sticking around to see about it! And if you've got any sense, you won't either."

Gray edged closer to the open window, his feet balancing precariously on the narrow rim of wood around the porch roof. The roof had a slight downward slant, and he had to hold to the window ledge with one hand so that the slick soles of his boots would not slip. From his vantage point he could see Trucklow's red hair. He had his back turned to the window as he talked to someone in the doorway, and when Gray heard the door slam as Trucklow abruptly dismissed the man, he made his move.

Tossing one leg over the window ledge, Gray slipped quickly and silently into the room. He paused by the window with his pistol aimed and cocked, waiting for Trucklow to turn around.

When the big man did, slowly, as if he sensed another presence, Gray motioned with the short barrel of the Peacemaker.

"Have a seat, Mr. Trucklow."

Trucklow stood so still it seemed as if he'd turned to stone, then he made a slow move with one hand.

"I prefer standing, Morgan."

"But the man with the pistol prefers that you sit."

Inclining his red head, Trucklow muttered, "I defer to the man with the pistol." When he'd slowly sat in a ladder-back chair and placed both hands on his knees—keeping a wary eye on Gray's pistol—Trucklow smiled. "How can I help you?"

"By joining me in Clanton for a little discussion with the sheriff, for one. And by giving a detailed confession, for another." Gray's smile was mocking. "I assume that you will, of course, tell all."

Trucklow's bushy red brows rose, and his mouth twisted in amusement. "You assume incorrectly, Morgan. I have no idea what you're talking about."

"Ah, are we referring to the abduction attempt, your shoddy attempts to raise money for a railroad by selling bonds in a nonexistent corporation, the midnight referendum before the voters could organize an opposition, or your success in persuading our town commissioners—fools all of them—to write out a bond note for one hundred and fifty thousand dollars at seven percent?"

"There's nothing illegal in that last!" Trucklow shot back with a scowl.

"Perhaps not, but you've hardly won friends in Comanche County by using such crude tactics. Did you discover that the good citizens of Clanton had hired me to get a court-ordered writ of arrest for anyone attempting to take possession of the bond certificates, by chance?"

Trucklow's jaw set. "That was you? How'd you know—"

"Easy," Gray interrupted. "One of your partners tried to persuade me to join your little group of swindlers. All I had to do was pretend interest, and I learned all I needed to know."

"Treena Lassiter," Trucklow growled, and Gray nodded.

"For some reason, she seemed intent on my being a part of your scheme."

"I told Treena not to involve you, but no!" Trucklow snapped. "Nothing would do but that she try to drag you in on it! I thought she was smart, but she's just a woman after all."

"Was a woman," Gray corrected, and watched Trucklow's eyes narrow.

"What do you mean?"

"She's dead."

Trucklow's jaw sagged, and he licked his lips. "Dead? Treena? How?"

"A fire.

While Trucklow digested this information, Gray edged toward the closed door, keeping his pistol trained on the man's chest. He could hear the vague rumble of voices downstairs and knew all Trucklow had to do was call out to bring his hired guns.

"Come on," Gray said after a moment, motioning for Trucklow to rise. The big man kept his eyes on the pistol. Gray reached around Trucklow to pull open the door.

Nothing was said for a moment as Trucklow preceded Gray out the door and into the hall. The hall was built like a loft and looked out over the main room downstairs. Cigar smoke drifted up, and lamps illuminated several men playing cards at a wooden table. When they heard footsteps, they looked up, then dropped their cards and leaped back from the table, hands flashing down for pistols.

"I wouldn't," Gray said loudly, "unless you want to see your boss full of holes."

"Listen to him," Trucklow told them when they hesitated.

"Tell them to back off and throw their weapons in the middle of the floor," Gray said, punching Trucklow with the Peacemaker when he hesitated a fraction too long.

"Do it!" Sweat rolled down Trucklow's face, and his eyes were bulging. "Do whatever Morgan tells you!" he shouted.

Reluctantly, the hired guns tossed their pistols to a pile in the middle of the floor, then backed away with hands held out.

"Now stay where you are," Gray said, giving Trucklow a slight shove toward the flight of steps. "The first man that moves gets Trucklow killed."

Heavily, one foot slamming down and then the other, Pierce Trucklow descended the steps to stand by the front door, Gray's pistol shoved in his back. Gray kicked the pile of pistols ahead of him, keeping his Peacemaker on Trucklow, deftly sweeping the surrendered weapons out of reach.

Before he could reach around Trucklow to open the front door, he heard footsteps on the porch. Instinctively, Gray stepped back, dragging Trucklow with him. The door swung open with a bang, and a struggling figure was framed in the doorway, a pistol held to his head. It was Matt.

"'Lo, Gray," Matt managed to say with a sheepish shrug. "I found Brogan."

"Looks more like he found you!" Gray shot back.

"Yeah, maybe so." Matt was shoved forward, Brogan's gun driving him. "Hey! Take it easy!"

Grinning, Brogan swaggered several steps forward. "Now, Morgan, I don't much care if I shoot this puppy. It all depends on you. If you want to let Mr. Trucklow walk away, then he can decide what to do with him. If not—" Lifting his pistol, Brogan squinted down the long barrel of the lethal .45 pressed against Matt's temple.

"He's bluffing," Matt said, and Gray shook his head. He knew better.

Swearing softly, Gray lowered his pistol. Trucklow gave a wheeze of triumph and snatched the Peacemaker from Gray's hand. Then his beefy fist slashed backhanded across Gray's jaw, making him reel before he caught his balance.

"Well, Morgan!" Trucklow snarled. "Looks like you've lost."

Gray could taste blood from a split lip, but his eyes fixed on Trucklow's florid face steadily. "Don't count on that."

"Take their guns," Trucklow said as his men scooped up their weapons, "and put these two in the barn for now. I'll deal with them as soon as I take care of some last-minute details."

Gray and Matt were shoved roughly to the barn and their hands tied to tall posts above their heads. They were hung on the posts by their wrists, their feet barely touching the hay-strewn floor. The posts were five feet apart, and Gray glanced over at his brother. Gray's arm and shoulder muscles were strained by the position, and he could tell from Matt's grimace that his were too.

"Sorry, Gray," Matt muttered when the men had left them there after a few cursory punches and kicks. His face was bleeding from one of the punches, and his left eye was blue and swollen.

Gray's head fell back against the rough post. He could feel splinters digging into his skin, another discomfort that made him curse softly before asking, "Sorry about what?"

"About getting us into this."

"You didn't get us into this. I did."

Matt shook his head. "No, if I hadn't let Brogan come up behind me like he did, you would have made it out of there with Trucklow, and we'd be on our way back to town by now."

"The night's not over," Gray said briefly.

Matt stared at him in the dim light afforded by a single lantern. "Do you really think we'll get out of this, Gray?" he asked in such a pleading voice it was hard for Gray to answer.

"Maybe," he finally said, and Matt let his head lean back against the post.

Shifting slightly to ease his strained muscles, Gray tried to think past the throbbing pain in his skull. One of the blows he'd been dealt had knocked his head back against the post, and he could feel the warm trickle of blood down his neck.

"Gray?" Matt asked into the growing silence. "Did you really love her?"

Gray briefly closed his eyes. He welcomed the pain in his body. It kept him alert, but he struggled against the decimating pain that Matt's words brought.

"Do we have to talk about that?" Gray snapped.

"I'd like to know before . . . in case we don't get another chance to talk." Matt cleared his throat, then added, "I did, you know."

Gray turned to look at him. Matt's gaze was fixed on the floor, his youthful features struggling for composure. Capitulating, Gray muttered, "I'm not sure I know what love is."

"Oh, I do," Matt said softly. "It's caring enough about a woman that all you do is think about her all the time. It's

caring enough to die for her but hoping you don't because it
would be too cruel to be taken away from her—or have her
taken away from you. It's not caring if you die once she's
gone..."

As his voice faded away and Matt gave his brother a
half-embarrassed glance, Gray realized that he felt everything
Matt had just said. "Yeah," he said after a few moments of
silence, "I guess I did love her, Matt."

"It's too bad you couldn't have told her," Matt said, and
Gray felt a choking sorrow well up.

Stifling it, he said shortly, "Yeah. Look, Matt, we need to
find a way out of this. Can you free your hands?"

"I tried. The ropes are so tight I can't even wiggle my
fingers."

"Me either."

"Do you think Trucklow's going to kill us?" Matt asked
after a moment.

"I don't think he's going to scold us and send us home,"
was Gray's laconic reply.

He was right.

When Trucklow swaggered into the barn with a wide grin,
Gray saw the thick coil of braided leather slung over his arm
and felt a queasy lurch in the pit of his belly. It was obvious
Trucklow was not going to make this clean and easy. His jaw
tightened.

"Well, Morgan," Trucklow said, and let the coil of leather
snake out of his hand to whisper across the dirt floor. He gave
it a twitch, watching Gray's face. One of his men hung
another lantern up, and Gray could see the ring of men behind
Trucklow. There looked to be seven or eight, and he wondered
where the other three were. Brogan stood out front, his
scarred face bisected by an evil smile as he toyed with a long
knife.

Trucklow's voice dragged his attention away from Brogan
and back to the coil of leather. "See this?" the beefy man
was saying. "I used to be pretty good with one of these. I
could peel the skin from an apple with it."

"That right?" Gray asked coolly. "I'm sure you were the entertainment at most fine establishments."

The coiled leather flicked at Gray with the lightning-quick motion of a striking snake, slicing through the thin material of his shirt and leaving a vivid red welt across his chest. Hissing in a sharp breath, Gray pressed his lips tightly together. His muscles tensed against the pain, cording in his arms as he pulled against the ropes holding him.

"You've been a thorn in my side long enough, Morgan," Trucklow was saying. "It's not enough just to kill you. I want you to feel death before it comes."

"Killing me won't get rid of your troubles in town," Gray said.

"No, but it will be a pleasant memory."

"Let my brother go, Trucklow," Gray said then. "He hasn't done anything to you."

"No, but he's too much like you to let live. I don't need any more Morgans harrassing me."

"Do you think we're the only two?" Matt burst out. "We're not! And as long as there's a Morgan alive, you won't be able to hide anywhere, Trucklow!"

Looking with amusement from Gray to Matt, Pierce Trucklow drawled, "Well, like I said, I'll have my memories to comfort me. And besides, I haven't noticed much mettle in the rest of the Morgan whelps."

"They might be a little more easygoing, but not a one of my brothers will let you get away with this," Matt began until Gray stopped him.

"Leave it, Matt. Let Trucklow find out the hard way."

"Speaking of the hard way," Trucklow mocked, snaking out the coiled whip again, "I need to get on with this. Time is running out."

Sweeping his right arm out to one side, Trucklow drew it back slightly, his wrist popping forward in an easy, almost lazy motion. The fringed end of the whip snaked out to bite into Gray's chest again, slicing skin and shirt as smoothly as a hot knife in butter. Gray steeled himself for the next lash, twisting against the post so it would catch him across his back instead of his chest.

Clenching his teeth, he tried to think of something else, anything else besides the harsh bite of the whip, the laughter of Trucklow's men, and Matt's white, agonized face as he watched helplessly. Pain rose and receded in crashing waves, dragging him along, then leaving him behind until the next soft whisper of leather split the air.

It felt like fingers of fire across his skin, and he suddenly thought of River, wondered if she had suffered before she died, and hoped she hadn't. Maybe it was best this way, that he die, too, because when he thought of long bleak years without her, it was almost unbearable. She had been too briefly in his life, a bright glimmer in the dark years since his father's death, and he wished he hadn't been so suspicious of his good fortune. Maybe if he'd been a little more trusting, hadn't told himself that life would only snatch her away, maybe things would have been different for them. Maybe.

River's burning memory cut deeper than the bite of the whip, and Gray writhed inwardly, not allowing a single murmur to escape. His body sagged against the rough wooden post, his reflexes driving him harder against it, as if seeking escape from the blurring crimson leather that rose and fell in sickening rhythm against his back. His shirt and skin were in shreds, and the sharp crack of the whip was duller as it tore across his bleeding back.

Then, as quickly as it had begun, it stopped. Dimly, as if he were underwater, Gray could hear the burst of gunfire and sudden shouts. He hung there, expecting to feel a bullet at any moment and somehow not caring. He was faintly disappointed to find himself still alive a few minutes later, and surprised to hear a familiar voice in his ear.

"Gray! Dammit, Gray, why don't you ever take any advice?" Robert Morgan muttered to his older brother as he cut him down from the post.

Gray staggered, then caught himself to keep from going to his knees. His blurred gaze shifted from the dead men sprawled in the hay of the barn floor to his brother's face. Robert was scowling, but his eyes were anxious.

Managing a pained smile, Gray murmured, "Glad you could make it, Robert," before he pitched forward to the ground.

Chapter 20

*

"This is foolish, Gray," Robert warned grimly. "You're not recovered yet."

"Trucklow skinned my back, not my shooting arm," Gray said, calmly brushing and saddling his stallion.

"Is Brogan worth it?" Robert snapped. His dark eyes shifted from Gray to Jamie and Chance, who sat next to Matt on a bale of hay. "You and Matt were almost killed out there, and if we hadn't shown up—"

"I'm grateful you did, Robert," Gray said, wincing slightly as he pulled the girth tight and his bandaged back screamed a protest. "I guess Trucklow is finally convinced that the Morgans stick together. I hope he lives to face trial."

"Doctor Parrott said he probably will," Matt put in. He glanced from Gray to Robert, then asked, "Gray, can I go with you?"

"No." Gray's reply was short, then noting Matt's face, he added, "This is my fight now." He slapped his stirrup down and tested the saddle with his weight, then looked up at his brothers. "I want Brogan, and I want Brogan to know why."

"He's probably in Mexico by now," Jamie said. "Why don't you wait until after . . . after the funeral?"

Gray's mouth tightened. "I don't need to be there."

There was a moment of awkward silence, then Chance said softly, "Doctor Parrott found her gold locket. The portrait of her mother was a little charred, but that was all."

He had meant it to be comforting, but Gray pivoted on his heel and led the stallion out of the barn without speaking. The others followed slowly.

It was dark, and a sketchy moon gleamed in the sky, shining across the broad, bare expanse of land and hills. The wind blew, whining mournfully across rocks and twisted scrub, and Gray could hear the distant wail of a coyote. A rush of loneliness swept over him, an emptiness that he knew would never fade, and he put back his head and let out a howl of pure pain, his voice ringing across the flat land. "River-r-r!"

River River River echoed back, and Gray closed his eyes against the pain.

He pursued Brogan relentlessly. He followed his tracks across rocky arroyos that cut deeply into the hills, using skills he had learned as a boy. The overturned rock, the bent twig or blade of grass, all left a trail.

He stopped only long enough to water the stallion and give it a handful of feed, then swung into his saddle and rode again. Night passed into the pale light of dawn, then into the bright glare of noon. The sun beat down, and Gray pulled his felt hat low over his eyes, squinting against the glare and ignoring his aching body as he followed Brogan's tracks. The pain kept him sharper, spurred his burning need for vengeance.

Gray pushed on, eating sparingly. He didn't care about eating and had brought a pouch of dried meat that he choked down to keep his strength. There was only one thing that mattered, only one thing on his mind.

Brogan. He'd hated the man for too long. The man was a hired killer, and he remembered Brogan from twelve years before . . .

It was almost dark before Gray rode into a sleepy Texas village of adobe huts and squat buildings. Lights glittered in the unshuttered windows of a cantina, and there were horses tied to the hitching rail out front. The dark street was deserted except for a few stray animals lurking in the shadows. He could hear the sounds of laughter and a guitar, and he dismounted in front of the bar.

Looping the weary stallion's reins over the post in a loose coil, Gray stepped over a snoring drunk and into the cantina. Smoke filled his nose, and noise filled his ears. It was close and stuffy in the room even with the windows open, and Mexican and American voices blurred together in a chaotic mutter.

He blinked as his eyes adjusted to the dim, smoke-filled light, and his gaze drifted over the men. A poker game was in progress in one corner, and several men hung on the bar.

Stalking across the floor, Gray approached the bar. "Whisky," he said.

"Looking for someone?" The swarthy man behind the bar gave him a quick frown.

"Sí."

After a moment's thought, the Mexican shoved a glass and a bottle toward Gray. When Gray tossed a silver coin into the air, the man caught it with a deft twist of his wrist and flipped it into a half-empty jar. He grinned.

Gray leaned back against the edge of the bar and surveyed the room from beneath the flat brim of his hat. It was tugged low over his eyes, and the rattles clacked slightly when he moved, catching the attention of a man across the room. The man paused with his drink half-lifted, then turned to nudge the tall, lanky man next to him.

Gray downed his whisky in a single gulp, grimacing at the harsh bite. It burned his stomach, but he didn't care. Not much could bother him now.

Two men beside him left, staggering out of the cantina and laughing. Gray looked around the room again, and his gaze narrowed on a tall man in the opposite corner. His lips thinned into a straight slash, and his muscles tensed painfully. It was Brogan.

Gently easing the leather thong from over his pistol, Gray stepped out from the bar to the middle of the room. He didn't care who was behind him, who was in front of him. All that mattered was the tall man who hadn't even seen him yet.

"Brogan." The word was soft, almost a whisper, but Brogan heard it. He stiffened, and kept his gaze straight ahead. Gray said it again. "Brogan."

Chairs were kicked back and tables overturned as the other patrons saw the deadly expression on Gray's face, and within a few seconds the room was almost clear. Only a few of the drunk or foolish remained to watch.

Turning slowly, Brogan faced Gray. His face tightened, and one hand made a reflexive move toward the gun he wore on his hip.

"Yeah, please go for it!" Gray said softly. "I don't need much of an excuse, but that will do!"

Brogan paused. "How's your back?" he asked in a mocking voice.

"If I were you, Brogan, I'd be more worried about my gun arm than my back."

Brogan's scarred face twitched reflexively. "What do you want?"

"I'm here for you, Brogan. And I don't care if I carry you back alive or not. It's your choice."

Brogan glanced around the room, but he was just as much a stranger as Gray and no one wanted to interfere. A rapid stream of Spanish from the man behind the bar indicated that the owner wanted them to go outside, but Gray ignored him. So did Brogan. The tall outlaw just stood there, his coat loose around his legs, partially covering his gun belt.

"At least give me a chance, Morgan. My gun ain't handy and you know it. It's almost like shooting an unarmed man."

"Well, you've had a lot of experience with that," Gray said in the same soft voice. "Twelve years ago. A cold night in March. You and about ten others stopped a man and a boy in a wagon. Do you remember that, Brogan?''

The outlaw shifted uneasily. ''I don't know what you're talkin' about—''

''Think. You'll remember it if you try. It was up around the county seat, Brogan, and you were still young enough to have peach fuzz on your face. But you were old enough to fire the first shot that killed my father—''

A cold sweat popped out on Brogan's forehead. ''You're crazy!''

''Oh, no, I remember that night like it was yesterday. I remember you now, though it took me a while. You fired the first shot, and you took away the rifle I was going to shoot you with. Well, my father is dead, I'm not fourteen anymore, and I have a pistol instead of a rifle, but you're welcome to try and take that.''

Brogan licked his lips, his eyes darting to each side as if looking for help.

''Why pick on me?'' he asked at last. ''There were ten men there, you say.''

''Because ten of those men believed in a cause, whether they were right or wrong. You were an outsider, just there for money. And it was your bullet that killed my father.''

Now Brogan saw the deadly intent in Gray's face, knew that he had not come to take him back to Clanton. He knew that Gray Morgan had come to kill him.

A slight grimace hooked Brogan's mouth, and he backed away a step. ''You aiming to play fair, Morgan? If you are, let me move my coat out of the way and we'll see who's faster.''

''I already know who's faster.''

The tall outlaw gave a snort of digust. ''Well, I ain't gonna draw on you, and if you shoot me that's murder. So how do you like that?''

Gray shrugged. ''Suits me.'' His hand dipped to his gun and had it out of the holster and leveled at Brogan before the outlaw could flinch. "Out here in west Texas, who's gonna care if I murder you?"

Caught, Brogan's face flushed a furious crimson. "Why, you're crazy, you son of a bitch!"

He half turned as if to leave, and when Gray barked an order at him to turn back around, Brogan's pistol was in his hand. It fired, orange flame spurting from the muzzle and the bullet crashing into the wall behind Gray. A lantern splintered with a loud cracking sound, and Gray returned fire instinctively.

Brogan staggered back, one hand moving to his chest and the other dropping the pistol to the floor. Slowly, he crumpled, his face creased in a shocked expression as blood seeped from a chest-wound. "Damn if you didn't shoot me," Brogan muttered, then pitched forward on his face and was still.

Gray looked down at him, his face emotionless. Then he strode back to the bar and poured himself another glass of whisky before he did what had to be done.

Dust puffed in small clouds, rising into the air behind Gray's horse and the bay carrying Brogan's body. He rode slowly down the main street of Clanton, wondering why it was so quiet and still. He'd ridden all around the town to approach from the end away from Treena's burned-out house. He hadn't wanted to see it, hadn't wanted to be reminded.

But he was reminded anyway, because the cemetery was at the opposite end of town, and he could see the two new graves being dug. Gray nudged his stallion into a trot and passed the cemetery without glancing at it again.

Sheriff Wentwhistle glanced from Gray's set, hard face to the body draped across the saddle and didn't ask any questions as he turned and went back inside. "Just leave him there for the undertaker," he said.

Gray followed him, his boots echoing on the sidewalk, then scraping across the office floor. Crossing his arms over his chest, Gray gazed at the sheriff until he looked away.

"Circuit judge will be back next week," Wentwhistle said.

"We'll have Trucklow's trial then. Guess you'll want to be the prosecuting attorney."

"You guess right."

The sheriff nodded. "Thought you might. Well, come round before then and we'll talk. Oh," he added as Gray started to ride away, "Tyler Templeton is over at the hotel in case you wanted to know."

Gray just looked at him, and something in his expression made the sheriff look away. Pivoting on his boot heel, he turned and walked out the door, shutting it behind him. For a long time afterward, Wentwhistle stared at the empty air where he'd been. There had been accusation and condemnation in Gray's cool gaze, and Wentwhistle blew out his cheeks with a long sigh. Then he slowly, steadily, unpinned the metal star from his chest and laid it on the top of his desk. For fourteen years he had been sheriff in Clanton, but he was done with it.

Coughing and sputtering, River pushed at the charred timbers barring her way. She was trapped. The fire had destroyed the entire house, and the ruins were still hot, with smoke rising in thin spirals. Somehow she had been spared.

The damp walls and the old mattresses she had piled on top of her had prevented fire or smoke from penetrating to where she cowered. Thank God for the stone above and around her, River thought, but now it was keeping her imprisoned.

She wondered how long she'd been unconscious. It had seemed as if she'd lain there forever listening to the crackle of the fire and the shouts from the fire brigade. No one had heard her cries above the din of the blaze, and she'd finally curled herself into a ball and put her arms over her head. Time had passed in a haze of smoke and fear, until she'd lost consciousness. Now she could see splinters of blue sky far above her.

Pushing at the timbers again, River tried to cry out. But her throat was parched, her tongue felt thick, and her voice weak.

River rested her head against one of the damp mattresses

and closed her eyes. Why weren't they looking for her? Why wasn't anyone there to rescue her? Even if they thought she'd perished, surely they'd try to recover her body.

"Ugh," River muttered at the grim thought. Sagging back against the stone wall, she looked up at the tiny blue slivers of sky that represented freedom.

She heaved a deep sigh of frustration. How would she ever escape. She tried to push at a heavy timber barring her exit, but it refused to budge. Frustrated, River gave a hard, angry shove at the boards blocking her exit. To her amazement this time they shifted slightly, so she shoved again. With a grinding noise, two of them toppled in a black shower of soot and ashes, covering River but freeing her.

She scrambled over the timbers, burning her palms but not caring. It took her several minutes, but she managed to clamber out, using charred timbers as steps, trying to ignore the pain from her burned hands and feet.

When she reached the top, she knelt in the blackened ruins and stared with awe. When she looked around her at the utter destruction of Treena's house, she realized how very lucky she was to have escaped alive. It had been a holocaust, and she could easily have been killed.

Weak from her ordeal, River made her way over black, burned timbers and unrecognizable lumps. She staggered slightly and had to rest several times before she got to the edge of Treena's once-neat picket fence. It had obviously been torn down by the fire brigade, and pickets lay tossed like matchsticks across the scorched yard.

The street was empty. Only a slight wind sent dust devils tumbling down the wide expanse, and they made an oddly whisking sound as they scratched past her. Pausing, she held to a hitching post just beyond Treena's house to wipe at the soles of her scorched feet. They hurt and had huge blisters on heels and toes.

Wincing, she put one foot in front of the other and limped down the main street, wondering at the air of desertion.

"It's so quiet today," she whispered, unconsciously lower-

ing her voice. No wagons rumbled down the street, and no
horses trotted down the wide thoroughfare. "How long was I
down there?" she wondered aloud. Her voice faded quickly
in the hot wind. "I feel like Rip Van Winkle," she said then,
reassured by the sound of her own voice in the quiet air.

Forcing herself forward one step at a time, slowly travers-
ing the distance between Treena Lassiter's burned house and
the hotel, River was disconcerted to find that no one was
there. The door was shut and a sign hung on it: Gone to the
Funeral.

Funeral? Whose funeral? she wondered, then realized it
must be for Treena and Juan Carlos. Her brain was still foggy
with smoke and fear, and she felt dazed as she tried to
concentrate on details. A funeral. Oh, yes. Of course. Everyone would be at the church or the cemetery.

Black crepe hung on doors and windows all down the
street, and River was faintly surprised. She hadn't known that
Treena was that well liked, and it appeared as if the entire
town had turned out for her funeral.

Spurred more by instinct than by any logical thought
process, River made her way from the Clanton Hotel across
the street. She could see the gleaming white spire of the
Clanton Methodist Church at the end of the street, and
suddenly it seemed a million miles away.

Wavering, she stood in the shadows a moment, struggling
for the strength to reach the church. A blinding sun seared the
street, making her burns sting even more, and she put up a
shaking hand to shield her eyes. The loose shirt and baggy
trousers she wore flapped slightly in a freshening wind, and
made a popping noise that startled her.

River finally pushed away from the wall behind her and
stepped back onto the sidewalk. The long walk seemed to dip
and sway, and she occasionally caught herself with one hand
outstretched against whatever offered support.

Slowly, determinedly, she made her way down the street,
wishing she would find her father or Gray before she fell into

a faint. As she drew closer to the end of town, she could hear the soft strains of a mournful hymn.

"We shall gather at the river..."

Pausing, River leaned on another hitching post to catch her breath. It sounded like the entire Sunday morning choir had gathered to sing sad farewells to Treena Lassiter. And where was everyone, she wondered fretfully. She was so tired and aching, and no one even cared enough to continue looking for her. Or even knew that she was still alive.

She wasn't quite right. Pierce Trucklow was watching River from the window of his small cell in the jail. He gave a hollow laugh as he saw her tottering down the street with smoke-stained clothing and a dazed expression.

"Some folks got more lives than a cat," he muttered to himself. His hands curled weakly around the window bars, and his mouth twisted with pain as he watched River reach the church at the end of town and push open the white picket gate to the cemetery. "Now, that's rich! Going to her own funeral." Trucklow laughed, then winced against the pain in his shoulder. The bullet had missed any vital organs. A pity, really, since he'd rather be dead by a bullet than hung. Maybe he'd made a mistake by not killing Morgan right off. His main consolation had been that the Templeton girl was dead, and now she wasn't. He laughed again, a hollow laugh full of mockery. It amused him more than anything had since the Morgans had delivered him to Sheriff Wentwhistle. "Yep, that's pretty damned rich!"

In the next cell, Riggs and Webster glanced out the window, their eyes widening as they saw River.

"What d'ya make of that?" Webster breathed with a growing smile, and Riggs came to stand at his shoulder.

"Well," Riggs said, "I think it's great that she's not dead. She was a nice girl."

"Yep!" Webster agreed. "The nicest girl we done ever kidnapped!"

Trucklow gave them a sour glance. "You two fools beat

everything, you know that? If you hadn't botched the job in the first place, I wouldn't be here right now!''

Webster recoiled, but Riggs thrust out his jaw and said, ''If there was ever anything to recommend botching up a job, Mr. Trucklow, your being in jail is it!''

Trucklow growled, and Riggs and Webster beat a hasty retreat to the opposite side of their cell in spite of Trucklow's weakness.

''I'm still glad she's alive,'' Webster said defensively. ''And I hope she likes her funeral!''

Even Riggs stared at Webster, who shrugged.

Pushing through the low picket gate that surrounded the sloping cemetery grounds, River was amazed at the large crowd. They stood elbow to elbow, dressed in their Sunday best, the women in sober dark colors and the men in suits. Children stood quietly, twisting their feet in the brown grass, eyes wide at this odd ritual of their elders.

A soft, plaintive hymn drifted solemnly into the air, and River stood back, suddenly shy, not wanting to intrude at Treena's funeral. After all, she could hardly be a true mourner since the girl had tried to kill her, and she felt it would be a mockery to pretend grief. Of course, these people had no idea of Treena's true nature, and now that she was dead it would be wicked to speak ill of her.

When peace, like a river, attendeth my way, when sorrows like sea billows roll, the mourners sang, *Whatever my lot, Thou hast taught me to say, it is well, it is well with my soul*.

River put out a hand to steady herself and then drew it back quickly when she realized she'd leaned upon the black-lacquered hearse that had borne Treena's body to the cemetery. The glass sides reflected her face, and she was shocked to see that she was almost unrecognizable. Her face was swollen and soot-streaked, her hair a mat of ash-covered tangles. She stared, then glanced quickly around to see if anyone else had noticed her.

As of yet, no one had, their attention trained upon the

black-garbed minister at the front. He stood on a small dais with his arms outstretched as the last hymn faded to a close.

Straining, she looked for her father and Gray in the crowd. There were so many mourners, and most of the men wore hats, so it was impossible to tell one from the other unless they were facing her. Reluctantly, she dragged her attention back to the service.

"... struck down in the prime of her life," the black-garbed man of the cloth was saying, and a general murmur of agreement rippled through the crowd. "So young, so beautiful, and with all her life before her."

Treena would have loved to hear how young and beautiful she was, River thought as she put a hand gingerly on one wheel of the hearse to keep from swaying.

"... leaving behind her loving family, from whose bosom she was snatched so prematurely ..."

River frowned. She'd thought Treena had said she had no family left.

"There the wicked cease from troubling, and the weary be at rest," the minister said. River thought that his words covered every situation quite nicely.

"And now it comes to this. Ashes to ashes, dust to dust, so we are all mortal," the minister intoned. "Our departed one has only been here in Clanton for a few months, but she has already left behind a great void. Her friends are legion, and all will miss her greatly in the years to come. Pray for her father, my friends, that he comes to accept his only daughter's death as God's will, and that he does not allow the bitter gall of vengeance to fall upon his head like the house of Samson was fallen—let the stones of wrath roll away like the stone away from the grave! Let us pray now, my friends, that God's will be done, not man's."

As the preacher bowed his head and the assemblage followed suit, River frowned. Her head ached so, and everything was so confusing. Treena had not had any family, had not had a father. Unless, of course, she'd lied to her, which was entirely possible. River's fingers coiled tightly around one spoke of the hearse's wheel, and she drew in a shaky breath.

Reality was fading, her surroundings were moving in and out as if shadows, and she knew she had to find her father or Gray before she fainted.

Elbowing her way through the crowd, River was vaguely aware of the stares swerving in her direction, the faint whispers and gasps, but she didn't care. She didn't care if her hair was matted and dirty and if Juan Carlos's clothes were torn and filthy and entirely inappropriate for a funeral. All she wanted was to see her father and feel Gray's strong arms around her, to have him hold her again, his handsome face smiling that mocking smile that she loved and resented at the same time.

"Excuse me . . ." She pushed past a heavy-set woman in a gray dress and large poke bonnet, almost tripping over the child at her feet, ignoring the mutter of annoyance the woman directed at her and the way she drew her skirts aside as if afraid of contamination.

Ahead, just a few steps more, was a tall man with broad shoulders and blond hair, and River's gaze riveted on him as she pushed her way through the press of people. But when she reached the man and he turned to glare at her with a scowl, she saw it was not Tyler.

Stumbling, she turned away, toward the minister and the crepe-hung coffin beside him. She would just ask him to announce that she needed her father, River decided in a haze of confusion and weariness. Limping, desperate, she thrust her way toward him.

As she reached the front of the crowd, River saw her father at last, and next to him stood Gray. Her vision blurred with hot, grateful tears, and she wedged her body through the press of mourners.

At last she stood beside Gray, just at his elbow, and her gaze drank in the sight of his long dark hair, stoic profile, wide shoulders, and narrow hips. As usual, he wore his gun belt and felt hat. Not even for a funeral would he change, she thought with a fond smile.

River didn't see the incredulous youth next to her, nor the nudge he gave his mother as River reached timidly up to touch Gray on the shoulder.

Without turning, Gray said in a hoarse whisper, "Can't you show some respect?"

"Of course," River murmured. She was somewhat taken aback by his vehemence. Didn't he care that she had returned from the very jaws of death? That at least *she* had escaped the grave? Had Treena meant so much to him that he couldn't spare an instant's attention for her?

In her confusion, River did not see Matt approach her, did not see Nancy Morgan right behind him, and did not see her father's slow turn and drooping jaw. All she could see, all she could feel, was Gray Morgan.

And as a distant buzz began in her ears and the world swayed, she finally saw Gray turn slowly and burn his silver eyes into her. A vague smile flickered for just a moment on her lips, and she whispered, "Gray," before slipping gracefully to the ground.

Chapter 21

*

For some reason Gray Morgan's reflexes did not work correctly. He just stared at River's crumpled form lying at his feet. It was Matt who lifted her up, who reached her even before Tyler.

"Get the doctor!" Matt shouted, his hard voice finally penetrated the protective haze clouding Gray.

Shoving people aside, Gray reached out for the girl draped in Matt's arms, and Matt did not protest. He relinquished her to his brother with only a soft sigh, then forced a path through the muttering crowd.

Nancy Morgan tugged at Tyler, whose ashen face was slowly regaining color, and they scurried right behind. The minister, astonished but realizing the situation, flicked only a curious glance at the closed coffin before asking loudly if the good doctor would be so kind as to attend the patient in his office.

It was a strange procession that hurried down the empty main street of Clanton to the physician's office. While Doctor Parrott attended River in his examining room, Gray waited in the outer room pacing the floor, his silver eyes shadowed.

"I can't believe it!" Nancy Morgan murmured.

"I can't either," Tyler said from his chair beside her. His big hands were clenched in his lap, and he shook his head slowly. Tears rolled unchecked down his cheeks, and he did not bother to wipe them away. "I thought she was gone forever."

Matt silently watched his older brother with narrowed eyes. Gray had said nothing. He'd made no observation nor had he exclaimed with relief or joy. Gray had carried River with his long-legged stride bordering on a run, but he'd said nothing. *Did he care?* Matt wondered. He'd once said he did, but that was when he thought he was going to die, thought she was dead. Did he regret that confession now?

The waiting room was lined with Morgans and those from the Double T, while outside the doctor's office a crowd jammed the sidewalk. The entire town was buzzing with talk of a miracle. It was a miracle.

"And to think," Nancy murmured more to herself than anyone else, "we would have left her there to die . . ."

Hearing her, Gray spun around on his heel and gave his mother a fierce glare, then stormed from the doctor's waiting room and shoved his way through the crowd anxiously awaiting word.

Startled, Nancy looked at Tyler, then at her remaining five sons. Only Matt had a vague notion of what was wrong with Gray, and he said nothing as he quietly slipped out after him.

Gray was almost at the end of town where his horse was stabled when Matt caught up with him.

"Where are you going?" Matt demanded a little breathlessly since he'd had to run to catch up.

Gray didn't answer. He kept walking, his long legs covering the ground with swift purpose.

Matt was right behind him. "What's the matter, Gray?" Matt finally taunted, and Gray whirled to stare at him with narrowed, dangerous eyes. "Can't you face the fact that you love her? That she's still alive and now you have to admit it? Is that what's bothering you? You don't want to admit a weakness? Can't you get used to the idea that you care about a woman?''

"Shut up!" Gray growled at last, and took a step toward Matt with his fists clenched.

Matt's chin jutted up defiantly. "That's it, isn't it? You're scared to be in love. The great Gray Morgan—scared of loving a woman!''

"Matt," Gray began warningly, and his hands curled into tight fists at his sides.

"Go ahead! Hit me if it makes you feel better," Matt said softly. "But it won't change it, will it?" He took a step closer. "All these years I thought my big brother Gray wasn't afraid of anything. I always felt as if I were less than you because there were things that frightened me, things you could do and I couldn't. But I don't feel that way anymore, Gray. Because at least I'm not too afraid to love."

Slowly relaxing his fists, Gray took a step back. His clear eyes studied Matt's flushed, angry face, and a small smile pressed the corners of his mouth.

"Well, now that my secret's out, I suppose I should just shoot myself," he said in a self-mocking tone that cut Matt to the quick.

"Is it so terrible to be in love?" Matt asked quietly, and Gray's bleak expression surprised him.

"Being in love isn't what's so bad, Matt. It's losing someone you love."

"Do you think you're the only one? Think about River. She lost her mother and her grandmother, yet she certainly hasn't stopped loving. She loves you, Gray."

"I know," he said, lifting his head to stare back down the street toward the doctor's office.

"Are you going to be there when she wakes up?" Matt asked after a few moments of tense silence.

Shrugging, Gray muttered, "I don't know."

"If you're not, Gray Morgan," Matt said in a strangely flat voice, "I don't ever want to see you again."

Matt turned and stalked back down the street, leaving Gray alone.

Gray stood there a long time, then he slowly turned and went into the stable. A few minutes later he rode his big gray out of the stable and out of Clanton, spurring his mount on as they reached the end of town.

"Gray," River muttered fretfully, "Gray!"

Exchanging glances over the bed, Nancy Morgan gave a regretful shake of her head and Tyler sighed.

River had drifted in a hazy half-world of consciousness for three days. Her ordeal had severely weakened her, the doctor said, and he had kept her under close supervision. No one had seen Gray.

Matt, ever-faithful, stayed close by River's bedside, and in those three days had somehow matured from a gawky, uncertain youth into a young man. His voice sounded deeper, and even his face seemed to have changed, hardening, with the boyish innocence and exuberance melding into the strong determination of a man. He held River's hand, and while she slept in that restless world, he read to her or quoted verses or just sat quietly watching her.

It was Matt who was with her when Gray finally returned. He opened the door and walked in with the haunted air of a man who has been to hell and back. Matt gazed at him coldly, his gaze flicking over Gray's unshaven face and rumpled clothes.

Standing uncertainly just inside the door, Gray looked at the still, pale figure on the bed. River's hair spilled over the feather pillow in a silken sheen that bore mute witness to the daily brushing it received. Her face—once sun-honeyed— now was pale and bore faint remnants of bruises like tiny purple flowers just beneath her almost translucent skin. Red splotches still dotted her bare arms, and Gray winced as he thought of the inferno she had survived.

His own scars were healing slowly, drawing tightly at times to remind him of his ordeal. Staring down at her, Gray had the grim thought that River may have decided she didn't love him anymore. After all, he hadn't been there for her when she woke, hadn't been able to come to terms with his own emotions until the night before.

"Where have you been?" Matt finally asked, and Gray was startled by his deep voice.

"With the Comanche," he replied.

Matt nodded. "I thought maybe that's where you were."

Gray wondered what River would have said if she'd seen him stripped to nothing but a breechclout and moccasins, sitting around a council fire with the Old Ones, smoking a pipe and speaking of dreams.

"She hasn't woken yet," Matt said into the silence, "but she's been calling your name."

A reply seemed unnecessary, and Gray remained silent, staring down at the slender girl in the bed.

"I want to sit with her," Gray said after a moment, and Matt didn't say anything for the space of a heartbeat.

Then he stood and faced his brother. "I'll wait outside until you leave."

Gray didn't reply. His gaze was fixed on River, and his throat was too tight to speak. He went and sat down in the straight-backed chair beside the narrow bed, watching her. He sat that way for a long time, watching the features he'd seen in his memory, memorizing them over and over. Dr. Parrott came and went, speaking low, telling Gray that she may come out of it and she may not.

"She's had a great shock, and some people never recover from it."

"She'll recover," Gray said flatly, so firmly that the doctor did not argue.

"I hope you're right, Mr. Morgan." After a brief hesitation, the doctor slipped out of the room again, and Gray did not even notice.

He must have fallen asleep sitting up, his arms folded across his chest. The hard back of the chair cut into the still raw welts in his skin, and Gray shifted uncomfortably, opening his eyes to find River staring at him. He gave a start, for her gaze was clear and lucid.

"River?"

She smiled. "I thought I'd never see you again," she said so softly he had to lean forward to hear.

His strong hands closed over hers. Gray's words stuck in his throat, and he had to clear it twice before he could say, "I'll never leave you again, River."

A slight smile curved her mouth, and her long lashes dipped briefly. "I know." She paused, then added in the same soft whisper, "You're my Ideal Man."

Somewhat taken aback because he certainly hadn't expected to hear that, Gray stared at her. "I thought you liked dark, brooding men," he finally said.

She laughed. "You'll never forgive me that, will you, Gray Morgan?"

"River, honest to God, I'll forgive you almost anything," Gray said, surprised to find he meant it.

River's hand lifted slowly to cradle his unshaven jaw. "You are my dark, brooding man," she whispered. "You are my everything."

She was astonished to see Gray's face soften, become almost tender. There were no mocking lights in his eyes this time, no mockery in his smile.

"River, I've been thinking a lot these past days. I know I don't say the things you want to hear, and like I told you a long time ago, I'm not much good with promises."

"Yes," she whispered, "I remember. The Comanche and the rattlesnake."

A faint smile touched his lips. "And you'll never forgive me that, will you?" he said before taking her hand between his and lifting it to his lips. "When you get well, I've got some things I want to tell you. To ask you."

River smiled tremulously. "The answer is yes!"

"I didn't ask you yet!"

Laughing softly, she said, "You will!"

Before Gray could say anything the door swung open and

Matt stood outlined in the doorway. His gaze took in Gray's hand holding River's, her soft expression, and the joyous light in her eyes, and he looked at his brother.

"It's about damn time."

"I didn't ask her anything yet," Gray shot back in annoyance.

"You will."

Grunting with irritation, Gray muttered, "I'm glad you both think I'm so predictable."

"Predictable?" River echoed as she pushed herself up on the pillow.

Matt was at her side instantly, holding her and plumping the pillow behind her head. At Gray's narrowed gaze, Matt shrugged and looked back at River.

She was staring at Gray. "You're not predictable," she said in an amazed voice that was closer to the old River. "You are the most maddening, mysterious man I've ever met!"

Gray looked at her. "Didn't anyone ever tell you that's the way it is with Ideal Men? Predictability is boring. And you like exciting men, remember?"

"I've loved you from the very first time we ever met, you know," she said, and he grinned.

"I remember. I couldn't imagine why you kept staring at me like you did."

Thinking of the afternoon in front of Delmonico's, River said, "I did not stare at you! I could hardly look at you because of Treena—'"

"That's not when I was talking about. I was talking about the *first* time we ever met," Gray said.

"But that *was*—"

"No, the first time was after that stagecoach robbery when Williams and Hotchkiss got into a fight over the water and I came along. Don't tell me you don't remember!" Gray added when River stared at him with an open mouth.

She shut it quickly. Her voice was a faint croak. "Did you know all along?"

Matt looked from one to the other with a frown. "What are you two talking about?"

"Drucilla Duckworth," Gray replied, and his mouth quirked in a smile. "I told you about it, Matt, remember?"

"Oh, yeah. You said Tyler's daughter was a plump, plain crow with glasses as thick as whiskey bottles."

"Did you know all along?" River repeated with rising indignation, and Gray laughed.

"No," he said. "I didn't figure it out until that day you were thrown from your horse."

"I wasn't thrown—"

"Fell then. I saw the Double T brand, and knew it had to be one of Tyler's horses, then I remembered that I hadn't met his daughter yet. When I saw you in town with him—a much different person—it kind of startled me. You changed a lot in three months."

"You didn't," River said tartly. "You were still the same arrogant, obnoxious—"

"Ideal Man," Gray finished for her. "But remember—you took me to church for my sins!"

She lay back on her pillows again. "Yes, I suppose that is true." After a moment, she asked, "And that night in the hotel? My first night in town?"

"Ah, when I made the fatal mistake of meeting Treena there." Gray shook his head. "I was drunk that night."

There was a long silence, then River asked slowly, "Was she . . . was she killed?"

"Yes," Matt replied when Gray remained silent. "The body they thought was yours was Juan Carlos's. The undertaker assumed it was you because of the necklace. It was burned so badly, and he didn't look any closer after . . . after he found the locket with your mother's portrait in it."

"Poor Juan Carlos," River murmured, then glanced up at Gray. "He was sorry for what he'd done, telling Treena where I rode so Trucklow could—Trucklow! Where . . . where is he?"

"In jail," Gray said tonelessly. It was apparent that he

didn't want to talk about Trucklow, so River let it drop for the moment. She wanted to ask about Brogan, but that could come later, too.

"Look," Matt said, "maybe we ought to go so River can rest. Now that she's awake, Doctor Parrott will want to check her over and all."

"No," River begged. "Please don't go yet! I'm just a bit tired, and that's all."

Uncoiling his long body from the chair beside her bed, Gray said softly, "River, I promised you I wouldn't ever leave you again." He lifted her limp hand in his and gave it a reassuring squeeze.

He was still holding it when the door opened again, and Tyler and Nancy slipped in, their grave faces altering to surprised joy at seeing River awake.

"River!" Tyler said as he strode forward to kneel at her bedside. His gaze took in Gray still holding her hand, and he flicked him a measuring glance. "It's about time, Morgan," he said, and Gray's mouth thinned.

"I haven't asked her yet," he repeated irritably.

"Oh!" Nancy Morgan said, dabbing at her eyes. "I'm so happy for you, Gray! A June wedding!"

"I haven't asked her yet," Gray repeated again.

Sandy Dennis, Consuela, and Maria hesitantly entered the partially open door, their faces lighting when they saw that River was awake.

"Señorita!" Consuela cried, rushing forward with Maria close behind. "Oh, you are getting better!"

A raspy bark sounded, and River peered over the edge of the bed to see the red dog limping toward her.

"We brought him, hoping he might be able to waken you, but I see that's not necessary," Sandy said when River exclaimed happily as she reached out to the dog. Sandy's eyes shifted to Gray, standing unshaven beside her bed, then noted the entwined hands. He smiled. "Well, Morgan, it's about time you came to your senses," he said.

Gray made a rude remark, then ground out from between clenched teeth, "I haven't asked her yet."

No one seemed to notice his irritation, and when the door opened and Dr. Parrott came in, telling everyone they would have to leave and let his patient rest, he noticed River's small hand tucked into Gray's. His face brightened. "Well!" Dr. Parrott burst out, "congratulations, Mr. Morgan, Miss Templeton!"

"I haven't asked her yet!" Gray said so loudly and so firmly everyone stopped talking and stared at him. A long, uncomfortable silence fell, and River stared up at him with her heart in her eyes. Had he changed his mind? Had he suddenly decided he did not want to marry her?

Matt spoke up. "Well, *ask* her!"

Incredulously, Gray said, "Here?"

"Why not?" Matt shot back. "What are you waiting for?"

"Yes, son," Nancy Morgan put in, "what are you waiting for?"

Gray raked a hand through his hair and shook his head, but a glance down at River's face stilled the hot words on the tip of his tongue. He looked back up at the crowded room and the full audience and shrugged.

"All right, dammit! I'll ask her!"

An expectant silence fell while everyone in the tiny room waited, then smiled as Gray turned abruptly to River and asked, "Will you marry me?"

For a moment she didn't say anything, wondering if he was being forced into something. But she recalled Matt once saying Gray never did anything he didn't want to do.

"Why?" she asked in a soft voice that had the same effect as a load of bricks falling into the room. No one spoke. Everyone stood still and shocked, looking from River to Gray and back.

"Why?" he repeated with a dangerous edge to his voice. "What do you mean by that?"

"Just what I said. Why do you want to marry me?" She gazed up at him, her chin tilted stubbornly.

Gray's eyes narrowed. "For one thing, it might keep you from being kidnapped again, or trapped in a burning house."

Shaking her head, River crossed her trembling arms over her chest. "That's not good enough. I can hire a guard or get some more dogs." She held her breath, staring up at him, realizing that she was taking a big gamble. But if he didn't say it, didn't say it *now,* she might never hear it. "Why, Gray?" she whispered. "Why do you want to marry me?"

Tucking his thumbs into his gun belt, Gray stared back at her, searching her eyes, the quivering line of her mouth, and her small, set chin.

"Why not?" he muttered. He glanced quickly at the carefully blank faces watching and listening.

"That's not a reason," River said, and he could see the crystal glitter gathering at the corners of her eyes.

"Oh, hell!" Gray said disgustedly, knowing what she wanted. "Do you have to hear it?"

River nodded mutely.

"Because I love you, dammit!" Gray growled. "I love you. Now—are you satisfied?"

"Well—"

"You better be," he shot at her, "because you're going to marry me whether you want to or not."

A half-sob burst from her throat, and tears streamed from her eyes as she smiled up at him. "Oh, yes, Gray! Yes, I'll marry you!"

And all my days are trances,
And all my nightly dreams
Are where thy gray eye glances,
And where thy footstep gleams—

POE, *To One in Paradise*

River's Dream

Tall, dark and handsome, that was her Ideal Man. And he was holding her in his arms, strong arms corded with muscle and yet gentle when he held her.

She sighed a soft, languorous sigh that slipped from between her lips and stirred silky strands of his dark hair. He smiled, and his brilliant silver eyes glittered in the pale light.

"You're beautiful," he whispered. His hands slid over her curves, pausing in all the most sensitive places until she moaned beneath him. "Umm," he husked against her ear, "I love all of you, but I think I like this place best. No, maybe that one . . ."

She arched seductively, leaning into his embrace with a happy sigh. "And I love you," she whispered back.

It was so wonderful to be with him, to know that he loved her and always would love her. Outside the wind blew softly, and starshine and moonlight filtered through gauzy lace curtains over the windows. Reclining on a satin-covered chaise, with clouds of silky hair spilling over her bare shoulders and her husband's arms, River Templeton Morgan thought how fortunate she was to be herself, and to have Gray for her husband.

Gray kissed her again, his mouth moving gently, then more persuasively over her lips, stirring storm clouds of desire and emotion. River kissed him back, closing her eyes, letting love take her far above the seaside hotel room where they were honeymooning. They lay blissfully lost in each other's arms. Ocean breakers crashed against the sand of the Galveston beach and filled her ears with their loud roaring. Through the tumult, she could hear a piercing cry that jarred her memory, and for a moment she was Drucilla Duckworth again, lying in her narrow bed and only dreaming of love.

Then the cry echoed again, and River realized it was only a sea gull, and that she was fully awake. This was no dream. It would never fade away.

A gust of salty air blew across them, and she could smell the sharp tang of the sea. Never, in all her dreams, had she dreamed of such happiness. Poor, unhappy Drucilla was gone forever, banished to that netherworld where she belonged. In her place was a confident woman, a beloved woman, a woman who preferred reality to her dreams.

Gray nibbled at her earlobe, and River shivered. "Cold?" he murmured, and she shook her head.

"No."

"Because if you are, I can warm you."

River shifted slightly so that she was looking straight up into his eyes. "Umm. Maybe I do feel a bit of a chill coming on . . ."

Sliding his hands over her body, Gray made good on his promise.

"Whoever said dreams don't come true was wrong," River observed later. Much later.

THE LATEST IN BOOKS
AND AUDIO CASSETTES